Spell Blind

David B. Coe

BAEN BOOKS
by David B. Coe

The Case Files of Justis Fearsson
Spell Blind
His Father's Eyes (forthcoming)

SPELL BLIND

DAVID B. COE

SPELL BLIND

Copyright © 2015 by David B. Coe

A Baen Book

Baen Publishing Enterprises
P.O. Box 1403
Riverdale, NY 10471
www.baen.com

ISBN: 978-1-4767-8024-5

Cover art by Alan Pollack

First Baen printing, January 2015

Distributed by Simon & Schuster
1230 Avenue of the Americas
New York, NY 10020

Library of Congress Cataloging-in-Publication Data

Coe, David B.
Spell blind / David B. Coe.
    pages ; cm. -- (Case files of Justis Fearsson ; 1)
Summary: "Justis Fearsson is a private investigator on the trail of a
serial killer in Phoenix, AZ. Justis is also a weremyste--a person with a
wizard's gifts and the ability to see into the paranormal world.
Unfortunately, weremystes also tend to go crazy on the full moon which is
why Justis is no longer a cop. But now an old case from his police
detective days has come back to haunt him, literally, as a serial killer
known as the Blind Angel strikes again. His signature stroke: burning out
the victims' eyes with magic. Now the victims are piling up, including a
senator's daughter, and Justis must race to stop Blind Angel before he,
she, or it kills again"-- Provided by publisher.
ISBN 978-1-4767-8024-5 (hardback)
I. Title.
PS3553.O343S68 2015
813'.54--dc23
                                    2014038692

Printed in the United States of America

10 9 8 7 6 5 4 3 2 1

Dedication

◎ ◎ ◎

For Nancy,
By my side, as I begin yet another journey

SPELL
BLIND
DAVID B. COE

CHAPTER 1

Ask most people to point at the moon, and they'll lift their gaze skyward, trying to locate it. Ask the same of a weremyste like me, and we don't have to search for it. We know where it is. Always, and precisely. As it waxes full, we can feel it robbing us of our sanity and enhancing the strength of our magic. Like ocean tides, our minds and our runecraft are subject to its pull.

I was on the interstate cutting across the outskirts of Phoenix, and already I could feel the moon tugging at my thoughts, subtle and light, but as insistent as a curious child. Three hours before today's moonrise, nearly a week before it would wax full, and its touch was as real to me as the leather steering wheel against my palms, the rush of the morning desert air on my face and neck.

I sensed the reservoir of power within me responding to its caress, like water to gravity. And I felt as well the madman lurking inside my head, coaxing the moon toward full, desperate to be free again.

I had five days.

And in the meantime, I had work to do.

Work for me means investigating. Once it meant being a detective for the Phoenix Police Department, but those days are gone. I was on the job for six years and eight months. The day I turned in my badge was, next to the day twenty years ago when my mother died, the worst of my life. Still, when I look in the mirror, I see a cop, a detective. I've heard it said among cops that once you're on the job, you're never really off. Some things are like that, they'll tell you. Some things get in your blood and that's it. You're never the same.

But being an ex-cop doesn't pay a lot of bills and after wallowing in self-pity for a while, I realized that wasn't much of a living either. So I hung out my shingle, went the ex-cop-becomes-private-investigator route. It's been done before, more often than not by ex-cops who are smarter than I am. But I have certain skills that paying customers find useful.

For the past year I've been owner, president, and principal investigator for Justis Fearsson Investigations, Incorporated, a one-man operation here in Phoenix. I've even got an ad in the phone book with my picture on it. I was going to make up a logo, but a friend—my old partner—said that I should use the photo instead.

"You're not unattractive for a white guy," she told me at the time. "That could work to your advantage."

So there I am in the yellow pages, smiling out from a quarter-page ad. My hair is sticking up all over the place, and the beard and mustache give me an unseemly look, but overall the picture isn't terrible. I have a website, too, but I haven't done much with it. I keep meaning to, but I don't get a whole lot of free time.

I had a rough go of it at first, trying to figure out how to run a business, how to know which cases to take. I turned to other former cops for advice, but soon learned that a good number of them didn't have any more sense of what they were doing than I did. Most of them were just scraping by—many were getting drunk before noon and staying that way until quitting time, which is likely why they had to leave the force in the first place. I read a couple of books and visited a bunch of websites, scanning articles for tips, but they weren't too helpful either. So, in the end I chose to teach myself.

Television shows about PIs make the profession out to be glamorous. It's not. In a lot of ways it's similar to being a cop. Cleaning up other people's messes. That's what Kona Shaw, my partner on the force, used to call what we did. And that's what I still do now. Except instead of working crime scenes, I work on the quieter cases, the ones people don't read about in newspapers or see on the late news. Early on I tried to stick to investigating insurance claims, and helping corporate clients identify employees who were spying for competitors or stealing inventory off of delivery trucks. It wasn't exciting work, but it got me started, paid off most of my debts, and allowed me to move the operation out of my home and into an office not far from where I live.

From the start, I tried to avoid the peeking-through-the-bedroom-window stuff. But PIs can't avoid the messier cases entirely, no matter how much we hate them. After following a cheating husband for several nights, or tracking down a runaway kid, or having to show a guy pictures of his wife and his best friend as they check into a motel on the outskirts of town, that work gets old. It's depressing as hell. It pays well, and God knows there's plenty of it, but it doesn't take long to figure out that the kid ran away because the parents were a nightmare, or the woman was cheating because her husband was a jerk. Most of the time, there are no good guys. I don't like that.

But the corporate cases have been few and far between, and working for the insurance companies isn't exactly a picnic. In the end, I had little choice but to go back to the personal cases. Which is how I found myself steering the Z-ster, my silver 1977 280Z, into a part of Phoenix's South Mountain precinct I never should have taken her to in the first place.

Two weeks ago I had been hired by Michael and Sissy Tyler to track down their teenage daughter, Jessie, who ran away from home. Tyler was one of the city's better-known businessmen. He had made a killing in the tech sector a few years back and wound up on the covers of magazines. He and his family lived in the Pinnacle Peak section of North Scottsdale, in a house that I might have been able to afford in twenty years if I scrimped and saved and gave up a few luxuries—you know, like food and shelter. Teenage runaways from homes of the rich and powerful are like private investigator cliches; we see them a lot. More often than not the kid winds up spending a night or two at a friend's house before returning to Mom and Dad.

Jessie's case was different. First, none of her friends knew where she'd gone. Second, she'd taken her wallet and had, within four or five days of her disappearance, used her ATM card to clean out the checking account her parents had set up for her: to the tune of about six thousand dollars. A couple of thousand of it went in cash and another three grand in purchases at stores all over the Phoenix/Scottsdale area. Nearly one thousand dollars had vanished without explanation, which made me wonder if she had hooked up with a myste. But all of it was gone. And third, according to her friends, her younger sister, and her parents, Jessie had been showing signs of what most folks in law enforcement and social services would call "self-destructive behavior." She was breaking rules at home and at school; she had gone from being a solid "B" student to flunking half her classes; and, though Mom and Dad were still in denial about this, the evidence I'd found suggested that she was experimenting with a variety of drugs. All she needed to complete the picture was the manipulative, perhaps even abusive boyfriend.

Early on in the case, I would have bet every dollar in my pocket that she had found him, and that he was the reason she'd left home.

It took me longer than usual to track her down, but eventually I found an addict who used to do some informing for me when I was with the PPD and who thought he had seen her near Esteban Park. I went to check out that lead, and found a second guy, another ex-cop as it happens, who had heard someone talking about a strung-out rich girl throwing money around in that part of town. I traced her to an abandoned building about a mile south of the Phoenix airport, in the growling shadows of Interstate 10. The building—an old service station garage—had become a den for users of Spark, a powerful and addictive hallucinogenic grown in the desert, which has become a Phoenix specialty for drug dealers and their clientele. I think it's nice when a local industry can expand and prosper.

By the time I pulled up to the garage, I was pretty sure she was inside. But "pretty sure" isn't positive, and since I don't have a badge anymore, it's not as easy as it once was for me to barge into places. The few windows on the front of the building were so filthy as to be opaque, at least those that were still glass. Several of the panes had been replaced with rough squares of plywood. A corrugated metal door blocked the mouth of the shop, its grooves covered with spray-painted gang symbols and names. Beside it was a smaller, windowless door that had a rusted padlock on it. Whoever was inside hadn't entered from the front.

Leaving the Z-ster at what was left of the curb, I tucked my Glock into my shoulder holster and started around toward the back of the building. I didn't want to have to use the weapon, but in this neighborhood there was no way I was going to leave it behind. As I walked I also began to recite a warding spell in my head, a simple one that would protect me from most anything some drug-crazed kid might throw my way.

As a weremyste, I could do such things.

Everyone's heard of werewolves. Weremystes work much the same way. We're mystes all the time, meaning that we can cast spells and feel magic when it's used by others of our kind. But for three nights in every moon cycle—the night of the full moon, and the nights immediately before and after—we lose control of our magic and ourselves. Our magical abilities strengthen, but our minds weaken. Some of us descend into a kind of quiet psychosis; others become violent. And many of us, myself included, fall in between those extremes.

I was born a weremyste; I didn't have to be bitten by one—that would be weird—and I didn't have a curse put on me, or anything like that. My dad was a myste, too. I've known I'd be one since I was fourteen. That was also when I learned the true reason my father went off the deep end every four weeks.

I'm more powerful than some; less so than others. And I'll be the first to admit that I'm not as skilled with my runecraft as I should be. But I can manage a good number of spells, particularly wardings. In the hands of a master, they could be more effective than a ballistic vest, without the bulk or weight. Of course, I'm not a master.

With the reassuring weight of the Glock tugging on my shoulder, and the power for my spell gathering inside me, I crept along the side of the building, past piles of rusted scrap metal and shards of broken bottles. I figured that most of the people inside would be stoned beyond consciousness, but still I placed my feet with care, in case someone was listening for cops. Or inquisitive PIs.

I found no door along this side, but upon reaching the rear corner of the building and peering around to the back, I spotted a steel door. It was closed, but had no lock.

A cold prickling on the back of my neck—premonition, or instinct honed by years on the force—made me pull out my weapon. I eased toward the door, holding the pistol in front of me. I also released the spell, felt the warding settle over me like a blanket. I reached the door, stepped past it so that I could swing it open and enter the garage in one quick motion. That was the plan, anyway.

I had forgotten about that vanishing money from Jessie's account and the possibility that she was with a myste. Stupid of me. And nearly fatal.

As soon as I flung the door open, I sensed the spell. It wasn't particularly strong, but it was an assailing spell—an attack—and whoever cast it had aimed it at me. I braced myself, hoped the warding would hold. It did, but the spell—it felt like an impact attack, meant, no doubt, to seem like I had been hit with a two-by-four—was strong enough to stagger me and to make the doorway shake. By the time I was moving forward again, I could hear footsteps retreating toward the front of the garage.

I followed, Glock ready, the power for a second spell already building inside me. This time I planned to cast an assailing spell of my own. I hate it when people use magic against me; makes me want to get even.

I hadn't taken five steps, before I slowed, then halted. The smell would have been enough to get my attention—feces, urine, vomit, sweat, fear, desperation—there could have been a body rotting in here. It was hard to tell.

But what I saw was every bit as bad. Worse, really. At least twenty college-age kids lay sprawled over the filthy cement floor, most of them unconscious. At least half of them were emaciated, their cheeks sunken, as if they'd been prisoners in this hell-hole for months. Others—the newcomers, most likely—might have been marginally healthier. But all of them wore stained, tattered clothing; all of them looked like they hadn't bathed in weeks or longer.

I spotted Jessie Tyler right away, but I couldn't help wondering how many of these other kids didn't have anyone searching for them.

I heard a loud crash at the front of the shop. Another glance at Jessie convinced me she wasn't going anywhere. I eased forward, gripping my weapon with both hands, considering what spell I ought to use. Assailing spells worked best with a precise target. I didn't have one, at least not yet, and I didn't want to hurt one of those kids.

Unfortunately, the myste I was stalking didn't have my scruples. Again, I felt the spell as soon as he cast it—the air was electric with magic. I sensed the heat before I saw the wave of flame rolling toward me. I backpedaled, scared, but also unwilling to ward myself and leave the kids to roast. Fire spells are rudimentary magic, but this myste, whoever he was, had poured serious power into this one. The temperature in the garage jumped twenty degrees. The skin on my face and hands flushed, like I'd been sitting way too close to a campfire.

The flames were almost on top of me when I cast my spell. Three elements, because that was how spells worked: the kids and myself, the fire, and a wall of magic in between. I recited the elements to myself three times, allowing the magic to build inside me. On the third repetition, I released it, the way I would a held breath.

The barrier winked into view and then shuddered as the attack hit it. But like my earlier warding, it held. That wall of flame passed over without burning any of us. There was nothing I could do, though, to keep the guy's magic from setting everything else in the garage on fire.

I started shouting for the kids to get out of the building. For the moment we still had a clear path to the door I'd used, but I didn't think that would last long. A couple of the kids managed to get themselves upright and stumble toward the daylight. Several more sat up and appeared to notice the flames. But they couldn't do more than that. Most of them didn't stir.

The air grew thick with dark smoke. I didn't think the building would come down on top of us; the walls were cinder block and the roof was metal. But it felt like we were in a giant oven.

Another pulse of magic shook the garage. I spun toward the front of the building, expecting to see more flames, but nothing came at me. The bastard had blown his way through that metal door, leaving the rest of us to broil.

I ran to the kids and started shaking as many of them awake as I could. Those who I could hoist onto their feet I helped to the door, two at a time. After that it became a matter of carrying the unconscious ones. They were filthy and rank; several of them had open sores on their arms and legs, faces and necks. When all of this was over I was going to bathe in a tub of hand sanitizer.

The smoke—black, choking, probably toxic as hell—continued to thicken, and the heat became nearly unbearable. But to my amazement, I managed to get all of them out without killing myself. Equally amazing, Jessie didn't run away while I was helping the others. She appeared dazed, her eyes wide but empty, her skin pink from the heat.

I heard the fire engines arrive a few minutes after I carried the last unconscious girl to safety. Moments later a trio of firefighters came running around the corner to the back of the building. Seeing the kids and me, they stopped.

"Good God," one of them muttered.

"Yeah," I said. "We're going to need a few ambulances."

"Spark den?" another guy asked, as the first radioed for help.

I nodded.

"And who are you?"

I pulled out my investigator's license. "Jay Fearsson," I said, holding it up for them to see. "I'm a PI." I pointed at Jessie. "Her parents hired me."

Jessie's eyes widened just a little, and her eyebrows went up, but she said nothing.

"You hurt?" the first guy asked.

"No."

"How'd the fire start?"

"There was another guy here—their supplier, I'm guessing. He started it when I showed up, and got away while I was carrying them out."

I didn't say more than that. Most people know that magic exists, but that doesn't make them comfortable with it, or with the people who cast spells. Filling in the details would have raised questions that I didn't feel like answering just then.

I heard more sirens in the distance, and figured at least a few of them were Phoenix Police. I'd be there a while answering questions. I walked to where Jessie sat and squatted down in front of her. It took a moment for her gaze to slide up to mine, and another for her eyes to gain focus.

"Jessie Tyler, right?"

She nodded. I thought I'd have to explain again who I was, but she was more cogent than I expected. "My parents really hire you?" she asked.

"Yeah. Does that surprise you?"

Jessie shrugged, stared past me.

"Who's your supplier, Jessie? Who was keeping you here?"

She didn't answer.

A couple of uniformed cops turned the corner. I saw them stop, take in the condition of the kids, and then speak to the firefighters, one of whom pointed my way.

The cops' questions were pretty standard. I hadn't done anything wrong, and they knew it. The fact that I had once been on the job helped too. They took Jessie and the others into custody, which I should have expected. Almost all of them would spend more time at the hospital than in jail, but still Jessie's parents weren't going to be pleased. Then again, they had hired me to find her, not to be her lawyer, so in the end they would have little choice but to pay me.

Once I was done giving my statement, the cops said I was free to go. I walked to the open door I had used to enter the garage, and examined it. The first spell that myste had thrown at me had rattled the door; there should have been some residue of magic on the door frame. All spells leave behind traces of power in the form of glowing luminance that clings to those things the magic has touched. And the magic of every myste manifests itself in a unique color. Thing is, only another myste can see it. I was hoping that Jessie's supplier had left behind the equivalent of a magical calling card.

But the Phoenix sun was bearing down on us at this point, bleaching colors, making it hard to see anything other than the sun's reflection on the dull steel. I thought I saw the faintest suggestion of beige or tan, like the color of dried grass, but I couldn't be certain.

"What're you looking for?" one of the cops asked from behind me.

I glanced back, then eyed the doorway again. The cop walked to where I stood.

"The guy who started the fire did other weird stuff, too," I said. "I think he used some kind of mojo on me. The first time he did it, I was right here by the door."

The cop stared at me for a moment, no doubt to see if I was joking. When I didn't smile or even glance his way, he began to study the door frame too. "I don't see anything," he said. "Do you?"

"No," I said. "Not a thing."

I walked away, heading back to my car. As I turned the corner, I saw that the cop was still scrutinizing the doorway. His partner, though, was watching me.

CHAPTER 2

I drove out to Pinnacle Peak, battling traffic the entire way. It was midday—nowhere near what used to pass for rush hour. But these days in Phoenix, rush hour started at dawn and lasted until way past dusk. I had called ahead to let the Tylers know that I had good news about their daughter, but I didn't want to explain the particulars over the phone. Especially because those particulars were not going to make them happy, and I wanted to get paid. It's a lot easier to ignore a bill than it is a guy standing in front of you.

By the time I got there, the police had called to say that Jessie was in custody. As I expected, Michael Tyler didn't take the news well, even if for now being in custody merely meant that Phoenix cops were keeping an eye on her while she was treated at Saint Luke's Hospital.

"How could you let this happen?" he demanded of me as he yanked open the front door. "I hired you to find her, not to get her arrested."

"I did find her, sir. She was in a spark den—"

"Oh, God," Missus Tyler said, voice trembling, a hand raised to her mouth. She sank into a chair in the front foyer.

"She was in a spark den," I started again, staring hard at Mister Tyler, "along with about twenty other kids. When I arrived, the guy who was supplying their drugs and taking their money lit the place on fire. I got your daughter out, and everyone else, too. But the fire department showed up, and so did the police. There was really nothing I could do."

"I want to see her," Sissy Tyler said. She stood again. "Right now, Michael."

Mister Tyler glanced at his wife and nodded. Facing me once more, he started to speak, stopped himself, then started again. "I suppose I ought to be thanking you. It sounds like you saved her life."

"I did," I said. "And you're welcome."

"What do I owe you?"

"Two hundred and fifty dollars a day, comes to . . ." I did the math in my head. "Thirty-five hundred, plus expenses. Let's call it an even four thousand, minus the five hundred you paid me when I started."

He nodded, cut me a check on the spot, and led me back to my car.

Holding out his hand, Tyler said, "I really am grateful, Mister Fearsson. Both of us are."

"Yes, sir," I said, gripping his hand. "I'm glad I was able to find her."

I climbed into the Z-ster and started the slow drive back to Chandler, where I have both my house and my business. Along the way I stopped to deposit my check, relieved to know that I wouldn't have to rely on overdraft protection to keep my rent check from bouncing.

As soon as I reached the office I tossed the newspaper and mail onto my desk, scrubbed my hands and arms up to my biceps, and washed down a couple of aspirin. Then I fired up the espresso machine.

My office isn't much to speak of. It's a single room on the top floor of one of those new sidewalk shopping developments that have grown up everywhere in recent years. It's well lit, with a bank of windows overlooking the street. It was originally intended for a local lawyer, who insisted on oak floors. He took a job with a big firm in downtown Phoenix a couple of months after the place was built and I happened to luck into it. I have a desk, a computer and printer, a pair of file cabinets, a small john off the main room, a couple of chairs for clients, one of those mini refrigerators, and my coffee maker, some Italian brand, which I remember costing more than all the other furniture in the place. I like coffee. Sumatran mostly, the stronger the better.

The computer doesn't see a whole lot of action. Mostly I use it for billing and writing up reports for the insurance companies. I'm not much for technology. Where most PIs these days rely on computers and cell phones and fax machines, I tend to do things the old-fashioned way, face to face, notepad in hand. It's not that I'm afraid of the fancier stuff or anything like that. I carry a cell phone, and use it when I have to. But I'll choose a handshake and a personal conversation over cell phones and social media any day of the week. I'm a purist at heart.

Of course, that begs the question, what is a purist doing with a seven-hundred-dollar espresso machine? I have no answer. My personal philosophy remains a work in progress.

My coffee was still brewing when the figure began to materialize in the corner by my doorway. It was insubstantial at first, a faint glimmering, like reflections of moonlight on a mountain stream. Gradually it grew more distinct, taking the form of a man, tall, broadly built. But always he kept that rippled, glowing appearance, as if he were composed entirely of luminous waters. If others had been there with me, they would have thought that a ghost had come to my office. And they wouldn't have been too far off.

To be precise, he was a runemyste, one of thirty-nine ancient weremystes who had been sacrificed by the Runeclave centuries ago, their spirits granted eternal life, so that they could be guardians of magic in our world. It's easier to call him a ghost, but he gets touchy about that. This particular runemyste—my runemyste, I guess you could say—was named Namid'skemu. I called him Namid. He was once a shaman, what most people would call a medicine man, of the K'ya'na-Kwe clan of the A'shiwi, or Zuni nation. The K'ya'na-Kwe were known as the water people, and they were, in their day, a powerful clan, steeped in the spiritual realm of their people. Today their line is extinct. Unless you count Namid.

I saw only a small fraction of what Namid did to guard against those who would use magic for dark purposes, and I understood even less. But one of his duties was to instruct me in the ways of runecrafting.

I can't say why Namid took an interest in me. As I've already admitted, I'm not the most powerful myste in the world; not even close. But I know that he was once my father's instructor and I think that on some level he held himself responsible for my father's descent into madness. I also know that he answers to a spirit council made up of his fellow runemystes, and from what I gather, they don't allow members of their council to engage in magical charity or indulge their guilt. So apparently, like my dad before me, I'm weremyste enough to have earned Namid's attention. I know for a fact that the magic is strong enough in me to have cost me my job. Namid would probably say that you couldn't measure sorcery by degrees, that you either were a weremyste—a runecrafter, as he called those who used magic—or you weren't. And he'd have been right. Being a weremyste was a lot like being a cop: once it was in your blood, that was it.

I nodded to the glowing figure. "Hey, Namid. What's up?"

"Ohanko," he answered, his voice fluid and resonant, like the rush of deep currents over stone. Ohanko was what he usually called me, although he had other names for me as well. All of them were in his language, and most of them he saved for those times when I'd really ticked him off. I only understood one or two of the others, but Ohanko I knew. It meant, roughly, "reckless one," and I guess I had earned it over the years.

He stood there, staring at me. His eyes shone from his face, like bright, cold flames reflected off the surface of a wind-swept lake. I'd never actually touched Namid—not to shake his hand, or pat him on the shoulder, or sock him in the mouth, which I often wanted to do. I wasn't even certain that it was possible. But I would have loved to try it, just once, just to feel what it was like. I imagined it would be like plunging my hand into an icy creek.

"Well?" I asked, uncomfortable under his gaze. "What do you want?"

"You need to practice your runecrafting."

"Not today, Namid. I have a headache." I grinned hoping to soften the refusal, and also to indicate that I was kidding. Namid's expression didn't change. He understood few of my jokes. He never found them funny. "Another time," I said, knowing this wouldn't satisfy him. My stomach had started to feel tight and hollow. I wasn't sure why; I knew only that I got this feeling whenever Namid demanded that I work on my craft. "Later," I said. "I promise. I'm wiped right now. I had an encounter with a myste this morning."

"You will tell me about that when we are finished. Now, we work. You have much to learn."

"Yeah, well, you're not going to teach me all of it in one day. It can wait."

The runemyste stepped to the middle of the room and lowered himself to the floor, his movements liquid and graceful. He eyed me expectantly. This was where he always sat when instructing me in the use of magic.

"No," I said, sounding like a whiny kid. "I'm not doing this right now." We'd had this argument too many times before. There was still a part of me that feared the powers I possessed. Though I had been casting spells for years, I understood little about the Runeclave and even less about Namid himself. And it was possible—likely, even—that I avoided these sessions because I'd seen what this same magic did to my father.

The phasings, those periods of each moon cycle when magic takes over our minds and bodies, turning us into crazed animals, are no picnic. The line between sanity and insanity, which much of the sane world takes for granted and thinks of as clear cut, feels disturbingly insubstantial to weremystes like me. Because while I consider myself sane most of the time, I also know what it's like to be insane. I've been tipping over into madness every month for half my life. And as bad as the phasings are, the long-term effects are worse. Turns out—big surprise here—putting one's mind through a psychic meat grinder every month takes a heavy toll. Most weremystes wind up permanently insane; a good number of them take their own lives before the descent into irreversible madness makes even that single act of will impossible. So, for good reason, I saw my magical powers as the source of my greatest weakness.

Whatever the root of my reluctance to train, I knew that sooner or later Namid would get his way. He always did.

"Is your scrying stone here or at your home?" he asked.

"It's at the house." Maybe there was a way out of this after all.

I should be so lucky.

"You can scry without the stone. Bring out the mirror from in there." He pointed toward the john.

"Namid . . ." I stopped, shaking my head. Then I got the mirror from the bathroom.

I hate scrying. People think of magic, and one of the first things that comes to mind is gazing into a crystal ball. That's scrying—or rather, that's Hollywood's take on scrying.

Except that scrying doesn't require a crystal ball, or even clear quartz. All you need is a smooth, lustrous surface. I use a piece of polished sea green agate, about the size of my hand, with a small crystalline opening at the center that's surrounded by thin, sinuous bands of blue and white. I didn't choose it because there's anything inherently magical about that piece of agate; I found it several years ago in a gem store at a Phoenix mall. I happen to think it's a beautiful stone, and I know its patterns and colors as well as I do the lines on my father's face.

Namid was right, though. In the absence of my stone, the mirror would work just as well. I sat cross-legged on the floor in front of him and laid the mirror across my lap.

"Look. Tell me what you see."

I gazed down at the mirror. "Is there really a crack in my ceiling?" I asked, peering up at the sheet rock above me.

The runemyste let out a low rumble, like the distant roar of flood waters.

"Sorry." I stared at the mirror again, concentrating on the surface of the glass, trying to ignore the inverted reflection of my office. For a while I saw nothing, and I let out a loud sigh, glancing up at Namid, hoping he'd agree that this was pointless. But the runemyste sat as motionless as ice, his eyes closed. I turned my attention back to the mirror, trying once more to ignore the reflections and see only the glass itself.

"Clear yourself," Namid whispered.

I nodded, and closed my eyes. Clearing was a technique the runemyste had taught me several years before, when he first started training me. It was a focusing mechanism that combined what many practitioners of magic call centering, with meditation, and we had worked on it enough that I could clear myself in mere moments. Once, early on, Namid had me visualize a time from my childhood when I remembered being happiest. I fixed on a camping trip with my parents in the Superstition Wilderness, east of the city. The runemyste made me describe for him every detail of the trip—what we ate, where we slept, what we did and saw. Gradually he steered me toward a single memory: a hike we took in the high country. My parents and I ate a late lunch on a crag that offered amazing views of the Sonoran Desert, stayed there for the sunset, and then returned to our campsite in the dim twilight, my father carrying me on his shoulders on the hike back down.

I remembered watching an eagle from that overlook. It was the first I'd ever seen, and it circled above the desert in front of us, the late afternoon sun lighting the golden feathers on its neck, the tips of its enormous wings splayed, its tail twisting one way and another as it rode the warm desert air.

"Whenever you need to clear yourself, I want you to summon the vision of that eagle," Namid told me. "When you hold that image in your mind, it should remind you of that day, of that feeling of peace. It should drive away all distractions."

And it did. At first, as I was still learning what Namid meant when he spoke of being clear, it could take five or ten minutes. But by now I could call the eagle to mind, and within a minute or two I was centered, my mind focused. As impatient as Namid was with me—as impatient as I often was with myself—I couldn't deny that I was learning.

"When you are clear," the runemyste whispered, "open your eyes again and tell me what you see in the mirror."

For a few seconds longer I kept my mind fixed on the vision of the great bird. Opening my eyes at last, I stared at the surface of the glass again. It felt as if I was alone with the mirror, that Namid had vanished, or rather, that I'd left him behind, along with my office, and Jessie Tyler, and everything else.

The vision began as a thin gray swirl, like a wisp of smoke embedded in the glass. Another appeared, and a third. Soon there were a least a dozen of them chasing one another across the mirror, reminding me of children skating on a frozen pond. The center of the image began to glow, faintly at first, then brighter, until I could make out the oranges and blacks and pale yellows of embers in a dying fire. And then a hand emerged from the cinders. It might have been dark red, the color of blood, but it was silhouetted against that burning glow. It wasn't taloned or deformed. It appeared to be a normal hand, long-fingered perhaps, but ordinary except for its color. Still, I knew immediately that it was . . . wrong; that it didn't belong here. For one thing, those wisps of gray smoke acted as though they were afraid of it. They kept as far from the hand as possible; when it moved, they did as well, matching its motion so as to keep their distance.

This continued for a while, the threads of smoke and the hand gliding over the embers, until suddenly the hand seized the strands of gray, capturing all of them in one lightning quick sweep across the mirror. The hand gripped them, the wisps of smoke appearing to writhe in its grasp. When at last the dark fingers opened again, what was left of the gray strands scattered like ash. And when those remnants touched the embers, they flared so brilliantly that I had to shield my eyes. By the time I looked at the mirror again, the image was gone. All that was left was the inverted reflection of my office.

The runemyste was watching me.

"What the hell was that, Namid?"

"What did you see?"

"You know perfectly well what I saw. You always know. What did it mean?"

"What do you think it meant?"

I shoved the mirror off my lap and stood too quickly; my vision swimming.

"Damn you, Namid! Can't you answer a simple question? Just once?"

"This is as much a part of your training as the summoning of that image. Scrying is more than seeing. Scrying is understanding what you see."

I hated it when he was right.

This was what made scrying so frustrating. The images came to me easily. Even Namid, who was a miser when it came to compliments, had once told me that the visions I summoned from my scrying stone were unusually vivid. Interpreting them, though, was another matter. Scryings were never clear or unambiguous. Rather they were shadows, portents, hints at the future. Frankly, they were a pain in the butt.

"I don't know," I said, beginning to pace the room. "That hand bothered me."

"It should."

I halted, surprised by the response. This was as close to a hint as he was ever likely to offer.

"Why, Namid? What does the hand mean?"

Before he could answer, the phone rang. Neither of us moved, and it rang again.

I kept my eyes on the runemyste, hoping he'd tell me more. The phone rang a third time.

"Someone wishes to speak with you."

A fourth ring and the machine would pick up. I strode across the office and grabbed the phone.

"Fearsson," I said, facing the runemyste.

"Justis."

I would have known that voice anywhere. Kona Shaw. But why would Namid care about a call from Kona? She called all the time.

"What's up, partner?"

"If you have to ask," she said, "you haven't read the paper yet."

Namid stared at me, those cold, impenetrable eyes locked on mine. I felt my gut begin to tighten again.

"Tell me." But even as I said it, my gaze flicked toward the calendar, and I knew. We were two days past the first quarter moon; five days until the full.

"We've found another body."

"Where?"

"South Mountain Park."

"Same guy?"

"Officially, I don't know yet," she said. "But yeah, it's our guy." I could hear the shudder in her voice. Kona was as tough as any cop I'd ever met. In all our years of working together I'd seen little that fazed her, including having a weremyste as a partner. But the Blind Angel murders would have made Jack the Ripper squeamish.

"Listen, partner," Kona said, "we're going to need your help on this one. Just to make sure it's him, you know?" Her voice was nearly drowned out by background noise—car engines, shouting, and at least one siren.

"You still at the scene?" I asked.

"No, I'm . . . I'm in Paradise Valley."

"What?"

"Read the paper, Justis. Or go online. This'll all make sense when you do."

"You've got to give me more than that."

No answer, though I could still hear the commotion behind her.

"Kona?"

"Yeah," she said. "This victim isn't like the others. It's . . . it's Claudia Deegan."

I would have done just about anything in the world for Kona, and I won't deny that I still lay awake at night thinking about the Blind Angel murders, even though I hadn't been on the job for a year and a half. But getting involved in an ongoing police investigation was dangerous enough for an ex-cop; getting involved in one that promised to be a media circus was more than I cared to deal with.

I would have told Kona as much, but abruptly I wasn't paying attention to our conversation. Namid had crossed the room to where I stood, and was staring at me. His color had changed. He had been translucent, his waters as clear as a quiet stream. But now he was clouded, roiled, like a river after a hard rain. His eyes were the same, though: intense and bright. He'd never shown much interest in any of my cases, but it seemed this one had caught his attention.

I put my hand over the mouthpiece. "What is it?" I asked.

He said nothing.

"Damn you, Namid! Would you tell me?"

He turned with deliberate grace and stared down at the mirror that still lay on my floor. After a moment he faced me again.

It wasn't much, but as I say, Namid wasn't one for giving hints. This was more than the runemyste had ever done before.

"Justis?" Kona said.

I removed my hand from the phone. "I'm here."

"I'm going to be tied up here for a while longer, and Margarite's got my car today. Can you meet me at the Deegan place? We can go downtown from there."

"All right," I said.

"Great. One hour."

I hung up and glared back at the runemyste, who was still watching me.

"Would you please tell me what this is about?"

You'd think by now I'd know better than to expect an answer.

Namid began to fade from view. "Tread like the fox, Ohanko. Be wary."

"Thanks a lot," I said, watching as he vanished. "Damn ghost!"

But he was gone.

I went to my desk and retrieved this morning's paper, which was folded beneath the day's mail. The story was right there on the front page. Top headline.

"Claudia Deegan Found Dead. Senator's daughter may be latest 'Angel' Victim."

I almost called Kona back then and there. I had just gotten through tracking down a runaway and dealing with the life crises of the rich and famous. Involving myself with the Deegans would be ten times worse. I didn't want any part of this case.

Or did I?

The PPD had been trying to solve the so-called Blind Angel murders for just shy of three years now. So had the Feds. The FBI came in with a lot of fanfare and press after the third or fourth murder and did their best to take over the investigation. After a while, though—after months stretching to years of being unable to find the killer—they began to lose interest. They cut the size of their task force in half, and then did so again and a third time, until they had basically ceded the investigation back to the Phoenix police.

If Claudia Deegan was this wack-job's latest victim, she would be number thirty-one, that we knew of. I had worked the case when I was on the job, and Kona and her new partner, Kevin Glass, were still part of the investigative team. Being a weremyste, I had realized from the very beginning that magic was involved: I could see the residue of power on the bodies. And it didn't take me long to figure out that every killing occurred around the same time in the moon cycle. I was convinced that our killer had taken a life every month for the last three years at least, and that there were still bodies out there as yet unfound.

Of all the cases I'd been working at the time I left the force, this was the one I most regretted not seeing through to the end. The idea of having another crack at it had definite appeal. On the other hand, as much as I missed being a cop, I didn't miss the jerks who had forced me off the job, who had assumed that my descents into psychosis each month were signs that I was a drunk, or an addict, or both. Even now, there were people in the department—men and women in positions of power—who would have loved to humiliate me all over again, to pay me back for disgracing the force.

In the end, I think that if Namid hadn't shown so much interest in my conversation with Kona, I might have called her back and told her

I wasn't coming. As much as I wanted to find the Blind Angel Killer, I didn't need the kind of heat this case was going to generate. But for whatever reason, the runemyste had made it clear that this was a job I had to take. I remembered my scrying, and that evil red hand. Namid seemed to think it was all related, and who was I to argue?

Yes, I had been a cop, and that would always be in my blood. But I'm still a weremyste, and I will be until the day I die. And for better or worse this was where my magic was leading me. I could tell that much from one glance in a mirror, be it a looking glass or a scrying surface.

CHAPTER 3

I read the rest of the article about Claudia Deegan, my insides winding themselves into knots as the details of the "Angel Murders" investigation flooded back into my mind.

Murder cases are never a picnic, but trying to chase down a serial murderer is about the worst part of a homicide detective's job. You feel that the killer is mocking you with every clue he leaves behind, and you feel responsible for each new murder he commits after you've taken on the investigation. But bad as that is, the worst part is the time in between killings, when you know another one is coming and that there isn't a damn thing you can do to stop it. It's no wonder that cops who investigate serial killings become obsessed with their victims and suspects, and that they're even more prone to drinking, drug use and emotional problems than their colleagues.

Kona and I worked the case from the beginning. We were the first detectives on the scene when Gracia Rosado was found in Red Mountain Park three years ago. It didn't take either of us long to realize that this murder was unlike any we had seen before. Gracia herself was all too typical of murder victims in the Phoenix area. Young, pretty, poor, Latino. She'd been involved with drugs for a couple of years and in the months leading up to her murder had started turning tricks to pay for her habit.

But in every other way, Gracia's killing was chillingly unique. Her body was found by a jogger in a small ravine deep in the park. She was fully clothed and there was no sign that she'd been sexually assaulted, which is pretty much the first thing you check for in a case like this. There were bruises on her neck, but I knew right away that her killer hadn't strangled her to death. Red magic shone like fresh blood on her face and chest, though I was the only cop working the scene who could see it. On the other hand, every cop and reporter there could see that her eyes had been burned out of her skull.

"Looks like we've got ourselves a new freak to track down," Kona said at the time, staring down at Gracia's body and shaking her head. "Just what Phoenix needs at the start of the damn summer."

"It's worse than you know," I said, keeping my voice low.

"What do you mean—?" She stopped and stared at me. "Oh, don't tell me, Justis, because I don't want to hear it."

Kona was the only person on the force who knew I was a weremyste. I'd told her early on, following number seven of my father's ten rules for being a successful cop: "Never keep secrets from your partner."

She hadn't believed me at first, but it hadn't taken more than a spell or two to convince her. And after my magical abilities helped us clear a couple of cases, she began to think of it as a good thing, even if it did render me useless three nights out of each month.

But on that morning in June, standing over what turned out to be the first of at least thirty murder victims—thirty-one, if the papers were right about Claudia Deegan—she wasn't amused at all.

"Talk to me, Justis," she said. She and my father were the only people who called me Justis rather than Jay. "What are you seeing?"

"There's red magic on her face and chest. Powerful magic—it's already starting to fade."

"If it's already starting to fade—"

"The faster the residue fades, the more powerful the sorcerer," I told her for what had to have been the twentieth time.

She nodded. "Right. I always get that backwards. So you're saying she was killed by magic. For sure."

"For sure."

"Well, that's just great. What do your magic senses tell you about that shit her killer did with her eyes?"

I shook my head. A white sheet lay over Gracia's body, but I could still see her ravaged face in my mind. In fact, I still can see it to this day. "I have no idea," I told her at the time.

The second body was discovered about a month later. Also a young woman, also killed by magic, her face mutilated in the same way. Others followed, some of them men, though most of the victims were women. All of them were young, and all of them died the same way. And, it turned out, all of the killings took place about a week before the full moon. Sometimes it took longer to find the bodies, but always the coroner put the time of death around the first quarter moon. I still have no idea what this means, but I know it's important.

Each body had been found in either Red Mountain Park, east of Mesa, or in South Mountain Park, on the west side of Tempe, so those of us working the case referred to our perp as the East Side Parks Killer. But the media fixated on the ritual aspect of the killings—the facial mutilation—and dubbed the killings the Blind Angel murders.

There had been no shortage of media coverage of the killings, but now that Claudia Deegan had been murdered it was likely to turn into a frenzy. Randolph Deegan, Claudia's father, was Arizona's most powerful and popular politician. Word was that he was running for governor this year, and that a presidential run might be in his future. Everything the Deegans did was news. Claudia's death would be on the front page of every paper in the country; the Arizona papers wouldn't be covering anything else.

Reading the article left little doubt in my mind that the Deegan girl had been murdered by the Parks Killer. The medical examiner claimed that she'd died two nights ago—the night of the quarter moon. Her body had been found yesterday in South Mountain Park. The article also mentioned that like so many of the other victims, Claudia Deegan had drugs in her blood and on her person at the time she died. Spark to be specific, which in addition to being addictive and expensive, also happened to be one of the drugs some weremystes used to suppress the effects of the phasings. As to the rest, the paper dealt with the details as delicately as it could.

A spokesperson for Senator Deegan's family refused to comment on the condition of Miss Deegan's body. However, sources within the police department confirmed that her face had been disfigured in a manner consistent with past Blind Angel killings.

The paper said nothing about magic, of course. It never did. No one at the scene would be able to confirm that magic had killed the Deegans' daughter. That was why Kona needed me.

For the second time that day, I drove back toward Scottsdale, this time heading into the foothills near the city. Traffic was starting to build again, but aside from the stop-and-go, the drive from my place in Chandler to the Deegan estate wasn't a difficult one. Still, judging from the difference between the neighborhood where I have my office, and the community in which the senator and his family live, you might have thought I'd entered another country.

The estate was located on a twisting road with more million-dollar houses than you could shake a stick at, all of them gated, all of them with clear views of Camelback Mountain.

As I rounded the last turn before the Deegan house I found the road half-blocked by a huge mob of reporters and cops. More than a dozen news vans lined the road; state patrol cruisers had been parked strategically to control traffic in both directions. There were sound booms and cameras everywhere—still and video. I slowed the Z-ster and crept past it all. As I did, the media people peered into the car, hoping to recognize someone famous. They all looked vaguely disappointed when all they saw was some guy in an old bomber jacket with wild hair and a three-day beard.

A uniformed cop stopped me and signaled for me to lower my window.

"You live up here?" he asked.

I almost laughed. "No. I'm a PI. I'm on my way to the Deegan place. Kona Shaw asked me to come. You can call ahead and check with her if you want."

He shook his head, straightened, and waved me on.

The Deegans' driveway was maybe thirty yards beyond the mob scene; nice for them, but I doubt their neighbors were thrilled with the arrangement. I guess it paid to be the most powerful man in Arizona.

The wrought-iron gate in front of the senator's place was guarded by two guys in navy slacks and powder-blue, short-sleeve dress shirts with the insignia of some security company I'd never heard of emblazoned on the sleeves. They were built like linebackers, with necks about as thick as my thigh. I also noticed that they carried

.40 caliber Glock 22s in their shoulder harnesses. A good choice; that's what I carry, too.

"Can I help you?" one of them growled at me through my driver-side window as the Z-ster idled in front of the gate.

"Jay Fearsson to see Detective Kona Shaw."

"License?"

I pulled out my wallet, flipped it open to my driver's license and handed it to him. As an afterthought I took off my sunglasses. Most security guys want to see your eyes.

He studied the picture, looked at me, and handed back my wallet. "They're expecting you." He nodded to his partner and a moment later the gate slid open with a low electrical whir. "Everyone's in the main house."

I nodded and steered the Z-ster to a spot next to about nine other cars. Four of them were worth more than I make in a year, even a good year. Of the other five, two were police cruisers and two of the others were cheaper models with police tags.

I didn't like this. Not at all. Aside from Kona, most of these people thought the worst of me. Many of them had nothing but contempt for what they thought I'd become; others pitied me, which might have been worse. A voice in my head screamed at me to leave now, while I had the chance. If not for the way Namid had pinned me with his stare when the phone rang, I would have. I got out of the car.

The driveway, if you could call it that, was an enormous cobblestone courtyard with a small bronze statue and fountain at the center. On the south side of the courtyard, arrayed in a semicircle, stood three buildings: two smaller ones—guest houses probably— flanking the main house. All the buildings were built in Spanish Mission style, which was popular among homeowners in Paradise Valley and throughout the Phoenix area. A cobblestone path to the front door of the mansion wound past an elaborate desert garden; hummingbirds darted among an array of glass feeders.

The door opened as I approached the front landing. I expected to see Kona. Instead, two people I didn't know emerged from the house. One was a short, slender man with thinning hair and tortoise shell glasses. He was wearing charcoal suit pants and a white dress shirt. His sleeves were rolled up, his tie loosened. He had dark rings under his eyes and a deep crease in his forehead, as if his face was stuck in a permanent grimace. He struck me as someone in the midst of a really bad day. Still, he managed a smile as he extended a hand to the woman standing beside him.

She was taller, and very attractive. She had long, curly brown hair that she wore pulled back from her face, and she wore dark-rimmed glasses with those small rectangular lenses that college professors tend to like. They were cute on her, though they made her look way too intelligent for a guy like me. Call it a cop's instinct, but I had a feeling that she was every bit as smart as she appeared.

"Thank you for coming, Billie," the man said. "I trust you'll be kinder to the senator than you've been recently. At least until we're through this."

"No promises, Mister Wriker," the woman said, smiling at him. "But I hope that you'll convey my condolences to Senator and Missus Deegan."

"I will. I'm sure they'll—" The man spotted me and stopped. "Who the hell are you? And how'd you get in here?"

The woman turned and eyed me with obvious interest.

"I'm Jay Fearsson. I'm here to see Detective Shaw."

The man narrowed his eyes, but then he began to nod. "Right. She said something about that. Forgive me, Mister Fearsson." He walked down the path to where I stood, the woman following.

"Howard Wriker," he said, as I shook his hand. "I'm Senator Deegan's chief of staff and a close friend of the family." He indicated the woman. "This is Billie Castle."

"Miss Castle," I said, shaking her hand as well.

"Are you a police officer, Mister Fearsson?" she asked.

I started to answer, but out of the corner of my eye caught a warning glance from Wriker.

"I'm an investigator," I said. Before she could ask me more, I faced Wriker again. "Where can I find Detective Shaw?"

"In the house," he told me. "I'll join you in just a moment."

I nodded once to the woman and hurried to the door. I couldn't say why, but I felt like I'd come through a shootout without being hit.

Stepping into the house, I saw that it was as impressive on the inside as it had been from the courtyard. The front foyer opened onto a large living room with oak floors that made the wood in my office seem cheap and dull. Opposite the entry was a bank of windows offering views of the mountain and, in the distance, the buildings of downtown Phoenix. My first thought was that this place had to be spectacular at night, not that it was bad now. The room was decorated tastefully with Native American art: pottery from Acoma and Jemez set on tables and shelves, Navajo blankets hanging on the walls, Kachinas in glass cases—not the cheap dolls made for tourists by the Navajo, but the real things, carved from cottonwood by the Hopi. I knew enough about the Southwestern tribes to understand that the Deegans had one hell of a collection, one that would have been the envy of many museums.

I was still admiring the Kachinas when I heard a footstep behind me. Turning, I saw Wriker close the door, a weary look on his face.

"That was well done, Mister Fearsson. If you can avoid talking to Billie Castle you should. For your sake and the senator's."

"Why? Who is she?"

Wriker frowned. "You don't know?"

I shook my head.

"You've never heard of 'Castle's Village'?"

"No. Should I have?"

"It's a blog," Wriker said, making "blog" sound like a dirty word. "A political one—probably the most popular of its kind in the Southwest. She has correspondents and opinion writers from all over Arizona, New Mexico, Colorado, Southern California, West Texas." He shook his head. "Suffice it to say that few of them are fans of the senator."

"And yet you allowed her in the house."

Wriker crossed to a wet bar in the near corner of the room. "You want a drink?"

"Water would be fine, thanks."

"You don't mind if I have a Scotch, do you?"

"Of course not. I'm sure this has been an awful day."

"You have no idea," he said.

"You and the Deegans have my deepest sympathies, sir," I said. There are only so many ways to tell the family of a murder victim that you're sorry for them, and over the years I'd used every one. But just because I'd said these words a thousand times that didn't mean I wasn't sincere. I'd never been a fan of Randolph Deegan; I'd never voted for him. But I wouldn't have wished this tragedy on my worst enemy.

"Thank you." He plunked ice cubes into a pair of tumblers, filled one from the tap, and poured a good deal of scotch into the other. "To answer your question," he said, handing me my drink, "yes, I let her into the house. Her readership is greater than the combined circulation of every newspaper in the state. And a little goodwill now might smooth things over for us later in the year."

I sipped my water. "Well, I know how hard a time this must be for the Deegans and for you. If you can just tell me where I'd find Ko— Detective Shaw, I'll be out of your way."

Wriker nodded and took a long drink of scotch, draining more than half the glass. "Of course," he said. "She's in with the senator and his wife right now, but I'll tell her you're here."

He put down his glass and walked through the front foyer to the other side of the house. Left alone, I crossed to the windows and stared out at the city. For the past year and a half, as I'd followed the Blind Angel case in the papers, poring over every article for details of the sixteen killings—now seventeen—that had occurred since I left the force, I had tried to put myself in Kona's shoes, to feel what she must have been feeling with every new murder. But I hadn't been able to. Losing my job had devastated me, but it had also released me from this one burden. The killings continued to haunt me, but that crushing feeling of responsibility I'd felt while still working homicide vanished once I was off the job.

Until now. Standing in Randolph Deegan's living room, I felt it returning; I could almost feel my shoulders bending with the weight of it. One phone call from Kona and the Blind Angel murders were mine again. It wasn't anything I wanted, and yet it felt strangely familiar, even comforting. I realize how twisted that sounds. As I said before, once a cop, always a cop.

"What the hell are you doing here?"

I knew that voice almost as well as I knew Kona's. Cole Hibbard: Commander of the PPD's Violent Crimes Bureau, and the man most responsible for forcing me out of the department. Before, when I said that I wouldn't wish the Deegan mess on my worst enemy, I had forgotten about Hibbard. I'd wish a whole load of crap on him.

I turned.

Hibbard stood in the entrance to the living room, looking like he had half a mind to pull out his weapon and shoot me then and there.

He was silver-haired, stocky, and pretty fit for a guy in his mid-sixties. There'd been a time when he and my father were close, but then my dad's mind started to slip and Hibbard turned on him, assuming that he was using drugs or drinking. I suppose it's understandable. Unless you're a weremyste, you really can't understand the intensity of the phasings. It's not something we like to talk about. Even those of us who are willing to admit that we're mystes are hesitant to tell the people around us that we're doomed to go insane. That's one of the reasons we use the word "myste" to describe ourselves rather than "weremystes." No sense conjuring images of werewolves howling at the moon; the reality is too close to that for comfort. Hibbard wouldn't have had any reason to suspect that one of his best friends on the force, a young, seemingly normal guy with a promising career ahead of him, was quietly going nuts right before his eyes.

Hibbard had it in for me from the start, assuming that I was trouble like my old man, and that it was just a matter of time before I screwed up, too. That he was right did nothing to make me hate him less.

"Hi there, Hibbard. Have you missed me?"

"Don't give me any of your crap, Fearsson. I want to know what you're doing here."

"I called him, Commander." Kona stepped around him into the room, with Wriker on her heels. It was like a big old family reunion; the kind you read about in the tabloids beneath headlines like "Grandmother Goes on Shooting Rampage."

You couldn't have found two people who were less alike than Cole Hibbard and Kona Shaw. Apart from the fact that they were both cops, they had next to nothing in common. Kona, whose real name was Deandra, was tall and thin, with skin the color of Kona coffee, which, as it happens, was just about all she drank. Hence the name. She was quite possibly the most beautiful woman I'd ever known, with big dark eyes, the cheekbones of a fashion model, short, tightly curled black hair, and a dazzling smile. She was also gay, in a department that was hard enough on women detectives, much less black, lesbian women detectives. That she had lasted in the department so long was testimony to how good a cop she was. If anyone needed further evidence, she had at least ten commendations to her name.

Kona had been my partner the entire time I was on the force. I can't say that she taught me everything I know about police work, because my father taught me a good deal before his mind totally quit on him. But if it hadn't been for Kona, I wouldn't have been half the cop I was.

"You called him in?" Hibbard said, glowering at her. "Where do you get off making a decision like that without clearing it through me first?"

"Sergeant Arroyo told me to call him," she said. Hibbard opened his mouth, no doubt to remind her that he outranked Arroyo. But she didn't give him the chance. "And he was acting on orders from the assistant chief."

"Latrelle? I don't believe it."

If it had been me, I would have demanded to know if the bastard was calling me a liar. But that was one of the reasons Kona still had a job on the force and I didn't. She flashed that gorgeous smile of hers, and said, "You're free to call him, Commander. But I promise you it's true."

Hibbard turned his glare back on me. For several seconds he said nothing. Then he shook his head and muttered, "Fine. Keep him the hell away from me."

Before Kona could answer, he stalked out of the room.

"What did you do to piss him off?" Kona asked, turning my way.

"Since when do I have to do anything? You know that Cole doesn't play well with others."

She lifted an eyebrow.

I held up my hands. "I swear, Kona. I said hello, and he acted like I'd been saying stuff about his mother."

Wriker cleared his throat, and both of us looked his way.

"I take it you used to be on the force," he said to me.

"Yes, sir."

"And now you're a private investigator?"

"That's right."

"Would you be willing to work for the Deegans?"

I exchanged glances with Kona. The PPD wouldn't be paying me for whatever work I did to help Kona with the case. They never did. But still, working for two clients at once on the same case was a bit sketchy ethics-wise.

She shrugged. "It doesn't bother me."

"What is it you'd want me to do?" I asked, turning back to Wriker.

"The papers are saying that Claudia was a drug addict, that she had drugs in her system and on her person when she died. We don't believe that."

I shook my head.

"Hear me out," Wriker said. "Either the medical examiner will say that she had drugs in her blood or he won't. But the police say she was carrying. We'd like to know where those drugs came from. If . . . if she was an addict, like the papers and television news say, we'd like to see the dealer who sold her the stuff put in jail."

I glanced at Kona again. She was staring at the floor, her lips pursed, as they often were when she had something on her mind that she knew she couldn't say aloud.

"Arresting drug dealers isn't the job of a PI," I told Wriker. "As to finding out where she bought her stuff . . ." I shrugged. "I'm afraid I don't see much point. Chances are the dealer was small time—maybe a college kid. I doubt it would do much good to go after him. Or her."

Wriker sighed, sounding exhausted. "You're probably right. Thank you anyway."

I took a breath. I'd never been fond of politicians, but in that moment I felt bad for the guy. Call it a moment of weakness. "I'll find out what I can, Mister Wriker," I said. "No charge. If I find anything of value, you can pay me then."

"Yes, we will. Of course. Thank you, Mister Fearsson." He pulled a business card from his shirt pocket, wrote his cell number on the back, and handed it to me. "Call me when you know something. Please."

"I will."

Kona and I thanked him for his time and left the house.

"No charge?" she said in a low voice, as we walked down the path toward the cars. "That your idea of a business plan?"

"You heard the guy. He was ready to hire me just so he'd feel like he'd done something."

She winced at the memory, then nodded. "Yeah, I know."

"I won't spend much time on it. But we know that our killer seeks out kids who are using. Maybe knowing where she scored her drugs will tell us something."

Kona looked impressed. "I hadn't thought of that. You must have been a pretty good cop, and you must have had one very good teacher."

"I did," I said, grinning. I waited a beat, then, "My dad taught me a lot."

"Shut up."

We both laughed. It was good to see her. Of all the things I'd loved about being a cop, having Kona as a partner was what I missed the most.

After a minute or two she grew serious again. "You ready to go over to the OME?"

OME. Office of the Medical Examiner. I needed to see Claudia Deegan's body, to confirm that she'd been killed by magic. It was amazing how quickly we could jump from the best part of my old job to the worst.

"Yeah," I said. "I'm ready."

I started toward the Z-ster, but Kona didn't move.

"You coming?" I said.

She remained where she was, watching me, a sly smile on her lips. "I've got something for you. Drop me at 620 before you park. We'll walk from there."

"What have you got?"

"It's a surprise."

I didn't answer; I just waited.

"Fine then. Claudia Deegan was arrested a couple of weeks ago at a political protest down at the military base in Florence. She put it together, apparently; they were demonstrating against some new bomber that her father had sponsored. She was trying to embarrass him, I guess." She shook her head. "Anyway, there was someone else arrested that day. I think you'll be interested in who it was."

Before I could ask her more, she climbed into the Z-ster and pulled the door closed. I had no choice but to get in and drive her to Phoenix Police headquarters.

CHAPTER 4

I let Kona out in front of 620, which is what cops call police headquarters, because it's located at 620 West Washington Street. I parked, and waited outside while she went up into HQ to get the list of arrested protesters. At some point I would get up the nerve to go back inside the building, but I wasn't there yet. Simply seeing the place was like running into an old girlfriend who I hadn't quite gotten over. I stood outside on the sidewalk trying to act like I belonged there, and avoiding eye contact with anyone going in or coming out.

As soon as I saw Kona emerge from the building, I started walking west on Washington, knowing that she'd catch up with me, knowing as well that she'd understand.

When she caught up with me, she handed me the list of names, but said nothing.

"Five pages?" I asked folding back the sheets. Names, phone numbers, addresses. This would be helpful, but I had no idea so many people had been arrested.

"It was a big protest," Kona said. "Deegan's daughter wasn't the only one who was ticked off about that bomber, or whatever it was."

"I guess not." There had to be two hundred names here. "So are you going to tell me who I'm looking for or make me figure it out myself?"

"I haven't decided yet."

The OME was only about a block from 620, on Jefferson. I started to read through the list as we walked, but none of the names jumped out at me, and before I knew it we were at the Medical Examiner's building, being buzzed into the facility by security.

Kona had on her ID from 620 and the guard waved us past his desk toward the autopsy lab, and the coolers where bodies were kept.

The M.E. was a guy named Pete Forsythe, who had been running forensics in Phoenix since before I joined the force. He was a crusty old goat, and not at all the kind of person who would have tolerated the presence of a PI in his facility. Fortunately, he liked to delegate work to his staff, and was rarely in the labs or cold storage this time of day.

"Have they done the autopsy yet?" I asked as we navigated the corridors, our footsteps echoing.

"I asked them not to," Kona said. "I thought you'd want to see her as we found her. They only brought her in last night and Pete was willing to wait until this afternoon."

I nodded.

We found a young woman in the anthrodental lab who was comparing dental records on a computer screen to a set of X-rays. I'd never seen her before, but Kona knew her.

"Hey, Caroline."

The woman looked over at us and smiled. "Hi, Kona." She was pretty. Red hair, freckles, blue eyes, a little on the heavy side, great smile. I noticed a big diamond on her left hand. "What can I do ya for?"

"This is my friend Jay Fearsson."

"Hi, Jay," the woman said. "Caroline Packer."

"Nice to meet you, Caroline."

"You new in Homicide? I haven't seen you here before."

"Jay's an investigator," Kona said before I could answer. "He's helping me out with something. I was wondering if we could take a look at the Deegan kid."

Caroline's smile vanished, along with most of the color in her cheeks. "Yeah, sure," she said. But she didn't move for a few seconds. She seemed to be gathering herself. "She's in CS," she said. "I can . . . I can show you."

"We know where it is," Kona told her, her tone gentle. "Just tell us which shelf."

"Fourteen. And you have to sign. The clipboard's outside the door."

Kona nodded. "Okay. Thanks."

"What he did to her . . . It's . . ." She broke off, swallowing and shaking her head. "I didn't used to think about this kind of stuff, but I don't like to be out after dark anymore."

"I understand," Kona said.

She turned and left the lab, and I followed her. The receiving cooler, where they kept bodies that had not yet been examined, was beside the autopsy room. We paused outside the door so that Kona could sign the access sheet, and then we stepped inside. It was a cold, stark, depressing place. Stainless steel walls and doors, hard fluorescent lighting, and a series of steel shelves on every wall for the bodies. Most of the shelves were empty, as usual, but there were white body bags on a few of them, including the middle shelf under the number fourteen.

A jar of mentholated Vaseline sat on a gurney near the door. Before opening the body bag we rubbed a small amount under our noses to guard against the smell. Then Kona unzipped the bag and spread it open.

My first thought was that the police had gotten the ID wrong. Sure she was a mess—there were burned out craters in her face where her eyes should have been. But this girl bore almost no resemblance to the Claudia Deegan I'd seen on the news and in countless newspaper photos. That girl had been blonde, athletic, tan: the all-American kid. This girl's hair was black, though peering more closely I could see that the roots were blonde. Her face was gaunt and she wore dark lipstick that gave her mouth a severe look.

"You're sure this is the Deegan kid?" I asked Kona, staring down at the girl.

"Yeah, we're sure. Why?"

I shook my head. "Doesn't matter."

Kona had brought me there to tell her if there was any magical residue on the body, and it was all over Claudia's face, neck and chest. Magic was similar to any other forensic evidence. Just as a gunshot at close range left powder burns on a victim, or strangulation caused bruising, magic left its mark as well. And just as fingerprints were unique, so was the color left by a weremyste's conjuring. Only another weremyste could see it, but to those of us with magic in our veins it was as obvious as a bloodstain or an open wound. Often, magical residue reminded me of fluorescent paint that had spilled wherever a runecrafter's spells had touched. It glowed and shimmered, the colors as vivid as summer wildflowers. At least at first.

The glow on Claudia's body had grown faint, and with the overhead lighting so harsh it was difficult to see. As I'd told Kona earlier, the more powerful the weremyste, the faster any remnant of his magic would fade. This probably seems backwards, but if you think of magic as having a half-life, like uranium, it starts to make more sense. Carbon 14 is a weak radiant with a slow half-life—well over five thousand years. Strontium 90, on the other hand, is powerfully radioactive and has a half-life of less than thirty years. In the same way, the stronger a spell, the faster its residue decays. At least, that's how I think of it. Then again, I'm not exactly a nuclear physicist.

Of course, there was a flip side to the fast decay thing: the more powerful the sorcerer, the more brilliant the color of his magic would be to begin with. I had seen the Blind Angel Killer's magic before; I would have recognized that shade of crimson anywhere. Still, even knowing how powerful he was, I couldn't help but be surprised—and scared—at how dim it had grown in a mere two days. I might not have noticed it as much working the case month to month, but in the time since I'd last seen one of his victims, the Blind Angel Killer had made himself stronger. Much stronger.

"Is it our guy?" Kona asked, watching me.

I nodded. "I think he's getting more powerful."

"Well, that's just what I want to hear."

"The color is nearly gone. Even at the eyes, where it should be most intense." I faced Kona. "I think whatever he gets from these kids is building him up. There's more to this than random killing."

"You've told me that before. But do you know what he's getting?"

"No." I turned back to Claudia's corpse. "If I knew that maybe we could find him." I stood for a moment, staring at the girl's ravaged face. "Let me try something," I said.

Three elements again: my magic, the red magic glowing on Claudia, and the purpose of the killer's spell. This last I didn't know, of course; I was hoping the spell would fill in that bit of information with some physical manifestation of the killer's magic. I had tried this before a couple of years ago, but I was a more accomplished runecrafter now, and I thought maybe I'd get a different result.

I didn't. I might have been better with magic now than I was when I worked for the PPD, but I wasn't yet a match for the Blind Angel Killer.

"Did anything happen?" Kona asked, looking back and forth between Claudia's corpse and me.

"No. We're going to have to find him the old-fashioned way."

"Not we, partner," Kona said in the same gentle tone she'd used with the girl in the lab. "That's not your job. I appreciate you coming down here with me, but we'll do the rest."

I said nothing, and I couldn't bring myself to meet her gaze. She was right, of course, but it wasn't like I needed to be reminded that I was no longer on the job. And Kona should have known that.

"I'm sorry, Justis. It's just—"

"I know," I said, my voice echoing sharply in the cold room. I turned away from the body and started for the door.

"Justis—"

"I should talk to that girl. Caroline. I should ask her about the whole drug thing. That's what the Deegans are worried about."

I left the room before Kona could stop me and went back to the anthrodental lab. Caroline glanced over as I walked in and gave a weak smile, but she was still pale.

I sat on an empty stool near her. "Can I ask you a couple of questions?"

She pulled her lab coat tighter around her shoulders. "I don't know much. I'm not working on . . . Until Doctor Forsythe does his initial autopsy, there's not much for the rest of us to do."

"I understand that. But I need some information; or I will when you start the lab work."

"I'm not sure—"

"It's nothing that the M.E. won't eventually give the press. I just need to know what kind of drugs she'd been taking, and anything you can tell me about their potency."

Caroline frowned. "Aren't you with the force? Kona said you're an investigator. Can't you get this from her?"

I forced a smile. "I'm asking you for it." I pulled out my wallet and gave her one of my business cards. "If you can, call me at that number . . ."

She was looking more frightened by the moment. "Um . . ."

"It's all right. I've known Pete Forsyth since you were in high school. He won't mind. And you can call me from your home, if you think that would be better."

"Stop it, Justis."

Kona didn't raise her voice. She didn't have to.

Caroline glanced past me, the relief on her face making me ashamed of myself. I turned, feeling my color rise.

Kona crossed to where I sat, wearing an expression that would have wrung an apology from a gangbanger.

"We're leaving," she told me. Turning, she said, "Sorry to have bothered you, Caroline. Tell Pete we're done here. He can go ahead with the autopsy."

Caroline nodded, seeming unsure of what had happened. Her gaze flicked from me to Kona.

I should have said something to her, but I was too embarrassed. I followed Kona out of the lab, through the hallways back to the main entrance. Once we were out on the street again, Kona turned to me, her hands on her hips.

"What the hell were you thinking, trying to play that poor girl like that?"

I didn't meet her gaze. "Wriker asked me to find out—"

"Don't give me that shit. He didn't tell you to go and bully some kid into getting herself fired."

I wasn't sure that Wriker or the Deegans would give a crap about Caroline Packer. But I knew that I didn't want to be measuring myself against their morals.

"I pissed you off," Kona said. "And you didn't want to have to get that information from me. So you went after her."

"Yes."

Kona stared down at her feet, her lips pursed. "I shouldn't have said what I did. You don't need me telling you what your job is, especially when you're still working this case and not getting any credit for it. The fact is, Latrelle wanted you here, but strictly on 'a consulting basis.' His words. I'm not even sure what he meant, and to be honest, I don't know how we're going to make this work. But I shouldn't have said it that way."

I shrugged, still not looking at her.

"Pressure's high on this one, partner," she said. "This guy's had our number for three years now, and that's bad enough. But you add in the Deegans, and suddenly everyone's on edge, you know?"

I could imagine.

"The damn FBI's back in town, acting as though they never bailed on us in the first place, asking why we haven't made more progress while they were gone." Kona paused, exhaled. "Anyway," she went on, "I'm sorry."

"It's all right." And it was. I'd never been able to stay mad at Kona for long, or her at me. Our friendship—our partnership—had always been too strong. I raised my chin toward the door we'd come through. "You'll apologize for me?"

"Yeah, sure," she said. "And I'll get that information to you as quickly as I can. I promise."

I nodded. "I know you will."

She glanced back toward the door. "Anything more you can tell me about what you saw in there?"

"Not really." We started walking back toward 620. "It's the same shade of red, but it's fading faster than it used to. Otherwise it's exactly like the other times. Mostly on her head and chest. No particular pattern, though it's strongest around the eyes."

"Nothing different at all?" Kona asked.

I shook my head, knowing where she was headed. "I don't think he had any idea that this was Claudia Deegan. She was just another kid to him."

"Yeah, well, that might have been true the other night. Not anymore. Things are about to get very hot for everyone involved in this case, including our friend with the red magic."

We fell silent, and after a few moments I pulled out the list of protest arrests Kona had given me.

"Check on page three," Kona said. "A bit past the middle."

I read several names before I saw it. I stopped dead in my tracks and gaped at her. She stopped, too.

"Robby Sommer?" I said.

"Interesting, don't you think? You're trying to find the source of Claudia Deegan's drugs, and look who gets his ass arrested at that protest Claudia put together."

Robby Sommer was a small-time drug dealer who I'd busted several years back. He catered to high-end, low-volume buyers; rich college students for the most part. Kids like Claudia Deegan, although he wasn't above selling to anyone he could find.

"You think he was connected to any of the other kids?" I asked.

"It's possible," Kona said. "A few of them were at the university; most of them were using."

"But this is the first time we've—" I smiled self-consciously. "That you've had any kind of link between Robby and a victim."

"Yeah. This is the first."

We started walking again, and I stared at Robby's name on that list. His address hadn't changed since I arrested him. "I guess you should go see him."

"Why don't you?" Kona said. "Kevin and I have more than enough to keep us busy, and this is the type of thing you'd be doing for Wriker anyway."

"All right."

I expected her to remind me that since I wasn't a cop anymore, I couldn't push Robby too far, but she didn't.

"I'll let you know what I find out," I said.

She nodded. "I'll do the same."

"Thank you, Kona."

We'd reached Washington again.

"No problem, partner. Talk to you soon."

She continued back toward 620; I turned toward the City Hall parking lot, my chest aching. I'd never begrudge Kona her badge, but at that moment I wanted mine back more than I wanted anything.

Nobody would be surprised to learn that a drug dealer like Robby Sommer was a screw-up. What always amazed me about the kid, though, was how lucky he'd been. In the years since I'd arrested him, he had been hauled in at least three or four more times. But he'd only been convicted once, and then on a reduced count. Something always seemed to go wrong with Robby's arrests—evidence was misplaced, procedures got fouled up. One time an assistant district attorney was found to have manufactured evidence in a number of cases—it was a huge scandal at the time—and while the evidence against Robby was completely legit, all of the perps in all of the assistant D.A.'s cases were released as a matter of course. This was the luckiest kid on the face of the earth.

I turned that thought over in my head as I drove to his place, amazed that this had never occurred to me before: What if Robby wasn't merely lucky? What if the punk had access to magic? What if he had been hiding it from us all these years? Most of the time I could identify a weremyste on sight. They usually appeared to shimmer and waver, as if there were heat waves in front of them. A powerful runecrafter might look like little more than a blur. I'd never noticed anything like this with Robby, but maybe he wasn't strong enough for me to notice, or at least hadn't been the last time our paths crossed. I thought of that faint hint of beige glow on the door of the building where I had found Jessie Tyler. Could that have been Robby? Had luck saved him yet again?

Maybe. But with Claudia Deegan dead, with drugs found in her backpack and in her blood, and with some connection established between her and Sommer, it was possible that Robby's winning streak was about to end.

Robby might have been thinking the same thing. As soon as I knocked on the door of his house, a small place on Hermosa, near the interchange of Highway 101 and U.S. 60, I heard a screen door fly open in the back. I leaped off the front stoop and sprinted around the house in time to see someone disappear over a cinderblock wall.

I went after him, knowing that I could clear the wall easily. But as I was about to throw myself over it, I felt magic. I stopped myself the only way I could: essentially by running into the wall. I didn't go over it, which was good because flames had erupted from its top—just like the flames I'd seen earlier that day at the spark den. I gathered that fire was Robby's attack magic of choice, which wasn't so surprising. Fire spells were about the most rudimentary assailing magic a myste could use.

Three elements: the cinderblocks, Robby's flames, and a magical blanket to snuff them out. The air around me hummed with the power of my own spell, and an instant later the flames on the wall died down. I climbed over, feeling the heat of the blaze still radiating from the stone. Once on the ground again, I ran on, following the retreating sound of Robby's footsteps.

It was my turn for an attack spell. I didn't try anything fancy; I wanted to slow him down, not kill him. My hand, his back, and a good hard shove.

I heard him stumble, then curse. Emerging from between two houses, I saw him scrambling to his feet half a block down the street. And yes, this time I did notice a faint blur around his face and neck. The son of a bitch was a runecrafter, albeit a weak one. He glanced back, took off again. I chased him across a couple of small yards, and followed him into another narrow alley between two ramshackle houses. This wasn't exactly textbook police procedure, but Robby had never been a violent kid. Just a slimeball, and not a particularly smart one at that. He broke out into a second open street and I ran after him; by now I was only a few steps behind. He dodged a kid on a bicycle; I tried to do the same, spun, and fell, tearing my jeans and most of the skin on my right knee.

I was on my feet again in a second or two, but I was limping now, and I was pissed off. I might have lost him, but he turned down a second alley that proved to be a dead end. Did I mention that Robby wasn't so smart?

I hobbled into the alley, glancing down at my bloodied leg and swearing loudly. Robby backed away from me until he bumped into the scalloped steel door of an old garage. He pulled something from his pocket and fumbled with it.

"Stay away from me!" he said, waving his hand at me. It took me a moment to realize that he was holding a small knife.

I stopped and considered drawing my Glock, which was still in my shoulder holster. I'm licensed to own it and Arizona law allows private citizens to carry a concealed weapon. And though I hadn't been on the job in some time, I still felt more comfortable with a weapon at the ready. In this case though, I figured I'd learn more from Robby if I got him calmed down.

"Put the knife away, Robby. You don't want to get hurt."

"I said stay away!"

I started walking toward him again. "You really are an idiot, aren't you?"

In a way I hoped he would try to cut me. My leg was aching and I was itching for an excuse to kick the crap out of him.

"I'm smarter than you think. I know that you guys want to nail me for dealing, especially now that Claudia's dead." His eyes were darting from side to side, searching for any way out of the alley. He might well have been desperate enough to attack me.

"Who do you think you're talking to? I'm not trying to pin anything on anyone."

"Bullshit, *cop!*"

"I'm no cop." He started to argue, but I raised a finger to silence him. "I was when I busted you, but I was kicked off the force a while back."

"Yeah, right. What for?"

I wasn't about to tell him that. "I beat a perp to death."

His eyes widened.

"Put the knife away, Robby. I just want to talk. I'm a PI now. A private investigator," I added, seeing his puzzled expression. "I'm doing a little work for the Deegans, trying to figure out what happened to their daughter."

Fear and uncertainty chased each other across his features.

"The cops are after me, though, right?"

"I honestly couldn't tell you. They know you didn't kill her. But they also know that you deal, and that Claudia had drugs with her when she died. Lots of the Blind Angel victims did," I added, eyeing him as I spoke the words.

Robby seemed to sag. The hand holding the knife fell to his side. "Shit," he muttered, eyes on the ground. I'm not sure that he heard my last remark. "I didn't do anything."

"No? What about Jessie Tyler?"

His gaze snapped back to mine. "That was you today."

"Yeah," I said. "Throw another spell at me and I'll break your neck."

"The Deegans, the Tylers. I guess business has been good."

"Did you know Claudia well?"

He glanced around again, still searching for some way out. At the same time, he let out a short breathless laugh. "Yeah, I knew Claud. She and I were a thing once."

"That right?"

Robby raised his chin, eyeing me. "You don't believe me."

I wasn't certain that I did. It's not like I thought girls would find Robby unattractive. He had a friendly face, shaggy dark hair, big brown eyes—the kind of down-and-out good looks that some girls like. But Claudia Deegan had been a beauty, and with her name and money she could have had any guy she wanted.

"Sure I do."

"No, you don't. To tell you the truth, I wouldn't either. I know who Claud was, before she became the woman I knew. If she'd been right with her family, she wouldn't have given me the time of day. I understand that, you know? I think she saw me as a way of getting at her old man. But I didn't mind." He stared past me; his expression had softened. "I . . . I liked her. A lot."

Maybe I did believe him. "What was she on?"

He met my gaze again, narrowing his eyes. After a moment's hesitation, he gave a little shake of his head. "Everything. You name it, she was into it. Spark, X, crystal, coke. It's not like she was short on money, you know?"

"Did she buy her stuff from you?"

"Is that what the Deegans told you? Them and that boyfriend of hers?"

"What boyfriend?"

"I don't remember his first name. Last name is Ruiz. He's some rich Mexican kid. But they all had it in for me. Blamed me for all of Claud's problems, which is bullshit. I mean, sure, we did some stuff, you know? But it's not like she'd never used before she started hanging out with me. It's not like she was a damn saint or something."

"Did you have any contact with the Deegans?" I asked. "Conversations, letters, emails?"

"Not her old man. He's not around that much, and anyway, his people probably wouldn't let him anywhere near someone like me."

I was sure Robby had that right.

"But Claud's brother came around once right after we broke up. Told me stay away from her. Threatened to have me thrown in jail if I ever went near her again."

"So did you stay away from her after that?"

He shook his head. "No," he said. "Couldn't. I went to that freakin' protest because I thought she'd like me more if I was into one of her causes, you know?" He laughed, sounding bitter. "That worked out great. She barely noticed me, and I wound up getting busted along with the rest of them."

"Did she buy her drugs from you?"

He chewed his lip, seeming to weigh whether it was safe to tell me the truth. "Yeah," he said at length. "I sold her Spark, coke, X. I don't deal meth anymore, so if she had any on her, it wasn't from me. But the rest probably was."

"What about the others?"

"What others?" Robby asked, growing wary.

"The other Blind Angel murder victims. Did you sell to any of them?"

"I thought you were working for the Deegans."

"I am. I'm trying to figure out why Claudia is dead. And if I can learn something about the other murders, too, all the better."

His gaze slid away. "Yeah, well, I don't know anything about that."

He was shutting down on me, so I turned the conversation back to Claudia, hoping that he'd open up again.

"Do you find it odd that this guy would go for Claudia? I mean, she's probably the most famous girl in Arizona, right?"

"He probably didn't recognize her," Robby said. "I mean, have you seen Claudia recently?"

"I saw her a little while ago," I said. "I've just come from the Medical Examiner's building."

He gaped at me, his face going white. "No shit?"

"I swear it."

Robby swallowed. "Well . . . well, then, you know. She changed. A lot. She lost weight—got really thin, you know? Unhealthy. And she dyed her hair black, used lots of eyeliner—went Goth. Actually it was a pretty cool look for her. It was like she was trying to be someone else, leave the blonde princess behind. That's what she called herself sometimes, when she was feeling especially anti-family, you know? Anyway, that was the weird thing about Claud. On the one hand she acted like none of the rules applied to her, you know? She thought she could get away with stuff because of who she was. And you just know that she got that from her old man, from being a Deegan. But at the same time, she was always trying to be someone else." He shook his head again. "Poor Claud."

I didn't pretend to be an expert on the subject, but I also didn't doubt that the guy loved her. Robby wasn't the brightest bulb on Broadway, but he'd given some thought to what made Claudia Deegan tick. It almost made me feel bad for him. Still, he hadn't answered my question, and I couldn't leave him alone until he did.

"What about the others, Robby? Did they buy from you, too?"

His gaze wandered away again. "I told you, I've got nothing to say about that."

"Well, I'll take that as a 'yes', and I'll be sure to mention it to my buddies at the PPD."

"You think I remember everyone who's ever bought from me? You're crazy! And I don't know the names of all the people this guy's killed."

"You'd remember if you sold to someone and heard a day or two later that she'd turned up dead. In fact, I think you do remember. And I think it's happened more than once."

"You're wrong." He kept his eyes down as he said it, and I could tell that he was hiding something, and that he was terrified. For a second I thought he might start crying.

"You're lying."

"Prove it."

"I don't have to," I said, taking a step toward him. "Like I said, I'm not a cop anymore."

He raised the knife again. "Stay away!"

"Which ones, Robby? Which victims bought from you before they died?"

"None of them did! And you can't prove different! Neither can your cop friends!"

I didn't believe him for a minute. But he was right; I couldn't prove anything, at least not yet.

"Fine," I said, relaxing a bit, checking my knee again. What a mess.

He regarded me, wary again. "Fine what?"

"I believe you didn't sell drugs to any of the other Blind Angel victims. You can go."

"That's it? I can go? Just like that?"

"What'd you expect? I told you I'm not a cop anymore. If I could throw you in the pen for a while let you stew on all of this, I would. For Claudia and for Jessie. But I'm just a PI. Even if you are lying to me, I can't do anything about it."

The smirk that curved his lips was way too smug for my taste. He let his blade hand fall to his side again. "Yeah, that's right. You can't do shit."

"Stay out of trouble. Watch your back. I might be done with you, but the cops aren't."

"Right," he said. "Whatever."

I frowned down at my leg once more, making like I was done with him. He started to saunter past me and as he did, I straightened and threw a punch, catching him full in the side of the face, right below his eye. He bounced off the wall of the house next to us and went down hard.

"God, dude!" he whined, sprawled on the ground, both hands on his face. "What the hell was that for?"

"My leg, those fire spells, pulling that knife on me, lying about the drugs. Take your pick." I started to walk away, shaking my hand and rubbing the knuckles—they never show it in the movies, but it hurts to hit someone like that. A lot.

"You are messed up, dude!" he called after me. "No wonder they booted you off the freakin' force."

I turned to face him, walking backwards out of the alley. My hands were shaking. To be honest, I wasn't sure why I'd hit him; I hadn't intended to. The best I can say in my own defense is that weremystes start to do strange things—stupid things—around the time of the full moon.

I suppose that could have been why Robby was throwing magic around like he was determined to set the city on fire. No myste was immune from the phasing. But I wasn't going to let him think I had any sympathy for him. "If I find out you've been lying to me, this'll seem like a picnic." I glared at him for a moment more, then left the alley.

"Hey, Fearsson!" I heard Robby call. "Fuck you!"

A few people stared as I walked by, but I ignored them. My hand and leg were throbbing and I didn't have much to show for my effort. I knew a bit more about Claudia, and I knew for certain that her drugs had come from Robby. I'd been hoping, though, that I would be able to connect Robby to the East Side Parks Killer. I should have known better. After all this time, leads in this case wouldn't come so easily.

As I approached the Z-ster, I was racking my brain, trying to think of other ways to tie Robby to past victims.

I was in the middle of the street when I felt it. Instinct. Suddenly the hairs on the back of my neck were standing on end. I spun around, pulling my weapon free as I did. Nothing. Sure, there were a few people milling around in their yards, looking at me as if I were crazy.

But I had been certain that someone was about to take a shot at me, and there was no one.

I took a breath, started to holster my Glock. But the feeling wouldn't go away. There might not be a gunman, but someone was watching me, and it sure as hell wasn't my guardian angel. I held on to my weapon until I was in the Z-ster with the engine running. Even then, I eased the car away from the curb, scanning the yards and houses as I drove. Only when I was out of Robby's neighborhood did I begin to relax. Still, I took special care to see that I wasn't followed as I headed back to my office.

CHAPTER 5

I had calmed down by the time I got back to Chandler, though I remained watchful as I made my way up to my office. Emerging from the brick stairway, I saw a woman standing by my door, and before I knew it, I was reaching for my Glock again.

"Mister Fearsson," she said.

I let my hand fall to my side and walked toward her, my steps deliberate. I even went so far as to take off my sunglasses. Still, it took me several seconds to recognize her.

"You're the blogger," I said, stopping in front of her

She smiled. "That's right. Billie Castle."

"Miss Castle, of course. Forgive me for not recognizing you right away."

"It's all right. I hope I didn't alarm you."

"No, I . . ." I held up my hands. "Never mind." I narrowed my eyes. "What are you doing here?"

"I found you in the phone book after we met at the Deegans. It's a nice picture."

I chuckled. "Uh-huh."

"You're a private detective."

"I am. And you're avoiding my question."

"Can I buy you lunch?" she asked.

I glanced at my watch and cocked an eyebrow.

"Fine," she said. "An early dinner?"

It occurred to me that I hadn't eaten anything since breakfast, and that I was starving. But I didn't think it would be a good idea for me to spend too much time with Miss Castle. I'm sure Howard Wriker would have agreed.

"I think I'll pass. Thanks, though."

A thin smile flitted across her face. "Wriker warned you away from me, didn't he?"

"I wouldn't put it that way."

"How would you put it?"

I felt like she was holding a microphone in front of my face.

"Look, Miss Castle—"

"What did you do to your leg?" she asked, staring at my bloodied knee.

"I fell down, running . . ." I clammed up, reminding myself again that I was talking to a reporter.

"Running?" she repeated.

"Yeah. Running. It's not important. But I was going to say, Miss Castle, that—"

"Billie."

"I think I'll stick with Miss Castle. I don't care much for politics or politicians, and I'm not interested in being famous. I'm trying to pay some bills and help out a friend."

"Are you a friend of Senator Deegan?"

I turned away from her, pulled out my key, and unlocked the door to my office.

"I'm writing a story, Mister Fearsson. A series of them, probably. And my readers are going to want to know why a private eye is involved with an ongoing murder investigation. They'll want to know why that private eye was forced to resign from the homicide division of the Phoenix Police Department nineteen months ago in the middle of the Blind Angel Killer case. Now I can leave it to others to answer those questions—Kona Shaw, Howard Wriker, Cole Hibbard . . ."

I couldn't help it. At the mention of Hibbard's name I bristled and shot a glare her way. She stared back at me with this innocent expression on her face.

"Or," she went on, "you can answer my questions yourself and make certain that I get your story right."

Just as I'd thought: smart as hell. Pretty, too. I probably should have ducked into my office, bolted the door behind me, and hidden in the shadows until she gave up and left. Instead, I sighed, locked the door once more, and turned to face her.

"An early dinner, eh?"

She nodded.

"You buying?

She grinned. "Sure."

There was a pizza place on the ground level of the complex, below my office. I took her there, and we ordered a small pie: mushrooms, green peppers, and sausage. I don't know if she was being agreeable so that I'd answer her questions, but we settled on the toppings in no time at all.

We both ordered Cokes as well, and carried them to a booth in the back corner of the restaurant.

"All right," I said. "What is it you want to know?"

She pulled a digital recorder out of her purse and set it on the table between us. Switching it on, she said, "Interview with Justis Fearsson, Private Detective." She glanced at her watch. "Five-twenty p.m., Monday, May fourteenth. What kind of name is Justis, anyway?" she asked me.

I shrugged. "Old English, I think. Probably my dad's idea. He wouldn't have settled for something normal. What about Billie?"

She smiled, though there was something forced about it. "My dad. He wanted a boy." She sat up straighter. "What were you doing at the Deegans' today?"

So much for the casual chit-chat.

"I was picking up a friend who was there to speak with the senator and his family."

"Kona Shaw, right? Your partner when you were on the force?"

She'd done her homework. I suppose I should have been impressed. Instead, I found myself growing annoyed. Who was this woman to investigate my life?

"Yeah," I said. "That's right. We had business downtown, and she didn't have her car with her. So she asked me to meet her there."

"What business did you have downtown? Was this police business?"

I shook my head. "I'm not—"

"Was this in connection with the Blind Angel killings? Did it have anything to do with the murder of Claudia Deegan?"

"I'm not going to answer that."

Her smile was smug. "By not answering, you tell me that it was."

I said nothing.

"You worked on the Blind Angel case when you were on the force, didn't you?"

I thought about this and realized in about half a second that my name was in articles about the murders published at the time. "Yes, that's right. Kona and I worked the case from the start."

"You investigated the very first murder?"

"Gracia Rosado. Twenty-one. Five feet, two inches; 127 pounds. Born in Hermosillo, came to the States with her parents when she was seven, lived in Mesa at the time she died."

Billie opened her mouth, then closed it again.

"To you this might be a great story, but I lived it for a year and a half. Longer, really. I'm not sure I've ever stopped living it."

"Can you do that with all the victims?" she asked in a hushed voice.

"Probably. Do I really need to?"

"No."

Before she could say more, a waitress arrived with our pizza. She eyed the recorder, put the pizza on the table next to it, and gave us both odd looks.

When she was gone, Billie sipped her Coke and leaned forward. "Why do you think he blinds them?"

Because he's a weremyste, like me. Because he's drawing power out of them in some way—through their eyes—and using that power to make his magic stronger.

A part of me wanted to say it, just to see the expression on her face. For all I knew, it could have been the biggest story her blog had ever seen. Because while most people knew that magic was real, few understood anything about the workings of spells, and fewer still could say that they knew a weremyste.

We were around, of course, in more places than most people would have guessed. We were cops and school teachers, doctors and lawyers. Hell, there were weremystes in the military. At one time, if the claims that flew around the magical community could be believed, back in the early '70s, and again in the early '90s, the Pentagon tried to create a special unit of magical Green Berets. It makes sense: combine that level of military training with spell-casting ability, and they'd have a force that was all but unstoppable. But as with all efforts to integrate weremystes and their magic more fully into American society, the effort foundered on the phasings and their effects on our minds. Special Ops guys went through vigorous psychological screenings. They lived violent dangerous lives, and they needed to be available at a moment's notice, 24/7. Throwing a three-day phasing into that equation created problems, both immediate and potential. As far as I know, the Magic Special Ops program never got off the ground. As far as I know.

And its failure pointed to the larger problem that weremystes faced. The stigma that surrounded mental illness in this country was a heavy burden, for those who were ill as well as for their families, in large part because mental illness was still so poorly understood. Well, so was magic. And as a result that stigma was far worse for those whose mental problems came from being weremystes.

This was why most of my kind used blockers to hide their abilities, and to spare themselves the effects of the phasings. Blockers were a family of drugs, the first of which came into use centuries ago. Many of them were legal; a few, like Spark, were not. But all of them, including Spark, affected weremystes the same way. Rather than getting us high, they guarded us from the psychosis of the phasings and suppressed our magic. If a weremyste was willing to give up magic, he could use blockers to avoid the phasings and the insanity that inevitably came with them. Seems like an easy choice, right? How many people could afford to lose their minds for three nights out of each month? How many people wouldn't do everything possible to avoid an otherwise inevitable descent into insanity?

But for a few of us, the choice wasn't quite so clear. Blockers were an all-or-nothing deal. I couldn't take them for the three days around the full moon and cast spells the rest of the month. That would have been great if it were possible, but as I had learned a thousand times, the world didn't usually make things that convenient for anyone, runecrafters included. In order for blockers to work, they had to be in our systems at a certain level for an extended period. If I wanted to escape the phasings, I would have had to give up magic entirely, and like my father, I wasn't willing to do that. So I didn't use blockers at all. I suffered through the phasings; I accepted as fate the eventual loss of my sanity. And I wielded my magic.

The truth was, even as I argued with Namid about mastering runecrafting, I liked being able to conjure. When I was a cop it gave me an edge over the creeps I was trying to put away, and now that I was a PI, it still came in handy. Maybe more to the point, it's who I am. I can't give up being a weremyste any more than I can give up being a Fearsson.

But I wasn't ready to share all of this with Billie Castle and her readers, and I'm pretty sure she wasn't ready to hear it.

"Mister Fearsson?" she said, eyeing me with what might have been concern.

"I think he blinds them because he's nuts," I told her. "I think he blinds them for the same reason another serial killer might rape his victims or dismember them or do something else that horrifies the rest of us. It gives him a sense of power, of control. It makes him feel like a god in his twisted little universe."

"And why do you think the police have had so much trouble tracking him down?"

Again, an honest answer would have come back to magic. We couldn't catch the guy because despite all appearances, he *wasn't* a typical serial killer. He wasn't crazy, and didn't secretly want to be caught, like some of those nut jobs you read about in the papers. He killed with purpose, he was sane and calculating and intelligent, and he had managed to leave no clues of value at any of the thirty-plus crime scenes we'd found. But I couldn't tell her all of that, either. So I tried to punt.

"I'm not on the force, Miss Castle. I haven't been for some time. Questions about the PPD's investigation should go to the PPD."

"You were with the force for the first year and a half of this case. I would think that you'd have some ideas."

I shrugged. "I think he's been clever," I said. "And I think he's been lucky. But I also think that his luck will run out sooner or later. It always does in these cases. The PPD will get him."

"Do you think they would have already if you'd remained on the job?"

I laughed, short and harsh, and reached for a piece of pizza. Taking a bite, I shook my head and said, "I'm not going to second-guess the detectives working this case."

"I'm not asking you to," she said, taking a piece of her own. "But I would think that you'd have spent the last nineteen months second-guessing the department's decision to fire you."

I stopped chewing and glared at her. Her gaze didn't flinch at all. Pretty, smart, and tough. At that moment, I wasn't sure which I wanted to do more: get up and walk out, or ask her out on a date.

I looked away before she did. "I'm not talking about this."

"Why were you fired, Mister Fearsson? Did it have something to do with the Blind Angel killings?"

"No." I said it automatically, my gaze snapping back to hers. As soon as I thought about it, though, I wondered if this was true. I was fired because of the phasings, because my erratic behavior and my inability to function for three nights every fourth week became too much for my superiors to tolerate, and too much for Kona to cover up. I was fired because I'm a weremyste. And wasn't that the same reason the Blind Angel Killer had evaded us for so long?

Billie must have seen the doubt in my eyes. "Did they blame you for the fact that they couldn't catch him? Is that what happened?"

I shook my head, resisting the urge to say, *You're getting colder.* "No. It wasn't like that at all."

"Then what?"

I bit into my slice of pizza and chewed.

Billie frowned and took a bite, staring right back at me, like we were kids daring each other to be the first to blink.

"Do you like prying into other people's lives?" I asked after some time, breaking a lengthy silence and reaching for a second slice of pizza.

"That's not what I do. I give people information. I tell stories about real-life situations. And occasionally I uncover truths that powerful people would prefer to keep hidden."

"That's what you think you're doing now, isn't it?"

She hesitated. "Yes, I guess it is."

"I think you're going for the cheap thrill. I think what you're doing here with me is no different from what the tabloids do, or what you see on those cheesy news shows that come on TV after the real news."

From the way she responded you would have thought that I'd

slapped her. Her mouth was open in a little 'o' and her eyes were so wide I thought she might cry. But that look only lasted for the span of a heartbeat or two. Then she pressed her lips into a thin hard line and the muscles in her jaw tightened. It's funny, but I didn't notice until that instant that her eyes were vivid green and as hard as emeralds.

"You know what I think, Mister Fearsson?" Her voice had gone cold. She wasn't trying to charm a story out of me anymore. "I think that all the stuff they wrote about you when you left the force was true. You're a drunk or an addict, or you're just too unreliable to serve in the PPD. I think you deserved what happened to you."

Others had said much worse to me. People I'd known for years, fellow cops who I'd respected. Her insults came too late and from too great a distance to hurt.

I put down what was left of the slice I'd been eating, took one last sip of Coke, and wiped my face with a napkin. Then I slid out of the booth and stood.

"Thanks for dinner."

I didn't wait for an answer. And she didn't try to stop me from leaving.

I went back to my office, intending to do a bit of billing work from my last few cases. I'd let it pile up, and I was still stewing over my conversation with Billie. This seemed as good a time as any to tackle a few mindless tasks. My hands were shaking, I was so mad. But I knew that would pass.

The answer machine was blinking—two messages. The first was from Kona and had come in around the time Billie and I were sitting down to eat:

"Hi, partner. Just got a call from Pete. The Deegan autopsy didn't turn up anything too surprising. Cause of death is 'sudden, trauma-induced cardiac arrest,' just like the others. It'll be a day or two before the toxicology report comes back, but Pete's convinced that Claudia was high on Spark when she died. Otherwise, nothing new. Our friend doesn't change much from killing to killing. Let me know what you found out from Robby. Bye."

"Sudden, trauma-induced cardiac arrest." I'd never heard the phrase before Gracia Rosado's death. Now it had become a morbid joke I shared with Kona. Basically, it was the medical examiner's way of saying "something really bad happened and it killed her."

The second message was from Howard Wriker, who wanted to know if I'd learned anything yet about the drugs Claudia had been using. I wasn't ready to tell him or the Deegans anything. I felt no need to protect Robby Sommer, but the last thing Kona needed was for the Deegans to be breathing down her neck about Robby, when we had no solid proof that he'd been involved in any way with Claudia's murder. Hearing his voice did remind me though, that I needed to tell Kona that Robby had been running a Spark den over in the South Mountain District. She couldn't arrest him on the little evidence I had for her, but she could pass the word to narcotics and they could keep an eye on him.

I called Kona at her home. Margarite answered, gave me a big hello, and insisted that I join them for dinner this coming weekend. I didn't bother reminding her that the full moon was coming up; even with friends, the phasings weren't easy to talk about. I asked for a raincheck. She said the following week would be good, and passed the phone to Kona.

"You been with Robby all this time?" Kona asked without saying hello.

"No. A reporter who I met at the Deegans' tracked me down at my office and asked me a bunch of questions."

"A reporter?"

"A blogger, actually. But Wriker was afraid of her, so I assume she's pretty big."

"You mean Billie Castle?"

Why was I the only person who'd never heard of her? I guess I needed to spend more time online. Or not.

"Yeah. You know her work?"

"Of course. Who doesn't?"

"Well, anyway," I said. "She wanted to know all about the Blind Angel case and why the PPD hadn't caught the guy yet, and what my firing had to do with it all."

"What did you tell her?"

"As little as possible."

I could almost see Kona nodding. "Good. How'd it go with Robby?"

"He admitted selling to Claudia. Seems they were an item for a while. But he denied having anything to do with the other victims."

"You think he was lying?" Before I could answer, she said, "Never mind. Of course he was lying."

"I doubt we can prove it, though," I said.

"Yeah, so do I."

"And speaking of things we can't prove, you should tell narcotics to keep one eye on Robby and another on a Spark den on 23rd near the freeway and the railroad."

"All right. Care to explain that?"

"Not really. Not now."

We both fell silent for a few seconds.

"Listen, Kona, I know this is the PPD's investigation, and I should stay away from actual investigating—"

"I never should have said what I did, Justis. It's not like we're tracking down leads or focusing in on suspects. We've got nothing here."

"Then you won't mind if I poke around a little, maybe check in with some of my kind?"

"Not at all," she said. "Let me know what you find out."

"Of course."

"And partner?"

"Yeah."

"Watch yourself. If you start getting close to this guy, he's not going to like it."

"Right. Talk to you tomorrow."

I hung up and took care of some of that paperwork. I would have preferred to head home, but I wanted to make sure that Billie Castle was long gone before I stepped outside again.

By the time I headed for the Z-ster, night had fallen and the moon was up. It was well past a quarter full and bone white in a velvet sky. And though we were still several days away from the full, I could already feel it tugging at my mind, bending my thoughts, making me shiver in spite of the warm air.

Describing the phasings to someone who wasn't a weremyste was like trying to describe color to someone who had been born blind. Words weren't adequate. The closest I'd heard anyone come to getting it right was something my dad told me not long after my mom died. We weren't getting along at the time, and his grip on reality, which had already become tenuous before Mom's death, was slipping fast. But what he told me then in anger still rang true to this day.

"It's like somebody reaches a hand into your stinkin' brain," he said, "and swirls it around, making a mess of everything. The thoughts are still there—your sense of who you are and how the people around you fit into your life—but they're scrambled. There's no order, no time or space or story line. The boundaries disappear. Love and hate, rage and joy, fear and comfort—you can't tell anymore where one ends and the next begins. And the worst part is, you know it's happened— you know that it all made sense a short while before, and that now it's gone. And there's not a damn thing you can do about it."

That was how it felt to me every time. You'd think after a couple of hundred phasings—three days a month for half a lifetime—I'd get used to it, or find some way to fight my way through. But each one feels like the first. I've tried to brace myself, waiting for moonrise the way I would a shot at a doctor's office. It doesn't do a damn bit of good. As soon as the full moon appears on the horizon, I feel those boundaries my dad talked about being sucked out of my mind.

That was the tug I felt now, with the moon shining down on me. It wouldn't happen until the end of the week, but already it was reaching for me, testing my defenses and finding them as weak as ever.

I was still staring up at the moon when I reached the Z-ster, which is probably why I didn't notice anything as I got into the car and put the key in the ignition.

"Ohanko."

"*Geez!*" I said, nearly jumping out of my skin.

The runemyste was in the passenger seat, his watery form glimmering with the pale light of a nearby street lamp.

"Good God, Namid! You scared the piss out of me."

"You need to use more care, Ohanko. Did I not tell you—?"

"Yeah, tread like the fox. I remember." I shook my head. My heart was trip hammering in my chest. "What the hell are you doing here, anyway? I never see you unless you're tying to get me to train."

He shrugged, or came as close to a shrug as a liquid ghost could. "I thought to see how you were faring with your investigation."

I stared at him.

"Have you learned anything?"

"Wait a minute," I said. "Are you telling me that you're checking up on me?"

"Does that surprise you?"

"You've never done it before."

He said nothing.

Abruptly I could see again the scrying I'd done in my office: that ghoulish dark hand, framed against the hot glow of embers.

"Is this about the vision I had this morning?"

Before he could answer, I thought of something else: crossing the street after my conversation with Robby, feeling so sure that someone was toying with the idea of killing me. I still had the instincts of a cop, and normally that was a good thing. But maybe in this case, without realizing it at the time, I had been feeling things a sorcerer would feel.

"You've never done anything like this before," I said again. "Unless that was you following me earlier today."

He frowned, the smooth waters of his face roughening, like when a sudden wind scythes across the surface of a calm lake. "What happened earlier? Tell me."

"I thought someone was watching me, an enemy. But I have no idea who it could have been."

The runemyste's nod was slow, thoughtful. He turned his head so that he was looking through the windshield at the street. "Good, Ohanko. Trust your senses."

Great. More riddles. Just once I wanted him to give me a straight answer. "You wouldn't tell me before what all this is about. Are you ready to tell me now?"

"No."

"Come on, Namid. You're interested in my case, though you never have been before. You're following me around, which you never do. Clearly something big is going on. You have to tell me what it is."

He faced me again, his eyes gleaming in the darkness. "You misunderstand, Ohanko. It is not that I refuse to tell you, but rather that I cannot. I do not know."

Well, there you go. That's a straight answer. Turns out I would have preferred another riddle.

CHAPTER 6

I know precious little about Namid's life as a Zuni shaman. I've studied the A'shiwi, as the Zuni people call themselves; I've studied most of the native peoples of the Southwest. But the K'ya'na-Kwe clan has been extinct for centuries, and since the ancient A'shiwi clans left no written histories, information on the runemyste's people is pretty scarce. And it's not as though Namid spends a lot of time talking about himself. I've asked him questions now and then, but he's about as forthcoming with information about his own life as he is about anything else.

In many ways I learned everything I needed to know about the runemyste the very first time I saw him. Most of my memories from those days are obscured by the residue of too many phasings, but this one remains as clear as fresh rainwater. I was at home—my old home, on the west side of the city, in Buckeye. I had started on the job only a few months before and was learning a good deal from Kona. We were in robbery detail then, although she was already angling to get us moved to Homicide. But I had yet to tell her that I was a weremyste and she was growing tired of having to explain to others why her new partner disappeared every few weeks. Friendship only goes so far, particularly when I'm nothing more than some dumb rookie cop, and she's well on her way to a promotion for which she's busted her butt some seven years. It was just a matter of time before she was going to dump me as a partner. No doubt I would have deserved it. Rule seven: Never keep secrets from your partner.

It was late, and the moon was full. I was in the midst of a hard, dark phasing, sitting on my living room floor, trying to resist the urge to grab my weapon and put a bullet through my head. Often my phasings are filled with delusions, and on this night my mom, dead some twelve years, was standing in front of me, telling me that I was exactly like my old man and that I'd wasted my life. And staring down at my hands, I could see that they were wrinkled and covered with age spots. The hair on them had turned white. Somehow there was a mirror beside me—at least I believed at the time that there was—and as I gazed into it, I saw that I was twin to my dad, my hair gray, my face slack. I remember crying, and screaming myself hoarse, begging her to go away. But she wouldn't leave me alone. I thought about using magic to burn my house to the ground. Really, I did. Magic is stronger during the phasings, and I could feel the power churning inside me. I was itching to use it. I had to remind myself that burning down the house would be a bad thing. Which is why I'd started thinking about the weapon. Not that shooting myself was much better, but at the time rational thought wasn't my strong suit. All I could think was that if I couldn't get her to leave, I'd leave myself.

But before I could climb to my feet and retrieve my pistol, my mother vanished, replaced by what appeared to be yet another delusion: a translucent figure, shimmering and liquid, and yet seemingly solid.

I didn't speak. I stared up at that face, at those glowing eyes, waiting for him to do or say something.

"Taking your own life would be a waste. You should reconsider." His voice was like rushing water, musical and random, soothing and exhilarating.

"Wow," I said, breathless. As delusions went, this was a good one.

"The moon-time is difficult for you, I know. I have seen it. But part of being a runecrafter is enduring the dark nights. What you call the phasings."

"What are you supposed to be?" I asked. I reached toward him with an open hand, wanting to touch his watery skin. I wasn't close enough, though, and I didn't have the strength to stand up.

"My name is Namid'skemu. I am a runemyste. Long ago by your reckoning, I was a runecrafter—a weremyste—as you are. More recently I gave aid to your father. I would do the same for you, but you must swear to me that you will not do harm to yourself."

"Namid'skemu," I repeated. "That sounds Native American."

"It is A'shiwi."

"A'shiwi?"

He nodded.

"You're Zuni?"

"I am of the K'ya'na-Kwe clan. The water people."

"The water people are extinct."

"Yes."

I let out a crazed laugh. I was starting to sound like my dad. "So you're telling me that I'm speaking to the ghost of some ancient Zuni?"

"I am no ghost," he said, sounding angry for the first time. "I was once what you would call a shaman, as weremystes often were. I am now a runemyste, chosen by the Runeclave to guard against the use of dark magic in your world. And I have come to you because I see great darkness in you. I fear that you will not survive this night."

I shook my head, averting my eyes, feeling ashamed that he had read my thoughts with such ease. "This is getting weird. I need something to drink."

I forced myself up, staggered into the kitchen and splashed water on my face. That helped some, but the tirade from my mom's ghost still echoed in my head. I knew that I couldn't kill myself; my new delusion had convinced me of that much. But I wasn't going to make it through the night if I didn't do something. Still leaning against the counter in front of the sink, I reached up into the topmost cabinet and pulled out a bottle of bourbon.

When I turned to get a glass, he was standing right in front of me. I should have been startled, but I wasn't. Somehow I had known he'd be there.

"That will not help you through this night," he said pointing at the bottle.

"You're wrong," I said. "It's helped before."

"That is an illusion."

I laughed. "You're one to talk."

"You believe I am an illusion."

"Delusion is the word I'd use. But, yeah, I do."

"You are wrong. I am as real as you are. Your father knows me."

"My father's a loon," I said, not meaning it kindly. "So we've had the same hallucinations. Not very surprising. I bet he's seen Mom yelling at him, too. Doesn't make her ghost real."

"I am not a ghost," he said again. "And you must ask him about me when you can. I assure you I am real, and I can help you, just as I did him. I can teach you to harness the powers you possess, to become a skilled runecrafter. But you must learn to endure the moon-times without resorting to alcohol and without doing harm to yourself."

I glared at him, but then I put down the bottle, walked back into the living room, and dropped onto the couch. Sleep. That's what I needed. Come morning, I'd feel better. The phasing still had one more night, and even the days of what my new ghost-friend called the moon-time were difficult—trouble focusing, forgetfulness, fatigue. They were better than the nights, though. And this hallucination would be over.

"You cannot escape me," he said. I opened my eyes and found him standing in front of the couch.

"Stop doing that! Leave me alone."

"Why do you refuse the Abri?"

I frowned up at him. "The what?"

"The drug that can keep you from suffering during the moon-time. Why do you not take it?"

Blockers. That's what he was talking about. My gaze slid away again; I had no easy answer. I could have said I didn't take them because my father hadn't taken them, but I'm not sure I was even ready to admit as much to myself. At that point, we didn't get along, and I blamed him for everything I hated about my life. I also could have said I wasn't ready yet to give up wielding magic, but I was still learning to cast spells, and back then I wasn't sure I believed I would ever become much of a runecrafter. The truth was, I sensed the runemyste wanted me to say that I was determined to retain whatever powers I possessed, and I didn't want to give him the satisfaction of being right. Even then I was a stubborn son of a bitch.

"You are a runecrafter," he said after some time, his voice as soothing as the sea at dawn. "You have some talent with magic. With my help you can become a more accomplished crafter."

"You're an illusion," I said, closing my eyes again.

"And you are a fool."

"Yeah, tell me something I don't know."

He said nothing and at last I opened my eyes again, thinking that perhaps he'd gone. When I saw him standing over me, as patient as the tide, I knew a moment of profound relief. I realized then that I wanted him to be real. I wanted to believe I could be a powerful sorcerer, that there was more to being a weremyste than these miserable nights around the full moon. But after suffering through the phasings for so long, I had lost hope. That month's phasing hadn't been the first time I considered putting my pistol to my head.

He still stared at me, and now he said, "You are trying to learn something of a theft. It has been many turns of the moon since last you learned anything of importance, but still you try. There is a single token from this theft that you possess; a knife with a broken blade. Get it now."

I started to say something, then stopped. He had described a robbery Kona and I had been struggling with for the better part of six months. His understanding of the case was crude, but detailed enough to be convincing. This proved nothing, of course. My delusion, my knowledge. But that broken knife was in the house, just as he'd said. Kona and I were certain it had been used to jimmy a window or door and had been broken in the process. But we'd yet to figure out where the thieves had entered the building. We had stopped by the warehouse again the day before. We wandered around for a while, but found nothing new. When we were done, Kona asked me to return the knife to evidence. I hadn't gotten around to it yet. I wasn't all that dependable in the middle of a phasing.

"Get it," Namid said, his voice like white water on the Colorado.

I retrieved the knife from my jacket pocket, pulled it from the evidence bag, and held it out to him.

"What do you see?" he asked, making no effort to take it from me.

I glanced at it, lifted it closer to my eyes. "Son of a bitch!"

"Tell me what you see."

I wasn't even sure how to describe it. A faint glimmer of yellow light danced along the edge of the blade, like fire. It was brightest at the broken end, but it radiated all the way up the hilt. How had I not seen this before? How had Kona missed it?

"It's glowing," I said at last.

"What color?"

"Yellow."

"That is magic, or to be more precise, the residue of magic."

"What?"

"Yellow is not a strong color. Had the conjuring been done by a more accomplished runecrafter, the color would be red or green, perhaps even blue. And it would have vanished long ago. Someone with true craft can mask his conjuring. You are searching for a crafter with the most rudimentary skills."

"You're making it do that. What am I saying? *I'm* making it do that. I'm imagining all of this."

"No. You see it because you are a weremyste. Your magic allows you to see what is left of spells conjured by others. It is part of your gift."

"Then why haven't I ever seen this before?"

"Because you did not know to look for it. And I was not there to show you. You will never fail to see it again."

I shook my head. "I'm not a sorcerer."

"Not yet. But you have power. If you did not, you would not see anything more than a broken knife."

Despite what Namid had shown me, I was slow to believe he was anything more or less than a product of my own psychotic imagination. I'd seen my dad lose his mind, the process slow and painful, and I had known for years that this was my fate, too. I knew my dad was a weremyste, and that I was as well, but I had never given much thought to what that might mean. I certainly hadn't ever believed that much good would come of whatever powers I possessed. Magic had been the source of too much pain in my life for me to see it in any other way.

After some time that first night, Namid left me, no doubt fed up with my stubborn refusal to acknowledge that he was real. But he appeared again the next morning and we resumed our argument. At first, I took his return as evidence that my descent into permanent insanity had already begun. But Namid was persistent to the point of relentlessness, and with time I came to believe that he was real and that all he'd been telling me about magic and my own gifts was true.

Even more, everything he said about the warehouse robbery turned out to be dead-on accurate. The knife hadn't been broken jimmying anything; it had been part of a talisman—a small statue of a Maori god—that the warehouse manager kept on his desk. Namid told me as much, and I confirmed it when I examined the idol more closely and found the rest of the blade imbedded in the stone base on which the figure stood. Namid also told me where we could find the man responsible for the break-in. Within a week, Kona and I had arrested Orestes Quinley, a small-time thief and weremyste, who'd stolen a bunch of stereos and TVs to cover the theft of that talisman. Turns out there are more weremystes in the Phoenix metropolitan area than one might think. They're not in the yellow pages, of course. Finding them can be tricky. You have to rely on word of mouth and, since most weremystes use blockers, and since those who don't aren't eager to be found, it becomes a matter of finding the right mouth, as it were. But there is a network of sorts, one that I've tapped into in recent years. Early on, though, I had to take a lot on faith. So did Kona. She was pretty skeptical about all of it, although Orestes' confession helped.

As I came to spend more time with Namid I began to sense an ulterior motive of a sort in the lessons he gave me. He himself had told me that he worked with my dad, and though he never admitted as much, I was convinced that he held himself responsible for my father's premature descent into insanity. I believe Namid felt that he had failed one Fearsson. He wasn't about to fail another. That was why he worked me so hard and so often. He wanted me to hone my power. From what I understood, as a runecrafter grew more proficient, he also developed some resistance to the long-term effects of the phasings.

But on this night outside my office, with the phasing still a few days off, and Claudia Deegan's murder on my mind, I was more concerned with what Namid had said to me in the car. In the years since he appeared to me that first night and kept me from killing myself, I had never known Namid to be wrong about anything. Until tonight I'd never heard him express even the slightest uncertainty. *I do not know* . . . It was like being a kid again and finding out my father wasn't stronger and smarter than every other man on the planet.

For the first time I'd bumped up against Namid's limitations, and I found it unnerving. I think he did, too. Along with his certainty on all matters relating to magic, Namid had also been fearless. He was a runemyste. He'd been chosen by the Runeclave because even in life his mastery of the craft had been exceptional. As a member of his council, his powers were beyond anything I could imagine, although as I understood it, he and the other runemystes were forbidden to use their magic directly on our world. Still, I couldn't imagine there was much that Namid feared. There could be no denying, though, that he had been scared tonight, or as close to scared as a runemyste could get.

Mercifully, Namid didn't stay with me long. The last thing I needed was a thousand-year-old ghost commenting on my driving. But long after he left me, I continued to think about our conversation.

I got home and cleaned my knee, first with water and soap, and then with hydrogen peroxide, which was no picnic. Usually these things look better once you wipe away the dried blood, but this one looked like hell even after I'd cleaned it up. I wished I had hit Robby harder.

Then I did something stupid. I went online, found Billie Castle's blog, and read her piece about the murder of Claudia Deegan. Most of what she wrote focused on the Deegans and the history of the Blind Angel killings, but she got me in there near the end.

> *Sources close to the probe indicate that Justis Fearsson, a private investigator and former Phoenix Police Department homicide detective, has been brought in to work on the case. Fearsson, who worked on the Blind Angel murder investigation before being forced to leave the department for undisclosed disciplinary violations, has denied having any connection to the Deegans, and refused to speculate as to why the case had not yet been solved. Others with connections to the PPD were less reticent.*

I wasn't mentioned again in the story, but my name was hyperlinked. Clicking on it, I was directed to another page that had some basic information about me—my service record, my office address and phone number, and a poor reproduction of the picture from the phone book. Considering the way my conversation with Billie had ended, I'd gotten off easy. But I had a feeling I'd be appearing in future articles at "Castle's Village."

I was tired and thought about turning in early. But my mind was churning. For the past few months, I'd managed to put the Blind Angel case out of my head. But with all that had happened today, it was front and center again, and I knew that sleep wouldn't come easily.

Instead, I put on a pair of jeans that wasn't torn and stained with blood, grabbed my bomber jacket, and left the house.

When I lost my badge, I also lost access to many of the sources a cop uses for information. But there was a whole other network in the city that had nothing to do with the PPD and everything to do with magic. Parts of that network were in neighborhoods that even I didn't like to visit at night; others were only available after dark. One of these was a place called, appropriately enough, New Moon.

The Moon was a small dive in Gilbert, not too far from my home in Chandler. It was open most nights, except when the moon was full, and it catered to weremystes and people who liked to pretend that they had magical abilities, or who just enjoyed hanging out with those of us who really did. Not much happened there. It wasn't like weremystes got together to plot a magical takeover of the world, or something like that. But at times there was something to be said for being able to talk about magic and the phasings with people who understood from their own experience, and who didn't shy away from me like I was already nuts. We tolerated the wannabes and groupies because they listened and they didn't judge us, and because they tended to buy rounds for everyone as a way of compensating for their lack of actual magical ability.

The bar was also where I went when I needed information about what was happening in the streets: new weremystes in town, rivalries among sorcerers, unexplained magical attacks, that sort of thing. My visits to the New Moon hadn't turned up anything about the Blind Angel Killer back when I was on the force, and I didn't expect this visit to be any different. But it was a place to start.

There were only about ten cars in the gravel parking lot and about the same number of people inside. A few of them tore their gazes from their gin and tonics and beers as I walked in, but they showed little interest in me and were soon focused once more on their glasses and bottles. I didn't recognize any of the customers. It had been a while since I'd been there.

I stepped to the bar and sat. The Diamondbacks were on TV, getting clobbered by the Giants.

"Jay Fearsson, as I live and breathe."

I smiled, as much at the New York accent as at the greeting. Sophie Schaller was about as unlikely a candidate to be tending bar in a place that catered to weremystes as a person could imagine. She was a Jewish grandmother from Brooklyn, who had moved out to Phoenix for the warm air and sunshine. She had to be in her late sixties; maybe even older. Most weremystes her age were already crazy, or they were dead. But she'd once confided in me that her phasings were milder than most, and I believed her. Her mind still seemed as sharp as the day I met her.

"Hi, Sophe," I said, leaning over the bar to give her a kiss on the cheek. "How are you?"

She shrugged. "Eh, not bad." She had white hair, warm brown eyes, and a smile that could melt glaciers. Like all weremystes, she had that slightly blurred appearance, though the effect was pretty weak on Sophie, probably because she wasn't a powerful sorcerer. I imagined that the Blind Angel Killer would have looked like little more than a smudge.

Sophie's face was lined and she wore too much makeup, but I could tell that she'd been a great beauty as a young woman.

"What'll you have, dear?" she asked me.

"Beer. The darkest you've got on tap."

She grinned, her eyes twinkling in the dim light. "We just got something new in. I think you'll like it." She had to use a step stool to get a mug down, and then she walked to the tap and started to fill it. "You here on business or out for a drink?"

"Business."

Sophie nodded, but didn't say anything more until she'd filled the mug and put it in front of me. "Whaddya wanna know?"

"You heard about the Deegan kid?" I asked in a low voice.

"Oy." She grunted the word, as if she'd been punched in the stomach. "'Course I have. Who hasn't?" She narrowed her eyes. "You still think those kids are bein' killed with magic?"

"Yeah, I do."

Sophie shook her head. "People around here didn't like it when you were saying that a couple of years ago. They won't like it any more now."

"I know." I stared back at her, waiting for her to tell me something, knowing that she'd give in eventually. Sophie had always liked me, and whatever the rest of the magical community thought of my efforts to find the weremyste responsible for the Blind Angel murders, she wanted this guy caught.

At last she sighed and began to wipe up the bar with a white towel. "Luis is in back," she said, her attention on her cleaning. "He's playing cards, but he'll talk to you. I think."

"Thanks, Sophe." I tasted the beer. "That's good."

She grinned. I dug into my wallet and threw a ten spot on the bar before walking to the back room. It was filled with cigarette and cigar smoke, which barely masked the smell of stale beer. Five men sat around a table playing poker with those old chips that always reminded me of Necco Wafers. Luis Paredes sat at the far end of the table behind a wall of chips, chewing on a stogie and staring hard at his cards. He was a short, barrel-chested Latino, with a scruffy beard and mustache, and dark eyes that were hard and flat, like a shark's. I saw that heat-wave effect with him, too, and with the other guys at the table. It was strongest by far with Luis.

The other poker players were all Latino, and they turned to stare at me as I stood in the doorway. I can't say that they made me feel welcome.

"Fearsson," Luis said. "You want to sit?"

"I want to talk."

Luis said to his friends, *"El gringo no tiene el cajones jugar con nosotros."* The gringo doesn't have the balls to play with us.

They all laughed. I kept my mouth shut.

Luis met my gaze again, his smile fading. I'd busted him years ago for possession of pot, and he'd managed to get probation and community service. Later, after I'd opened my business, I helped him track down an employee who had stolen from the bar. So he had as many reasons to like me as not. And he knew that I wasn't someone who would have shown up here without good reason. At last he muttered, *"Maldita sea,"* and put his cards on the table, face down. *"Nos dan cinco minutos."* Damn it. Give us five minutes.

The other men eyed me again, with even less warmth than before. Then they put down their cards, stood, their chairs scraping on the wood floor, and filed out of the room.

Luis indicated the chair nearest his own with an open hand. "*Mi amigo*," he said. "What can I do for you?"

I sat and sipped my beer. "You've heard about Claudia Deegan?"

Luis' expression hardened, if that was possible. "*No tengo nada hacer con eso.*" That's not my problem.

"I know that, Luis. But I think she was killed by magic, like all the other Blind Angel victims. So that makes it a problem for all of us."

He scowled, but after a moment he nodded for me to go on.

"You know of anyone in town who's been playing with dark magic? Maybe showing signs of power that he shouldn't have?"

Luis shook his head. "No."

I would have preferred that he give the question more thought, but I didn't sense that he was hiding anything from me. Even if I had, I wouldn't have been fool enough to call him a liar in his own place, with his friends in the next room. Luis was as skilled with his magic as I was with mine, maybe more so. And I didn't think the weremystes listening from the barroom would be siding with me if it came to a fight.

"Can you think of any reason why someone would kill with magic on the night of the quarter moon?"

He sat forward. "The first quarter?" Clearly I'd gotten his attention. "*El Angel Ciegos?*"

"Yeah," I said. "Every time."

He sat back again, rubbing a hand over his mouth.

I took another sip, watching him. "What does that mean, Luis?"

"*No estoy seguro.*" I'm not sure. "The first quarter—that's a powerful night. Not like the full, but strong, you know? If I was doing magic and I needed it to be just right—*perfecto*, you know?—that's when I'd do it."

"I think he's using these kids to make himself stronger," I said. "I have no proof, and I don't know what kind of magic he'd have to do, but that's what I think. Call it the hunch of an ex-cop. I'd appreciate any help you can give me."

"I don't talk to cops, Jay. You know that. And private eyes are no different in my book. But this . . ." He shook his head. "*Esto suena mal.*" This sounds bad. He stared at the table for several seconds, seemingly deep in thought. "You talked to Quinley yet?"

"Brother Q?" I said with genuine surprise.

Luis laughed. "Yeah, Brother Q." He said it in a way that made me think he didn't like Q very much.

Orestes Quinley was the weremyste Kona and I arrested after my first conversation with Namid. He was a minor conjurer then, still new enough to his power that a jail would hold him, and he served a couple of years at Eyman State Prison.

Within a few months of his release, he started getting in trouble again; small time offenses primarily. He'd never been a violent guy, and for the most part he was accused of stealing esoteric stuff—strange pieces of jewelry, unusual gems and stones, rare herbs and oils. On several occasions, the victims dropped the charges as soon as they recovered the stolen goods. Many of them seemed reluctant to tell us too much about why Orestes might have wanted them, or why they were so anxious to have them back. Even in those cases where the charges weren't dropped, it never seemed that we could find enough evidence against him to get a conviction. And since I was the one guy in the PPD who could track magical crimes, after I left the department he stopped getting caught at all. Those twenty-six months at Eyman still represented the only time Orestes had ever done.

To this day, whenever something strange happens in town—strange in a magical sense—Kona will ask me to go around and speak with Orestes. On a few occasions he had been able to help us out, but always for a price, and, of course, never in any way that implicated himself. To be honest I was glad I hadn't been able to prove anything against him. I liked Orestes, and despite the fact that our friendship began with me arresting him, I believe he liked me, too. But I hadn't talked to him about the Blind Angel case since I'd left the force, and before then he hadn't been particularly helpful.

"You think he has something to do with this guy?" I asked.

Luis gave a noncommittal shrug. "I just said you should talk to him."

"Yeah, all right." I drained my beer and stood. "Thanks, Luis."

A sly grin carved across his face. "You sure you don't want to play a few hands?"

"Weremyste poker, huh? I don't think so."

He laughed. "By the time we're done for the night, the cards are glowing with so many colors you can barely tell which suit is which."

"Yeah, I'll bet," I said. "Goodnight, *mi amigo*."

"Jay."

I halted in the doorway. His expression had grown deadly serious.

"This guy—this killer . . . he *loco peligroso*. Crazy dangerous, you know? Watch yourself."

I nodded once, and left, pausing at the bar long enough to give Sophie my empty mug and wish her goodnight.

Once outside, I had to resist the urge to jump in the Z-ster and drive straight to Q's place in Maryvale. But it was late and I'd had a long day. I'd find him soon enough, and if it turned out he'd been lying to me when I was on the job and asking him about the Blind Angel case, he was going to wish he'd never left Eyman Prison.

CHAPTER 7

I woke up early, not because I was so eager to see Orestes Quinley, but because after working for the PPD for eight years and getting to work first thing in the morning, I was no longer capable of sleeping late. Besides, this was Tuesday, and every Tuesday morning I drove out to the desert north of Wofford to see my dad.

I started doing this several years ago, when I was still on the job. It had become clear to me that while he could take care of most of the day-to-day stuff—cooking his own meals, getting an occasional load of laundry done, keeping his trailer somewhat clean—he couldn't handle anything that involved interacting with the rest of society. The way the shifts worked after Kona and I moved to Homicide, Tuesday mornings were my free time, and since Dad had no one else, I gave them to him.

I went to the market first to get his shopping done. He still received a small pension from the department, and that paid for his place and some of his food. We also had some family money—from my mom's side. It went to my dad when she died, although ultimately I think it was meant for me. These days though, I made enough to get by, and my dad needed the money more than I did.

He liked steaks, New York strips mostly, and chicken salad, the kind that came in cans like tuna. He ate raisin bran for breakfast every day, but only one particular brand. And, man, could he tell if you tried to slip in the wrong one. He loved ice cream at night before he went

77

to bed, and he didn't care much what kind, so I liked to surprise him with something different most every week. I also picked up basic supplies for him as he needed them: paper towels, toilet paper, laundry detergent, soap; stuff like that. And I usually brought him a six-pack of beer. Two, if I intended to stay with him for dinner. He no longer drank the way he had in the years after my mom died—though of course he'd quit many years too late—and his doctors said an occasional beer wouldn't hurt him, as long as he didn't have too much. The funny thing was he never did. For a guy who'd accelerated his own psychological decline by boozing, my father was now pretty disciplined. He allowed himself one beer a night. No more.

He was funny that way, a study in contradictions. I never knew from one visit to the next what I'd find when I reached his place. Some days he was sharp as a tack; other times it seemed like his brain and his mouth weren't connected, so that he'd be carrying on a normal conversation, except that nothing he said made any sense at all. There were times when he was jovial and talkative, and times when he acted so depressed, so withdrawn, I was afraid to leave him alone, and I'd end up spending the night curled up on his couch. And sometimes he'd have what he called his "piss and vinegar days" when he was ticked off at the world. Those days were no picnic.

The tricky thing was there were endless combinations with all of these moods. He could be pissed off and incoherent, or lucid and utterly cheerless. Each visit was a crap shoot.

For the first several years, I resented every second I spent with him, every mile I drove to get there and every mile I had to drive to get away again. He hadn't been the best father in the world. It was tough on cops to begin with, what with overtime, schedules that were less than family-friendly, and the occasional stakeout. Add in a difficult personality and the effect of the phasings, and my dad was never a nominee for Father of the Year.

Things grew far worse after my mother's death. I still don't understand all that happened. I know she had an affair with another man, and eventually both of them wound up dead. Some people said my father killed them both, but I can't imagine it. For all his faults, and despite all the damage to his mind, my father was no murderer. Most assumed that my mother and her lover killed themselves when their affair became public knowledge. Whatever the truth, there could be no denying that my father loved her. After she died, he started drinking all the time and his mind began to go. Soon he had lost his job as well as his grip on reality, and I was left effectively orphaned by the age of fifteen. Is it any wonder I hated him?

I should have ended up in foster care, and who knows where I'd be now if I had? But the cops in my dad's unit took me in. I got passed around from family to family, from home to home, but they were all good homes and good families, and they all took care of me, got me through high school, helped me get state aid to go to college. And after I went to the academy, they made sure I got a job on the force.

It was only then, as I started to live a cop's life and learn what it meant to be a weremyste, that I came to understand my old man. I'm not naïve enough to think that I'll ever forgive him entirely for the things I went through as a kid. Those old resentments die hard. But for better or worse, he's my dad. And those days when I find him upbeat and clear are priceless.

I got an early start on this day and finished most of the shopping before eight in the morning. It had been a comfortable night, but I could tell that the day would be scorching hot. It was already warm and the morning sun felt like one of those heat lamps in a fast food restaurant.

A hard, hot wind blew out of the west, sweeping clouds of dust and tumbleweeds across the Phoenix-Wickenburg Highway and making the Z-ster shudder as I cruised past the pale, baked houses and gas stations of Peoria and El Mirage.

Phoenix had crept farther and farther into the desert over the years, new subdivisions and shopping malls fanning across the landscape like flame spreading across paper. But Wofford remained much the same: a small, bland little town with a gas station, a post office and not much else. A single road off U.S. 60 cut through the town and one mile north of the town center, such as it was, you were back in the desert again, following an endless line of sun-bleached telephone poles and watching dust devils whirl above the sage.

My dad lived on a small rise a short distance off this road, at the end of a rutted dirt track. His trailer had been nice once, but it was old now, and he didn't do much to keep it up. A couple of years ago I'd rigged a little covered area for him outside the front door, using a sturdy tarp and a frame I built out of two-by-sixes. It flapped some in the wind, but it had made it through three winters with only a few minor repairs. He sat out there every day on an old lawn chair, sipping iced tea and staring at the desert waiting for God-knows-what. He knew his birds, and he often had a pair of old Leica binoculars at his side.

He was out there already today, his chair angled eastward, toward the New River Mountains, which were partially obscured by the brown haze hanging over north Phoenix. He was dressed in jeans and a torn white t-shirt. He'd put on his old tennis shoes, but hadn't bothered with socks.

My dad was a little like a scrying stone. There were signs I could watch for, portents of his mood and state on a given day. No socks was never a good sign. Neither was a mess anywhere in the house. He kept things neat when he wanted to, and when he could manage to clean up after himself. If there were dirty dishes in the sink or clothes strewn about in his bedroom I knew that he'd been out of it for a day or two.

I got out of the Z-ster, grabbed the bags of groceries from the back, and pushed the door shut with my foot.

"Hey, Dad!" I called.

He didn't answer. I could see that he was muttering to himself, his white curls stirring in the wind, his hands gripping the plastic arms of his chair. He sat slouched, long legs stretched out in front of him, his belly, once as flat as mine, gathered in folds beneath the threadbare shirt.

I let myself into the trailer and started putting things away. The dishes and pans from the previous night's dinner were still in the sink. I saw no evidence to suggest that he'd had any breakfast.

"I got you Rocky Road this time. You seemed to like it when I got it for you last month."

Nothing.

When I'd finished with the groceries, I cleaned up his kitchen. Then I joined him out front, unfolding another lawn chair.

I kissed him on the forehead, then sat. "How you doin', Pop?"

"This wind means rain," he said, not bothering to tear his gaze from the desert hills.

I glanced up at the sky. There wasn't a cloud over the entire state of Arizona.

"I don't know, Pop. They're saying clear skies all week."

He mumbled something else that I couldn't hear.

"How are you feeling today?" I asked, studying him.

No answer. He was squinting, but his eyes were clear, and his color was good. The doctors told me to check him closely when he was nonresponsive like this. Most times he'd be fine—this state of mind was as normal for him as any other. But they said that if he ever did have any physical problems, his mind would be the first thing to quit.

My father was the only weremyste I'd met who didn't appear even the slightest bit blurry to me. No heat-wave effect at all. I've thought about this a lot and wondered if maybe people in the same family vibrate on the same frequency or something like that, so that to me he'd look normal. But that's just a half-baked theory. I could ask Namid about it, I suppose, but I figure I'd get another riddle in response. Whatever the reason, I could see him well enough to know that there was nothing wrong with him physically.

"Did you have any breakfast?" I asked.

He nodded, then frowned. "I'm hungry."

"I'll get you some cereal," I said, standing and going back inside the trailer, grateful for something to do.

I filled a bowl, added a bit of milk—he didn't like too much—and brought it out to him with his favorite spoon.

He took it from me and began to eat, spooning it slowly into his mouth, his eyes still fixed on the mountains.

A hawk circled in the distance.

"Swainson's," he said, without even lifting his binoculars.

I had no doubt that he was right.

"So I was in Randolph Deegan's house yesterday, Pop. You know, Senator Deegan? There's . . . there's a new case and . . . Well, anyway, I got to go to his house. You should see it. It's huge and it's got this great view of—"

"Used to be you'd see Harris's Hawks up here, too. Not for a while now. That brown air scares 'em off."

I exhaled, deflating like an old balloon. "That right?"

"I remember cottonwood leaves being yellow in the summer before the rains came, and the doves would sit in the trees watching the leaves shrivel and fall. There wasn't any rain for that long. Birds just died. The wind would blow like it is now, but it didn't mean a thing. It was just dry, and blue, and yellow leaves, and doves looking like they were shivering. But it was hot. That's all it was. Nothing else. Just hot."

"When was this, Pop?"

"Dad and Mom drove me to water, to cottonwoods. But there were none to see. None with anything on them. None that weren't yellow already."

"So you were a kid? This was with Gran and Pappy?"

"'S different now. Wind and rain. That's what they say. Wind and rain. When it rains, at night, the sky over there is orange." He pointed with the spoon, dripping milk on his jeans. "The colors are confusing now. Yellow and blue, brown and orange. Used to be I understood better."

Something in the way he said this made me sit forward.

"When was that?"

He dropped his gaze, but now he knew I was there.

"Before."

"Before what? Before you left the job? Before Mom died? Before I was born?"

"'S harder now." He glanced out at the desert once more. "It's been a long time."

"Do you remember Namid, Dad?"

I'm not certain what moved me to ask the question, but as soon as it crossed my lips he turned his head and looked right at me. Even after all these years, after watching his decline, after feeding him, and helping him take a piss and change into his pajamas on those really tough days, I still found his gaze arresting. Those pale gray eyes were so similar to my own that it was like staring into a mirror and seeing myself thirty years from now. The rough white beard and mustache, the long, lean face—it was me; me as I will be.

"Namid?" he said.

"You do remember him, don't you? The runemyste. He taught you how to do magic. He might have come to you sometimes during—" I stopped. We hadn't spoken about the phasings and magic in almost fifteen years, since I accused him of being a drunk and stormed out of the house. I'd never told him that I could conjure, or that I understood now what it was like during the full moons. After all these years, I still didn't know how to start that conversation. "During a case," I finally said, knowing how lame it probably sounded; knowing that he wouldn't notice. By then I'd lost him again. He'd turned away and the glimmer I'd seen in his eyes had vanished. They were unfocused again, the way they had been when I arrived.

"There was lightning. It was gray and cool, and lightning cut the clouds in half. The wind blew then. Colder than it is now, but it blew the same. And birds soared by like leaves. They couldn't help themselves and they couldn't fight it. They just flew by, black against the gray. I couldn't hear them, but I saw them. They went sideways, like they were caught in some current, like white water. . . ."

I made myself sit through it, like I did every week. There were times when staying with my dad was a pleasure, when the hours passed as easily as an afternoon in the mountains. Most days, though, were like this one. I'd long ago given up trying to decipher all that he said, although I did think it interesting that as soon as I mentioned Namid he started talking about rain and white water, as if he could see the runemyste in front of him, fluid and as changeable in his moods as the sea. But after a time, even this thin thread was lost, and he rambled on about the desert and hawks and the damn wind.

At midday I went back inside the trailer and made a couple of sandwiches. Dad barely touched his, but I ate mine, happy for any distraction. After cleaning up the dishes and cutting board, I stepped back outside.

"I should get going, Dad. I've got work to do."

"They treating you well?" he asked. "They made you a sergeant yet?"

He forgot sometimes that I'd left the force. I had told him several times, of course, and we'd had plenty of conversations about my work as a PI. But, hell, at least he was speaking to me instead of at me.

"No," I said. "Not yet."

"You can trust Namid, you know?"

I gazed at him, not knowing what to say. He was like this sometimes: incoherent one moment, lucid as can be the next.

"You hear me?"

"What do you remember about Namid, Dad?"

He shrugged. All the while he kept gazing at the mountains, but he was frowning now, wrestling with memories.

"Not much," he said at last. "It's all muddled today. But he was a friend when others weren't." He cast a look my way. "Know what I mean?"

I nodded. "Yeah. I know."

"Get going," he said. "Go work."

I kissed his forehead again, and he gave my hand a squeeze.

"I'll see you soon," I said, and left him.

Funny how even that little bit of a connection can make the whole damn visit worthwhile.

I drove back to my office to check for mail—it was all bills and junk—take in the paper, and get my phone messages. The *Republic* led off with another story about Claudia's death, but there was nothing new in it except a more detailed statement from the M.E. and the announcement that her family was putting up a twenty-five-thousand-dollar reward for the capture of her killer. For the most part, the article repeated details from yesterday's story and gave a lengthy recap of the facts from previous Blind Angel murders. Still, I read through all of it, scanning the piece for any mention of me, but it seemed that Billie Castle was the only reporter in Phoenix who found me interesting. I wondered if I should be flattered.

I was on my way out the door to go see Orestes Quinley when the phone rang. I thought about letting the machine get it, then reconsidered. I reached it on the third ring.

"Fearsson."

"Justis." Kona's voice.

"Hey, partner. What's up?"

"You can tell just from seeing a guy if he's a . . . you know, like you, right?"

"You mean, if someone's a weremyste?"

"Right. You can see it, can't you?"

"Yeah," I said. "Why?"

"I need you to come down to 620 and take a look at someone for me. Right away." She sounded excited and abruptly my heart was pounding, too.

"You think you've got him?" I asked.

"Maybe. We're working blind here, partner. No pun intended. We need your eyes on this one."

"Yeah, all right. I'll be there as soon as I can."

I hung up and hurried down to the Z-ster.

As Phoenix moves through May into June, two things in the city become constant: traffic and heat. Driving downtown in the middle of the day I had to struggle with both.

It took me the better part of an hour to get from Chandler to 620, even though it was no more than a twenty-five-mile drive. As I walked from the lot to HQ, a hot wind swirled around the street lifting scraps of paper and plastic wrappers into the air. There were cops everywhere, of course. Men and women arriving for work, others leaving, guys on duty bringing in perps. 620 was always a busy place, and even now, a year and half after leaving the force, I hungered to be part of it.

I recognized some of the faces, though not all. It's not easy being a cop; the hours suck, it eats up your personal life, and no one with integrity is going to get rich on the job. Not surprisingly in a city as big as this one, there's a good deal of turnover at any one department. So as I entered the building, a fair number of the cops inside ignored me. A few others eyed me with cool indifference, but said nothing.

To be honest, I was shaking all over; I would have preferred that no one see me. I wanted to feel like I still belonged, but I didn't, couldn't. And so what I really wanted was to be somewhere else—anywhere else.

"Hey, Jay! What brings you back here?"

Carla Jaroso had been the front desk officer at 620 for as long as I could remember, as if in defiance of all that turnover. She was short and round, with the friendliest face you ever saw. Her hair was almost pure white now, but her skin was the color of dark rum, and still as smooth as the day I met her.

I took a deep breath. "Hi, Carla. You look great."

She stepped away from the window and emerged from a side door to give me a hug and kiss. "Liar. You behaving yourself?" she asked.

"When I can."

"You here to see Kona?"

I nodded.

"Should I phone up?"

"No," I said. "It's all right. She's expecting me." I gave her another hug. "It's good to see you, Carla."

She returned to her desk and I started to walk away. Then I

stopped, remembering. When I faced Carla again, she already had the visitor's badge in her hand.

"Sorry, hon," she said. "Rules. I'll need your driver's license, too."

Such a little thing, trivial when it came right down to it. But it felt like a fist to the gut.

"Yeah, sorry, Carla. I forgot."

She smiled, sympathy in her dark eyes. "I know you did, hon."

I clipped the badge to my shirt and took the stairs up to the third floor, where the Homicide unit was located. The last thing I wanted was to get stuck in the elevator with one of the detectives I knew from my time on the job.

The smell of a police station is something a cop never forgets. It's like the perfume of that old girlfriend I mentioned before: stale coffee and sweat, nitrocellulose and old paint. It doesn't sound like much, or like anything a normal person would want to smell. But to me it was like the smell of home.

When I walked into the detectives' room, Kona was sitting at her desk, talking on the phone. A number of years ago, when I first joined the force, detectives had their own offices. Now they had cubicles, like horse stalls in a big barn. It made no sense; Kona needed to be able to lock up files at night, and in fact, since the changes, many detectives had gone out and bought those fire-safe lock boxes they sell for important documents. It was ridiculous that cops should have to pay for these themselves, but the politicians cutting police budgets didn't see it that way.

Kona was playing idly with a long, elaborate earring, which she had taken out so that she could talk on the phone. Kona and her earrings. None of the ones she wore conformed to regulations for proper attire. Our sergeant, Iban Arroyo, had been on her about her jewelry for years now. But Kona did things her own way, and she was too good a cop to get busted for the little stuff.

Seeing me, she smiled and waved me over. I sat in the chair beside her desk, waiting until she hung up.

At last she ended her call and beamed at me. "This just gets better and better," she said.

"Tell me."

"His name's Mike Gann. We picked him up at Robo's last night. He wasn't supposed to be there because Randy Deegan plays there with his band, and our friend Mike isn't supposed to go anywhere near the Deegans. Not any of them."

A vague sense of discomfort crept over me, but I said nothing.

"Well?" she asked. "Don't you want to know why?"

"Yeah, sure."

"He used to work for the Deegans. Odd jobs: yard work, small projects around the house. Handyman stuff, you know? But then he was fired because—wait for it—he started hitting on Senator Deegan's daughter. She told him to get lost about a dozen times, and he kept at her. Over time he started to get angry about all the rejections. He even threatened her. So they fired him, got a restraining order to keep him away from Claudia and from the house. Eventually he got a job as a bouncer at Robo's. But then he got fired from that job, too, because Randy and his band started booking gigs there. So then he had another reason to hate the Deegans."

"When was all this?" I asked her.

"He was fired by the Deegans three years ago. It's been about ten months since he lost the job at Robo's."

I nodded, though I wasn't convinced. "Kona—"

"Hold on, Justis. There's more." She nodded toward the phone. "That was Kevin." Kevin Glass, Kona's new partner. "He's at Gann's place now. Says it's filled with all sorts of oils and herbs and those little talisman things that your friend Q used to steal." She smiled. "We think the guy's a damn sorcerer."

"Even if he is, you're making the Blind Angel murders all about the Deegans, and you and I know better than that. Everyone is so caught up in the fact that Claudia Deegan was killed, that they're forgetting about the other thirty victims."

I regretted that last bit as soon as I said it.

"You think I'm forgetting the other victims?" she demanded, the words clipped, her voice like ice.

"No. I shouldn't have said that."

"I've been working this case for three years now, Justis. Even you can't say that. I never—*never*—forget any of the kids this guy's killed."

"I know you don't."

For some time neither of us said a word. She stared at her phone; I studied at my hands.

"He lives in West Chandler," she said, breaking a brittle silence.

"Did I mention that? He's, like, ten minutes from South Mountain Park."

"Still—"

"I hear you. Really, I do. And it's not like I'm booking this guy's room on death row. But you have to admit that we've got an awful lot of coincidences at work here."

I took a breath. "Yeah, you do."

She frowned. "Isn't it possible that when the Deegans fired him— when Claudia got him fired—something snapped and he began this string of killings that culminated in her murder?"

Put that way, it did make some sense.

"So you want me to use my magic eyes," I said. "Tell you if I think he's our guy."

"Would you know if he was?"

I thought about Sophie at the New Moon, and how subtle the blurring effect had been with her.

"Yeah," I said. "I'd know."

She smiled and stood. "Then come on."

We walked to the interview rooms, where suspects were interrogated and stopped first at the observation room. Each interview room had video cameras in the ceiling corners. The signals from the cameras came here. The room was brightly lit and it seemed to vibrate with the hum of fluorescent bulbs. Four television screens lined one of the walls. Three of them were off. The fourth showed a large, muscular man with a military style buzz cut and a square face. He sat on a metal chair in front of an empty table. The TV was black and white, and the signal wasn't the best, so I couldn't tell from here whether he was a weremyste, much less one who was powerful enough to have left that vivid crimson wash of magic on Claudia Deegan's face and body.

Gann was antsy. He was slouched in his chair, one of his legs bouncing, his eyes flicking up toward the camera every few seconds.

Kona watched me, expectant.

I shook my head. "I can't tell anything from here. I'm going to have to see him in the flesh."

"Yeah, I was afraid of that."

"Hibbard?"

"Damn right, Hibbard. I'd rather the Federal boys didn't see you here either, but I'm more worried about old Cole. Calling you to the

Deegan place was one thing. But if he finds out that you were here, meeting with his suspect . . . ?" She shook her head. "One day you're going to have to explain to me again why it is he hates you so much."

"I'll keep my mouth shut and you can tell Gann I'm visiting from one of the precincts, or something."

We made our way back to the interview room and went in. Gann sat up as soon as the door opened, his gaze darting back and forth between us. I leaned against the wall near the door, and stared at him. Kona began to pace the perimeter of the room, her lips pursed, her eyes on the floor. This was how we'd always started our interviews. Kona and I hadn't been in one of these rooms together in a year and half, and yet it felt like no time had passed.

After a few moments of silence, Gann started to get real nervous. He stared at me and narrowed his eyes. I guessed that he could tell I was a weremyste. But it also seemed he didn't want to admit that if he didn't have to. After a moment or two, he turned his attention back to Kona.

"Who the hell are you guys?"

"We're priests, Mike," Kona said, still pacing, still not looking at him. "We've come to hear your confession."

"I haven't done anything wrong."

"The guys at Robo's say different."

I watched him as his eyes followed Kona. He was definitely a weremyste. I could see a faint shimmering around his face and shoulders. It might have been somewhat stronger than the blurring I'd seen on Sophie and on Robby Sommer, but it wasn't as obvious as what I'd seen on Luis. It wasn't even close. And Luis' power was no match for that of the Blind Angel. There was no way this guy had left that magical residue on Claudia. Asking him to cast a spell that powerful would have been like asking a ten-year-old little leaguer to hit a home run off a major league pitcher. He didn't have the strength or the skill to pull it off.

"I just went in there for a minute," Gann said. "I heard music and I wanted to see who was playing."

"It said out front who was playing, Mike. Randy Deegan's name was on the marquee, in the windows, on the door. Unless you can't read, you couldn't have missed it."

Gann glared at her, but didn't answer.

"What were you doing there?"

He crossed his arms and stared at the table.

Kona flicked a glance my way, a question in her eyes. I shook my head, drawing a frown.

"All right, Mike," she said, sounding like a parent who's disappointed in her kid. "You give that question some thought, and I'll be back."

Kona and I stepped out into the hallway and she closed and locked the door. I knew better than to say anything right away. We started back down the corridor toward the detective's room and once we'd put some distance between ourselves and Gann, she glanced my way.

"Well?"

Before I could answer, two guys came around the corner in front of us. One of them I didn't know. The other I recognized, but couldn't name. He must have remembered me, because he stared at me the way he would a guy he knew from a wanted poster. He muttered a hello to Kona, but his gaze kept swinging back in my direction. I'm not one to feel self-conscious, but in that instant I wanted to make myself invisible. Had I been more comfortable with the spell, I would have spoken it.

A moment later, we turned that same corner and were alone again. I exhaled.

"Justis?"

"Yeah," I said. "He's not our guy."

She did nothing to mask her disappointment. "You're sure?"

"Pretty sure. Unless he's found some way to dampen his magic and make himself appear to be less of a weremyste than he really is, it couldn't be him. I didn't see that much power in him."

"Is what you just said possible? That part about dampening?"

I shrugged. "I'm not sure, Kona. I wouldn't know how to do it, but that doesn't mean it can't be done."

She started to say something, then stopped, shaking her head.

"You really think he's our killer?" I asked.

Kona rubbed her eyes with her thumb and forefinger. "Maybe," she said with a sigh. "He's the best prospect we've had since that groundskeeper at Red Mountain you and I brought in two years ago." She smiled faintly. "But that's not saying much."

"If this was a normal case I'd agree with you," I said. "But whoever this guy is, he'd not a typical serial killer. He's smart and he's ruthless and he has a specific goal in mind. A magical goal. He's building up to something. I don't know what it is yet, but there's more to this than trying to get back at the Deegans. And there's more to our killer than I saw in Mike Gann."

"I'm not the only one who likes him for this," Kona said. "Hibbard is giddy as a little girl who just got her first pony." I snorted and she grinned. "Yeah, and I can tell you, that's not a pretty sight."

I laughed.

"The Deegans are convinced he's guilty," she went on, her smile disappearing, and her voice falling to a whisper. "And the Feds are about this close"—she held her thumb and forefinger a hair's breadth apart—"to taking him themselves. They're leaning pretty hard on Latrelle and Hibbard to release the guy into their custody and be done with it. And with the assistant chief and the commander of violent crimes pushing us, that's probably what's going to happen. I've never seen pressure like this. Randolph Deegan is one powerful man."

"Do you want me to keep poking around?" I asked, whispering as well. "Hibbard doesn't have to know. Whatever I do, I can claim that I'm working for Wriker and the Deegans."

She eyed me. I could tell she didn't like the idea, but she was considering it just the same. "Where would you go?"

"I'd start with Robo's, maybe learn a bit more about Gann. And then I'd go see Brother Q." I hesitated, but only for a second. "Truth is, I was planning to see Q anyway. I talked to Luis Paredes last night, and he seems to think that Q might know something about our guy."

"And when were you planning to tell me all of this?"

I smiled. "I hadn't decided yet."

Kona shook her head. "I don't like putting the future of this case in the hands of Orestes Quinley, Justis. The man's certifiable."

"He's eccentric."

"My grandma's eccentric. Q is nuts."

I didn't say anything; I didn't have to. All I needed to do was watch her make up her mind.

"Yeah, all right," she said. "Let me know what you find out at Robo's."

"And Q?"

She rolled her eyes. "Sure, tell me what he says, too. Just keep him the hell away from me."

"You're starting to sound like Hibbard," I said with a grin.

"Great," she said. "That's what I want to hear."

CHAPTER 8

Robo's was one of the hottest music and booze joints in Tempe. It was upscale enough to serve all the best beers and trendy drinks, and to provide its bands with a professional stage and quality sound equipment. But it was also seedy enough around the edges to seem cool to the university kids. On nights when there was live music—Thursdays, Fridays, and Saturdays of most weeks—the line to get in could stretch all the way around the block.

When I got there, the doors to the place were closed, including the second set of glass ones past the window where patrons paid the cover charge. As Kona had told Gann, the marquee read "Electric Daiquiri: Featuring Randy Deegan and Tilo Ruiz." Inside one of the windows was a black and white picture of the band standing in front of some vague photo studio backdrop. Randy stood at the center, wearing jeans and an untucked dress shirt. The guys around him came across as cool and a little unsavory, which I'm sure is what they were going for. But Randy couldn't help but look like an all-American kid, even with that serious, "I-really-am-a-badass" expression on his face.

It didn't surprise me at all that a place like this would be interested in having Randy Deegan's band headlining for it. What did surprise me was that a buttoned-down guy like Randy would stoop to play there. Then again, from all I'd seen in the papers and on television over the past year or so, I had the sense that Randy wanted to follow in Dad's footsteps, and maybe he figured anything that made him out to be a regular guy would help.

Despite the locked doors, I could hear music coming from inside, so I knew the place wasn't empty. I knocked several times until at last a large man in a Robo's t-shirt came to the door and tried to shoo me away. I pulled out my private investigator's ID, which has a terrible picture of me and looks official enough to impress.

"My name's Jay Fearsson. I'm doing a little work on behalf of the Deegans."

He frowned, glanced back over his shoulder, clearly unsure of what to do. But then he shrugged, perhaps figuring that I was Randy's problem and not his. He let me inside.

The music was cranked to an ear-splitting volume, but I could tell right away that Electric Daiquiri was a decent band. They were in the middle of an up-tempo instrumental piece with a Latin beat and a lot of tonal modulation. Randy played bass but was obviously the group's front man—not that I would have expected anything different. The band also included a guitarist, a drummer, a keyboardist, and a saxophonist, who was in the middle of a blistering solo. The stage lights were on, but the rest of the place was dark and I doubted that any of them could see me. The sound guy acknowledged me with a quick nod, but then went right back to fiddling with the mixing board. I took a seat in the back of the bar and listened to the rest of the piece, which went through a keyboard solo, a drum break, and a final go-round of what must have been the original melody. All of it was very tight, and when they finished I clapped.

Randy shielded his eyes from the spotlights. "Who's that?" he asked, squinting against the glare.

"My name's Jay Fearsson," I said. "I was at your house the other day."

"The guy Howard talked to?"

"That's me."

He glanced at the guitar player, and then at the other musicians. "Let's take a quick break, guys."

Randy and the guitarist took off their instruments, hopped down from the stage, and joined me at my table. The rest of the band wandered backstage.

I shook hands with Randy, and he introduced the guitar player as

Tilo Ruiz. He was a tall, good-looking Latino kid, with black curly hair and large dark eyes. He was rail thin and was dressed like a model in his black jeans and white t-shirt.

"You were Claudia's boyfriend, right?"

"That's right," he said with a puzzled frown. "How'd you know that?"

I didn't think it would be too smart to bring up Robby Sommer, so I shrugged. "Must have read it somewhere. You both have my deepest sympathies."

"Thank you," Randy said, sounding anything but grateful. "I have to tell you Mister . . . uh . . ."

"Fearsson."

"Right. Mister Fearsson. I think it was a mistake for Howard to even talk to you the other day. He shouldn't have asked you to do any work for us. I'm not comfortable with that at all, and neither is my father."

"I understand. But first of all, he never gave me any money, so he didn't hire me in any true sense. And second, even if he had, I'm bound by both ethics and the law to keep any work I do for you completely confidential."

"That didn't stop you from talking to Billie Castle."

My smile was reflexive; I would have preferred to smack the kid in the mouth. "If you read her piece the other day, you would have seen that I told her nothing, and that she was feeling pretty snippy about it."

"And now you're here," Randy went on, as if he hadn't heard me.

"Yes, I am. You probably know that the police have a man in custody."

"Mike Gann," Tilo said.

"Right. I came here to learn what I can about him. The fact that I happened to find you here is a coincidence. You have my word."

Randy had narrowed his eyes. "You're doing work for the PPD?"

"You read Billie's article. I used to be a homicide detective. I worked the Blind Angel case for a year and a half before I left the force."

The Deegan kid still wasn't ready to declare me his closest pal, but my explanations seemed to have satisfied him, at least for the moment.

"You think this guy Gann is the Blind Angel Killer?"

An honest answer would have raised questions that could get Kona in trouble. "I don't know. He certainly had it in for your family."

"Yeah," Randy said. "I'm sorry if I came on too strong just now. It's been . . ." He averted his gaze. "It's been a rough week."

"I understand. I won't trouble you anymore. But can you tell me who I should talk to about Gann? I have a few questions about his work here and how he got along with his coworkers. That sort of thing."

Randy nodded. "Kenny Moore is the person you really want to talk to. He's the manager. But he's not in today, and he won't be again until Thursday night." His expression brightened. "You should come then. We're playing, and I can reserve a table for you up front."

"I'm not sure I want to be that close to your speakers."

Tilo laughed.

"In back then," Randy said, grinning. "But that's your best bet for finding Kenny." He furrowed his brow. "The other person who might help you is Doug Bass. He's the janitor, and he's been here forever. He'd have known Gann."

"Is he here now?"

Randy nodded. "In back."

"All right, thanks." I shook hands with both of them, and started toward the back of the club.

"I meant what I said," Randy called to me. "Come Thursday night. There'll be a table reserved for you."

"Thanks," I said. "I'll try to make it."

I found Doug Bass in the alley behind the club, sitting on an old, rusted metal folding chair, smoking a cigarette. He was a big African-American man with white hair and a mustache to match. He eyed me suspiciously and didn't seem at all impressed with my PI license. When I told him Randy had recommended that I talk to him, he stared straight ahead and took a long pull on his cigarette.

"I ain't never voted for his old man."

I laughed. "Yeah. Me, neither."

No response.

"I can't make you talk to me," I told him, pulling out my note pad and pencil. "But the police are getting ready to charge Mike Gann with the Blind Angel killings, and while I don't think I'd want Mike for a friend, I also don't think he killed all those kids."

Doug studied me through squinting eyes. Then he took one last puff on his cigarette, dropped it on the street, and crushed it with his sneaker toe. I thought for sure he was going to get up and leave me there. But he didn't.

"Mike Gann's a fool," he said in a deep voice. "Bigoted son of a bitch, too. But he ain't the Blind Angel Killer."

"What makes you say that?"

"This Blind Angel fella—he's smart. He'd have to be, the way he's been avoiding the police for so long. Like I say, Mike's a fool. He'd have got himself caught a long time ago."

"Did you ever notice anything . . . weird about Mike? Stuff he did, or stuff that happened around him, that you couldn't explain?"

"You mean like magic?"

I opened my mouth, closed it again. After a few seconds I gave a little laugh. "Yeah," I said. "Like magic."

"Mike talked about magic all the time. Used to tell me and anyone else who'd listen that he could do stuff. Spells, you know? Now, I believe in all that. I seen folks do it down in Mobile, where I grew up. I saw some shit on full moons that would have scared you half to death. But I never saw Mike do much more than light a match without strikin' it. Rest was all talk."

"Could he have been holding back? Maybe he didn't want to show too much."

Doug shrugged. "Then why all the talk?"

Good question. "Did you ever see him around the full moon?"

The old man shook his head. "He made himself scarce around then. Didn't want no one to see him."

I knew how he felt. "Was there anything else strange about him, anything that made you nervous or made you want to stay away from him?"

"Nah," Doug said. "He was a typical poor white boy. He said some stupid stuff now and then, stuff that would have made me hit a white boy I didn't know. But he was all right most of the time. The one thing that set him off was the Deegans. Any mention of them, and he got all quiet and intense, you know? It wouldn't surprise me at all to find out he killed that girl. But there's no way he killed all those other kids."

I nodded, jotted down a few last notes, and put the pad and pencil away. I started to reach for my wallet to give him a few bucks for his time, but Doug shook his head.

"No need for that," he said. He stood, his body unfolding slowly. He was bigger even than I'd thought. He stood a full head taller than me and he was broad in the shoulders and chest. I would have bet good money that he'd played football in college. Maybe even in the pros, back when athletes had to work for a living after they retired.

"Thanks," I said, holding out a hand.

He gripped it, his hand appearing to swallow mine. "No problem."

He limped back into the club and I followed. Electric Daiquiri was working their way through another song, the music so loud it hurt. I let myself out of Robo's without bothering to say goodbye to Randy and Tilo. Once on the street, I began walking back toward the Z-ster, my ears ringing.

I hadn't taken three steps, though, when I felt it again. I was being watched, tracked. I imagined myself in the crosshairs of a rifle. Except this time I knew the feeling for what it was: magic. I made no effort to find the sorcerer; I didn't even alter my gait. But I began to mumble the words to a deflection spell, which was one of the most rudimentary wardings I knew. In essence, it redirected any conjuring aimed at me toward something else, an object of my choosing, in this case an SUV parked along the curb in front of me.

But the attack never came. It almost seemed that someone—the Blind Angel Killer?—was playing with me, trying to make me flinch. Or maybe he wanted to see what I was capable of doing before he tried in earnest to kill me. Whatever the explanation, I was growing tired of it. And, to be honest, I was scared. So scared, that by the time I reached the Z-ster, there was sweat on my forehead and neck.

True, I was pretty good at warding magic. But I figured any weremyste who could make his presence known to me in this way wouldn't have had too much trouble mastering a deflection spell.

I began to relax once I was in the car. This made no sense whatsoever—it's not as though my 280Z has some magical property that protects me from assailing spells. But sometimes the illusion of safety is enough to get a person through. I started the Z-ster up, pulled away from the curb, and drove down University toward the campus. As soon as I could, though, I doubled back and cruised the street a second time, hoping that maybe I'd catch my secret admirer unawares. But though I made two more passes down the same block, and though I saw a couple of people who shimmered with magic, none of them possessed enough power to be a threat. Either they were small-time conjurers or weremystes who were using blockers to suppress the phasings, and their abilities with them.

I was about to give up and drive over to Orestes Quinley's place, when I spotted someone of a different sort, though no less interesting.

Billie Castle.

She was stepping into a coffeehouse, a thermal coffee mug in one hand and a computer case slung over the other shoulder. Alarm bells went off in my head. I knew that I should keep driving, keep as far from the woman as I could. She was a reporter, and all she had wanted from me yesterday was information. But I couldn't deny that there was something intriguing about her. Maybe that was a fancy way of saying that I found her attractive. Intriguing, attractive, a challenge: pick your reason. I thought about stopping to see if I might wrangle a dinner date out of her.

Then I thought better of it.

Then I parked the car and made my way to the coffeehouse.

By the time I was inside and in line, she had her coffee and was setting up her work space at a table in the back. She didn't notice me, which was probably a good thing. Given the way our last conversation went, I figured the element of surprise was about all I had going for me.

To my amazement, the place served Sumatran coffee. I took it as a sign.

I got my cup and walked back to her table. She had her computer out and was already engrossed in her work. Her hair was down today; it was longer than I'd remembered. She wore a beige linen sports jacket with the sleeves pushed up, and a black t-shirt underneath. Silver and malachite earrings flashed within her curls, and a matching necklace lay against the t-shirt. Tastefully stylish, as well as pretty. I admit it: I was smitten.

Most of the tables in back were open, and I thought about sitting at a table nearby and trying the whole "what-a-coincidence" thing, but she was too smart for that to work. Instead, I went with the direct approach.

"May I join you?"

She glanced at me, did a double-take. "Mister Fearsson!" Her expression turned guarded; I think she expected me to yell at her, or maybe throw a punch.

"I read your article."

"Is that why you're here?"

"No. I . . . had a meeting nearby and I saw you come in. I thought I'd say hello."

"What kind of a meeting?"

A reporter to the core.

"The kind that I'm not going to tell you about." I reached for the chair opposite hers, and raised an eyebrow. "May I?"

She started to say something; I expect she was going to tell me she was working and didn't want to be disturbed. But then she smiled. "Sure," she said, setting her computer aside. "Be my guest."

"Thank you." I sat and sipped my coffee. It was pretty good, almost as good as my own.

"How's your investigation going?"

"I don't think I'm going to tell you about that, either."

"So you're going to sit there and drink your coffee and not say a word?"

"No," I said. "I was thinking that we could talk about something other than Claudia Deegan and the Blind Angel murders."

She shook her head. "Bull. You're just like me. You don't want to make small talk. You don't want to chat with me about the weather or this coffee or the Diamondbacks—"

"You're a baseball fan?"

"My dad wanted a boy, remember? My point is, you miss being a cop. You're back working on a case that I'll bet you've been thinking about constantly for a year and a half. You're as absorbed in your work as I am in mine."

"Is that so?"

"Yes," she said, her green eyes dancing. "You *want* to talk about Claudia Deegan and the other murders."

"I do?" I asked, laughing.

"Yup. So why don't you tell me about your meeting and what you've learned, instead of playing these games."

I leaned forward. She did, too, eager, eyes fixed on mine.

"No," I whispered, and sat back.

Her expression soured. "What is it you're hiding?"

"I'm not hiding anything. That's the problem I have with reporters. You assume that I have to be hiding something simply because I don't want to share the details of my investigation with your readers. Isn't it possible that I have other reasons for keeping these things to myself? Did it ever occur to you that I could actually compromise the investigation by revealing too much?"

She shook her head, a smirk on her face. "That's an old excuse, Mister Fearsson. Politicians and bureaucrats have been hiding behind that one for a long time. 'We're keeping the truth from you,'" she said, in a deep mocking voice, "'but it's for your own good.'"

"It's not an excuse." I leaned in again. "What if the Blind Angel Killer reads newspapers and blogs?" I asked, my voice low. "I don't know if he does, but it's possible, right? I don't want to tip him off. I certainly don't want to give him any hints about who I'm talking to, for their sake and mine, too."

"What about the rest of us?" She gestured toward the front window of the shop. "People out there are terrified of this guy. Don't they have a right to know how this investigation is going, and how soon they can expect you to catch him?"

"I guess you and I have different priorities. I think it's more important that people be safe than informed."

She gaped at me, wide-eyed and clearly disgusted. "You truly think that's the choice?"

"Yes, I do."

Her laugh was harsh and abrupt. "Well, good for you, Mister Fearsson! You've stumbled across the same excuse for suppressing the media that Hitler and Stalin used! Maybe you'd feel safer living in North Korea!"

People were watching us, some craning their necks to get a better view, which was good, because this wouldn't have been as much fun without an audience. "I didn't say anything about suppressing the media," I told her, keeping my voice low. "I was just pointing out that sometimes giving people too much information can do more harm than good."

"Well," she said. "I don't believe that."

I took a breath. Too late, I realized that coming into the coffeeshop had been a bad idea. Mental note to self: next time your instincts tell you to stay away from a woman, do that.

"Well, I'm sorry to have troubled you, Miss Castle. I guess I should be on my way."

"Yes, you should," she said, already turning back to her computer. "I have work to do."

Right. I stood and picked up my coffee, having every intention of walking away. But I didn't.

"You know what?" I said. "I don't want to go."

She blinked. "You don't."

"No, I don't." I sat down again. "I'd rather stay and fight with you."

She considered me for several seconds, wondering, no doubt, if I was nuts. Then she burst out laughing.

"That's the stupidest thing I've ever heard in my life!"

"Yeah," I said, grinning. "I guess it is."

Her laughter faded until she was just looking at me, a quizzical smile on her lips. "Justis is a very odd name for a private detective."

"What would be a normal name for one?"

"I don't know. Joe. Dave. Bob. Dick."

I raised an eyebrow.

"As in 'Tracy,'" she said grinning. "You know what I mean. Justis sounds so . . . formal." She shook her head. "That's not the right word. I guess I'm saying that you don't seem like a 'Justis' to me."

"That's why I go by Jay."

She squinted. After a while she shook her head. "I'm not sure Jay works, either."

"So you're going to keep calling me Mister Fearsson?"

"Maybe. We'll see."

I watched her for a minute, until at last she dropped her gaze, her cheeks coloring. "What?" she said.

"I was thinking that Billie suits you well."

She had gone shy, but a smile tugged at her lips. "Thank you."

I glanced around. "This is a pretty upscale coffeeshop. I didn't think bloggers made any money."

"Sure we do. I sell ads on my site. For a lot. I probably make more than you do."

"Everybody makes more money than I do."

She laughed.

"Did you always want to be a reporter?"

Another laugh escaped her, this one self-conscious and breathless, but her eyes met mine again. "Not always, no. You don't meet too many kids who want to grow up to be journalists. But once I started college I knew."

"What did you want to be before then?"

"A ballerina. A movie star. An airplane pilot." She shrugged. "Little girl stuff."

"Except the airplane pilot."

She grinned, nodded. "Right. I wanted to . . . to go places. Travel."

"Where was home?"

Her smile turned brittle. "Home? Connecticut."

Two words, but I sensed that there were layers upon layers to her story. I could tell from the tone of her voice and the pain lurking in her eyes. And I found that I wanted to know all of it. Every detail.

"Well you managed to get pretty far away at least."

"Pretty far," she repeated. "How about you? Did you always want to be a private eye?"

The way she said "private eye" made it sound far more exciting and exotic than it was.

I grinned and shook my head. "I wanted to be a cop."

"Of course. Sorry. I forgot."

"It's all right. We're off the record, right?"

She gaze remained locked on mine and her smile warmed once more. She reached up and closed her computer. "We're off the record."

"Thank you," I said.

"Leaving the force must have been hard."

"Yeah, you could say that."

"I did. What would you say?"

I hesitated, wondering how much to tell her.

"We agreed that we're off the record," she said. "I'd never lie about that. But that doesn't mean I can't ask you questions, does it?"

"No," I said. "Leaving the force almost killed me. I was a cop for six years, eight months." I tried to keep my smile from turning bitter, but I'm not sure I succeeded. "I can give you the weeks and days if you want them. It's lousy work most of the time. You keep bad hours, you get paid next to nothing, and you see things that . . ." I shook my head. "That no one should have to see." I shrugged again. "And I loved every minute of it."

"Why?" she asked, making no effort to hide her bewilderment.

"Because I was helping people. Because when Kona and I were working a case, it was like we were solving a puzzle, putting each piece where it belonged, watching as a picture emerged. I liked that."

"Still, the bad stuff: doesn't it get to you after a while?"

"It's part of the job. You live with it." I sipped my coffee. "Besides, every job has it's share of crap to deal with. Being a reporter—a journalist," I corrected, using her word. "It can't be all flowers and sunshine, right?"

"Oh, it's not. Especially running my own site. It took ages to establish an audience, to get my writers, to get enough advertisers that I could make some money. It was easy to forget that I was a reporter."

"And now you get to interview guys like Randolph Deegan."

She smiled. "Deegan was nothing. I've interviewed the president."

I couldn't help but be impressed. "Really?"

"Really. The president," she said, counting on her fingers. "The prime minister of Great Britain, the prime minister of Israel, the chancellor of Germany, the Russian president. There are others who I'm forgetting. I know I've interviewed at least eight heads of state."

"So was I your toughest interview?"

"You wish!"

She had a great smile and a better laugh, and I was content to spend the next hour just talking to her, listening as she described her work. I had to admit that it was far more interesting than I'd expected. Partly—mostly—because of the way she lit up as she spoke. It was her passion, and as she explained all of what she did—the interviews and the writing, the management of her site and its reporters—I began to understand how she could be so jazzed about what I'd always dismissed as nothing more than "the news." She and her reporters were doing investigative work, too; they were detectives like I was. When she'd finished, I said this, and she seemed to like the idea of it. A lot.

"Do you really believe that?" she asked.

"I do. See that?" I said. "I bet you didn't think we'd have this much in common."

She eyed me, still smiling. "No, I didn't."

Cops don't tend to be romantics. We see too much crap on the job—too many killings, too much abuse, too many kids whose lives have been ruined by violence or drugs or sex. It doesn't leave a lot of room for dreams of romance. This isn't to say that cops don't fall in love and get married and all the rest. Of course we do. But Hollywood romance? No. I might not have been a cop anymore, but the job had left its mark on me. Add in that I was the son of a crazy old weremyste and was on my way to becoming one myself, that I'd lost my mom way too early, and that I'd been forced to quit the one job I'd ever loved doing, and I was about the least romantic person I knew.

But in that moment, sitting across from Billie Castle, watching her watch me, I would have done it all to win her over: the flowers, the candlelit dinners. Hell, I would have taken her dancing, if that's what it took. I couldn't remember the last time I'd been with someone. I don't mean for a night. That was easy enough to find, if you knew where to look. I'm talking about something serious, something that makes you think about the future.

How weird is that? Twenty-four hours ago I thought she was the most annoying person I'd ever met. An hour ago we were fighting. And here I was getting way ahead of myself. Thinking about it, I realized it wasn't weird so much as stupid. But that didn't stop me from opening my mouth again.

I glanced at my watch. Five thirty. "I know it's a little early," I said. "But would you like to get some dinner?"

She opened her mouth to reply, her forehead wrinkling a little, and I knew before she said a word that she was going to turn me down.

But at that moment I heard a voice—a man's voice, of course— call out, "Billie!"

She peered past me, I turned.

He was tall, handsome in a nerdy sort of way. Straight, fine brown hair, parted on the side, dark-rimmed glasses that resembled hers so much it was a little scary. Blue eyes, square chin, blah, blah, blah. He was your basic nightmare in a tweed jacket and jeans. Forced to guess, I would have said that he was a professor at the university. My first thought—after who the hell is this?—was that he had to be every bit as smart as she was, which meant he was way smarter than me. I. Whatever.

I turned back to Billie, and was glad to see that she appeared mortified.

"I'm sorry," Professor Stud said. "Am I interrupting?" He had stopped a few feet from the table and was eyeing me with a kind of proprietary concern. It's times like these when I find it dangerous to carry a weapon. The temptation to use it is too strong. But I was good.

I could tell that Billie was gearing up for introductions, and I wanted no part of that. I'm sure her friend was a great guy; intelligent, friendly, articulate. I didn't want to know about it. I didn't want to know his name. I didn't want to find out that he had a solid handshake and a winning smile. In this case, ignorance really was bliss.

When faced with an untenable situation, beat a quick and graceful retreat.

I stood. "Thank you, Miss Castle," I said in my best Dick Tracy voice. "If you think of anything else, feel free to call me."

She didn't say anything. After a few seconds, she nodded.

I stepped away from the table, nodded once to Billie's friend, and left, hoping to God that I didn't trip over someone's bag or try to push the door open when I was supposed to pull it.

See? This is why cops and PIs aren't romantics. Because we know what the real world is like. And in the real world, these things never work out the way you want them to.

CHAPTER 9

Walking from the coffeehouse back to the Z-ster, I remembered in a rush the weremyste who had been testing my magical defenses as I left Robo's. I tried to sense him, to open myself to his magic, but I felt nothing. As far as I could tell, I was the only weremyste in the area who wasn't using blockers. I suppose a sorcerer as powerful as this guy could have hidden himself, but he hadn't been shy before about letting me know he was nearby. I couldn't see why he'd start now. Reaching the car, I climbed in, drove one more circle around Robo's, and headed for home.

My house in Chandler is in a nice family neighborhood near Arrowhead Meadows. It's not a big place, but it's more than I need. Two bedrooms, a decent sized kitchen, living room, dining room, two bathrooms. I got a good deal on it and had intended to turn one of the bedrooms into a home office. Then the other office fell into my lap, and I never got around to it.

It was built about twenty years ago, but the previous owners remodeled the place—redid the kitchen and bathrooms, tore out the old carpet and put in oak. Then they got divorced and rather than one of them staying, they sold it and split the money. It's a good place. Well lit and open. Usually I like it a lot. But this evening, for some reason, it felt big and empty.

Until Namid materialized in the kitchen.

I had just gotten a beer from the refrigerator, though I hadn't opened it yet.

He took form right in front of me, his waters rough and wind blown.

"I expected you long ago," he said.

"You my mother now?" I asked with a small laugh.

I started to open the beer, but he shook his head. "Do not drink that now. If you need to drink, have water."

"Good God, you are my mother."

"We need to work, and you must be completely clear."

Strange that my mind should need to be clear and free of alcohol in order to practice magic that was driving me nuts. But he was right. I returned the beer to the refrigerator, poured myself a glass of water, and followed Namid into the living room.

"I felt it again this afternoon. The sense that I was being watched."

The runemyste turned. "I have no doubt that you were."

My eyes widened. "Have you learned something about the weremyste who's following me?"

"No. But it does not surprise me that he tracks you."

"He? Do you at least know that it's a man?"

Namid shook his head. "I know nothing, Ohanko. I have told you this already."

"Yeah, I remember."

"Two times now," he said. "You understand why he does this?"

I nodded. It hadn't occurred to me until then, but as soon as he asked the question, I knew. "Yes. I warded myself with a deflection spell, in case whoever it is tried to attack me. But nothing happened."

He said nothing.

"A deflection spell wouldn't have helped, would it?"

"A deflection spell is easily defeated," the runemyste said, seeming to choose his words with some care. "A skilled runecrafter would have little trouble overwhelming such a warding."

"So what should I have done?"

He stepped to the middle of my living room floor and sat, eyeing me like an expectant cat, his head canted to the side. More training.

For once I didn't argue.

"Do I need my scrying stone?"

"No." He indicated the floor with an open hand that glowed like starlit waters. "Sit."

I lowered myself to the floor in front of him.

"Clear yourself," the runemyste said, once I was settled.

I closed my eyes and summoned the vision of that eagle in the Superstition Wilderness. As I did, everything else melted away. The Blind Angel Killer, Claudia Deegan, Cole Hibbard, Billie Castle, my dad. All of it seemed to dissipate, like a vaporous breath on a cold day. In moments, I was clear, centered.

"Now," the runemyste said, "defend yourself."

It was like meeting up with your best friend and having him haul off and punch you right in the mouth, for no reason at all.

One minute I was sitting there, and the next, it felt as though I'd been stung on the legs and arms by twenty hornets.

"Son of a bitch! What was that for?"

"Defend yourself," he repeated, as calm as you please.

The stinging started again, on my neck and chest this time.

I jumped up, swatting at bugs I couldn't see. The pain stopped.

"What the hell are you doing?" I asked, my voice rising.

"I am teaching you to ward yourself."

"You could at least give me some warning!"

"Will the crafter who tracks you be so courteous?"

That brought me up short. "Of course not," I said.

"Then why should I?"

There wasn't a person alive who could make me feel foolish and young the way Namid could. I guess that came with hanging out with a being who was centuries old. "I thought we were going to be training, that's all. You caught me off guard."

"You cannot be off guard," he said. "Ever. Not anymore."

"You're scared, aren't you?"

"I fear nothing for myself. But I would rather you did not die. I have spent too many days teaching you. It would be a waste."

"Thanks, Namid. I'm touched."

"Sit down, Ohanko. Clear yourself, then ward."

I sat once more, took a moment to clear myself, and then started to recite the deflection spell from earlier in the day, just to see what it could do.

I hadn't gotten two words out before the stinging began again. Chest, back, legs. God, it hurt!

"Damn!" I said. "You're not giving me a chance!" I raised a hand before the runemyste could answer. "I know. Neither will the other sorcerer."

Namid nodded once. "Defend yourself."

I knew that I should have been able to do what the runemyste was asking of me, that my inability to ward myself was a symptom of my greatest weakness as a weremyste. I still thought of spells as being the same as incantations, as something spoken. The fact is, they don't have to be. Namid, who was driving me crazy with these damned hornets, had not moved or made a single sound. But this did nothing to weaken his magic.

On the other hand, my need to speak spells was weakening me, leaving me vulnerable to his assault. Of course spells involved words. But spells for an accomplished weremyste could be as immediate and powerful as pure thought. The words of a spell had no inherent power beyond what they meant to the weremyste using them. One sorcerer might use a rhyming scheme, while another might just use three words. I usually used a simple list of the elements of the spell, repeated as often as necessary. I also tried to limit my spells to three elements or, if that was impossible, seven. There was power in certain numbers: three, seven, eleven, and some larger primes.

Mostly though, I tried to fix my mind on the magic I was attempting. Casting, like the simple act of clearing, required focus and concentration. The rest was a matter of style.

My goal in casting spells—Namid's goal for me—was to get to the point where I could conjure without words, without fear or doubt, without hesitation.

And I wasn't there yet. Not even close.

Not to make excuses, but it's hard to focus when you're being stung by dozens of invisible, magic hornets.

I tried to cast the deflection spell again, though I knew it wasn't the right defense against this attack. It was the warding I knew best, the one I turned to when I didn't know what else to do, and at that moment, I couldn't even get it to work. I should have tried a simpler conjuring. There are lots of warding spells. One of them sheathed the body in a sort of magical cocoon; another, which I'd yet to learn, allowed a weremyste to transport himself somewhere else. Ideally I would have liked to try a reflection spell and sick the vicious stinging bastards on Namid. Somehow, though, I knew it wouldn't work. The problem was, I couldn't come up with anything that would.

After a few minutes, the stinging stopped and Namid just sat there with his eyes fixed on mine.

"You are not even trying."

"Yes, I am," I said, sounding like a bratty little kid. "I'm out of my depth here, Namid. The magic we've done before and what you're asking me to do now. . ." I shook my head. "They're totally different."

"They are not different at all. You need to be clear and focus. Otherwise you cannot defend yourself and you will be killed. It is that simple."

A book flew off one of my shelves and sailed right at my head. I ducked. The book hit the opposite wall and fell to the floor.

"Damn! You're crazy! You know that?"

"You warded yourself."

"No, I didn't. I just ducked."

"Did the book strike you?"

"No."

"Then you warded yourself. You did so without craft, but it was a warding nevertheless."

"What's your point, ghost?"

His expression didn't change at all. I needed to find a new way to get him riled.

"That you ducked without a thought. You simply acted. That is how magic should be. You think too much, Ohanko. And at other times you do not think at all. You are a most difficult man."

I had to grin. "Yeah, well, you're the one who always shows up uninvited."

"Clear yourself."

I did. And this time when the attack came, I resisted the urge to speak the deflection spell. Instead I envisioned his attack bouncing off of me, two dozen watery hornets clattering against the walls. My body, the hornets, the walls. Three elements. I didn't bother repeating them three times. I inhaled, feeling the magic build within me, and released it.

I wasn't stung once.

"Better," he said. "You knew how I would assail, and when. But still, that was better." He paused. Then, "Defend yourself."

Fire this time. Aqua green flames licking at my hands and arms. I almost panicked. But instead I managed to turn that fear into craft. Deflection wouldn't work, so I went with the cocoon. Shielding, it was called. Once more, three elements: my body again, the fire, the cocoon. It worked.

"Good," the runemyste said, sounding surprised. "Defend yourself."

A second later, I saw movement out of the corner of my eye. I turned just enough to see, then froze. Not two feet from where I sat, a snake lay in a tight coil, its head reared back to strike. I didn't have time to mark what kind it was, or whether it was venomous. This was Namid I was dealing with. I assumed the worst.

This time at least, I had a pain-free second in which to think. Camouflage spell, but with a twist. Snakes hunted by smell, using their tongues to taste the air, and they waited for motion before striking. So I had to make myself invisible and scentless. Pit vipers could also sense temperature, but I didn't know how to lower my body temperature to match the air in the house.

Camouflage wardings were the most complicated spells I knew, almost as difficult as some of the simpler transformation spells. I visualized myself blending with my surroundings, so that to the snake I would appear in every way to be nothing more or less than empty space. I slowed my breathing, and recited the spell to myself.

The snake. My body. My scent. The air around me. The wall behind me. The picture hanging on that wall. Back to the snake again. After a few moments, the snake's posture changed. Its tongue flicked out three times, as if it were trying to find me again. I eased my Glock free.

Before I could shoot it, the snake vanished.

"Good, Ohanko. Very good."

I closed my eyes.

"Clear yourself."

"Let me rest a minute."

I thought he would argue, but he nodded and sat there.

"Are there other warding spells you can teach me?" I asked.

"You must master the ones you know."

"I understand that. I'm asking if there are more."

"Of course. There are always more."

I laughed. "Always? You never run out?"

"Never," he said, without a trace of humor. "If you cannot remember one, you must create one yourself."

"Wait. You mean I can make up my own spells?"

"You are a runecrafter. How do you think the spells you know came into being?"

I shrugged. "I guess I thought that you made them up, or brought them from the Runeclave, or something like that."

"Magic is a craft, and though it might not seem so, it is a living craft." Something resembling a grin crept over the spirit's face. "Your father created a spell."

"My father?"

He nodded.

"Teach it to me."

"I do not know that you are ready for it."

That stung. "He was that much better than me?"

"He was older when he created this spell. And at that time, yes, he was a far more accomplished crafter than you are now."

"Teach it to me anyway."

It was a complicated spell. Impressive, but complicated. My father had found a way to combine two different kinds of transporting spells, one which allowed him to move himself a short distance, and another which in effect transported an object—in this case his weapon—to his hand. The trick, of course, was to carry off the two spells simultaneously, so that he could go from being unarmed and vulnerable to being armed and protected in the blink of an eye.

Try as I might, I couldn't do it. It was good practice. After several tries, I'd nearly mastered a basic transporting spell. But my pistol always wound up lying on the floor in the spot where I'd been. I gave up on that one for the time being, vowing to practice it on my own later. Namid had other spells to teach me, and for once I was eager to learn. Maybe it was the stark memory of feeling so vulnerable on the street earlier in the day. Maybe it was hearing that my father had been better at this than I was. Whatever the reason, on this night I worked my craft as I never had before.

I was in the middle of trying a new assailing spell when I heard a knock at the door. Namid's glowing gaze locked on mine.

"Are you expecting someone?" the runemyste asked.

"No." I glanced at my watch. Almost nine-thirty. We'd been working for close to three hours. Whoever it was knocked again. I stood and started toward the door.

"Careful, Ohanko."

I glanced at him and nodded. Then I crossed to the door, unlocked it, and prepared to pull it open, all the while reciting a shielding spell in my head.

But when I pulled the door open, I found myself face to face with Billie Castle. Looking past her, I saw that the street and sidewalk were wet. It had rained while I was working with Namid. Seems my dad was right about that wind after all. The sky had cleared and the gibbous moon shone through the Acacia tree growing in my front yard. Even from the doorway, I could feel the moon's pull, more insistent than last night, hinting at the power to come. Friday night. That's when the phasing would begin.

Billie opened her mouth to say something, but then stopped herself, seeming to take in my appearance. Only now did I realize that I had sweated through my shirt and that my face was damp. Working spells for hours on end was hard work.

"Good God, Fearsson, what have you been doing?"

"Um . . . Working out."

"Are you going to invite me in?"

"Sure." I opened the screen door and she stepped past me into the house. I glanced at the moon one last time, then closed the door. Billie turned a full circle, surveying the living room, and stared right through Namid, who couldn't be seen by those not descended from the Runeclave.

"Nice place."

"Thank you. You want anything? Water? Coffee? Beer? Wine?"

"No, thanks." She faced me. "You certainly took off in a hurry this afternoon."

I shrugged, scrutinizing my coffee table as if it were the most interesting thing in the world. "I didn't want to get in the way."

"Boy, I expected you to be tougher than that."

"What's that supposed to mean?"

"Well," she said, and now it was her turn to avoid my gaze. "I had the feeling that maybe you were, I don't know, interested in me. You certainly were flirting and, well, you started to ask me out to dinner, and . . ." She shrugged, her eyes meeting mine again. "And then Joel shows up, and you run away like a frightened little boy."

"Joel?"

She began to walk a slow circle around the room. "Joel Benfield. He's one of my contributing writers. He teaches history at the university and writes about environmental issues and Western politics."

"I'm sure he's very nice. And I wasn't frightened, I was just—"

"You assumed that he and I were already involved."

"Well, aren't you?"

She stopped right in front of me. I hadn't noticed before that she smelled faintly of lavender, or that her eyes were actually two shades of green—forest green nearer the center, brightening to emerald around the edges.

"Boy, Fearsson," she said. "I sure hope you're better at detective work than you are at figuring me out."

I grinned. "Fearsson. Is that what you've decided to call me?"

"I'm thinking about it. You mind?"

"No," I said with a small shake of my head. "I like it."

"So are you going to take me out to dinner tomorrow night?"

I laughed. "I don't know. Are we still off the record?"

"Until we say otherwise."

"Then I guess I am."

"Good. Come by my house at six."

"Where's your house?"

"In Tempe," she said. "Near Cyprus Park." She crossed to my telephone table, found a pad and pen, and wrote down her address. "Here," she said handing me the paper. "Do I need to pin this to your shirt?"

"No, I think I'll manage to hold onto to it for twenty-four hours."

"Good." She crossed to the door and pulled it open.

"Where are we going?" I asked.

She rolled her eyes. "I found your house, for God's sake. Do I have to figure out everything?"

"Fine. Six o'clock."

"Don't be late," she said, stepping outside.

"I wouldn't dare."

I watched her walk back to her car, waved once as she started up and pulled away from the curb, and closed the door. Turning, I saw that Namid was watching me.

"What?" I said.

"You should be concentrating. You might well be in danger. The woman is a distraction."

"Distractions can be a good thing now and then."

The runemyste frowned.

Before he could say anything more, the phone rang. I recognized the number on the caller ID. Kona, at 620.

I switched on the phone. "You're working late," I said, not bothering with a hello.

"Don't give me any crap, Justis. I'm not in the mood."

"Sorry. What's up?"

"Mike Gann has formally been charged with Claudia Deegan's murder."

"Damnit, Kona! He didn't do it! There's no way he's the Blind Angel Killer!"

"I believe you," she said, lowering her voice. "But it's not like I can tell Hibbard that my friend the weremyste, the person he hates more than anyone else in the world, told me Gann's not our guy, so we should let him go."

I exhaled. "I know that."

"What did you find out from Orestes?"

I winced, feeling guilty for the time I'd spent with Billie. "I haven't seen him yet. I went to Robo's and talked with a guy who'd worked with Gann. This guy knew that Gann was a weremyste, but what he told me confirmed what I saw in the interview room today: Gann's not powerful or skilled enough to be a threat to anyone. I can't talk to the manager until Thursday, but I'm not convinced that anything he'll tell me will change my mind."

"So you talked to one guy at Robo's?" Kona said. "What have you been doing with yourself all afternoon?"

I felt my cheeks burning and was glad she wasn't here to see me.

"Justis?"

"I had a . . . well, sort of a . . . a date."

"No shit?"

I grinned. "No shit."

"Well, give me some details. You know Margarite's going to ask me, and I have to have something to tell her."

"What do you want to know?"

"Let's start with her name."

"Her name's Billie. Billie Castle."

"Huh. You mean like that blogger-lady?"

"Just like her."

"Are you dating a celebrity?"

"Yeah," I said. "I guess I am."

"What's she like?"

"She's . . . I don't know. She's pretty, she's smart, she's pushy and opinionated and stubborn. You'd like her."

"Well, damn. Ain't that something? You had a date."

"It's not that big a deal."

"No? When was your *last* date?"

"All right. Point taken."

We both laughed and then fell silent.

"Randolph Deegan has got some serious pull, Justis," she said. "I'll do what I can to slow things down, try to keep Hibbard from executing the dude himself. But you need to give me something to go on. Anything."

"I'll find out what I can, partner. I'll see Q tomorrow. Promise. And maybe I'll go out to South Mountain, and see if I can find anything there. Is there still tape up where Claudia was found?"

"Yeah. It was that same ravine where we found the Santana kid. Slightly north."

"Okay, thanks. I'll be in touch."

We hung up and I turned to Namid. "The police think the guy they have in custody is the one who killed all those kids with magic."

He didn't respond.

"They're wrong, aren't they?"

"Do you think they are?"

"I'm sure of it."

"Then why do you ask me?"

I laughed. "I don't know. I'm pretty wiped. And I've got a lot to do tomorrow."

"Until next time, then. Watch yourself, Ohanko," he said, as he began to fade. "You trained well tonight, but the danger remains."

I nodded, watching him vanish. That much I'd figured out for myself.

CHAPTER 10

The idea came to me in the middle of the night. One moment I was sleeping, deep and dreamless. The next I was awake, my mind racing.

A few months before, when I was working on a corporate espionage case and trying to learn what a suspect employee had been up to the day he disappeared from his office, I tried some new magic that Namid had taught me. I went to the employee's office, and, using my scrying stone and holding something that belonged to the guy, I was able to see in the agate an image of him stealing the files and then concealing what he had done by altering the user logs on his computer.

So why couldn't I do the same thing with Claudia Deegan? Why couldn't I go back to South Mountain Park and scry what she had seen in the last moments of her life?

All I needed was some way to link her to my scrying.

I managed to get back to sleep for a few hours, but was wide awake by six. I went for a run to clear my head, and after a shower, a bite to eat, and two cups of Sumatran, I checked the time again. Eight fifteen. That would have to be late enough. I called Howard Wriker's cell. He answered on the third ring.

"Wriker."

"Mister Wriker, this is Jay Fearsson."

It took him a minute. "Mister Fearsson! The PI, right?"

"Yes, sir."

"You have some information for me?"

"Nothing yet, I'm afraid." I still wasn't ready to share with him what little I knew. I didn't want the Deegans to crush Robby Sommer and leave me without any way of tying the other Blind Angel victims to a potential drug source. Better to lie to the man, at least for now. "I'm still looking into it and I need a little help from you."

"From me?"

"It's nothing difficult and nothing that will link the senator to the investigation. I simply need Claudia's address. I'd like to . . . to search her place for anything that might help me."

"Yes, all right." He sounded uncertain, and I wondered if he regretted asking me to learn the truth about Claudia's drug use. "Ah, here it is," he said after several moments. "She lived with a girl named Maddie Skiles." He gave me the address and phone number, both of which I wrote down in my note pad, along with Maddie's name.

"Thank you, Mister Wriker."

"You heard that the police made an arrest?"

"Yes, sir, I did."

"It's a great relief for all of us. For all of Phoenix, really. At least the madman who did this is off the streets."

I should have agreed and hung up, but I couldn't help thinking about what Kona had told me the night before. Someone close to the Deegans needed to hear that the pressure they were putting on the PPD wasn't helping matters. "We can hope, sir," I said.

"You don't think they have the right man?" He sounded defensive. I wondered how much of that pressure had come from Wriker himself.

"No, sir, I don't. I know that he threatened Claudia, and that he hated the Deegan family. But for three years the Blind Angel murders had nothing to do with the Deegans. To assume that this man is responsible for all those killings, just because he had it in for Claudia, doesn't make much sense to me."

"Well, Mister Fearsson, it would seem that the Phoenix Police Department disagrees with you."

"Yes, sir. It wouldn't be the first time."

He didn't seem to know how to respond to that. "Yes . . . well . . . good day, Mister Fearsson."

"Thank you, sir."

Not the most comfortable phone conversation I'd ever had, but I'd gotten the information I needed. I gathered a few items in a backpack—two water bottles, my knife, my scrying stone, and a couple of granola bars. Then I left the house and drove back to Tempe.

Claudia had lived east of the campus, near Hudson Park, in a neighborhood that most college students couldn't afford. The small yard needed some work—the flower gardens were overgrown with weeds and the grass was wispy and baked brown—but it was a nice house.

There were a few press people camped out front, but most of them ignored me, even after I parked in front of the house.

"Who are you?" one woman called to me.

I ignored her and strode up the walk to the front door. I got out my wallet and rang the bell. After waiting a bit, I rang it twice more and was ready to give up when at last the door opened a crack.

"Yeah?" said a young woman. Her hair was a mess, her face pale and puffy, like she'd just woken up, or maybe like she'd been crying. She wore a pink t-shirt and drawstring pajama pants.

"Miss Skiles?"

"Who are you?"

"My name is Jay Fearsson." I showed her my PI license. "I'm a private investigator. I've been asked by the Deegan family to investigate the circumstances surrounding Claudia's death."

She frowned. "Claudia's parents hired a private eye? I don't believe it." I had a feeling she was about to close the door on me. I'm sure she'd had to put up with a lot of crap the past few days.

"Howard Wriker did," I said the words tumbling out of me. "I talked to Randy and Tilo yesterday."

She chewed her lip for a minute, and opened the door a hair more. "You did?"

"Yes. They even invited me to see them play Thursday at Robo's. They want to know where Claudia got her drugs," I said, my voice as gentle as I could make it. It was like trying to get a skittish dog to eat from my hand. "Do you have any idea?"

She eyed me for a minute, then nodded, her gaze flicking toward the cluster of reporters. "Yeah, I know," she said. She wiped a tear off her cheek. "I don't want to get in any trouble, you know?"

I nodded. "I understand. I'm sure this has been a rough time for you. I'm sorry for your loss." I waited a moment, and then asked, "When did you see her last?"

"That morning. She left here saying she was going to the library. But I'm not sure she went there." The door was opened halfway now and she was leaning against the edge, relaxing a little. "She wasn't the studious type, you know. She didn't have to be. She was really smart." She bit her lip again. "Most of the time."

"Sometimes smart people do stupid things."

"Yeah," she said. "That was Claud."

I nodded. "Listen, I'm sure the police have searched this place top to bottom—"

"They have. It's been, like, *such* a pain in the ass."

"I don't doubt it. But could I take a quick look around? I won't take long, and it could be a big help."

She tipped her head to the side and twisted her mouth. But she'd stopped crying, and I could tell that I'd won her trust, at least for the moment. "Yeah, I guess," she said. She opened the door the rest of the way and stepped back to let me in.

It was a typical college student's house, although a bit nicer than most. The furniture was all good quality, but nothing matched. The kitchen, which was off the living room, was filthy. The dish drain was full, as was the sink, and the entire house smelled faintly of cigarette smoke and rotten vegetables.

"This is a nice place, Miss Skiles."

"Thanks. And it's Maddie, all right?" She walked into the kitchen. "I'm going to have some coffee. You want anything?" She turned to me, and I could see that she was holding a jar of instant.

Coffee sounded good, but not that coffee. I admit it: I'm a coffee snob.

"I'm fine thanks." I peered down a corridor. "Which room was—?" I stopped, seeing the yellow crime-scene tape stretched in a large "X" across the doorway on the left side of the hall.

"Yeah," she said from behind me. "That's Claud's room. I wish they'd finish up already, you know? That tape creeps me out."

"Have they searched in there a lot?"

"A couple of times. But they haven't taken much away."

No doubt they were hoping to uncover something that would link her to the other victims. If my experience working on the case with Kona was any guide, they'd find nothing.

I started down the corridor.

"You're not allowed in there!" Maddie called after me. "They told me that it was against the law even to open the door."

"I know," I said, smiling back at her. "I won't tell if you won't."

I could tell she was unconvinced, but I didn't wait for her okay. I had enough experience with crime scenes to know what I could get away with and what I couldn't. I even went so far as to untuck my shirt and put it over the knob so that I wouldn't leave prints on it when I opened the door. Then I slipped through the lower part of the "X" and shut the door behind me.

I wasn't stupid. I had no intention of touching anything, at least not anything important. But I needed something small of Claudia's for the scrying I planned to do at the crime scene.

Her bedroom had a lot in common with every other college kid's bedroom I'd ever seen. There was a futon in the far corner on a simple pine frame that must have cost three hundred dollars at the Futon Shoppe in Tempe. The walls were covered with posters, some of them political, others showing various alternative rock groups— Psychic Currency, Stealth Hype, TorShun. Her stereo sat on a peach crate near the bed, and a set of cinder block and pine bookshelves lined the wall beside an old desk. There were a few framed photos of her and Tilo on a dresser opposite the door, but none of them could have been too recent; in all of them her hair was blonde, and his was to his shoulders.

Some of the drawers in both the desk and bureau were half-open, and her closet door stood ajar. Several pairs of shoes lay scattered on the floor. Most of them were high-top sneakers and combat-style boots, but a few might have been dressier. I wasn't really an expert.

I found what I needed on her bureau. A hair brush sat next to one of the photos, a tangle of black hair caught in the plastic bristles. I pulled out several strands, all of them blonde near the root, wound them around my finger, and placed them in one of the small plastic evidence bags that I still carried in my bomber pocket. Old habits die hard. I scanned the room one last time, then let myself out, again taking care not to disturb the police tape.

Maddie was waiting for me in the hallway outside the door, her forehead creased. "I shouldn't have let you in there," she said, as soon as she saw me. "You're going to get me in, like, so much trouble."

I shook my head. "No, I'm not. I promise."

Her frown deepened.

"I used to be a cop. I know how to treat a crime scene. I didn't touch anything. No one will ever know I was in there."

"You sure?"

"Absolutely."

"You find anything?"

"Not really. But I didn't search as thoroughly as I would have liked." I smiled. "Because I didn't want to get you in trouble."

That coaxed a reluctant grin from her. "Thanks."

"You said that you knew who had sold Claudia her drugs. Can you tell me now?"

Her smile disappeared and she seemed to shrink back from me.

"Was it Robby Sommer?"

She gaped. "You know him?"

"I busted him once. Did Claudia buy drugs from him?"

"All the time," she said. "He's a creep. I told her to stay away from him, but she couldn't, you know?"

"Did she buy from anyone else, or just from Robby?"

"I think just from Robby. But I don't know for sure. We didn't talk about it, because she knew I didn't approve."

"All right. Thanks." I pulled a card from my wallet and handed it to her. "If you think of anything else that might help me out, give me a call, all right?"

"Yeah, sure," she said. She glanced at the card. "Justis?"

"Yup," I said, walking to the door.

"Weird name."

"I know. Bye, Maddie."

"You going to bust Robby again?" she asked, stopping me.

"I'm not a cop anymore. But Robby isn't the smartest guy on the planet. He'll get himself busted before long."

She grinned, and I left.

I drove to the south end of South Mountain Park and hiked into the center of the preserve, where Claudia had been found. It was a warm, clear morning, and usually I would have enjoyed being out. Rock wrens scolded me from atop boulders by the trail, bobbing up and down and flitting into the brush whenever I stopped to rest or take a drink of water. Tiny blue butterflies fluttered around the brittlebush and rattleweed.

But this wasn't a walk to be savored. Too soon I reached the ravine where, two and one half years ago, the Blind Angel Killer left the body of Maria Santana, his fourth victim.

About two hundred yards farther up the trail, I saw the crime scene tape marking the spot where Claudia had been found a few days ago. It shone in the desert sun, shockingly yellow, strung among the palo verde trees. No one else was around, though the trail was lined with fresh bike tracks. I pulled out my scrying stone and the evidence bag that held those strands of Claudia's hair.

The magic I'd come all this way to try was called a seeing spell. Like scrying, it was a kind of divination magic; if it worked it would allow me to see what Claudia had seen the night she died. As always with magic, though, there were a couple of catches. To cast the spell correctly, I needed something that belonged to Claudia. That was why I had taken those strands of hair. Clothing would work, too, but hair was better, and body parts probably would have been ideal. Don't laugh. Over the years, sorcerers had resorted to all sorts of stuff.

The other catch was that the spell only worked if Claudia had been in this place, alive. I couldn't do a seeing spell for Claudia from my house, because she'd never been there, and standing here in South Mountain Park, I couldn't scry what Claudia had seen, say, at her parents' home. Seeing spells were specific to a given place.

I knew that Claudia had been here, on this trail. I didn't know for certain if she'd been alive at the time, or if the weremyste had killed her before bringing her here. All the forensics from the other killings pointed to her being alive up until the moment that the sick bastard burned the eyes out of her skull. But I couldn't be sure until I tried the spell.

Holding the scrying stone in my hand, with the strand of her hair coiled beneath it, I cleared myself and summoned a vision of what she had seen. Three elements to the spell: Claudia, this place, and my stone. As simple as a spell could be.

The blue and white lines in my piece of agate faded, so all that remained was a reflection of the blue sky and dark leaves above me. And then the image darkened. At first I thought that I'd wasted my time, that she was already dead. I saw nothing in the stone, heard nothing in my head. Or did I?

There was sound. Shallow breathing and a low whimpering noise that made my stomach clench itself into a fist. And something else: footsteps on a hard trail of rock and sand. Shading the stone with my free hand, I realized there was an image on the surface, too, though it was murky. I could make out the ground below me as it would appear at night, illuminated by the weak light of a quarter moon.

My pulse quickened. Claudia had been here, alive and with her sight intact.

I moved into the shade of the palo verdes, still staring hard at the vision I'd summoned to my scrying stone. I couldn't make out much. It seemed he was carrying her over his shoulder, and that she was only semiconscious. She continued to whimper as he walked; her vision remained dim, muted, maybe because of the drugs in her body.

After several minutes of this, the footsteps stopped. An instant later, the vision in my stone heaved and spun. I heard the sharp crunch of stone, a hard grunt, and then a low moan of pain. The trail had vanished, swallowed by darkness. But after a few seconds, Claudia's eyes fluttered open again, and I saw starlight. I saw the moon, glowing high overhead.

And I saw him—the Blind Angel Killer—looming over her, blocking out the stars while the moon kept his face in shadow. I leaned closer to the stone, desperate for any details I could make out—his face, his hair, his body-type. He seemed tall, although that could have been Claudia's perspective. His hair, if he had any at all, was short; a buzz-cut, maybe. But even with the agate only inches from my nose, I couldn't make out his features.

He reached toward her face, his hand dark against the night sky, long-fingered, graceful. And I gasped at the sight. I knew that hand, those elegant fingers. I'd seen them in my office mirror a few days before, gliding over a burning glow, chasing wisps of gray smoke. My scrying.

In my mind I heard Claudia scream. My stone flared crimson—the color of fresh blood, so bright I had to turn away. And when I squinted down at my scrying stone again, it was just a piece of sea-green agate with twisting bands of blue and white.

"Damnit!"

I tried to summon the image again, and failed. I pulled out a second strand of Claudia's hair and spoke the spell aloud. But the stone remained as it was. I closed my eyes, cleared myself, repeated the spell. Nothing. I didn't know if seeing spells couldn't be repeated, or if I was too appalled by what I'd seen to cast the spell a second time. I closed my eyes once more, this time attempting to commit to memory what I'd been able to make out of Claudia's killer. He was lanky. His head appeared shaven. And his hands . . . I would never forget those. I knew, though, that this wasn't much to go on. His most distinctive characteristic was the color of his magic, and I had a feeling that if I saw one of his spells coming at me, it would be too late for me to do much of anything to stop him.

I surveyed the crime scene for another moment, searching for anything that Kona might have missed, or any stray signs of magic. Nothing caught my eye. Feeling weary and frustrated, I turned around and began the long walk back to the Z-ster.

This was one of those times when I would have been willing to ignore my aversion to cell-phones. I needed to talk to Kona, but I had no signal out on the trail. I walked fast, and was sweating like a marathoner by the time I reached the parking lot. But here I had three bars on my phone. I dialed Kona's number.

"Homicide, Shaw."

"Hey, partner."

"Justis, I've been trying to call you all morning."

"I—"

"Have you got anything for me? Hibbard and Deegan have managed to get Gann's arraignment moved up. He'll be in court tomorrow. The way things are moving, they'll have him tried and convicted by the end of the week."

"I saw him."

That stopped her. "Saw who?" she asked, although I could tell that she already knew.

"Our guy. I used a kind of scrying magic—a seeing spell."

"You're losing me, Justis."

I grinned. All those years ago, Kona had struggled to adjust to the fact that I was a weremyste. Acceptance had come harder for her than it would have for most people. She could be stubborn, and as a detective she had been trained to trust in logic, to believe only what her eyes could see. So placing faith in my abilities had been a stretch for her. That she had done so at all spoke to the depth of our friendship. But in all the years we'd known each other, she had never gotten used to hearing me talk about magic and spells. It confused her, butted up against that rational training. Sometimes I talked about this stuff just to bug her. This time I'd been too excited to remember.

"I went out to South Mountain Park," I told her. "And I used that stone I carry to see what Claudia saw in her last moments." I skipped the part about the hair; she didn't want to hear those details, and I would have felt like a ghoul telling her that I'd taken hairs from Claudia's brush.

"You can do that?"

"I learned this magic in the past few months. Otherwise I would have done it long ago."

"And you saw him?"

"It was dark; I only saw him in silhouette. He's tall, lean. I think he might be bald, and . . . and he has long thin hands." I hesitated. "I know that's not much."

"No," she said. "But it's something. Would you recognize him if you saw him?"

"I don't know. Maybe. I'd know the color of his magic, and I'd know his hands."

"What's all this about his hands?"

"I scried them once before. They made an impression. I'm not sure why." I took a breath, knowing what I had to say, knowing that it wouldn't do Kona any good. "Gann's not our guy. I'm sure of it now. For all intents and purposes, I saw the person who killed her."

"Yeah," she said, the word coming out as a sigh. "I hear you. But how do we prove it to Hibbard?"

"We catch the right guy, and we hope that Gann manages to get himself a decent lawyer."

"Right. Where are you going next?"

"Q's place. I'll let you know what I find out."

We hung up and I pulled out my weapon to make sure that it was fully loaded. I didn't know if bullets would work against this weremyste or not, but I'd seen him now; he felt more real to me than he ever had before. And I'm not above admitting that I was scared of the guy.

CHAPTER 11

South central Phoenix, from the 91 area of the Cactus Park precinct, through the Maryvale precinct, and into Estrella Mountain includes some of the toughest beats any cop in the city has to face. This part of Phoenix comprises maybe fifteen percent of the total area of the city and is home to a similarly small percentage of the population. But its beats account for more than a third of the violent crimes committed here. Maryvale itself is tiny when compared to other precincts, but in any given year, it sees more assaults and murders than some precincts many times its size. Parts of Estrella Mountain are even worse.

I was never good at math, and I'm no expert on crime numbers, not like some of the men and women in statistics, who can quote figures and percentages off the tops of their heads. But I understand stats well enough to know that when one small area of a city sees the lion's share of its murders and aggravated assaults, that area has a problem.

I wouldn't want to single out the worst of Maryvale's beats—they are all bad—but I was headed to the 813, which was about as ugly as it got. Rundown houses broiling in the sun, storefronts that looked like they hadn't seen business in years until you realized that they were still open, streets strewn with shattered beer bottles, kids' playgrounds turned into havens for junkies and hangouts for gangs. I'd been down here plenty of times while I was still on the job, but I rarely drove these streets by choice.

I was hoping that Orestes Quinley would be able to tell me enough about the Blind Angel Killer to make the trip worth my while.

In the last few years, after his many brushes with the law, Brother Q had made some effort to join legitimate society. He'd opened a place on Thomas Street called Brother Q's Shop of the Occult. Not exactly a name that rolled off the tongue, but I'm not convinced that he expected the business to appeal to a large clientele. He sold stuff that any small-time sorcerer might need: used books on magic, Wicca, and shamanism; many of the same powders, herbs, and oils he'd once been accused of stealing; and various stones, jewelry, and other items that might be used for conjuring. His was the only shop in Phoenix where a person could find Tuberose and Styrax oils. His prices were outrageous, and in all my visits to his place, I had never seen another person shopping there. But Orestes didn't seem to mind. He had his store, he lived in the apartment above it, and he was content to sit outside in his old wooden rocking chair, smoking contraband clove cigarettes and watching the world go by.

That's what he was doing when I pulled up to his place in the Z-ster. Even in the brilliance of the Arizona sun, Orestes' storefront glimmered faintly with the light of his magic. This was not the flat yellow gleaming of his early conjurings. It was more a golden orange, the color of the sun as it sits balanced on the desert horizon. Orestes had grown more powerful and more skilled since our first encounter. And if I could see the magic on his place now, it must have glowed like a bonfire at night. He had enough wardings in place to hold off a horde of weremystes. I had a feeling he was worried about one in particular.

Apart from developing a bit of a gut, Orestes hadn't changed much over the years. He claimed to have been born in Haiti, and he spoke with a heavy West Indian accent. He wore his hair in thick braids, and he often had on a pair of wire-rimmed sunglasses, the lenses of which were far too small to serve any practical purpose. Today he was dressed in old khaki shorts, a pair of beat-up sandals, and a Coca Cola shirt that had been tie-dyed so many years ago that the colors had all faded to various shades of gray.

"Justis Fearsson," he said, as I got out of the car. "Come a-callin' over Brother Q's way. To what does Q owe the pleasure on this fine, sunny day?"

Two things to know about Orestes. First, he was one of these people who referred to himself in the third person. Drove me up a wall. Second, on occasion, for no apparent reason, he liked to speak in verse. I used to find this annoying, too. In recent years I'd decided that it was funny, in a really weird sort of way. Still, despite his quirks, Q wasn't a flake and I didn't think he had started losing his mind yet, although Kona would have argued the point. He was smart enough to have survived on these streets for years, and in all the time I had been coming to him for information he had almost never steered me wrong. But he'd developed this persona, and while it might once have been a put-on, at this point I wasn't sure he could have set aside the rhymes and the way he spoke even if he'd wanted to.

"Hi there, Orestes," I said. I walked to where he was sitting and patted his shoulder. "You staying out of trouble?"

"Always, Brother. Always."

I smiled. "Right."

He pulled a folding chair out from behind his own and handed it to me. I unfolded it and sat.

"You here to buy or to talk?"

"Talk."

"Good," he said. "Then Brother Q don't have to get up. Heat like this make a brother wilt. Seems they had no AC when this place was built."

"The rhymes need a little work."

He shrugged. "Maybe. You try it sometime. Ain't as easy as it sounds."

"You know why I'm here?"

"Brother Q can guess. There's only one thing people in this town are talkin' about these days. Brother Q ain't never seen weremystes so scared. But why would the Deegan girl bring you to Brother Q? You know that Q wouldn't have anythin' to do with a killin'."

"True, but I also know that you keep your ear to the street. If there was something going on that you didn't like—maybe a sorcerer gathering more power than anyone ought to have—you'd tell me about it. Wouldn't you?"

"Brother Q keeps an eye out," he admitted, avoiding my gaze. "Purely out of curiosity."

"Sure," I said. "I understand. You remember me coming around to ask you about the Blind Angel case when I was still a cop?"

"Of course. Brother Q remembers everythin'."

"Then you also remember what you told me."

"Q told you the truth," he said pointedly, facing me at last. "Q told you that he didn't know anythin' about the killin's, which was true."

"At the time, you mean."

"Right. At the—" He clamped his mouth shut.

"What do you know now, Q?"

He stared out at the street, his eyes tracking a low-riding roadster with a group of Latino kids in it. He still had his lips pressed thin, and I could tell that he was angry; angry with me for tricking him, and angry with himself for letting me. Luis was right, though: Q knew something.

"Thirty-one kids now," I said, my voice low. "Those are the ones we know about. And you can be sure that Claudia Deegan won't be the last. If you know something you've got to tell me."

"Brother Q knows nothin' for certain," he muttered.

"But you have an idea of who's doing this, don't you?"

He peered at me over the top of his sunglasses. "Who are you askin' for, Brother J? Yourself or the cops?"

"Does it matter?"

"What matters and what doesn't depends on where you stand. Brother Q might feel different with some green in his hand."

I had to laugh. "That was pretty good." I reached for my wallet and pulled out two twenties. It was more than I usually gave to any informant, including Orestes. But after three years, we were getting close. I felt it in my blood, in my bones. And I was still shaken by what I'd seen in my scrying stone on the trail. The money was the least of my worries. I held the bills up, but I didn't hand them to him. Not yet.

"You're hungry today, aren't you, Brother J?"

"I need a name."

"Brother Q doesn't have a name to give."

I lowered my hand. "Then what do you have?"

"What do you know about this sorcerer you're after?"

"Not a lot. I know the color of his magic. I know that he's taken an interest in me and my case. I know that he carried Claudia Deegan out into South Mountain Park and killed her there."

"How you know that?"

"I scried it," I told him. "A seeing spell."

"Good for you!" he said, sounding like he meant it. "A seein' spell. That's high magic." He glanced up at the sky. "But you're right: you don't know much."

The last thing I needed was Q telling me how much I did and didn't know. I examined his shop again, noting the orange light that danced along the roof line and around the windows and doors. "What are you so afraid of?"

He twisted around in his chair. "What do you mean? Brother Q ain't afraid of nothin'."

"No? Then why all the warding spells? Your place is glowing like the magical equivalent of Fort Knox."

"There's a lot of crime on these streets. You know that." He forced a smile. "Things aren't as safe around here since you left the force." He wasn't very convincing.

"What's going on, Q?"

The smile faded. He regarded me for a minute. Then he motioned with his head toward the shop, stood up, and walked inside.

I followed.

"Close the door," he said.

The shop was lit by a single light bulb in an old fixture, and it smelled of incense smoke and oils. I recognized the frankincense as soon as we got inside, but it was mingled with something harsher, more bitter.

"Is that petitgrain?" I asked.

"Very good, Brother J. You're learnin' well."

Petitgrain and frankincense. Among herbalists, both were thought to be powerful guardians against dark magic. Orestes could deny it all he liked, but he was scared.

"What's all this about, Orestes? Frankincense, petitgrain, all those wardings; it's like you're preparing for a war."

"A man can't be too careful."

"Why not? What's out there?"

He shook his head. "Brother Q doesn't know."

"Damnit! I don't have time for this. Some sorcerer is out there stalking me, making me look over my shoulder every two seconds!"

"Brother Q is tellin' the truth. Q swears it. He hears whispers, wind in the trees, nothin' more."

"What kind of whispers?"

He licked his lips, glanced around the shop. "There's a new player in town. A real badass. You know what Brother Q is sayin'?"

"But if he's new—"

"Brother Q doesn't believe he's new. It's the same guy you've been after for three years. But he's gettin' stronger. That Q does believe." He shook his head. "People are scared, J. People are real scared."

"Who is he?"

"No one knows. He's got no name. Nobody ever sees him, or at least they don't talk about it if they do. He comes and goes and no one knows where he lives or where he's come from." He leaned forward. "Some are sayin' he comes from Hell itself," he said, his voice dropping to a whisper.

"How long have you been hearing about this guy?"

"Not long. Can't say for certain. But not long."

"Why does he kill? What's he getting from these kids?"

"I don't know that either."

"Come on! You've got to be able to tell me something about this guy, other than the fact that he's a badass weremyste."

"He ain't like other weremystes. He's more than strong, you understand? He's *different*."

I felt cold suddenly and had to keep myself from shuddering. "Different how?" I asked, though I wasn't sure I wanted to hear his answer.

He shrugged. "Q don't know. He's just different. His magic's stronger than it should be. Some people are sayin' that the moons don't bother him, though I don't know nothin' about that."

"Yeah, all right," I said. I believed Q was trying to help me, and would have, had he known enough. "Who else can I talk to about this guy?"

"No one other than Q is gonna talk to you about him. They're all too scared."

"Leave that to me. Give me a name. Someone's had dealings with him, right?"

He hesitated. "Some say he's done business with an enchanter near here." Orestes said the word "enchanter" as if it were something dirty. To those skilled in the use of magic, enchanters were weremyste wannabes, people who dabbled in conjuring but had learned little craft. He might as well have called the guy a fraud. "A boy named Antoine Mirdoux. Another brother from Haiti."

"Mirdoux," I repeated. "Sounds familiar."

"He's been around a little while, but he's just a kid. Calls himself 'Toine. Thinks he's goin' to be somethin' big, you know what Q's sayin'? Thinks he's goin' to be the next Brother Q." He shook his head. "But the boy ain't got the chops."

"Where can I find him?"

"Like I said, it's not far. He has a place just off of Thomas; I think it's on 18th. It's white, but it needs paint. There's —" He stopped and waved his hand, in the general direction. "You'll see the wardings on it. Pale green; very weak."

I handed him the two twenties. "Thanks."

"Did you mean what you said before? Is this hell sorcerer really targetin' you?"

I rubbed the back of my neck, wishing I'd kept that bit of information to myself. "Yeah," I said. "At least I think it was him. It felt like someone was about to use assailing magic against me. I warded myself both times, but no attack ever came."

"Both times," Orestes said. "It's happened twice?"

I nodded. He grimaced.

"Have you considered whether you might be better off leavin' him be?" he asked.

I didn't bother to answer. Instead, I reached for the door. "Thanks again."

"Brother Q has one favor that he'd ask of you . . ."

This one I'd heard before; his standard parting line. "Please don't tell a soul that you heard it from Q," we said together.

"You got it," I told him. "Stay safe."

"You, too. Keep your head down."

Right. I got back in the car and drove east on Thomas and then turned onto 18th. Antoine Mirdoux lived in Mountain View's 733 beat, another garden spot. To a civilian—one crazy enough to be walking these streets—there wasn't a whole lot of difference among the beats in this part of town. A person could drive from one to the next without knowing it. But to the cops working the neighborhoods, each beat had a personality, a flavor. I'm sure the 733 was like that, a place that cops came to know and even like, in a perverse sort of way.

To me though, these were just streets and ramshackle houses, places where a dark sorcerer could be waiting, watching for me. The area around Orestes' place I knew; I'd been there enough times before to make even those rough streets feel familiar. But as I drove the Z-ster up and down 18th, looking for a house that glowed with pale green magic, I felt like a soldier entering an urban war zone for the first time. These streets were alien to me, and I could almost feel the danger crawling up my arms and legs, making me shiver. As I drifted past, kids and old people stared at me, grim and hostile. They knew I didn't belong there; they might even have sensed an ill omen in my coming. I kept my speed the same, trying not to make eye contact as I searched for Antoine's house.

I spotted it about a block short. Like Orestes' house, it was dripping with magic—between Orestes and Antoine, I was beginning to feel like I should go home and put a few spells on my place. It seemed there were some heavy clouds looming on the magical horizon.

I couldn't tell for certain in the daylight, but Antoine's magic did appear to be a very pale green, about the same color you might see on a traffic light. At least I knew that he wasn't our killer.

I drove past the house and parked two doors down, not wanting to spook him. I tucked my weapon into my shoulder holster, walked to the door, and knocked.

No answer. I raised my hand to knock again, and as I did, several things happened at once.

I felt a pulse of magic aimed at me through the door—an assailing spell—and without even thinking, I warded myself. When in doubt, go back to what you know best. I used a deflection spell.

I didn't know what 'Toine had in mind for me when I redirected his assault at the first thing I thought of: his door, to be precise. But given the way the door exploded inward, I guessed that he wanted me blown up. The wood shattered with a sound like thunder from a too-close lighting strike and fragments of the door and flecks of old white paint flew through the house like flakes in a snow globe.

My initial thought was that Orestes had sold the kid short, making him sound like some kind of hack conjurer. He wasn't a master yet—if he had been, I'd have been killed by the explosion—but he was better than Orestes had made him sound. I should have recognized Brother

Q's attitude for what it was: professional jealousy. 'Toine was every bit the sorcerer Orestes had been the first time I busted him. Give the kid a few years, and he'd be a force in this town.

In the next instant I realized that I'd heard another sound after the door vaporized. A second door had opened on the far side of the house and a moment later a screen door had slammed shut. I sprinted through the house and out the back in time to see a young black man disappear around a corner. It was Robby-freaking-Sommer all over again. And my leg still hurt.

But 'Toine had tried to kill me, and I was pissed. It was amazing what a bit of anger could do to strengthen a person's magic. Turning that same corner, I saw Mirdoux running away from me, and I tried the most basic assailing spell I could think of, something so simple that he never would have expected it, something so harmless that if he reflected it back at me, it wouldn't do any damage.

Three elements. My hand, his foot, his momentum. As I've said, the words don't matter; it's all visualization.

'Toine went down in a heap, the way he would have if I'd been close enough to grab his foot in the middle of his stride.

I ran toward him, warding myself as I did. I almost pulled out my Glock, but then I thought better of it. I didn't want him panicking, and I didn't want to give him another target for his magic.

As I got near him, I slowed to a walk. He had sat up, and was glaring at me. I expected him to cast a spell my way at any moment.

"Don't even think about it, Antoine," I said, still easing toward him. "I'm a better conjurer than you are."

"The hell you are, man!"

"Have you seen your door lately?"

He said nothing, but if he'd been able to turn that glower into magic, I'd have been little more than ash.

Antoine couldn't have been more than twenty-five years old, and he was surprisingly clean-cut for a kid who'd tried to splatter me all over his front steps. His hair was short and neatly cut, his face was square, his skin smooth. It was hard to tell with him on the ground, but I don't think he would have stood much more than five-six or five-seven. He was broad in the shoulders and lean, and he wore a diamond stud in his left ear.

"Who the hell are you?" he asked. 'Toine may have been from

Haiti, but he had no accent, and I had the feeling that he could have spoken like a news anchor if he'd chosen to.

"You're trying to kill me, and you don't even know?"

"I know you don't belong 'round here. I know you got no business knockin' on my door."

"So you'd have tried to blow me up even if I'd been selling Bibles?"

"You don't look like no Bible salesman."

"No? What do I look like?"

"A cop."

I guess it never really goes away. It's not like I could argue with the kid. "It would have been pretty stupid to blow up a cop."

"Man, what are you talkin' about with that blowin' up shit? I didn't try to blow up nobody."

"No? Then what was that spell you threw at me through what used to be your door?"

"Nothin' you ever heard of, man." He grinned. "It's one of my own. It would have felt like somebody shattered a beer bottle on your head. Would have put you out cold." The smile vanished. "Instead, you gotta go and destroy my house."

Either he was lying or I was far more powerful than I'd ever thought and had unwittingly found some way to amplify his assailing spell. Guess which one I was betting on.

"I'm not a cop, Antoine," I said. "I'm a private investigator." I pulled out my wallet and showed him my PI's license. "My name is Jay Fearsson. I'm doing some work on the Blind Angel murders."

He stared past me. "Never heard of them."

"No? Maybe you heard that Claudia Deegan was killed."

"Never heard of her, neither."

Well, now I had to reconsider, because 'Toine was about the worst liar I'd ever met. What the hell *had* happened to his door?

"You know what? I think you're full of shit. I think you ran away from me because you're into something that you can't handle and you're scared out of your mind."

"Whatever, man."

"Claudia Deegan was killed with magic."

"Bad luck."

"Every Blind Angel victim was killed with magic."

His eyes narrowed. "How do you know that?"

"I used to be a cop. And I'm a weremyste, too. Remember? I saw the magic on them."

"Then you know it's not mine, don't you?"

"Yes, I do. I know that it belongs to someone with real power."

"Fuck you, man!"

"The magic that killed those kids was red. Deep red, almost the color of blood. And the magic on Claudia Deegan had faded nearly to nothing in the span of about two days. There can't be more than five people in the entire country with power like that."

He refused again to meet my gaze. But he was clenching his jaw, and I had the sense that he was considering another assailing spell.

"Like I said, man, if you cast, then you know what my stuff is like. It ain't red, and it don't disappear after no two days. So you know it wasn't me."

"Maybe, but I think you know who this sorcerer is."

"You think wrong, then, *cop*."

I squatted down and got right in his face, forcing him to look me in the eye. "Like I said, little man, I'm not a cop anymore. But I've still got friends on the force. And who do you think they turn to when they're working cases that involve magic?" I tapped my chest. "Me. All I have to do is give the word and they'll be all over you. You'll spend the rest of your life rotting in jail, wishing you were a good enough conjurer to get yourself out, and wondering why you were so stupid as to piss me off."

He was working up to another attack. I could see it in his eyes; I could hear it in the rasp of his breathing. I pushed hard enough, and I got exactly what I expected. For all his talent and potential, 'Toine was still just a kid, playing with toys he didn't quite understand.

The spell he threw at me was similar to the one Robby Sommer had used against me—a basic fire spell. Rudimentary stuff. But he was angry enough that this time he might have been trying to kill me, and so I went with *deflection* rather than *reflection*. I didn't want to hurt him. But he needed to know that he didn't want to be screwing around with me. I aimed the bounce at the wall directly behind him, so that 'Toine's own fire flew past the side of his head, missing him by maybe an inch and blackening the wall with the sound of sizzling fat.

"Shit!" he spat, ducking away.

"Next time, I won't miss," I told him. "Tell me who this guy is, or

I'll bring the cops down on you. I'm a PI; I just want to get paid. And all the cops care about is clearing the case. None of us gives a crap if you go down for it. Hell, if I tell them that it's your color on Claudia Deegan, they're not going to know any different." I shrugged. "Now, as far as I'm concerned, I've got nothing against you. I'd rather see this other guy off the streets. And I bet you wouldn't mind using a bit less mojo around the house."

"I don't know what you're talkin' about, man," he said. "I don't know any red magic sorcerer."

"I don't believe you."

"Who sent you here, anyway? Somebody got it in for me?"

"Who is he, Antoine? Why is everybody so afraid of this guy?"

For a second I thought he'd spill it all. He was scared, terrified even. I glimpsed it in his eyes—I'd seen that fear before, in little kids who were being abused by their parents. Terror, helplessness, the memory of pain, the desperate desire to end the abuse, but all of it overmastered by the belief that no one could end the cycle and the certainty that if he tried, if he dared tell a soul, he'd be punished even more severely than before. 'Toine felt trapped, and he had no faith that I could set him free.

At last he fixed his eyes on the street. It was almost like he expected to see the sorcerer strolling past. "I don't know nothin'," he muttered again. "Whoever told you I did was bullshittin' you."

He was lying. But again, as with Robby, I couldn't do anything about it.

I stood. "Fine." I fished out my business card, and tossed one down to him. It was a waste of time and paper, but what the hell. "If you reconsider, give me a call."

He laughed. "Yeah, right, man. I'll be callin' you."

I started to walk away.

"We can chat, man," he called after me. "Like we're old friends, you know?" He laughed again.

I made my way to the Z-ster, Antoine's laughter still ringing in my ears. I had been preparing myself all day, planning what I'd do if I felt the Blind Angel Killer's power again. But like an idiot, I allowed the kid to throw me off balance.

And so, when the red sorcerer suddenly had me in his sights again, I was utterly unprepared. I tried to ward myself, knowing as I did that anything I came up with he could defeat, knowing as well what he was trying to do with these teasing encounters. But I made the effort anyway.

The feeling was much more vivid this time. I knew he was close. Too close. I turned a quick circle, but I also knew that I wouldn't be able to find him. The hairs on my neck and arms stood on end and my skin grew cold, as if I was in shadow and the rest of the city was in brilliant sunlight. If he had wanted to kill me in that moment, he could have, though I would have put up a fight.

But he was toying with me. For a split second, I thought I could hear laughter. Not 'Toine's, though I heard that, too. This was deeper, more menacing, more elusive. I turned again, trying to pinpoint where it was coming from. But it was everywhere. Around me, above me, below me. It was in my freaking head.

You're mine now, I thought I heard someone say.

And then it was gone. The laughter ceased, the sun shone on my face and arms, a warm wind touched my skin.

Three times. Once outside of Robby Sommer's place, once outside of Robo's in Tempe, and now here, in front of Antoine Mirdoux's house. Was there a connection there, something linking the three of them to one another and to this sorcerer with the blood-red magic? Or was it mere chance, the random choices of this bastard who was hunting me?

I should have been concentrating on those questions, trying to figure out what Robby, Robo's, and Antoine had in common with the Blind Angel victims.

But all I could think was that he'd done this to me three times now. He'd touched my mind with his magic; he'd tested my defenses and seen how I would respond to an attack, how I would ward myself.

Three times.

There's power in numbers. He knew me now. I was his. And the next time, if he chose to attack, there would be precious little I could do about it.

CHAPTER 12

I drove back to Chandler, my heart pounding out a salsa beat, and my hands sweating so much the steering wheel grew slick and I had to wipe my palms on my jeans every few seconds. I spent more time glancing up at my rearview mirror than I did looking ahead. I don't know what I was watching for—maybe some red glowing car, driven by the bald guy I'd seen in my stone. Every time a car drew too close to my rear bumper I started to hyperventilate.

By the time I reached my office, I'd stopped shaking, for the most part. But I was still jumpy; walking from my car to the office, I must have glanced back over my shoulder a dozen times. I hated this. I'm not one to go through life scared; I'd spent too long on the job for that. But this sorcerer had gotten into my head.

More than anything else, I was mad at myself for letting him get the better of me. I knew full well that I couldn't stay locked up in my house or office and still do my job.

Usually when I was in a mood like this, Namid was the last person I wanted to see. But as soon as I was inside my office, I called for him, something I had never done before. I didn't even know if it would work.

It did.

His name was still echoing off the walls and wood floor when he began to take form in the middle of the room.

"Ohanko," he said. "You summoned me."

I took a breath. "Yeah, I did. He found me a third time."

"It was inevitable that he would."

For reasons I couldn't explain that made me feel better. "I know that. But . . . I'm not sure what to do now."

"You do what you always do." I thought I saw a smile creep over his glimmering face. "You tread like the fox, and you do your job."

"I heard him laughing, and I heard his voice."

Namid didn't seem overly impressed by this, but he asked, "What did he say to you?"

"Just that I was his now."

"It means nothing."

I nodded, glanced toward the bank of windows. Why had that gray sedan slowed as it drove past?

"Listen to me, Ohanko."

I faced him.

"It means nothing," he said again, his tone more pointed this time.

"We both know that's not true."

"Yes, yes," he said. "Three times. He knows you now. This increases his ability to do you harm. But he had that ability already. His main purpose in doing this is to track you, to know what you do from one moment to the next."

"So he can do that?"

The runemyste nodded. "He can."

"And this is supposed to make me feel better?"

"Yes, Ohanko," he said, the way he might if he were explaining something to a ten-year-old. "If he wanted to kill you, he would have already. He tracks you to follow the progress of your investigation. There may come a time when his purpose is darker. You must be wary. You must learn to ward yourself at all times, with spells more effective than deflection. But this was true already."

I walked to the windows. The gray sedan was gone. It was just another day in Chandler, and no one on the street seemed the least bit interested in me or my case.

"So then, I really do keep going about my business."

"Is that not what I said?"

I laughed. "Yes, it's what you said."

He sat, that familiar, expectant expression on his face. "You need to work on your craft. Now more than ever."

I checked the clock. It was a few minutes past two o'clock. I felt like I'd been awake for thirty hours.

"Yeah, all right," I said, sitting opposite him. "But not too long. I have a date tonight."

He frowned. "Distractions," he said.

I grinned. Then I closed my eyes and summoned that clearing image of the golden eagle. After a few moments, I opened them again.

The runemyste nodded once. "Defend yourself."

For the next two hours, Namid threw a wide variety of assailing spells at me—the stinging and fire spells he'd used the night before, a suffocation spell, which scared the crap out of me, and one spell that blinded me temporarily. That one was frightening as well, not to mention frustrating. It took me several minutes to come up with a warding that would defeat it, and all the while Namid was using his power to throw books and CDs at me. By the time I could see again, I was covered with bruises and my office was a mess.

Despite all that, however, Namid seemed pleased when we were done.

"You conjured well, today," he said, as I stood and stretched my back. "You are starting to cast by instinct."

I was sweaty and tired, but I felt good, the way I would after a long workout. "Well, you don't give a person much choice."

"I will leave you," he said. "You have a big date."

I laughed. "Yes, I do."

He started to fade.

"Namid, wait."

The fading stopped, and a moment later he was as substantial as he ever is. Once more I had the urge to reach out and touch him, just to see what it was like. He was staring at me, and I realized he was waiting to know why I'd stopped him.

"What you told me before about the red sorcerer—is it true?"

"About him tracking you?"

"About him not being able to hurt me anymore now than he could before. I thought that once an enemy tested you three times—"

"We call it 'sounding'."

"Sounding," I repeated. I'd heard the term before, though in my fear I hadn't yet connected it to what the red sorcerer was doing.

"Well, he's sounded me three times. I thought that means he can do anything to me, and I'm powerless to stop him."

"A runecrafter can always ward himself." He paused, eyeing me, perhaps trying to decide how honest he could be. "The danger to you is greater, it is true. But your skills are increasing as well. And as this crafter learns more about you, you also learn more about him. You are linked to each other now. He can hurt you more easily, but you can sense him sooner. The sounding is not without risks for him as well."

"He must be pretty confident then. He probably knows that I can't hurt him."

"You are more than you think you are," Namid said. "You would be wise to take precautions; keep yourself warded. But he would be wise not to underestimate you."

"Thanks. Really," I added. "I mean that. Thank you, Namid."

He tipped his head to me, and then started to fade again. This time I let him go.

I drove home, showered and changed before getting back into the Z-ster and driving to Tempe. It was early still, but I hoped that maybe Billie would be done with her work already. I kept an eye on the mirrors, but no one was following me. I tried to make myself relax. Even without any reassurances, I knew that Namid was right. I was getting stronger, and just as magic was an act of visualization and of will, so too was it a product of faith, of belief in oneself. If I convinced myself that this red sorcerer had power over me, I wouldn't survive his next attack. If, on the other hand, I believed that I could protect myself from whatever he threw at me, I at least gave myself a fighting chance.

I found Billie's house without too much trouble, and parked out front. I started to climb out of the car, but then stopped myself, making certain once again that I hadn't been followed by the red weremyste. Satisfied that he wasn't nearby, I walked up the path to her door and knocked. The house was small, built in Spanish Mission style, and it seemed to have been well cared for, at least from the outside. There was a little garden out front with flowers and a few small cacti, and a small lawn that had recently been cut.

Billie came to the door in a t-shirt and jeans, her hair pulled back in a ponytail. Seeing me, she gave a puzzled smile, her forehead creased. "Hi!" She peeked at her watch. "I know I told you not to be late. . ."

I shrugged. "Yeah, sorry. I'm kind of through for the day, and I thought maybe, if you were, too, we could get an early start. But if you're still working I can come back later."

"I have a bit left to do. Not much. What did you have in mind?"

"I was thinking about a walk in the desert."

She wrinkled her nose. "The desert?"

"You've never taken a walk in the desert?"

"Well, no. I mean, why would I?"

I stared at her, shaking my head. "Amazing. Why did you come to Tempe if not for the desert?"

"I came for a job," she said. "An editing position at a publishing house. I stayed for the sunshine. But the desert . . ." She gave a shrug of her own. "I guess I'm kind of a city person. A Northeastern city person."

"One walk in the desert will change that," I said. "You game?"

She smiled at me, and I knew she'd say yes. "You still taking me to dinner?"

"Of course. No sense walking in the desert if you're not going to eat afterward."

"All right," she said, pushing the door open so I could come in. "I need ten minutes to finish and post the piece I'm writing."

"What's the piece about?" I asked, stepping past her into the house. Her smile faded as she stared at me, and I knew. One question: that was all it took to put me on my guard. "It's about the Blind Angel case, isn't it?"

Billie nodded, as wary as I was.

"Do you mention me in it?"

"No. We've been off the record, and I've been focusing on other aspects of the story."

"Like what?"

"The Deegan family mostly. The senator is getting a lot of sympathy right now, but the fact that his daughter was using drugs might come up eventually. I'm writing about the risks his opponents would be taking by raising the issue, and how he might deal with it if they do."

"Sounds interesting," I said, relaxing a bit.

She exhaled, her relief palpable. "Thanks. I won't be long. Make yourself at home."

Her computer sat on what appeared to be her dining room table, surrounded by piles of papers, several magazines, a newspaper, and a dictionary. She sat down in front of it, stared at the screen for a minute, and then began to type.

I wandered around the living room. The house was as nice inside as it had appeared from the street. Wood floors, high ceilings; she didn't have much furniture, but all of it was tasteful. Her walls were covered with framed black and white photos of people and city scenes. None of them was signed, and I wondered if they were Billie's. I turned toward her to ask, but she was typing furiously, her brow furrowed in concentration. I figured I'd be wise to leave her alone.

After about ten minutes she sat back. Still she frowned at the screen for another few seconds, before hitting the 'return' key.

"Okay," she said, standing and grabbing her denim jacket off the back of her chair. "I'm ready."

"Will you get lots of comments on your blog?" I asked.

She nodded. "Hundreds probably. Some of them will say that I'm brilliant; others will call me a stupid bitch. I make a point of not reading them. I get to have my say with the article. My readers can say what they want after I post it."

"That's a mature attitude."

She smirked. "Don't sound so surprised."

We walked out to the Z-ster, with which she appeared only mildly impressed. Not a car person. That was okay. She wasn't a desert person either, but I was about to cure her of that. I started up the car and on the spur of the moment decided to go south. I put us on Interstate 10.

"So, where are you taking me?" she asked after we had driven for a few minutes in silence.

"Sonoran Desert National Monument. It's between here and Gila Bend on State 238."

She nodded. "All right." Another brief silence. Then, "Tell me what you like so much about the desert."

"What?"

"Well, I want to know what I should be looking for."

I considered this for some time, taking the exit off the interstate and getting on the state road.

"Fearsson?"

"Yeah," I said. "I'm thinking. It's a bit like asking me why I like chocolate."

"But that I understand."

"The desert is uncompromising. It's so severe and it forces everything that lives there to be the same way. It says 'die or adapt.' There's no middle ground, no getting by. And yet, it's also incredibly beautiful. Some of the beauty is harsh, austere, you know? And some of it is as delicate as a spider web." I glanced over at her, only to find that she was watching me, her expression unreadable. I faced forward again and shrugged. "Anyway, that probably doesn't really explain it very well."

"Sure it does. You've spent a lot of time at this place we're going to? Sonoran Monument?"

"Some. I've spent more time in the Superstition Wilderness, but that's a longer drive."

"Is that where you took the last woman you wanted to impress?"

I laughed. "Is that what you think this is about?"

"Isn't it?"

I shook my head. "No, it's not. To tell you the truth, I can't remember the last time I took a woman anywhere." I smiled. "At least not one who I wanted to impress."

"Why is that?" she asked.

Because I'm a weremyste who doesn't take blockers. Because my father's nuts and someday I will be, too. Because my life is wrapped up in so many secrets that I can hardly tell anymore where the mask ends and where the real me begins. "It's complicated," was all I said, staring at the road once more.

"You're strange. One minute you're as open as a kid, and then bang, it seems like you shut some door somewhere inside you and I find myself staring at a wall."

"It's not intentional."

"Isn't it?"

See? This was the problem with getting involved with smart people. Or maybe it was the problem with getting involved at all.

"We're still off the record, right?"

"Yup."

"All right," I said, eyes fixed on the double yellow. "Then what do you want to know?"

She didn't answer for several seconds, and I started to hope that she'd let me off the hook. No such luck.

"What's the real reason you stopped being a cop?"

Smart. That was the $64,000 question, wasn't it? That was the one that led to every other secret in my life.

I glanced at her. "After this it's my turn, right? I get to ask questions, too?"

She hesitated, then nodded.

"All right," I said. Deep breath. "I left the force because I was going to be fired. The department's Professional Standards Bureau had determined that I was incapable of fulfilling my duties as a police officer."

"Why?"

"Because I was having psychological problems. Breakdowns, sort of."

Silence. I chanced a quick glance at her, expecting that she would be gaping at me with fear and pity. But she was just sitting there, chewing her bottom lip, watching the scenery slide by.

"Are you still?" she asked, her voice very low.

There was an easy answer to this, a cheap out. And I took it, because at this stage of our relationship explaining the phasings and my choice to endure them seemed unthinkable. "Problems like that never fully vanish," I told her. "You learn to control them, to live with them."

Billie nodded. "Are you on medication?"

"No. The drugs I could take have . . . side effects." *They'd make my magical abilities go away.* "And I'm not willing to deal with them."

"So these problems can be dealt with through therapy?"

I wasn't sure how to answer that one. Were my training sessions with Namid a form of therapy? Were my visits with my dad? In the end I decided that they were. I wasn't seeing a therapist, but Namid was better equipped to help me through the phasings than any psychiatrist on the planet. Again, it was a cheap way out, but I didn't want her thinking that I was doing nothing to take care of myself. "Yes," I said. "I have someone who helps me through the rough patches."

"Good. Thank you."

"For what?"

"For telling me the truth."

"You're welcome," I said, knowing that I had cheated and gotten away with it. I felt unclean. "Do you want me to take you back? I'd understand if you did."

"No." She shifted in her seat, turning so that she was facing me. "Your turn."

"Okay," I said. "Why were you so eager to leave home? Connecticut, right?"

She blew out a breath through pursed lips and ran a hand through her curls. "Wow, Fearsson."

I smiled in sympathy. "Now you know how it feels."

"I guess. Why was I so eager to leave Connecticut?" She shook her head and regarded me with something akin to admiration. "How did you even know that I *was* eager?"

"From the way you talked about home the other day."

"I hardly said anything."

"Yeah, well, I guess I noticed that."

"I think you must have been a pretty good cop." She ran a hand through her hair once more. She seemed to do that a lot. "I suppose the short answer to your question is that I wanted to get away from my dad."

I waited, knowing there was more.

"He drank," she went on. "A lot. And most times when he was drunk, he'd end up beating my mother."

"I'm sorry," I said.

Billie shrugged. "Mom eventually got up the nerve to kick him out. I think it broke her heart. She really loved him, and when he wasn't drinking, he was a decent guy. But by the end, we only saw him when he was smashed. He'd go on a bender and show up at our door, and Mom would let him in. She'd try to take care of him, get him sobered up. But it always ended the same way, with Mom crying and sporting another bruise, and Dad leaving again. I got to the point where I didn't want to be anywhere near either one of them."

"Your dad still drinking?" I asked.

She shook her head. "He died about ten years ago. Liver gave out on him. If you ask me it was a mercy killing."

I had no idea what to say, so I kept my mouth shut.

"Guess we're both damaged goods, huh?" she said.

"Do you know anyone who isn't?"

"That's awfully cynical."

"It's realistic," I said. "There isn't a person alive who doesn't have something lurking in their past or in their family that they'd rather ignore or erase. Life is about coping with all the crap that comes with being human. Some of us cope better than others. That's all."

She shook her head. "Maybe you're right. But that seems like an awfully dark view of life."

"I guess it is," I said, feeling that I'd failed some test. We had turned off of the main road onto the rural two-lane that would take us into the monument. "Listen," I said, "should I keep on driving, or turn around now?"

"God, what is it with you? Have you decided you don't like me or something?"

"No!" I said, taken aback. "Not at all. I just—"

"Have I done anything to make you think that I don't like you?"

I opened my mouth. Closed it again. "We were arguing," I said weakly.

She did that half-smile, half-frown thing again. I was starting to like it. "We were not! We were talking, expressing opinions, disagreeing with one another. You mean to tell me you never disagreed with your partner when you were a cop?"

"No, we disagreed all the time. But that was different."

"Why? Because he was a man?"

"Actually, she wasn't."

That brought her up short. "Oh. Right. Kona Shaw."

I had to laugh. After a moment, she did, too.

"You enjoyed that, didn't you?" she said.

"Very much."

"I deserved it. But still, I can't spend time with someone who's not willing to disagree with me. I'll get bored. And you don't seem like the kind of person who'd bore me."

"I'll try not to," I said. But I sounded uncertain.

"Arguing is normal," Billie said. "Didn't your parents fight?"

"Not that I remember. My mom died when I was twelve. After that it was just my dad and me, and he wasn't around a lot."

"Oh. My turn to be sorry." She seemed at a loss as to what else to say. "Well," she finally began again, "take my word for it. People argue.

Everyone except my mom. She refused to fight at all. She accepted everything, and look where it got her."

"So," I said. "When I think you're full of crap, you want me to say, 'You're full of crap'? Just like that?"

She liked that a lot. God, I loved the way she laughed. "Yes!" she said. "Exactly!"

I shrugged. "I can do that."

We both fell silent and she looked out the side window. We were near the entrance to the monument now. There were saguaro cacti everywhere and in the distance we could see the ridges of the North Maricopa Mountain Wilderness.

"My God!" she said. "This is gorgeous."

I was starting to fall in love.

A few minutes later we entered the monument. Billie hadn't said another word, although she kept mumbling something that I couldn't quite hear. There were several new trail heads in the monument that had been developed in the years since the area's designation as a national facility, and I stopped at the first of these.

Even after I had turned off the Z-ster, she continued to sit and stare, shaking her head and muttering to herself.

"What is it you keep saying?"

Her head whipped around in my direction, her eyes widening. "Was I saying that out loud?" she asked.

"You were saying something. I couldn't make it out."

She gestured vaguely at her window. "This is so beautiful. And I can't believe I didn't bring my camera."

"So you *are* a photographer," I said. "I saw the work in your place and I wondered if it was yours."

"It's mine. But I'm hardly a photographer. I have my dad's old Nikon FE and I fool around with it some. I wish I had it now."

I grinned. "We can come back."

Billie nodded and smiled, and we got out of the car.

It was hot still, though the sun was low. It angled across the hills, casting long shadows and bathing the sandstone and saguaros in rich, golden light.

She was wearing her denim jacket and she took it off now. I chanced a quick peek at her shoes, realizing that I hadn't even bothered to check if she was wearing something suitable for hiking.

Turns out she was wearing flat soles, which, while not the best for a desert walk, were far better than, say, heels. I hadn't thought that she was the stiletto type.

I still had my pack with me and I grabbed that now. The water I'd put in the bottles this morning would be warm, and would taste of plastic. I didn't expect us to walk far enough to get thirsty, but a person should never go into the desert without carrying water, and I wasn't a skilled enough weremyste to conjure a spring for us if we needed it.

We started up a small hill and, clearing it, descended into a shallow basin filled with saguaros and ocotillos, teddy-bear chollas and prickly pear. A lizard sunning itself on a rock scuttled out of sight, and a canyon wren sang from some unseen perch, its call cascading downward, liquid and melodic. Billie stopped, and shading her eyes with an open hand, turned a full circle, drinking it all in.

"It always looks so empty from the road," she said.

"It does," I agreed. "You can't appreciate the desert from a car. You need to wade out into it. Feel the heat, smell the air, listen to the sounds. I think that's another reason why I like it so much. You have to work at it a little bit. You have to earn it."

We walked on, neither of us talking. The sky was shading to azure, and everything seemed to be glowing in the late afternoon light. A red-tailed hawk circled lazily overhead, twisting its tail in the wind.

"You know what all these are called?" Billie asked, pointing at the ocotillos and chollas.

"Most of them, yeah."

"So, tell me."

I started rattling off the names, pointing out each plant to her. A pair of sparrows popped up on top of a brittlebush and then vanished again just as quickly.

"Black-throated sparrows," I said.

"How do you know all this?"

"My dad taught me a lot when I was young, and I've spent a lot of time hiking. You pick stuff up."

"I like that you know it."

I smiled. "Then you'll love this."

I pulled out one of the water bottles, walked off the trail to a cluster of bright green shrubs, and poured some water over the leaves.

Instantly, the air was redolent: a sweet, pungent scent that I couldn't possibly describe.

"My God! What is that?"

"Desert creosote."

She frowned. "I thought creosote came from coal."

"Some does. Some comes from trees. But this is different. Creosote is the name of the plant. I forget the Latin name. But if there's a single scent that makes me think of the desert, this is it. After a rainstorm the entire basin would smell like this."

We walked on, crossing through a second basin and then climbing another gentle incline to a rocky ledge that offered a clear westward view. The sun hung low above the horizon, and already the breeze was growing cooler.

Billie's face was flushed from the climb, but she didn't seem at all winded. I had the feeling that she worked out.

"I thought we'd stop here," I said. "Maybe watch the sun go down before driving back for dinner."

She nodded. "Sounds great."

We sat on the stone, which was still warm. A nighthawk flew over, bobbing and weaving on narrow wings, and a yellow butterfly floated past. It occurred to me that I hadn't thought about Claudia Deegan or the red sorcerer since driving out of the city.

"This was good for me," I said. "Thanks for coming along."

She was sitting cross-legged, and she had her eyes closed and her faced tipped toward the sun. "Thanks for bringing me." After some time she turned to me, shading her face with a hand once more. "Can I ask you about your investigation? Off the record?"

"I suppose."

"Do you think this man they arrested is the Blind Angel Killer?"

"I know he's not," I said, without thinking.

Her eyebrows went up. "You know it?"

Trust and comfort could be dangerous at times.

"What I mean is I'm pretty sure he's not the guy. He had his reasons for hating the Deegans, but that doesn't explain the murders that came before Claudia. I just don't think it's him."

I didn't know if she agreed with my assessment or not, but I could tell she was curious about the certainty with which I'd answered the question. To my relief, she didn't press the issue. Instead she asked,

"Don't you find it depressing spending so much time investigating killings like these?"

"I wouldn't call it depressing," I said. "There's something sad about any crime, and killings are the worst. But when you're investigating a murder, you don't think about it that way. You try to figure out why and how, and who, of course. It's a puzzle. And when I solve a case I feel like I've given something to the victim, and to the victim's family." I tried to smile, but I don't think I succeeded. "These days, though, I mostly work for insurance companies, and corporations, and families falling apart at the seams." I glanced at her. "This is the first time I've worked a murder since leaving the force."

"Really? So then I suppose you're sort of enjoying yourself."

I gave a reluctant nod. "Yeah. Sick as that probably sounds, I'd rather be doing this than insurance work."

The sun was slipping down behind the distant mountains—the Sand Tanks and the Saucedas, the Craters and the Mohawks—coloring each ridge line in successively paler shades of blue and purple, and painting the western sky orange and red.

"I draw," I said, blurting it out. As soon as I spoke the words, I felt my face begin to color.

A small smile touched Billie's lips. "Excuse me?"

"I said that I draw. I'm not sure why I told you that. I was watching the sun go down and it popped into my head."

"What do you draw?"

I shrugged. "Landscapes mostly. Desert scenes. I use colored pencils and charcoal. Sometimes I use watercolor paints, too."

"Can I see your drawings?"

"Sure," I said. "And I'd like to see more of your photos."

Billie nodded, then turned back to the sunset.

There wasn't a cloud in the sky, which is fine until twilight rolls around, at which point it makes for somewhat plain sunsets. But Billie seemed happy, and as we walked back to the car in the deepening blues of dusk she slipped her hand into mine.

I glanced down at our hands and then at her, unable to hide my surprise.

"Do you mind?"

"Hardly," I said.

"So where are we having dinner?"

"Your choice," I said. "My treat."

She grinned. "All right. I know just the place."

"The place," turned out to be a Mexican dive in the western part of Mesa, on a side street off of Southern. I had to hand it to her: it was one of the few Mexican restaurants in this part of the Phoenix area that I didn't know, and it was crowded with a mix of university students and Latino families. I had no doubt that the food would be excellent

Upon returning to the city, though, I felt myself growing tense again. I made us wait for a table in the back of the restaurant, though there were a couple of open ones near the front when we arrived. And then I insisted on sitting against the back wall, so that I could watch the door and windows.

By the time we were seated and the waitress was handing us our menus, Billie was frowning at me. No half-smile either. This was all frown.

"What was that all about?" she asked.

"What?"

"That bit with the table? The fact that you practically raced me over here so that you could sit in that chair?"

"I don't like to sit with my back to the door," I said, trying to keep my voice light. "I'm sure you've seen enough detective flicks to know that I'm not the first person to be like that."

"That's a load of crap, Fearsson. What's this about?"

I put down the menu and met her gaze. "I really don't like to have my back to the door. And since this case has started, I've had the feeling, at times, that I'm being watched, followed." *Hunted.*

"Do you think you're . . . in danger?" Her frown deepened. "I feel so weird even saying it. Now I feel like I'm *in* one of those movies."

I rubbed a hand over my face. "I didn't mean to scare you."

"I'm scared for you, not for myself."

Hadn't Namid said much the same thing? Nice to know everyone was so worried about me.

"I appreciate that. I don't know if I'm in danger or not. I haven't been threatened or anything like that. I haven't even seen anyone following me. It's a feeling; nothing more." I picked up the menu again and shook my head, eager to find some way—any way—to reassure her. "Who knows? Maybe it's the strain of working a murder case again. I'm getting paranoid."

She still wasn't reading her menu. "Was that a problem for you before? Paranoia?"

"No."

"I didn't think so. You don't seem like the paranoid type. And you also don't seem like the type to act this way unless you were really concerned."

Did I mention that she was smart?

"You're right," I said. "That's why I wanted to sit back here, and why I feel better having a view of the door and the street."

"Should we leave?"

I shook my head. "No. That would be giving in to my fear, and that's exactly what I don't want to start doing."

She nodded.

"So what's good here?" I asked.

Billie smiled and picked up her menu. "Everything."

As it turned out, the food was great and the place had Dos Equis Amber on tap, which you don't find in a lot of restaurants. We stayed for two hours, talking, laughing a lot. We even spent a little time just sitting, looking into each other's eyes. I swear. I don't think I'd ever done that with anyone.

After dinner, I drove her home. I went so far as to walk her up to the door. My dad would have been proud.

She got out her keys, but then leaned against the door frame. "What are you doing tomorrow, Fearsson?"

"Not sure yet. I have some more digging around to do, and I have to go see a band play tomorrow night."

Her eyebrows went up. "A band?"

"It's work, not pleasure. I need to speak with the manager of Robo's about the guy the police have arrested, and as it happens, Randy Deegan's band is playing there."

"Hmmm," she said. "I like music."

I laughed. "I told you it was work."

"But don't you need a cover, someone to make it seem like you're a regular guy going for the music?"

"You mean my girl Friday?"

"Something like that."

"Sure, why not? Eight o'clock?"

"It's a date."

Silence. Our eyes locked again.

"This was fun," she said. "More than fun. It was . . ."

"It was the best day I've had in a really long time," I said for her.

"For me, too." She stepped forward and kissed me lightly on the lips. "Good night, Fearsson."

"Good night."

I waited until she was in the house before walking back to the Z-ster. As I approached the car I slowed, trying again to sense the red sorcerer. Once more, I felt nothing. He was out there, of course. Somewhere. But for tonight at least, he had let me be.

I peered up at the moon, which was radiant and big, shading toward full. Just seeing it made my head start to throb. I climbed into the Z-ster and closed my eyes, taking long, slow breaths.

One more night. I'd have my date with Billie at Robo's. And then the phasing would begin.

CHAPTER 13

Often on the cusp of a phasing, my dreams become fragmented to the point of incoherence, as if the insanity that's about to be brought on by the moon has crept into my sleep. But not this night.

All night long I dreamed of the red sorcerer, and in every dream he was tracking me, hunting me down. I'd wake from one dream, fall back asleep, and slip right into another; my mind was like a flat stone skipping along the surface of a pond. At one point I dreamed that I was back in the monument with Billie, running along a dried river bed, leading her, pulling her by the hand. I kept staring back over my shoulder, expecting to see the red sorcerer. I could feel him behind us, and as much as I wanted to get away, to get Billie away, I also wanted to see his face, to find out who he was.

We reached a bend in the riverbed, and I hesitated, though now Billie tugged at my hand, trying to get me to run on. She said something to me that I didn't hear, and I turned to her. And as I did, I saw her eyes widen at something she could see past my shoulder. She screamed, and I spun to look.

Which, of course, is when the phone rang, waking me from the dream. I groped for the receiver, missed it the first time, got it the second.

"Fearsson," I mumbled.

"Sleeping late, I see," Kona said. "You alone, or did you have another date?"

I grunted a laugh. "Both."

"Good. What do you have for me?"

"So much for the social niceties."

"You're lucky you got as much as you did. I'm having a bad day, partner. It's not even nine o'clock and my day's shot to hell."

I sat up, running a hand through my tangled hair. "Tell me. Maybe I can help."

"It's nothing you don't already know. Gann is being arraigned right now, and I've got no way of proving to Hibbard or Arroyo or anyone else that he's innocent."

Right. "I'll see what else I can find," I said, forcing myself awake. "I didn't get much from Q or Luis, but there's another place I can go today."

"We don't have much time."

I chuckled humorlessly. "Don't I know it."

"Meaning what?"

"Meaning that our friend has taken a particular interest in me. I don't know why; I guess he knows I'm after him. But he's taken the measure of my warding three times now and—"

"You've lost me, partner. It's that mumbo-jumbo stuff again."

"Sorry. He's been testing me in a way, and he's done it three times, which in magical circles basically means that he owns me. The next time, if he wants to hurt me, or kill me, or turn me into a toad, he can pretty much have his way."

"And you're guessing it won't be the toad thing."

I grinned, despite the tightness in my gut. "Yeah, something like that."

"Well then, watch yourself," she said.

"I will."

I hung up, showered, and was soon on my way back to Mesa. There was a small park near Falcon Field where I knew other weremystes would be gathered today in anticipation of the full moon. The drive was as slow as one would expect on a weekday morning, and by the time I was parking the Z-ster I could see the crowd gathered among the small tents and plywood stalls.

Passersby would have thought it nothing more than another small farmers' market, of which there was no shortage in the Phoenix area. This market, though, was far from typical. We referred to it as the

Moon Market, because it only turned up for a few days right before the phasing. Rather then selling produce and jams and homemade salsas, the sellers at the Moon Market sold herbs and oils, crystals and talismans, elixirs, incense, and bundled blends of flowers and native plants that resembled the sage sticks burned by the Pueblo people. Many of the items were similar to those Q sold at his place, only in far greater numbers and varieties, and often at much better prices. Some peddled their own spells, which they taught to other weremystes for a fee. Some sold knives or candles that they claimed to have charmed.

As usual, there were as many wannabes circulating among the tents as there were actual weremystes. Sometimes tourists stumbled across the market as well. They took pictures of the various displays and bought the occasional geode or quartz spear. But it was always easy to spot the weremystes in the crowd, even if direct sunlight obscured the wavering effect from their magic. They weren't there for the fun of it, and they weren't shopping for pretty trinkets. They moved around the market with quiet urgency, seeking something— anything—that might take the edge off the coming phasing.

I'd tried a few of the herbs early on: sachets of stargrass and alyssum that I was told to leave near all the windows and doors of my house; blends of anise, bay, pennyroyal, and rosemary that I was supposed to put in pots of boiling water. Once I even bought a wand made of mulberry. As far as I could tell, none of them had done anything to ease the pull of the moon.

But other weremystes swore by remedies like these, and who was I to argue? I knew cops who used one kind of aspirin, but not others. Different people have different headaches; same with phasings.

I wandered through the market, searching for people I knew, people who might be able to tell me something about the Blind Angel killings. A few vendors and shoppers appeared to recognize me, but most of them refused to make eye contact. They probably thought I was still a cop.

The first person I saw who both knew me and appeared willing to speak with me was an old Navajo named Barry Crowseye, who sold crystals at the market, and jewelry in a small shop in Tolleson. He waved me over when he spotted me and stood to shake my hand, reaching across a long table that was covered with baskets of polished stone—petrified wood, tiger's-eye, citrine, jasper, bloodstone, malachite, and a dozen other stones I couldn't identify.

I'd known Barry for years and he hadn't changed at all. As far as I could tell, his hair had always been silver, and he had always worn it in a long ponytail. He was a big man, with a chiseled face that could have come straight off of a coin. If I'd been making a western and needed to cast the part of Indian chief, I'd have tracked him down simply because he looked the part. His skin was the color of cherry wood, and his eyes were almost black. He was wearing jeans, a pale blue Los Lobos t-shirt, and a brown leather vest. And as always, the shimmer of magic around him was so strong that his face, neck, and shoulders were blurred.

"Good to see you, Jay," he said, smiling at me, a gold tooth glinting. "Been a while."

"You too, Barry. Things going well?"

He shrugged, then lowered himself back onto a folding canvas chair. "I suppose. You interested in buying?" he asked, pushing a few stones around on his table until satisfied with his display. In addition to the polished rocks, he also had agate geodes, pendants of various sizes and colors, and amethyst, quartz, and fluorite crystals. Like the herbs and oils I'd seen elsewhere, his selection of stones was weighted to those said to offer magical protection and psychic strength.

"No, thanks," I told him.

He gave a sage nod. "Information, then."

I laughed. "Guess I'm getting predictable."

He shrugged again. "I haven't seen you around here in more than a year. And even back when you were a regular, you were never as interested in protection as you were in information."

"You'd make a good PI."

He chuckled, but quickly grew serious again. "People here don't want to talk about the murders. They didn't when you were a cop, and they don't now. Can't say as I blame them."

"How'd you know I'd be asking about that?"

Barry regarded me in a way that made me feel like the biggest idiot on the planet.

"Yeah, all right," I said, my voice dropping. "If you knew anything, would you tell me?"

"Yes," he said.

I believed him.

"Who else should I talk to?"

"I don't know that, either."

"Well, thanks anyway," I said. I started to leave, but then stopped. Barry knew as much about magic as anyone I'd met, aside from Namid. And unlike the runemyste, Barry was willing to give me a straight answer now and then. "What do you know about dark magic?" I asked, turning to face him again.

"Not a lot. Some. I did a little when I was younger. And my brother played around with some nasty stuff once upon a time. Why?"

I asked him the same question I'd asked Luis Paredes a few nights before. "Can you think of any reason why a weremyste would kill on the night of the first quarter moon?"

His eyebrows went up. "First quarter moon is a powerful night. Any spell would be stronger then."

"So I've heard. But what spell would require a murder?"

"Lots of them do," he said, his voice and expression grim. "Why do you think they call it dark magic? Sacrifice is just another word for murder, and there's not that much difference between killing a goat and killing a person. Except that human blood amplifies the magic more."

"Could he be using the kids he's killing to make himself stronger?"

Barry gave a small frown. "I suppose."

"But you don't think he is."

"I don't know enough about the guy to think anything. But I've never heard of a weremyste making himself stronger with magic. We cast spells, we hone our craft, we practice. But using magic to strengthen our magic?" He shook his head. "I'm not sure I believe it."

"Yeah, all right. Thanks, Barry."

"No problem. And don't be such a stranger," he called after me.

I walked away, raising a hand as I went. I made my way around the rest of the market, unsure as to what, exactly, I was trying to find. I figured I'd know it when I saw it.

I was right.

Near the back of the market, as far as possible from where I had parked, a woman sat under a small white tent selling an odd assortment of oils, herbs, and stones carved into animal shapes: owls, snakes, bears, wolves. They resembled Zuni fetishes in a superficial way, but I could tell they were knock-offs. In fact, her entire display could have come from one of those New Age stores in a mall; I doubted that any of what she was selling had much value for a weremyste. I noticed a small sign taped to one of the tent legs; it said "Renewing Designs, Shari Bettancourt." It gave a website and PO address in Tempe.

I no more than glanced at the woman as I gave her table a quick scan and prepared to move on. Then I froze, eyeing the woman once more, my gaze settling on a pendant that hung around her neck. She wore a long multi-color batik dress with a v-neck. The necklace was barely visible beneath it. But I could see a small stone and the silver setting around it. And I was certain that the stone glowed with a faint shimmering of crimson magic.

The woman was speaking to another customer, and at first paid no attention to me. I stared at the stone, stepping closer to her table. The other customer walked away, but I hardly noticed.

"May I help you?"

I tore my eyes away from the pendant, forcing myself to look at her. She appeared to be in her forties. There were small lines around her mouth and eyes, and her short, dark hair was streaked with strands of gray. She had a pleasant, round face and pale blue eyes.

"Yes," I said, finding my voice. "I was . . . I was admiring your necklace."

"Isn't it pretty?" she said. But her smile tightened and she adjusted her dress so that it covered the pendant.

"Yes," I said. "That red stone is quite remarkable."

"It's garnet," she told me. "It's a healing stone, and a protector."

I nodded, meeting her gaze again.

"I have some garnets here," she said, pointing to a small wooden box that contained a few pieces of raw red crystal. Compared to the glowing pendant, they appeared dull, lifeless. "Of course, they need to be polished to shine like mine."

"Yes, of course. Where did you find yours? Shari, is it?"

Her gaze wavered; her smile vanished. "Yes, I'm Shari. I . . . I don't remember where I got it. I think it was a gift, but I've had it for a very long time."

She wasn't a very good liar.

"Can I see it again?"

Shari hesitated, then drew the pendant out from under her dress and held it up for me. I noticed that her hand trembled.

"That's a lovely stone," I said. "It's so bright, it could almost be glowing."

She slipped it back into her dress. "Trick of the light," she said.

"I'm not sure it was. I think it was magic." I kept my tone light, trying to make it sound like an observation rather than an accusation, but you wouldn't have known it from her response.

"Well, I think I'd know if it was magic, wouldn't I?" she said her tone turning brusque. She dismissed me with a flick of her eyes and spied an older man walking near her tent. "Good morning," she called. "How are you today?"

The man offered a vague smile and half-hearted wave as he continued by. But Shari had made her point: our conversation was over.

"I'm sorry if I offended you," I said. That was a lie, too. I'd meant to spook her.

She scrutinized her goods, and made a show of rearranging several of the items. "You didn't," she said, her voice clipped.

I watched her a moment longer, then turned and walked away. I left the park by way of a nearby path that led onto the street running behind her booth, and went so far as to walk past her tent once more, so that she might see me over the small hedge growing there. I wanted her to think that I'd come on foot. Once I was sure she couldn't see me anymore, I circled back to the Z-ster, pulled out of the parking lot, and then positioned it along a curb where I could watch the market entrance.

As I expected, Shari didn't stay there much longer. I'd scared her too much. She came out a short time later wheeling a large, battered suitcase that must have held her goods. Her folded tent was tied to it with bungee cords. She walked hurriedly to a small hatchback, heaved the suitcase into the back, and pulled out of the lot. I kept low as she drove by me and then followed at a safe distance.

She drove straight back to Tempe, sticking to back roads, and eventually pulled into a driveway beside a small house near the sports complex south of the University. I parked nearby and waited until she was back in her house before walking up the path to her door and knocking.

Shari was slow to answer, and I began to wonder if I'd scared her too much. But then the door opened a crack and she peered out at me over the chain.

"Yes? What—" Her mouth fell open. "You," she whispered. "How did you—?"

"I followed you."

"You had no right!"

I showed her my license. "My name is Jay Fearsson, Ms. Bettancourt. I'm a private investigator. I'm doing some work on the Blind Angel killings. I need to ask you some questions."

She shook her head. Opening the door a bit more, she looked past me into the street, her eyes wide and fearful. "You have to leave. Now, before he sees you."

"You mean the man who gave you that necklace? The one who used his magic on it?"

Her eyes snapped to me and she opened her mouth, then closed it again. "You have to leave," she said again, and started to close the door.

"I'll tell the police to speak with you," I said, blurting it out.

She'd nearly gotten the door shut, but now she opened it again, appearing even more frightened than she had before. "You can't!"

"I will. I have to. We have to stop him."

The woman laughed, sounding half-nuts, as if her phasing had already begun.

"You have no idea what you're dealing with," she said. "You can't stop him anymore than you can stop the moon from rising."

"He's a powerful weremyste, I know. But . . ."

I broke off. She was laughing again, though there were tears in her eyes.

"You're an idiot. Get out of here before you get me killed. Please!"

"Who is he? What's his name? You have to tell me something! Anything!"

She shook her head, scanning the street again.

"He'll kill again, Shari. You know he will. But we can stop him."

"No, you can't!" she said, her tone fierce. "No one can! He's much, much more than you think he is."

"What do you mean? Tell me about the magic he used on your necklace."

Her hand strayed to her chest, where the pendant lay beneath her dress. Then she gripped the door again. "You have to go."

"I'm not going anywhere," I said. "You know what this man's done. You know how many people he's killed. You have to help me stop him."

She hesitated, and I wondered if maybe I had gotten through to her.

"I will," she said. "Really. But not now, not here. You have to go. Please." This last she whispered. There were tears on her face.

I didn't want to. Kona and I had been after the Blind Angel Killer for three years, and here at least was someone who knew him, who could describe him, tell me his name. She might even have known where he lived. He'd done more than give her a pendant. I was sure of it. That stone still glowed with his magic, which meant that he had done something to it recently. Red's magic faded too fast for that glow to be from an old spell. Was he communicating with her in some way? Was she helping him? If I could convince her to let me into the house for a moment, I was confident that I could get something of value out of her.

"Just a few questions," I said, pleading with her. "Tell me his name. His address if you know it."

"I can't." She started to push the door closed. Then she stopped, her face contorting.

"Oh, my God! He's here! You fool! You let him follow you!"

I started to tell her that I hadn't been followed, but in that instant I felt him, too. The air around us seemed to come alive with magic; it felt charged, the way it does in a desert lightning storm.

She backed away from the door without closing it.

"No!" she said.

I felt his power, but it wasn't directed at me, as it had been outside Robo's or Robby's house or Antoine's.

"Let me in!" I shouted. "I can protect you if you let me in!"

"No!" she said again, but it wasn't directed at me. She said a name—it sounded like Cower, but that wasn't quite it. "Please, no!"

A moment later she screamed, clutching at the pendant or at her chest. She dropped to the floor, her body convulsing, her head jerking from side to side.

"Ms. Bettancourt! Shari! Let me in!"

She screamed again, the sound strangled this time. I considered kicking the door in, but thought better of it. I didn't think I could get to her fast enough to ward her from whatever magic he was using. Instead, I pulled my weapon and whirled, searching the street. I was frantic; he had to be close.

And this time I saw him.

He stood at the corner on the far side of the street and he bore little resemblance to the bald man I'd seen in my scrying stone the day before while standing on the spot where Claudia Deegan died. He had long white-blond hair and a thick beard, and he was dressed in tattered jeans, a t-shirt, and an old army coat. But as soon as I spotted him, I knew it was the same guy. He shimmered and wavered like a mirage on a desert highway.

He must have seen the recognition in my eyes, because an instant later I felt his magic turn itself on me. I tried a warding spell, but knew that it would fail. Desperate, acting more on instinct than on rational thought, I raised my Glock and fired.

My aim was true. I'm sure of it. In all my years as a cop, and even in my academy days, I'd been great with a pistol. But somehow I missed this time. Instead of hitting him square in the chest, the bullet struck the street sign above him and to the left. A deflection spell, probably. If he'd used reflection magic instead, I'd have killed myself.

He glared at me, pale eyes blazing like stars in a night sky. Then he turned and ran. I spared only an instant for Shari, who I could see through the narrow gap in her doorway. She lay crumpled on the floor, as still as death, her hands folded over her chest.

There was nothing more I could do for her. I whirled and ran after her killer.

CHAPTER 14

Shooting at him had been stupid—useless as well as dangerous. On the other hand, it had made the sorcerer run, and might well have saved my life, at least for the moment. The rest was all nuisance. Someone was going to call the police, and I'd have to explain why I'd discharged my weapon, and what role I'd played in Shari's death. Given the chance I would have called 911 for her, of course, but I would have done so anonymously. No chance of that now.

But those were matters for later. In that instant I was interested only in the blond-haired, bald man who had killed her.

He's much, much more than you think he is . . .

What had she meant by that?

I knew he was a more powerful weremyste than I was. He might have been the strongest sorcerer I'd ever encountered. And I guessed he was strong physically, too. He appeared to be at least half a foot taller than me. He had the build of an athlete, and I couldn't help remembering how far into South Mountain Park he'd carried Claudia. I also couldn't deny that he was pulling away from me as we ran, much the way Antoine had the other day.

But I had a feeling that Shari had meant more than all of that.

It occurred to me that given the ease with which he'd tested my defenses those three times, chasing after him might not have been the best idea.

Even as I formed the thought, he stopped and turned to face me.

I slowed, then halted, too, holding my weapon loosely at my side. I had a feeling that shooting at him again would be pointless, that he would be able to save himself with magic. The same magic he could use to attack me.

Defend yourself!

It was as if Namid was right beside me, shouting warnings. I sheathed myself in a shielding spell, the same protective cocoon I'd used against against Namid's magical fire. At the same time, I raised my pistol again.

The sorcerer laughed.

The touch of his magic was about as light as one of those lead aprons the dentist gives you for x-rays. It draped over my mind, pressing down on me. I couldn't move my arms or my legs. I stood on the sidewalk, my weapon still aimed at the man, and I couldn't even bring myself to pull the trigger.

"You should have left it alone," he said. He didn't shout or call back to me. He spoke the words, and I heard them as I would if he had been standing beside me, whispering in my ear. He had an accent of some sort, but at that moment I couldn't place it. "You should have stayed away."

My shooting hand started to turn. I fought to keep the Glock trained on him, but I might as well have tried to make the sun move west to east. I had no control over my own body. In a tiny corner of my mind I wondered what spell he was using on me; it was beyond any magic I knew. Panicking, I tried everything I could think of to throw him off. I recited wardings in my mind. I threw assailing spells at him. I even attempted my father's transporting spell. Nothing worked. The weapon was turned toward me now. I opened my mouth and stuck the muzzle in, tasting the tang of metal and the bitter residue of gunpowder. I wanted to gag, but I couldn't even do that much.

I felt my trigger finger twitch, and I closed my eyes, tears streaming down my face.

I heard Namid's voice again. *Defend yourself!*

Yes. I refused to die here, killed by my own pistol. I had thrown every spell I knew at the guy, but maybe that was my mistake.

Three elements: the sidewalk, his feet, and a great big crack in the cement. I knew I couldn't hurt him, but I didn't need to. I only needed to knock him off balance for a second.

And I did. I opened my eyes in time to see him stumble, then right himself.

His magic wavered for an instant, long enough that I managed to pull the weapon from my mouth, nearly retching. I pointed the Glock at him again, though my hand was unsteady and my legs felt like they were about to give way.

"Hey! What the hell are you doin'?"

The voice came from the house to the right of me. I glanced that way, but wasn't willing to take my eyes off the sorcerer for long. I saw anger flash across the killer's face, and then I saw him laugh again.

He ran, vanishing around a corner. I couldn't tell if he'd gone past the point where I could see him, or had used a spell to make himself disappear. To be honest, I didn't care. I sank to my knees, my chest heaving.

"Hey, mister? You all right?"

I looked over at the man who'd saved my life. He was wearing old cutoff-jean shorts and a sleeveless undershirt. His hair was black, but he had a grizzled beard.

"You shouldn't play with your gun like that," he said, frowning at me. "Scared me half to death."

"Yeah," I said, my voice ragged. "Sorry."

"Who was that guy, anyway?" he asked, standing on tiptoes and craning to peer down the street after the sorcerer. "The one you were talking to."

"I don't know." I forced myself back to my feet, though my legs still felt rubbery. "You need to call 911," I told him. "Something's happened to Ms. Bettancourt."

"Shari?" the man said, concern in his voice, his brow knitting.

"Yes."

"Did he do it? That guy?"

"Call 911. Please."

He stared at me a moment longer. Then he hurried back inside.

I walked—staggered really—back to Shari's house, sat down on her front steps and placed my Glock on the top step next to me. If the sorcerer had come back, I'm not sure I would have had the strength even to lift the pistol, but having it near at hand made me feel better.

A squad car arrived a few minutes later, stopping first in front of the neighbor's house and then pulling up to Shari's place. I didn't move.

Two uniformed guys got out of the car, one Latino, one white, both of them young and burly. The Latino cop spotted my Glock first and reached for his weapon.

"Hands up!" he said, leveling his weapon at me.

I raised my hands and stared back at him as he and his partner—now with his pistol out, too—hurried up the path. The Latino cop kicked the Glock beyond my reach.

"He's all right!" the neighbor called, running up the street toward the house. "He didn't do anything! It was the other guy."

"Who are you?" the Latino cop asked, his weapon still aimed at me. The badge he wore identified him as Roberto Torres.

"My name's Jay Fearsson," I said, my voice even. "I'm a PI. I used to be on the force."

"The Glock's yours?"

I nodded. "I fired it once at the man who killed Shari Bettancourt. I hit that street sign over there." I pointed with my chin, keeping my hands as they were.

"You hit a street sign?" the other cop asked.

I wasn't about to explain that the guy I'd been aiming at used a deflection spell to steer my bullet away. I nodded, and tried to ignore their shared grins and raised eyebrows. But while they both had me pegged as a lousy shot, they also seemed convinced that I wasn't a threat. Both men holstered their pistols.

Torres stepped past me to the doorway.

The white cop—Allen Marra, according to his badge—said, "I'll need to see your license, Mister . . ."

"Fearsson." I pulled out my wallet and handed it to him.

I heard his partner rattling the door.

"This is chained," he said. "How'd he kill her?"

"I don't know. You need to call Kona Shaw in Homicide. She knows me, and she knows what I'm working on."

"Do you know the guy's name?" Torres asked, ignoring what I'd said.

"I heard her call him 'Cower,' or something like that."

"And why are you here? Did you have a relationship with the victim?"

"No." I said. "I met her this morning at a . . . a farmer's market. I talked to her for a while there, and then followed her back here to ask her a few more questions. While I was talking to her, the other guy showed up."

"And he killed her."

"Yes."

"Is that what you saw?" Torres asked, speaking past me to Shari's neighbor.

"I didn't see any of that," the man said. "I saw this guy and the other one. This guy was chasing him, and then he stopped. They both did. And then this guy puts his gun in his mouth, and then pulls it out again, and that's when I yelled at them. The other guy ran away." He hesitated. Then, "Is Shari really dead?"

Marra still held my wallet, and now he frowned at the man. "Fearsson put his weapon in the other guy's mouth?"

"No. He put it in his own mouth."

Marra grimaced. "Why the hell would you do that?"

"It's hard to explain," I said, sighing the words.

Torres descended the steps and planted himself right in front of me. "Give it a try," he said.

"The other guy made me do it. I couldn't help myself."

"What the hell is that supposed to mean?"

"Please, call Kona Shaw. She'll know what I'm talking about."

"First you explain this."

"The guy's a myste. A sorcerer. He used some kind of mojo on me."

Torres raised an eyebrow, drawing a roll of the eyes from his partner. I figured I was about thirty seconds away from an all-expenses-paid trip to the psych ward.

"Please call Kona," I said. "You have a dead woman in there. I've told you that I didn't kill her, and that's been corroborated by another witness. The rest I'll explain to the homicide detectives."

"We can run you in anyway," Torres said.

"Yeah, you can. But you'd be wasting your time." I took a breath. "I'm working on behalf of the Deegan family, and so my investigation is connected to the Blind Angel killings. I worked the case when I was still on the job, and now I'm working it again. Kona was my partner. The guy I was after—the guy who killed this woman—I'm pretty sure he's the Blind Angel Killer."

"The Blind Angel Killer is already in custody."

"Gann's not your man," I said.

"Holy shit," the neighbor said in a hushed voice. "That was the Blind Angel Killer?"

"I swear to God, Fearsson," Torres said, wagging his finger in my face. "If you're bullshitting me, I'm going to make your life a living hell."

"I'm not. Call Kona."

Torres considered me, the muscles in his jaw bunching. After a moment he nodded to Marra, who hurried to the squad car.

"Holy shit," I heard the neighbor whisper again.

It took Kona and Kevin, her partner, some time to get there, and then they spent several minutes speaking in low voices with Torres and Marra. The forensics team had arrived in the interim and after cutting through Shari's chain lock, had entered the house. I moved off the stairs to a shady corner of her yard. Kona and Kevin joined me there now, both of them grim-faced.

Kevin was younger than Kona and me, and had only been in Homicide for three or four years. He'd shaved his head since the last time I saw him; it looked good on him. He was a handsome African-American man, with dark eyes, a lean build, and an easy smile. I'd tried to be as nice to him as I could since meeting him about a year ago, but both of us remained wary of each other. I think he felt that I was critiquing him all the time, measuring his performance as a cop against my own. I wasn't. I just found it hard to think of Kona working with anyone other than me.

"You all right?" Kona asked me.

"Yeah, I'm fine."

"You sure this was our guy?"

My eyes flicked toward Kevin. He didn't know I was a weremyste. "Pretty sure," I said.

"There isn't a mark on the woman," Kevin said. "No sign that anyone broke in. Is it possible she died of . . . of something natural?"

"I don't think so," I told him.

"Kevin," Kona said, "why don't you go see what they're doing in there. Make sure they're not messing with my crime scene. I'll be in soon."

Kevin eyed us both. It wasn't the first time one of us had contrived to speak in private with the other while he was around. "Yeah, all right," he said, his voice flat. "Catch you later, Jay."

"See you, Kevin."

Kona and I watched him walk away.

"You're going to have to tell him eventually," I said.

"I keep hoping you two will become friends so that you can tell him yourself." Her eyes raked over me. "You look like hell."

"I thought I was dead. This guy's stronger than any weremyste I've ever seen. He made me . . ." I broke off shaking my head.

"So it is our guy."

I managed a smile, but it was fleeting. "It better be. If there are two sorcerers walking around with this kind of power, we're in trouble."

"And the pistol in the mouth thing?"

I shook my head again. "Don't ask." Taking a long breath, I said, "He killed her, Kona. I saw him do it, although I can't tell you how it happened. She said his name—Cower, I think it was. She knew he was there. She felt him. And then she was dead."

"She was a weremyste, too?"

I nodded. "I saw her at the Moon Market this morning. She had on a necklace that was glowing with his magic. That's how I knew to follow her." I followed a passing car with my gaze, my mouth twitching. "I guess I got her killed."

"We're going to need a statement," she said. "You know that."

"You'll have to take it. This guy's magic is unlike anything we've gone up against before. No one else will believe me."

"Who says I do?" She smiled to soften it.

"You're going to get a description from the neighbor," I told her, as we started to walk back toward the house. "It'll be nothing at all like what I told you yesterday."

"He was disguised?"

"I think he's a chameleon. He can look like anything and anyone he wants."

"I'm starting not to like this guy, Justis."

"Yeah," I said. "Tell me about it."

Between waiting for Kona to finish her work at the Bettancourt house, and going back to 620 to give her my statement, most of my afternoon was gone. The only thing that could have made my day worse would have been running into Cole Hibbard before I managed to get out of the building.

So, of course, that was exactly what happened.

When old Cole found out I'd been at the scene of a murder, he practically wet himself. When Kona told him that I'd only been a witness, he started trying to find ways to charge me with the killing anyway. I left as soon as I could, and was seething the whole way home, not only for myself, but also for my father.

Hibbard and my dad had been close. In fact, for a while Hibbard and his wife had been my parents' closest friends. I still remembered them coming over to the house and staying up late playing Spades, smoking cigarettes, and drinking daiquiris. I was supposed to be sleeping, of course, but I'd spy on them from the stairway, mostly because I thought Hibbard's wife, whose name I've forgotten, was the prettiest woman I'd ever seen.

Eventually the phasings started taking their toll on my father, and though Hibbard was his friend, I gather that Dad wasn't able to confide in him about the magic and Namid and all the rest. Or maybe that's an excuse that both he and I have used too often. I did confide in Kona, and in the end it changed nothing.

After a while, Hibbard turned on him. I suppose he had cause. My mother turned on him, too, in her own way. Hell, so did I. To Hibbard, it must have seemed that his friend had lost it, had burned out right before his eyes. When my mother and her lover died, Hibbard was one of those who believed my father had killed them both. And when my father went all the way over the edge, leaving me without a family or a home, Hibbard and his wife were among the few couples who refused to help me out. I guess that's understandable, too. The Hibbards had lost their two closest friends in a tragic, ugly sequence of events. The last thing they would have wanted was a living reminder of both Dara and Leander Fearsson haunting their home.

But try telling that to a fifteen-year-old kid who'd lost his parents. That's when I started hating Cole Hibbard. One of the reasons I so wanted to be a cop, and not just a cop, but a homicide detective, was to show Hibbard and all the others who had turned their backs on my father and me that we deserved better. I had a lot to prove, and I'm sure that I came into the force with an attitude to match. It's not surprising that Hibbard had it in for me from the start; I had it in for him, too.

In the end, the only thing he had done to me that I couldn't forgive was to refuse to accept that maybe I could be a decent cop and wouldn't necessarily become my father.

Of course, I understood all this in my calmer moments, when I could reflect on all that happened back then. At other times, though, I couldn't get past the fact that Hibbard was such a jerk.

By the time I reached my office, I'd worked myself into quite a state. I'd watched a woman die, nearly been killed myself, and had been shown, in no uncertain terms, that whatever magic I wielded was nothing next to the power of the Blind Angel Killer.

The *Republic* was still running stories about Claudia's death above the fold. It had a picture of Gann on the front page, too, beneath a caption that read, "Is This the Blind Angel Murderer?" I wondered if Torres and Marra believed what I'd told them about Shari's killer being the one who'd killed Claudia Deegan. Maybe that was the one good thing that would come out of this day.

I dropped the paper in the trash and rubbed my eyes. After a moment I stood again and started to pace.

Where was Namid when I needed him? I was eager to train, to work some magic and get the day out of my system. The runemyste would have told me that this wasn't a proper use of magic, that the purpose of clearing prior to conjuring was to keep emotions and frustrations from intruding on the spells. Whatever. I wanted to break something. Failing that, I wanted to use my magic against someone, even if it was Namid and I couldn't hope to do any real damage. In fact, better that it be him, for that reason.

"Namid!" I called.

After a few moments, he materialized, as smooth and clear as a mountain lake in early morning.

"I am not your servant, Ohanko. I am not to be summoned like one."

"I know that," I said. "But I need to train, and I . . . I thought maybe we could work on some more wardings." I winced at what I heard in my voice. I sounded like some willful spoiled kid ordering around a playmate. "If you'd be willing to help me, I mean," I added, knowing it was too little too late.

He considered me, his face placid. Then he shook his head. "No. You are clouded."

"I can clear myself."

"No," he said again. "I do not think so. Not now. I sense much anger in you. Restlessness. This is not a good time for you to conjure."

It only helped a little that I'd known he would say something like this. "Yeah, all right," I said. "I'm sorry I called for you."

He inclined his head and began to vanish.

"Tell me about my father," I said, on impulse.

Namid grew more substantial again. "What do you want to know?"

"Anything."

"You know much about him already."

"Maybe. Sometimes I feel like I don't know him at all."

"You are much like him. The good and the bad."

"Will I end up like him?"

"That has yet to be scried."

"But I'm headed in that direction. Isn't that right?"

The runemyste seemed to weigh this. Then he sat down on the floor right where he'd been standing. I sat as well.

"Magic exacts a price. You know this. And still you have chosen to conjure rather than block your power with Abri."

"Right. Like Dad did. And now he's nuts."

"He made his choice. He lives with the consequences of that."

"You make it sound so . . . simple," I said, anger creeping into my voice. "This is my sanity we're talking about, Namid. It's my life. I don't want to wind up like my dad."

The runemyste gazed back at me, still glasslike. "Then take the Abri. Block your magic, and you will be free of the moon's pull. You will not have to worry about going . . . nuts." The word sounded strange coming from him.

"You know I can't do that."

He widened his eyes. "You cannot? Why is this?"

I started to answer, then stopped myself and chuckled. "All right," I said. "I get it. I've made my choice. That's what you're telling me. So I should stop complaining, right?"

"You have made your choice for today, Ohanko. As you did

yesterday. You can change your mind whenever you wish. The Abri will always be there, waiting for you."

"I'm not sure I could give up being a sorcerer."

"That is your decision to make."

"I almost died today," I told him. "I was face to face with this weremyste we're after. He killed a woman with some kind of spell, and then used his magic to make me put my weapon in my mouth. He would have made me pull the trigger."

The runemyste's appearance clouded, his waters becoming turbulent. "He made you do this," he repeated. "What do you mean?"

I shrugged. "Just what I said. He made me. He didn't say anything that I could hear, but suddenly I had no control over my body. I wanted to run. I wanted to shoot him. But I couldn't do anything at all. None of my wardings worked against him."

Namid was scowling. "He controlled you."

"Yes."

"How is it you are still alive?"

I grinned. "I defended myself, like you told me to. I couldn't attack him, so I cracked the sidewalk beneath his feet. It wasn't enough to hurt him, but it broke his hold on me."

The runemyste nodded. "That is good. You will be a runecrafter yet." He eyed me again. "What else can you tell me about this man?"

"He can change his appearance. He's bald and clean-shaven, and then he has long hair and a beard. His eyes are pale though. Almost white. And I have a feeling that they don't change at all." I thought for a moment. "He speaks with an accent. I'm not sure what kind. European, I think. Maybe French? And I heard the woman call him Cower."

"Cower," Namid said, with an intensity I'd never heard from him before. "Could it have been Cahors? A French name?"

"Maybe," I said. "Do you know him?"

"There is much I need to learn," he said. "I must go." He began to fade.

"Namid, wait!"

He solidified once more, though I sensed his reluctance. "Do you still think I can protect myself from this guy?"

"I think you have no choice."

I exhaled. "Right."

"I must go now."

"Of course," I said. "Thank you."

He frowned. "For what?"

"Being honest with me."

"You expected less?"

I smiled at that. "Not really, no." I stood. "I'm sorry I called for you that way. I won't do it again."

"Be well, Ohanko." He faded from view.

I stared for a moment at where he'd been and then considered the pile of papers and unopened envelopes on my desk; most of them were unpaid bills. They could wait. As Namid might have said, I had a big date tonight, and I had enough time to get home, eat a little dinner, and change before I had to start back toward Tempe to pick up Billie. I started toward the door, but before I reached it the phone rang.

I strode back to the desk and picked up the receiver. "Fearsson."

Silence.

"Hello?" I said.

"Yeah, this is um . . . this is 'Toine Mirdoux."

He kind of mumbled it, and at first I had no idea what he'd said.

"Who?"

"*Antoine*? Remember, dog? You blew up the door to my house?"

"Right," I said. "How's it going, Antoine? You calling for that chat you were going on about?"

"What?" he said. Then he allowed himself a half-hearted laugh. "Oh, yeah. That's right. I wanna chat."

Something was bothering him. I found myself wondering if whatever business he'd had with the red sorcerer had gone sour. There was a good deal of noise in the background and I had the feeling he was calling from a cell or maybe even a pay phone, if you could still find one in this city. Wherever he was, he definitely wasn't home.

"Great," I said. "Let's chat."

"Not on the phone, man. I need . . . I need some help. I'm in some trouble here."

"What kind of trouble, Antoine?"

"Not on the phone."

I checked my watch again. I didn't have time enough to get to the Mountain View precinct and back, and still make it to Tempe by eight, not if my talk with the kid was going to take any time at all.

"I can't now, Antoine. How about later tonight?"

"How much later?"

God, he sounded scared, like a little boy left alone in a dark house.

"Tonight. Eleven, at your place."

"My place?"

"You still have it warded, right?"

There was a long silence, and after a while I started wondering if the connection had gone bad.

"Antoine?"

"Yeah, man. All right. My place. Eleven."

"Keep your head down until then, all right?"

"No shit, man."

The line went dead. I returned the phone to its cradle and shook my head. Mountain View's 733 at eleven p.m. Not even close to the way I had hoped to end my evening. But it seemed that now I had two dates. One with Billie, and the other with 'Toine Mirdoux.

CHAPTER 15

I made certain to get to Billie's house precisely at eight. She seemed to place a premium on punctuality. I rang the bell and a moment later she opened the door. My jaw dropped.

Don't get me wrong. I already knew that Billie was beautiful. I liked the way she dressed. I loved the glasses and the pulled-back hair. But I wasn't prepared for this. Her hair was down, dark curls spilling down her back, and she'd yet to put on her glasses. She had on a close-fitting black blouse, a flowing print skirt, heels, and a pair of long, glittering turquoise and silver earrings. It was like she had transformed herself into a movie star.

I'd showered again before coming and I'd shaved, which I only did when I had to. I'd even put on a pair of black jeans and a button-down shirt under my bomber, instead of the usual blue jeans and t-shirt. But I felt like I ought to go home and put on a tie and jacket.

"Hi," I managed to say.

Her eyes sparkled. "You're on time."

"Always. You look incredible."

"Thank you." She spun around once, making her skirt swirl. "You're going to take me dancing."

"Whoa!" I said, shaking my head. "I'm taking you to hear a band. I never said anything about dancing."

She walked away from the door, leaving it open for me. "Geez, Fearsson!" she called over her shoulder. "What do you think people do at these clubs?" She poked her head out of one of the back rooms. "I mean aside from investigate crimes."

"I'm not much of a dancer," I said, wandering around her living room, knowing that this was a fight I was going to lose.

"Well, I'm Ginger Rogers, so I guess I'll be good enough for both of us."

I grinned.

She came into the living room a few moments later, still no glasses on her face. "Ready," she said.

"Don't you need to . . . to be able to see?"

"I have my contacts in."

"I didn't know you had contacts."

"I don't wear them a lot. They're kind of uncomfortable. But I figure this place is going to be pretty crowded tonight, and a lot of my readers are students. I don't want to make it too easy for them to recognize me."

She was just about my height with the heels on, and I found myself staring into those incredible green eyes.

"What's with you tonight?" she asked, smiling at me.

"Nothing." I laughed. "You really look great."

"You're surprised?"

"Not at all. I'm wondering what you're doing with me."

She rolled her eyes, then took my hand and led me toward the door. "Come on, Fearsson. We're going dancing."

We drove to the club, though the walk from where we were able to park was only a few blocks shorter than it would have been from Billie's house. The moon shone overhead, and I tried to ignore the way it seemed to be tugging on my mind, muddying my thoughts. As we walked, I asked her about her day, and she asked me about mine, almost like normal people. Except that I glossed over my conversation with Shari Bettancourt, and I couldn't tell her a thing about Shari being murdered, or the red sorcerer nearly getting me to blow my brains out, or the things I had discussed with Namid. I wouldn't have thought it possible, but I was already reaching the point where I didn't want to keep anything from her at all. I had too many secrets, and they were burning a hole in my chest.

By the time we arrived, the line outside of Robo's already stretched halfway down the block. Apparently Electric Daiquiri had a good reputation. Most in the crowd were college students, the girls decked out in party dresses and heels, the guys dressed with studied indifference in jeans and untucked tees or dress shirts.

"Hey, you're Billie Castle!" one of the girls called as we got on line. "I love your blog."

Billie laughed. "So much for going incognito."

The press was there, too, clustered across the street. Anything the Deegans did was a big deal in this town, this week more than ever.

We could hear the band doing a sound check inside. They sounded good. Billie said something to me, but in that moment I wasn't paying any attention. The last time I'd been at Robo's, Red had been here, too. I sensed that he was nearby again, and I started mumbling warding spells to myself, trying to figure out how I might extend my magic to protect Billie as well. I wasn't even sure it was possible, though I couldn't imagine why it wouldn't be. Act of will, right? Well, I'd kill myself willing her to be safe if it came to that.

"Fearsson, are you listening to me?"

I grimaced. "No, I wasn't. I'm sorry. What were you saying?"

"What were *you* saying? I heard you muttering something."

"I was thinking about work." Too many lies, too many secrets. "This is more than dancing, remember? This is a work night for me."

"Right!" she said, a conspiratorial smile lighting her face. "I'm your girl Friday."

"That's right."

"Who are we here to talk to, boss?"

I laughed and shook my head. "This isn't a game, you know. I probably shouldn't have brought you at all."

"Why not?"

Yeah, Jay, why not? Sometimes I'm pretty stupid. "Because this could be dangerous," I said, feeling again like I was in a "B" movie. At least I was telling her the truth, though.

She sobered. "Really?"

"Really. I need to speak with the club's manager, and the last time I was here, also to speak with him, I had the feeling that I was being followed."

"That stuff really happens?"

"Not usually, no. But this has become a pretty weird case."

"All right," she said, with a small nod. "I'll stop making jokes."

I shook my head. "No, don't do that. I want you to have fun. I want to have fun, too. But understand that I'll be working." I slipped my hand into hers. "And also know that I won't let anything happen to you."

"Wow, Fearsson," she said, grinning. "That was damn near heroic." She pointed to her arm. "Check it out: I have goosebumps."

She did.

Billie started to say something else, but then stopped herself, and whispered, "Oh, crap," instead.

I frowned, but before I could ask her what was wrong, I saw that Professor Stud from the other day was walking down the street, straight toward us.

"Hey," I said. "Isn't that—?"

"Joel. Yes. Don't say anything. Maybe he won't recognize me."

"Billie?"

"I don't think your disguise is very good," I whispered.

Billie giggled. "Hi, Joel," she said, schooling her features.

Good-looking-professor-boy stopped in front of us, glanced at me, but then turned his full attention on Billie. "I didn't know you liked . . . this kind of music."

"Yes, very much."

Joel opened his mouth to say more, but I stuck out my hand, and said, "Hi. Justis Fearsson. How are you?"

He shook it with some reluctance. "Fine, thank you. Joel Benfield."

"Nice to meet you, Joel."

"Are you with the university, Mister Fearsson?"

"No, I'm a private detective." I used my Dick Tracy voice again. I figured I'd let him know what he was up against. Compared to private eye, professor of American history didn't sound all that glamorous.

"Did you say your name was Justis?"

"Yeah. Kind of weird, huh? You can just call me Fearsson, though. Everyone else does."

Billie burst out laughing.

Joel didn't seem to know what to make of us. "Well," he said with false brightness. "I should be going. Billie, nice to see you again." He shot me one last less-than-friendly glance. "Nice to meet you, Mister . . . uh . . . Justis."

"You, too, Joel. Take care."

"You're awful!" Billie said, after Benfield had walked away. But she was still laughing.

The line started to move, and a cheer went up from the college kids.

"All I did was introduce myself. You were the one who couldn't stop giggling."

She gave my hand a hard squeeze.

The cover charge was twenty dollars per person, which seemed a bit steep for a college band. But I didn't let Billie pay her own way. When she objected, I shook my head. "I told you: this is business."

Inside, Robo's was a lot like every other college-town bar in the world. It wasn't a big place, and I had the feeling that an accurate head count of the crowd would already put them over whatever limits Phoenix's fire marshal had placed on occupancy. There was a bank of different-colored spotlights mounted on a scaffold above the band, a small, parquet dance floor in front of the stage, and a bunch of round, wooden tables scattered around the rest of the place, one of which was supposed to have my name on it. It was hot and loud, and it smelled of stale beer and sweat. But I could feel the excitement as soon as we stepped inside.

Electric Daiquiri started their set with a couple of up-tempo instrumentals, including the piece that I'd heard them play a few days before. They sounded great. True to her word, Billie wasted no time dragging me out on to the dance floor. Oh, well. Hadn't I told myself that I'd be willing to take her dancing if that's what it took to win her over? Truth is, it was kind of fun, in large part because I got to watch her. She might not have been Ginger Rogers, but she did dance very well.

"I thought you couldn't dance," she shouted to me at one point, her voice barely carrying over the music.

"I can't," I shouted back.

"Clown!" She smiled.

The first set went by quickly. Randy did most of the talking for the band, though Tilo, as the lead singer and guitarist, was the focal point of much of the music. It made sense: Tilo was a quiet kid, and Randy did a good job as front man. At one point he spotted me in the crowd and he sent a smile and nod my way. Other than that, though, both he and Tilo ignored me.

Late in the set they played a ballad that their keyboardist had written, and before I knew it, Billie was in my arms and we were dancing close.

"So why don't you like to dance?" she asked, her breath stirring my hair and warming my neck.

"Because I look stupid doing it."

She pulled back so that she could see my face. "Who told you that?"

"No one had to tell me. I just know it."

She shook her head and nestled against my chest again. "You're wrong."

The set ended with a funky, upbeat instrumental that really got the place jumping. When they finished, the band vanished off the back of the stage, and some prerecorded music was piped through the sound system.

"That was fun," Billie said, flushed and smiling, a fine sheen of sweat on her face. "You want a beer?"

"Sounds great. But I have to go work now."

"Right."

"Will you be okay?"

"Yes, Mister Fearsson," she said, her voice like that of a dutiful schoolgirl.

I smirked.

"I'll be fine. Go do your thing." She smiled. "Then we can dance some more."

"All right."

I could see the manager's office from the club floor. It was an elevated room with glass walls; a narrow stairway led to the door. I fought my way through the crowd toward the stairs and soon found myself face to face with a bouncer.

He was about six-four and he had the build of a professional wrestler. His head was shaved and he wore a black Robo's t-shirt that must have been three sizes too small. He had on one of those small headsets that allowed him to communicate with the rest of security.

"Sorry, buddy," he said, blocking the stairs. "No access beyond here."

"I need to speak with Mister Moore," I said. I pulled out my wallet and showed him my license. "I'm a PI and I've been asked by the

Deegans to learn what I can about Claudia Deegan's murder. I'm here as Randy's guest tonight. He told me that Moore would see me."

His entire bearing changed, as if he hadn't considered the possibility that I might have a legitimate reason for going up those steps. "What'd you say your name was?"

"Jay Fearsson."

"Fearsson," he repeated. "Wait here." He turned and went up to the office.

It occurred to me that Randy might have forgotten to mention my name to Moore, but after only a few seconds the bouncer opened the office door again and waved me upstairs.

Moore was at his desk and speaking on the phone when I entered the room, but he hung up a moment later and stood to greet me.

"Mister Fearsson," he said, holding out a hand. He was about my height and weight, with brown curls and a receding hairline. His skin was rough and pockmarked; I guessed that he'd had bad acne as a kid.

I shook his hand and tipped my head toward the window, which offered a clear view of Robo's stage. "Those guys are great."

"Glad you're enjoying the show," Moore said. He pointed to a chair in front of his desk, and both of us sat. "Randy said you wanted to talk to me about Mike Gann."

"That's right."

"He also said that you're a private investigator, not a cop. I'm a little uncomfortable talking to you about a former employee. Especially since I've already told the police everything I know about him."

"I understand," I said. "I used to be on the force, and I know how they work. I expect my questions will be a bit different from the ones they asked you."

He frowned at that.

I pulled out my pad and pencil. "Did you ever see Mike do magic?"

Moore laughed. "You're kidding, right?"

"No, I'm not."

His smile faded. "He always talked about stuff like that. To me, to Doug Bass, to the musicians. He wasn't shy about it, but all of us thought he was crazy."

Doug Bass didn't, but I kept that to myself.

"You never saw him do anything that you couldn't explain? Nothing that seemed . . . magical?"

"Not a thing."

"Was he a good worker?"

"He was all right. I probably wouldn't have fired him if Randy hadn't insisted. Truth is, I didn't want to do it. But when I mentioned that Electric Daiquiri was going to be playing here, Mike got real weird about it. After that, I understood what Randy was so worried about, you know? So I let him go."

"Did he ever work on nights when the moon was full?"

He frowned again. "You're right, Mister Fearsson: your questions aren't at all like the ones the police asked me." He sat back, eyeing me for a few seconds. "No, he didn't work full moons. It was a pain in the ass if you want to know. If Doug hadn't volunteered to cover for him whenever the moon was full, it would have caused me real problems. As it was, I didn't pay him for those nights. But I assumed it was part of the whole magic thing, one more delusion. You think there was something to it?"

"I don't know," I said. "Did he miss other nights? Quarter moons, maybe?"

Moore shook his head. "No. Just the full ones. If he'd missed more than that I definitely would have canned him sooner."

I jotted down a few notes. The fact that Gann had worked on the nights of quarter moons could help prove that he hadn't killed the other Blind Angel victims. Kona and I would have to match murder dates to the club's payroll records, but it might be the evidence we needed to save Gann's neck.

The piped-in music stopped and a cheer went up from the crowd on the dance floor.

"I think that's my cue to leave you alone," I said, getting to my feet.

Moore stood too, and I shook his hand.

"Thanks for taking the time to talk to me."

"You're welcome."

I crossed to the door.

"Do you think Mike really could do magic?" Moore asked before I could pull it open. "Real magic?"

"I don't know, Mister Moore. I'm just trying to figure out what happened to Claudia Deegan."

He nodded, though he looked troubled. I let myself out of his office, descended the stairs, and waded through the crowd toward the bar.

I found Billie there, speaking with four or five college kids. As soon as she spotted me, she waved and started pushing through the throng to get to me. She glanced behind her once or twice, seeming to make certain that she wasn't followed. The kids waved to her, and eyed me with obvious interest.

"Fans?" I asked.

She rolled her eyes again. "I was hoping to avoid them and instead it was like I stumbled into a nest of sorority kids." She handed me a bottle of beer. "Here. It might be a bit warm by now."

"Thanks," I said, taking it from her and sipping some. It wasn't too bad.

"How did the work go?"

I shrugged. "Not bad, I guess. I learned a couple of things that might be helpful."

At least I thought I had. I found myself wondering if I should have asked more of the club's manager. Only now, working this case alone, did I realize how much I had come to depend on my give-and-take with Kona when doing police work. We used to challenge each other, offer competing theories and then dissect them until we had figured out what happened. Working alone was like sitting solo on a seesaw. I wasn't sure I was asking the right questions or following the right leads.

"You okay?"

I smiled at her, and while I was frustrated by these doubts, the smile was sincere. "I'm fine."

Electric Daiquiri began their second set, and Billie and I made our way back onto the dance floor. We hadn't been dancing long, though, when I felt him again. The red sorcerer. He was close, and he was intent on me.

The panic I'd felt earlier, when he made me turn the Glock on myself, flooded into me again; I felt the blood drain from my face. I stopped dancing, cleared myself, and began to chant wardings in my mind.

"Fearsson?"

It wasn't going to be enough. Whatever I came up with wouldn't keep him from killing me, and Billie, too. I grabbed her hand and pulled her off the dance floor. We were nearer to the back of the club, so I made for the exit I'd used to find the janitor the last time I'd been here.

"What are you doing?" she called to me.

"We have to get out of here."

"Why?"

"Remember when I told you I was followed? Well, he's here again."

"You're sure?"

I scanned the club, trying to spot anyone who shimmered with enough power to make me feel this way. No one did.

"Pretty sure."

We were almost through the crowd when I felt the heat of his magic hit me.

"Oh, shit," I had time to mutter.

"Fearsson?"

I could hear Billie's concern, but it was all I could do to ward myself and try to save her. I couldn't risk saying a thing for fear of distracting myself. There were people all around me, so reflection and deflection spells were out of the question. I tried to shield the two of us with a conjuring that would absorb his magic, so that no one else would get hurt, but while I knew in theory what to do, the spell was beyond me.

An instant later, I was in agony. It felt like someone had thrust a flaming torch into my chest, as if this bastard sorcerer was trying to burn my heart right out of my body. This was what Shari Bettancourt felt, I told myself. And then the pain obliterated every other thought in my head. I doubled over, clutching both hands over my chest, folding in on myself. Somehow I sensed that I was on the floor, writhing, my teeth clenched, my eyes squeezed shut. I tried again to ward myself, but I could barely remember who I was, much less whatever conjuring I'd been trying a moment before. I heard Billie screaming my name, but I couldn't tell if she was doing so out of fear for me, or because she was being tortured, too. Not that I could have done a damn thing about it.

He had me. Three times. Power in numbers. I was going to die on this rank floor, with strains of Latin fusion blaring in the background, with people dancing and getting drunk all around me.

I tried to fight him, but I had no weapons, and he'd already carved through the shield I'd tried to summon. Magic may be an act of will, but it's also an expression of power and knowledge, and I didn't have enough of either. I wasn't even close. And I was growing weaker by the second. I could feel the life seeping out of me. I could hear my heartbeat slowing, I was aware of the blood laboring to flow through my body. I thought I heard laughter again.

And then I heard a voice.

"Ohanko."

It was as soothing as the laughter had been harsh, as welcome as rain on a parched landscape.

"Namid?" I croaked.

"Be still," he said. I could feel cool water coursing into my chest, dousing the fire that had raged there seconds before.

"I didn't know you could do this," I whispered.

"I cannot. There will be a cost. Now, please, be still."

I lay there on the floor, savoring whatever it was the runemyste was doing to me, amazed that I was I alive, grateful for the ability to inhale and exhale without pain. After a time, I opened my eyes and saw that Billie was kneeling beside me, her face as white as bone and her lips pressed thin.

"Thank God," she said. She ran a rigid hand through her hair. "Stay still. There's an ambulance on the way."

"She is right," Namid said. "Do not try to move yet."

"I don't need an ambulance," I said, the words coming out as a rasp.

Billie frowned. "The hell you don't."

The music hadn't stopped, but there were quite a few people standing around, staring at me.

"Hurry up, Namid," I whispered.

"What?" Billie said.

The runemyste rumbled like surging flood waters. "You must rest."

"Not here, though."

"What are you saying, Fearsson?"

After a few moments more, the flow of soothing waters over my heart ceased. As soon as it did, I felt the pain return, or at least a shadow of it. I could only assume that my chest would be sore for a while.

I sat up, which made my head spin. But I met and held Billie's gaze. "I'm all right."

"No, you're not. What was that? What happened?"

"I'll try to explain it to you," I told her. "But not here."

I thought she'd argue, but after gazing at me for a few seconds, she nodded once. She still looked pale and scared, but I could tell that she hadn't gone to pieces. She was too strong for that. She stood, helped me to my feet. It hurt to move at all, but I didn't want to be anywhere near here when the ambulance arrived.

Billie started toward the back door again, and I followed, my steps stiff, like those of an old man.

One of the college kids stared at me. "Dude, you okay?"

I laid a hand on his shoulder as I walked past him. "Yeah, thanks."

The air in the alley behind Robo's felt cool, and I leaned against the cinder block wall for a moment, taking deep breaths.

"What happened to you, Fearsson?" Billie demanded again.

I straightened and started walking. "Not here," I said.

She didn't move. "Yes, here."

I walked back to her. "I'll try to explain this to you. I swear it. But we're still not safe. I want to get as far—"

"Wait a minute," she said, eyes narrowing. "Are you trying to tell me that what happened to you in there was . . . was done *to* you?"

"I guess that sounds pretty strange, doesn't it?"

Billie nodded, her mouth a dark gash on her ashen face. "Paranoid, even."

I sighed. "I'm not nuts." *Not yet, at least.*

"I didn't say you were," she said. I could tell she was trying to keep her tone gentle. "I'm trying to understand."

I didn't want to have this conversation now. I was spent and sore, and even if I had been ready to tell Billie everything, I wasn't certain that she was ready to hear it. I'd only had to explain all of this once before, to Kona, years ago. And that had been right after we solved the warehouse robbery cases and collared Orestes. She would have been willing to believe pretty much anything at that point.

Other than Kona, I'd never had to tell anyone about all of it— Namid, the craft, the phasings. My father already understood, and my mother would have as well, having lived with my father. There were a few street sorcerers, like Orestes, who knew, but again, they hadn't needed an explanation. Billie wouldn't understand much of this at first. She might not even believe me; some people didn't believe magic was real.

By the same token, she deserved some explanation for what she'd seen in the club. And before long I wanted to tell her everything.

"Fearsson?"

But not tonight.

"Can we walk while I try to explain?"

She hesitated, then nodded. We started down the alley. I tried to sense the sorcerer, but he wasn't around. Maybe Namid had driven him off before doing whatever he'd done to ease my pain.

"Do you believe in the occult?"

"The occult? You mean witchcraft? Voodoo? Stuff like that?"

"Yeah, basically."

"I've heard people talk about it. I guess you could say that I'm a skeptic."

"I figured you'd say that."

She stopped walking. "You're telling me that was voodoo?" she said, gesturing over her shoulder at the club. "Come on, Fearsson. You can do better than that."

I stopped as well, and turned to face her. I didn't have the energy for this. "Not voodoo precisely," I said. "But that's kind of what we're talking about."

"You're serious, aren't you?"

She was frowning now. I thought she even seemed a little bit afraid of me.

"I could lie to you. I could tell you that my father had a heart attack when he was in his thirties, and now it's my turn. But I don't want to do that."

She started walking again. When she reached me, I fell in step beside her.

"Voodoo," she muttered again.

"It's not voodoo," I said. "Stop saying it like that. Voodoo is a religion. Some of its practitioners dabble in the craft, but for the most part voodoo is a word that people use to describe things they don't fully understand."

"The craft?" she said. "Wasn't that a movie?"

I shrugged. "It might have been."

"You said when we got to the club that your work tonight could be dangerous, and that you thought you'd been followed before. Did you know something like this would happen?"

I almost said, *Yes, but I hoped I could ward myself.* But I stopped myself in time. "I was afraid it might," I told her. "I didn't know how bad it would be."

She eyed me. "How bad was it?"

I stared at the street in front of me. "It was pretty bad."

"You're closing down on me again, Fearsson. How bad was it?"

I took a breath and looked at her. "I'm not entirely sure why I'm still alive."

For a long time she didn't say anything. Finally, she nodded, and faced forward again. "That's how it seemed."

I could tell she still didn't know what to make of all this, or whether she should even believe me. But she hadn't dumped me yet, so I figured I was doing all right.

"I bet dates with Joel aren't this exciting," I said, chancing a joke.

She wasn't in the mood for that yet.

"Why would someone who . . . who does . . . ?"

"Magic?" I offered.

"All right. Why would they be after you?"

I didn't answer; I could see that she was working it out herself.

"Unless magic had something to do with what happened to Claudia, and with the murders of all those kids." Her eyes went so wide it might have been funny under different circumstances. "Did it?"

"I think it's possible."

She shook her head. I could see her racing to catch up with each new implication. "But you understood what was happening. You anticipated it. So this isn't new for you. Somehow you're used to this."

"There's more magic in the world than you might think. More than most people know."

"Do you know how crazy that sounds?"

"Why?" I asked. "You know that there are sorcerers in the world. Is it really that much of a surprise that some of them are here in Phoenix? Just because most of us don't see magic in our everyday lives, that doesn't mean that it's not out there."

"Don't get all philosophical on me. That's a different conversation."

"I'm not sure it is. Ask yourself why you're having so much trouble believing all of this. Is it because you think I'm lying to you?"

"No."

"Is it because you think I'm crazy?"

"I'm still working that one out."

I laughed. She didn't.

"I'm not crazy," I said again. How many times did a person have to say that before it stopped being true? "I know crazy. My dad is . . . I believe the clinical explanation is that he has psychotic episodes."

"You told me that you've had psychological problems before. And now you're saying that you have a history of mental illness in your family?"

I could tell I was starting to lose her.

"His problems were a lot like mine," I said. "And the delusions he has started much later in life."

"He has delusions?"

Good move, Fearsson. "Sometimes. But that's not what happened to me tonight. He's never imagined pain like that. I promise you."

She seemed to consider this, though I could tell she wasn't convinced. Not by a long shot. "Okay," she said. "Let's assume for a moment that this was magic, that someone put some kind of hex on you."

"All right."

"And let's assume as well that whoever it was really did want you dead. Why are you still alive?"

God, I hated lying to her. But this didn't seem like the time to introduce the concept of Namid, the magical ghost who only I could see. "The spell failed," I said instead.

It was circular logic, like saying that I woke up because I stopped sleeping. But Billie was on unfamiliar ground, and she let it go.

"That happens?"

"Of course. That's why it's called a craft. It's not automatic. The effectiveness of any magic is limited by the abilities of the person wielding it."

We were almost back to the Z-ster. Again I tried to sense the sorcerer, but it seemed that we were still safe. Billie said nothing until we got to the car and I unlocked the door for her—the Z-ster was a vintage car; no automatic locks. I started around to the driver's side, but Billie caught my arm.

"I'm going to need some time, Fearsson."

My heart sank. I understood, but I'd hoped that somehow we could get past it. I should have known better.

"I know," I said, putting on a brave smile. "We're in no rush here."

She let me go.

I drove her back to her house and walked her to the door. Neither of us had much to say.

"How are you feeling?" she asked, after we'd stood in awkward silence for a few moments.

I told her the truth. "I feel like I've been worked over."

"You really thought you were going to die?"

"I was pretty sure of it."

She reached out and rubbed my arm, concern and fear and sadness all mingling on her features, until her face resolved at last into a slight frown. Her hand lingered on my arm, though. "You should get some sleep," she said after a while.

"I'd like to, but I have someone I have to see." Checking my watch, I saw that it was already ten-thirty. "Soon."

"What?" she said. "Who?"

"A guy named Antoine Mirdoux. He called me earlier. Said he needed to talk to me about the case."

"Is he a magician?"

"Most people call them sorcerers, sometimes mystes. And yes, he is."

She blinked. "I was kidding."

"I know you were. But he is."

She raised her eyebrows and nodded once. "Okay, then. This has been an interesting evening." She turned and unlocked the door to her house.

I waited until she turned to face me again, and then I leaned toward her and kissed her forehead. "Don't give up on me yet, okay?"

"Wouldn't do me a bit of good anyway. You'd just slip me a love potion."

I grinned, and so did she.

"Would you rather I didn't call for a while?" I asked.

"I'll call you," she said.

"All right. Good night."

I walked back to the car.

"I really will call," she said.

I reached the Z-ster and glanced back at her. "Good."

Namid was sitting in the passenger seat when I got in, but I ignored him until I had pulled away from Billie's house. No sense in throwing more fuel on the fire by appearing to talk to myself.

"You are all right, Ohanko?" he asked.

"Yes. Thank you. You saved my life."

"I told you the woman was a distraction."

I cast an angry look his way. "That's not fair. He would have attacked me whether she'd been there or not. And we both know that I'm nowhere near strong enough to fight him off."

"You are wrong. You could have warded yourself if you had been prepared. But you tried to ward her as well, and you almost died."

I couldn't argue. "You told me that there would be a cost," I said after several seconds, the memory seeming to come from a great distance. "You were saving me, and I said I didn't know that you could. And you said, 'I can't.' What did you mean?"

"We runemystes are not supposed to meddle so in the affairs of humans. We are not even supposed to have that ability. I sensed though that I could this time. I do not know what it means. I do know that when I saved your life, I went against the laws of my kind. Already the others know of this, and have called for a conclave to speak of what I have done."

"Will you be punished?"

"Possibly."

I wondered how one punished a runemyste. Could they take away his powers? Could they hurt him? I almost asked, but Namid was always tight-lipped about these things. He'd already told me more than I would have expected.

"I'm sorry," I finally said.

"You must be careful. I will not be able to intervene again. If this runecrafter makes another attempt on your life, you will face him alone."

"I haven't sensed him since the club. Did you do something to him?"

"It is enough that I showed myself. My kind are feared by the dark ones. He knows now that you and I are linked, and he will be more careful the next time he assails you. But assail you he will. You are more of a threat to him now. Our bond will give him pause, it may even make him fear you. But ultimately it will make him ever more determined to kill you."

A joke leaped to mind, but I kept it to myself. Most of the time Namid thought my humor inappropriate, and tonight I was inclined to agree with him.

"I'll tread like the fox," I said, trying to smile.

Namid nodded. Then he vanished.

CHAPTER 16

I wanted nothing more than to go home, take a hot shower, and curl up in my bed for a day or two. Even as I began the drive into Mountain View, I considered blowing off my appointment with Antoine. It wasn't as though he and I had hit it off the day we spoke. Let him handle his own damn problems. That's what I told myself anyway.

As if in response, I heard again his voice on the phone. He'd been terrified. The guy hated me; he wouldn't have made the call if he hadn't been desperate. Besides, I probably wouldn't get any sleep anyway. I had a feeling that it would be a long time before I could close my eyes without reliving those terrifying moments on the floor of Robo's.

Driving through this part of Phoenix by day was depressing. It didn't take a genius to see that hope had abandoned these neighborhoods years ago, leaving a residue of despair and bitterness that seemed to coat the homes and shops, even the streets themselves, like dust from a desert wind storm. But at night, this area, like Maryvale and Estrella Mountain and parts of Cactus Park, became something else entirely. Hopelessness gave way to fear; misery turned to rage. Violence, as Mick Jagger once put it, was just a shot away. Even cops didn't like to venture here after dark. Kona and I had investigated more murders in south central Phoenix than I cared to count, but I'd never gotten used to it.

Now I was alone, and I didn't like it at all. I started going over my phone conversation with Antoine in my mind, searching for any indication that this might be a trap. Maybe Billie was right and I was getting paranoid. The first time I met the kid, though, I thought he might be working with the red sorcerer. And here I was, maybe an hour after Red had come within a hair's breadth of killing me, going to meet Antoine at his home. Either I was too stupid for words, or . . . well, that was the only option coming to mind.

I decided that I would park a short distance from the house, like I had last time, and approach on foot. I didn't want Antoine trying to kill me again, and the Z-ster didn't exactly blend in on these streets.

As soon as I turned the corner onto Antoine's street I knew that I wouldn't have to creep up on the place after all. I parked in front of the kid's house and sat there, staring at the ruin, my stomach knotting like wet rope.

I knew without getting out of the car that Antoine was dead. All of his wardings were gone. I assumed they had been torn to shreds by the pulsing crimson magic that now covered the house. But there wasn't even a trace of them left. Had he been alive there would have been something. It was one of the fundamental principles of magic: spells died with the sorcerer who crafted them.

That red glow seemed to be a message in and of itself, a marquee of sorts, announcing to all who had the power to see it that there was a new act in town. It clung to the windows. It shone from the twisted hinges and shattered remains of Antoine's new front door. And it glimmered from within the house as well, flickering like some weird red television screen. Yet, for all the magic I could see, I sensed nothing at all. The red sorcerer had been here—there was no doubt about that—but he wasn't around now, unless he had managed to mask himself somehow.

To be safe, I pulled my weapon from under the driver's seat, where I'd hidden it before leaving home, got out of the car, and approached the house. I glanced around, but saw no one. My weapon held ready, I walked up the cracked cement path to the door.

The inside of the house looked no better than the outside. What little furniture had been there was in shambles. The television had been knocked to the floor, the tube smashed and gleaming red with the sorcerer's power. A table lay in pieces near the kitchen, and two chairs had been overturned.

I found Antoine in the bedroom, and upon seeing him had to fight to keep from being sick. His chest had been blackened; I assumed the red sorcerer had killed him with the same burning magic he had used to cauterize my heart. There wasn't much left of his face, either. It was hard to tell in the dim light where his blood ended and the gleaming remains of the sorcerer's magic began.

The bedroom was in far better shape than the living room had been. Forced to guess, I would have said that Red had charged into the house intent on killing Antoine; he cornered the kid in the back of the house, at which point he had no reason to do any more damage. He wanted Antoine, and once the kid was dead, he left.

I made a quick search of the house, hoping to find anything that might link Antoine to Claudia's death or to the other Blind Angel murders. But Antoine's home was modest; there were few places to hide anything, and fewer still that remained in one piece. I knew enough about crime scenes to stay clear of Antoine's body.

I had the scrying stone with me—I had decided before leaving home to pick up Billie that I'd be wise to carry it with me at all times, like a real sorcerer. I tried a seeing spell now, hoping that 'Toine might be able to show me the red sorcerer. At first I used a shirt from the kid's bedroom to link the magic to him. It worked initially. He was watching TV and rolling a joint. But then there was a noise outside the house that seemed to catch 'Toine's attention. He stood, and at that point the images stopped. I went back to 'Toine's body and, feeling like a ghoul, dabbed a bit of his blood on the underside of the stone. Blood should have given me a stronger vision than clothing. But when I tried the spell a second time the same thing happened. Either 'Toine had blacked out, or the red sorcerer had found some way to block my seeing spells. I was betting on the latter.

After I'd convinced myself that there was nothing to be found in the house, I grabbed a paper napkin from the kitchen. Then I went to the phone, took the receiver off the cradle, taking care to keep the napkin between my hand and the plastic, and punched in 911, again using the napkin to avoid leaving any fingerprints.

I heard the emergency operator come on the line, her voice thin as smoke as she asked if anyone was there. I left without responding. They'd dispatch someone to the house soon enough, and I wanted to put some distance between myself and the crime scene before the police arrived. Hibbard was eager for any excuse to mess with me, and a fresh corpse would have been like manna from heaven for him.

I got back in the car and started for home. Three blocks from Antoine's house, I turned due west, deciding in that moment to check on Orestes. Call it a hunch. Brother Q had sent me to Antoine Mirdoux, and Mirdoux was dead.

Two blocks from Q's place, I floored the gas. Already I could see the red glow lighting the sky. There was some orange mingled with it, though not much. Orestes was still alive.

I had my Glock in the pocket of my bomber, and as I jumped out of the car and ran toward Q's door, I pulled it out again.

"Orestes?" I called.

From the outside, the place looked like it had been bombed. His door, like Antoine's, had been ripped off the hinges and shattered. Windows were broken, and some of the building's siding was blackened, as was a good portion of the roof.

The inside of Orestes' store had been trashed. Broken vials of oils and herbs covered the floor, and the place smelled like two armies of conjurers had done battle with nothing but incense and brews. The remnants of Brother Q's wardings still bordered the cracked windows and the door frame, but they flickered and hung there, weak, dim, limp, like the tatters of old orange curtains in a long-abandoned house. Red magic gleamed everywhere. A trail of it led toward the back of the store. I followed.

The small room behind the cash register was in shambles as well— more broken jars and dark stains on the old wooden floors from spilled oils and ointments, their smell mingled with the heavy stink of smoke. A narrow stairway, lit by red and orange conjuring, led to the second floor. I began to climb, holding my weapon with both hands, the stairs creaking beneath me.

As I neared the top of the stairway, I peered over the edge of the floor into Orestes' small apartment. And as soon as I did, I felt the pulse of power. It was hot and moving fast and aimed directly at my head. I ducked. It flew over me and slammed into the wall of the stairway, raining burning pieces of wood and charred plaster down on me. I smelled burning hair, and brushed a flaming fragment off my head. Only then, thinking about it, did I realize that the magic I'd seen hurtling toward me had been orange.

"Orestes, you idiot! It's me, Jay Fearsson!"

"Show yourself then!" Orestes called. "Let Brother Q see!"

He was talking in third person; he couldn't have been hurt too badly.

"No way! You'll try to blow my head off again!"

Q didn't answer, and I started to wonder if he was gearing up for another assailing spell. I pulled my wallet free and flipped it open to my PI license.

"I'm going to hold up my ID, Orestes. Don't blow my hand off, okay?"

Still no answer. I took a deep breath and lifted my hand.

After several seconds I heard, "Brother J? That really you?"

"It's me. You all right?"

"Brother Q in a bad way, boy. Nearly got himself blown up today."

I think it was an attempt at verse, but I couldn't be sure. "I'm coming up, all right?"

"Yeah. All right."

The apartment was even more of a mess than the store had been. Shards of glasses and old plates covered the floor, crunching like snow under my feet as I crossed to the bed. Q's pine and cinder block bookshelves had toppled, littering much of the room with old books and crystals. His mattress had been burned black, and was still smoking.

Q sat on the floor on the far side of what remained of his bed frame, his back against the wall. Blood from several deep gashes covered his face, and he had a nasty burn on his left cheek and temple. One of his legs was fractured; a bloodied, jagged end of the bone protruded through his pants leg. From the way he was holding his right arm, I guessed that it was broken, too.

"You don't look so good, Q."

There was a large pool of blood around his leg, and a good deal more soaked into his jeans. I knelt down in front of him and studied his eyes. They were glazed over, but it was too dark to see if his pupils were dilated. He might well have been in shock, or at least on his way.

"Where's your phone?"

"Q ain't seen it," he said. His voice sounded strong enough.

"Is there even one up here?" I asked, surveying the damage.

"Most of the time."

I found it under a pile of books. For the second time that night I dialed 911. When the operator came on, I told her to send an ambulance to Orestes' address.

"It might be a good idea to send the fire department, too," I added, before hanging up.

Returning to Q, I examined his leg with more care. Because of the compound fracture, I couldn't apply any pressure to stop the bleeding, at least not without causing him a lot of pain. I tore a strip a cloth from the bed sheets and tied a tourniquet a couple of inches above the break. I didn't tie it too tight—I didn't want him to lose the leg any more than I wanted him bleeding to death.

"Why did he attack you, Q?" I asked as I worked.

"It was that badass," he said. "Remember the one Q told you about?"

"Yeah, I remember. I recognized the color of his magic. But why'd he do it? What'd you do to piss him off?"

"Q still doesn't know. Q hasn't even met the man."

I paused in what I was doing. "You're telling me that you don't know this guy at all?"

"Brother Q told you that last time."

"You ever hear the name Cahors?" I asked him.

"Ca-what?"

"Cahors. It's French."

He shook his head. "Never heard it before."

"Then why would he attack you? Why would the guy come in here, and bust up your place, and leave you half-dead if he doesn't even know you?"

"Q has no idea. He was just mindin' his own business and that man came and blowed down Q's door like the big bad wolf, y'know?"

"Did you get a look at him?"

"Brother Q saw his eyes," he said, his voice dropping to a whisper. "There's evil in that man."

"What color were his eyes?" I knew the answer. At this point I was trying to keep him talking.

"They were light. Blue. Gray maybe. They was almost white. Strange, scary, you know?"

"What else? Is he white?"

"Did you ever see a brother with eyes like that?"

I heard a siren approaching, but it kept going past. I wondered if it was a cruiser on its way to check out Antoine's place.

"Tell me more. I need to find this guy."

"He's tall, lanky, you know?"

"Hair?"

"Nope."

I laughed. "He was bald again, huh?"

"What do you mean, 'again'?"

"I've seen him twice: once with hair and once without."

"Well, he's shaved now. To Q that doesn't always look right on a white man, but it worked for this guy. Made him look mean."

"All right. Thanks. That should help."

"Stay clear of this guy, Brother J. Let someone else bring him down. He's bad to the core."

"I know he is. He's had a busy night. He's already been to Antoine's place. Kid wasn't as lucky as you were."

Orestes had closed his eyes, but he opened them now. "'Toine's dead?"

I nodded.

"Damn. Boy that young should never get mixed up with a dude like this. 'Toine wasn't ready for big time."

"He almost killed me, too. He attacked me at Robo's."

Orestes appraised me with a critical eye. "You don't look so bad."

"I should be dead. My runemyste saved me."

His eyebrows went up. "You've got a runemyste? Q didn't know that." He gave a slow nod; I'd impressed him. "There's more to Brother J than meets the eye."

"That's between you and me."

"Yeah," he said. "All right."

I glanced at my watch. Where the hell was that ambulance? I untied the tourniquet, allowing some blood to flow into Q's leg. Then I tied it again. I thought about trying a seeing spell, but I didn't figure it would work any better here than it had at 'Toine's.

"Is there anything else you can tell me? Any idea why a weremyste this powerful would be killing kids on the quarter moon?"

"Q told you already. He doesn't know anythin' about that."

"I remember you saying so. But look around you. This is serious now. If you've got any connection with this guy, any at all, now's the time to tell me."

"*You* look around, Brother J. Q's got somethin' now. Least, he did. House, store. Why would Q wanna mess that up by gettin' involved with this Blind Angel dude? That'd just be dumb."

I rubbed a hand over my face. He was right.

"Then why'd this guy come after you?"

Orestes shrugged. I heard another siren in the distance, approaching fast.

"That'll be your ambulance."

"Q ain't got money for an ambulance."

"You need to see a doctor. We'll deal with the rest later."

He didn't argue, and we listened to the changing pitch of the siren.

"The other day when I came here, what made you think 'Toine had something to do with this guy?" I asked him.

"Q hears things," he said, his eyes closed. "'Toine was into all kinds of bad doin's. Not just drugs. Word was he did some pimpin'. An' word was your badass was after kids, ones who had trouble, you know?"

Something clicked into place in my mind. Of all the things that Q could have told me about Antoine, that made the most sense. A guy like Red wouldn't want to take a chance on finding a suitable victim on the night of the quarter moon. Not if he was planning some kind of magic that had specific demands. He would have wanted to have a target picked out ahead of time, and even being able to disguise himself, he would have stood out too much in the neighborhoods he needed to frequent to find the kids he wanted for the killing spells he'd been casting. 'Toine could do that for him.

But what, if anything, did Shari Bettancourt have in common with Antoine Mirdoux? Was she finding kids for him, too? Was that why she had that necklace? And even if she and 'Toine were helping the guy identify possible victims, how had they found Claudia Deegan? I would have liked to go back to 'Toine's house to search for something that resembled Shari's pendant. But by now the place must have been crawling with cops.

"What are you thinkin' there, Brother J?" Q asked.

I shook my head. "I'm playing catch-up. This guy's been way ahead of me from the start, but I may have finally figured something out."

The siren wailed outside the house, then died away. I heard the rasp of a radio and then, a few seconds later, the slamming of the ambulance doors.

"Hello?" a voice called.

"Up here," I shouted in return. "Stairs are in the back."

I could hear another set of sirens now. Probably the fire department.

Two EMTs came up the stairs and hesitated as they took in the scene.

"Man, what happened here?" one of them asked.

My eyes met Q's. "Stove blew," I said after a few seconds.

"How long this tourniquet been on?" the EMT asked me.

"Since I called. But I released it once a few minutes ago."

He nodded. "Good deal."

I stood. "You're going to be all right, Q. I'll see you soon."

Orestes grabbed my hand. "Q won't forget this, Jay. He mean it. From now on, if you need to know somethin', Q will tell it, no charge, no shit."

I smiled. "Thanks." To the EMTs I said, "You're taking him to Samaritan?"

"Yup."

I nodded, and winked at Q.

He let my hand go, and I started down the stairs.

"Wait a minute," one of the guys said. "The stove's electric."

I heard Q chuckle, low and deep.

A crowd had gathered around Q's house, and they eyed me as I walked past to my car.

"What happened?" someone called to me.

Another voice said, "Is Brother Q all right?"

"He'll be fine," I answered and climbed into the Z-ster.

I started her up, but then sat idling, watching as the crowd parted and the fire trucks pulled up. Something other than that glowing gibbous moon was tugging at my mind, trying to make me see what should have been obvious. The moon was clouding my thoughts, making me feel sluggish and stupid.

"Think, Jay," I muttered, gripping the steering wheel.

If 'Toine was finding victims for the Blind Angel Killer—and that was just a guess on my part—he couldn't have been the only person doing so. I couldn't imagine that Claudia Deegan and Antoine Mirdoux had ever crossed paths. Claudia wouldn't have gone that far, no matter how much she might have wanted to rebel against her old man.

And that's when it hit me. Robby Sommer had been Claudia's dealer.

CHAPTER 17

I'd been at 'Toine's the third time I felt the sorcerer test my magic, and now the kid was dead. I'd been outside Robo's the second time, and I'd nearly died there a couple of hours ago.

The first time I'd felt the red sorcerer's magic, I'd been at Robby's house.

I threw the Z-ster into gear and raced away from Q's place, my tires screeching. It was a long drive back to Tempe from Maryvale, but by now the freeways were clear and I made good time.

When I arrived, though, it seemed that I needn't have bothered rushing.

Robby's place looked much the way it had the last time I saw it. There was no sign of the violence I'd seen at Orestes' house or at Antoine's. The door was still on its hinges, the windows were intact. There was a light on inside, which was a bit strange, given how late it was. But for all I knew, Robby was a night owl.

I got out of the car and walked up to his door. I'd even gone so far as to raise my hand to knock before I noticed that the door was already unlatched, and that there was a small but brilliant flare of crimson magic on the knob and lock. Seeing this tiny bit of craft, I was reminded once more—as if I could have forgotten—of how powerful this red sorcerer was. The stronger the magician, the faster the traces of his sorcery fade from view. The magic at Q's house had seemed bright, but compared with this, it was flat and dull. This magic, though, was as fresh as warm blood.

Once more, I pulled out my pistol and prepared to push the door open. I knew he could use magic to deflect bullets, but I also knew that I didn't have enough knowledge of assailing magic to hurt him. The Glock seemed my best bet.

My hands were shaking and I was breathing hard. Back when I was on the force, I was no braver than any other cop. I was no more a coward either. You learn to accept fear as part of the job, to manage it and live with it. But right then, I was really scared; as scared as I had been in years. Just the thought of going up against this guy so soon after Robo's made my chest ache. I tried to sense him and knew in an instant that he was near, though I wasn't sure that meant "in the house." I wasn't sure it didn't, either.

I took a breath and kicked the door open.

Robby was sprawled on the couch, his eyes open and fixed sightlessly on the ceiling. A bag of Spark lay beside him, his pipe sat on the coffee table in front of him. The television was on, but the sound was turned down low. Making as little noise as I could manage, I stepped through the living room and peeked around the corner into the kitchen. Nothing. Still holding my weapon, still expecting to be attacked at any moment, I followed a corridor toward the back of the house, edging along the wall. I reached a door, counted to three in my head, and kicked it open. It appeared to be a spare room. An electric guitar leaned against one wall, an amplifier beside it. A bike was propped against the closet door. Otherwise the room was empty. I checked the closet but found only a few cardboard boxes filled with books and junk. The bathroom was across the hall from this room. It was empty, too, as was Robby's bedroom, which was all the way in the back.

I exhaled, relieved. As much as I wanted to catch this guy, I didn't want to face him tonight. I tucked my Glock into my belt against my back and returned to the living room.

I checked Robby for a pulse, but I knew I wouldn't find one. There was a small but bright red glimmering around his head and neck, but to anyone who couldn't see magic he would appear unmarked.

I'd had enough of this guy killing off my leads and hurting my friends. I wasn't crazy about him attacking me, either. But most of all, I resented the fact that he always seemed to be one step ahead of me.

I reached for the phone to call the police yet again, but then I stopped myself. Robby wasn't going anywhere, and it was possible that a quick search of the house might turn up something tangible that would connect Robby with 'Toine and Shari.

My first thought was to use the scrying stone, but I knew from 'Toine's place that it wouldn't work here. Then something occurred to me. I pulled out the stone and fished in my jacket pocket for the evidence bag containing Claudia's hair. I still had it with me. Whatever else this case might have done for me, it was making me an expert at seeing-spells.

I chanted the spell to myself, and a moment later, there was Robby, sitting on the same couch he was lying on now. He was adjusting a scale, measuring out Spark for a sale.

I told you this was good stuff, Claud, he said, his eyes fixed on the balance. *It costs, too. So I gotta make sure that the bags are right, you know? I don't wanna be giving away too much, and I sure don't want someone coming back at me claiming that I shorted them.*

I wouldn't do that.

He glanced up at her and smiled. *I know you wouldn't. But I wouldn't want to shortchange you, you know? You least of all.*

She didn't answer and a moment later she started to glance through his DVD collection. I had the feeling she didn't like the turn their conversation had taken.

Just hurry it up, she said, her voice low.

You still with that Tilo guy?

Don't, Robby. You and I are history, and I'd like to forget about it, all right?

I'm just asking.

You're not just asking. You never just ask.

He said nothing, and a moment later he turned his attention back to the scale. He fiddled with it for a few seconds. Then, with utmost care, he brushed the Spark he'd laid out into a bag and handed it to her. *Check that out.*

For severals moment Claudia stared at it.

Eyeing the stuff lying beside Robby's body, I understood why. In all the years I'd worked narcotics I'd never seen Spark like this. The color was so deep, so rich, it reminded me of desert dirt, the kind you might see in Monument Valley or the Superstition Wilderness.

Where did you get this? she asked.

Usual place. My scalper said he'd found some great stuff, and, man, did he ever. I've tried it, he said, his eyes widening. It's amazing. He nodded. *You want some now? On the house?* He was lying to her. Spark was a blocker—it wouldn't have gotten Robby high; it might have made the phasing less intense, but he wouldn't have gotten off on it. Of course, she wouldn't have known this.

I better not, she said. *Thanks, though.*

She rolled up the bag and put it in her pack. Then she pulled out a wad of twenty-dollar bills and handed it to Robby.

There you go, she said. *Three-sixty.*

Robby made a quick count and smiled at her. *Thanks, Claud. Always a pleasure taking your money.*

I don't like your new prices. I might have to start shopping elsewhere.

You say that now, but after you try this stuff you won't think twice about what it cost. I promise. Cleanest burn you ever had.

At one-eighty a 'g' it better be. She swung her pack onto her shoulder, walked to the door and pulled it open. *Later, Robby. Thanks.*

Close the door, Claud! You want the whole neighborhood to see what I got here?

She laughed. *Hey, everybody!* she called, raising her voice. *Check out Robby's stuff!*

He jumped up, yanked her back into the house, and slammed the door.

Claudia pulled her arm out of his grasp and rubbed it. *Geez, Robby!*

Geez, yourself! You think that was funny?

Yeah. It was just a joke.

Robby shook his head. *You're unbelievable. That kind of shit might be funny for a Deegan, but for the rest of us, it's not. In case you didn't know, this stuff's illegal. If I'm caught dealing again, I'll probably get thrown in jail for the rest of my life.*

I know it's illegal, she said, sounding sullen.

Well, you don't act like it. I guess you think Daddy will pull your ass out of the fire if anything happens, right?

Fuck you, Robby!

He seemed to deflate, and he twisted his mouth. *Sorry,* he said. *That was outta line.*

Yeah, it was. She pulled the door open again, though not too widely this time. *I gotta go.*

Right.

Claudia left, closing the door behind her, and the image faded.

So she had bought her drugs from Robby, and Sommer had been telling the truth about their relationship. He hadn't mentioned, though, that she'd ticked him off the last time he saw her alive, and it seemed he'd lied to me about knowing the Blind Angel Killer. I didn't think it had been Robby's intention to point out Claudia to Red. He cared about her too much. But I'd have bet every dollar in my pocket that the sorcerer had been watching Robby's house, and had chosen her from a distance, without knowing who she was. That was the only way to explain why Claudia Deegan would have ended up a victim of the same murderer who'd killed Gracia Rosado, Maria Santana, and the others.

I didn't want to take too much more time here, but I wanted to search all the rooms before I dialed 911 yet again. Maybe Robby had a red stone, too. I started in the living room—a bit of a misnomer with a corpse in the middle of it, but I tried to ignore that. There was drug paraphernalia everywhere. The open bag of Spark next to Robby was one of several lying in plain sight. A couple of the others were pretty big; glancing around the room I could see close to ten thousand dollars worth of the drug. The scale was still there on the table, and beside it a box loaded with empty plastic bags, waiting to be filled. All of it struck me as being a bit heavy-handed. It was almost as if the red sorcerer had left Robby as an offering to the PPD.

Robby wasn't wearing a pendant, and I didn't know where he would have kept a stone like Shari's. Not that it had to be a stone; I would have been satisfied with finding anything—other than Robby himself—that had red magic on it. But after a few minutes of this I stopped in the middle of the room, staring at the body again. I had that same dull feeling in my head—the damn moon. Why would Red care what the police thought about Robby's death? He'd had a busy night: trying to burn a hole in my chest, destroying Q's place, killing 'Toine and Robby. But he hadn't made any effort to hide the rest of what he'd done. He'd tried to kill me in a crowded club. His attacks on the two street sorcerers—Q and 'Toine—had been brutal, spectacular even. He'd left their homes in shambles.

He could have blown the door off of Robby's house, too. But his touch here had been as gentle as it had been rough in Maryvale and Mountain View.

I surveyed the room, trying to see it as I would if I was still a cop. The drugs scattered all over the room, Robby dead on the couch. And me standing right in the middle of it.

Once again it came to me in a rush. "Damn!"

I crossed to the phone in two quick strides, intending to bypass 911 and call Kona's direct line.

Before I could pick up the receiver, I heard a light footfall outside the window. I dropped into a crouch and again pulled my weapon free, which seemed at the time like a perfectly reasonable thing to do. Turns out it wasn't such a great idea.

Every light in the house went out. I heard both the front and back doors being rammed open at the same time, and seconds later there were several bright lights shining in my eyes and a number of guys carrying what appeared in the darkness to be very large weapons ordering me to drop my pistol and lie down on the floor.

They identified themselves as Phoenix Police, and I had no reason to doubt them. This had the feel of a narcotics bust. And here I was, an ex-cop who'd left the force amid rumors of drug and alcohol abuse, with my pistol drawn in the house of a known dealer, who happened to be dead on the couch. I could imagine the big, shit-eating grin on Cole Hibbard's face when he heard about this.

By the time the lights came on again, I had been cuffed, and a guy was standing over me with his foot resting on my back and his shotgun aimed at the nape of my neck.

Another cop squatted down next to my head. He was a big guy, mid-forties maybe. Sandy hair. I didn't recognize him. He was in plain clothes, but he had on a dark blue windbreaker. I'd seen jackets like that before—I was pretty sure it had "PPD NARCOTICS" stenciled on the back.

"What's your name, buddy?"

"Jay Fearsson," I said. "I'm a PI. My license is in my wallet."

"Fearsson?"

"Yeah. I used to be on the job."

I saw him nod, but he didn't seem in a hurry to take off my cuffs and invite me out for coffee and doughnuts.

"That your car out front?" he asked. "The 280Z?"

"Yeah, that's mine."

"How long have you been here?"

"Maybe fifteen minutes. I found the door unlocked."

"So you just thought you'd let yourself in."

"At this time of night, I thought something might be wrong, so yeah, I walked in. Listen, can you at least help me up. Carrying on a conversation with my face on the floor isn't as much fun as you might think."

The cop glanced up at the guy standing over me and nodded. A moment later, I was hoisted to my feet.

The cop I'd been talking to began to inform me of my Miranda rights.

I cut him off. "I understand my rights," I said. "I'll answer any questions you have."

"You're waiving your right to have an attorney present at questioning?"

"Yes, I am. Ask your questions."

The two cops exchanged glances.

"How do you know the kid?" the cop asked me, taking out a pencil and pad.

"I remembered Robby from when I was a cop. I knew he'd been dealing for a while, and when I was hired by the Deegan family to look into Claudia Deegan's death, I came to him, to find out if he sold Claudia her stuff. They were an item for a while."

"Sommer and Deegan?" the cop said.

I nodded.

"How'd he die?"

"I have no idea. He was dead when I found him."

"Can you account for your whereabouts tonight?"

"I was at Robo's from about eight to ten. I dropped off my date at ten-thirty and drove to the Maryvale eight-thirteen to see a friend. Turned out there'd been an accident at his place and he was hurt. So I called 911 and waited with him until the ambulance arrived. Then I came here."

"Busy night," the cop said.

"Busier than I would have liked."

"What's your date's name?"

"Billie Castle. She's a political blogger. Maybe you've heard of her."

He ignored that. "And the hurt friend?"

"Orestes Quinley."

That got his attention. "Quinley?"

"Q and I have been friends for a long time. I'm the only cop who's ever arrested him and gotten the charges to stick."

The cop grinned. "And that's the basis of your friendship?"

"When I was still on the job, he helped me out a few times. I still go to him for information."

"All right, Fearsson. You know we have to take you in, right? I mean, the kid's dead, you're in the house, you're carrying a weapon."

"I understand." He nodded to the other cop again and started to walk away.

"Tell me something," I said, stopping him. "What are you guys doing here?"

"We've been watching Sommer for a while now—several months. Like you say, he's been dealing for a long time."

"Yeah, but why bust in on him tonight?"

"We got a call, a tip. Said there was a big deal going on here tonight."

"When did the call come in?"

"Maybe an hour ago."

"What time is it now?"

He squinted at his watch. "A little bit after one."

An hour ago. Red must have made the call moments after killing Robby. He might even have made the call from here, maybe after retrieving his red stone. Had he taken one from 'Toine's place, too? Was that why he'd torn it apart? Regardless of the rest, I was sure that he'd set me up. Was I being that predictable?

"Thanks," I said. "Listen, can you do me a favor?"

The cop frowned.

"It's nothing big," I told him. "Just give a call to Kona Shaw in Homicide. Tell her I've been arrested, and where, and under what circumstances. She'll do the rest."

His expression remained sour and for a moment I thought he might say no. But I was an ex-cop, and that still counted for something. And I don't think he believed I'd killed Robby. He was covering all the bases by having me taken in. I would have done the same in his position.

"Sure," he said. He even pulled out his pad and pencil again. "Kona Shaw, you say?"

"She was my partner."

He wrote it down, then nodded to me. "I'll make the call."

"Thanks."

He walked toward the back of the house, then stopped again. "You touch anything?" he asked.

"I kicked in a couple of doors down the hallway, thinking I might find someone here. Other than that, no."

The other cop led me outside and put me in a squad car. A crowd of people had gathered outside Robby's house, and I could feel their stares as I sat in the cruiser, waiting to be driven to central processing. Even knowing that I'd done nothing wrong, I couldn't help but feel humiliated. A couple of people yelled things at me, but I tried not to listen. I kept my head down, refusing to make eye contact with anyone. It occurred to me then that every cop should be put through this at least once, so that they could know how it feels to be on the other side.

When two of the cops finally got in the front of the car and we pulled away from the curb, I leaned back and closed my eyes, glad to be putting some distance between myself and the crowd. I never thought I'd be so pleased to be on my way to jail.

CHAPTER 18

True to his word, the cop from narcotics called Kona. And she did the rest, just as I'd known she would.

In this case, doing the rest meant placing a call to Mateo Fuentes, in the public defender's office. Mateo had been working in the P.D. office for several years now, and I can tell you as a former cop that I hated it when Mateo worked one of my cases. The guy was tenacious, brilliant, articulate, and sneaky as hell. In other words, he was the perfect trial lawyer. He could have made a mint in private practice, but he never went that route. Don't get me wrong: public defenders are, as a rule, good people and they tend to be good lawyers—competent if not spectacular. But generally speaking, the shining stars in the P.D. office can find better jobs with the D.A. or in private practice. Public defense is crap work. At least half the time the lawyers there find themselves defending people they know or suspect are guilty. The pay is low compared with what most lawyers make, and the hours are nothing special.

Most guys with Mateo's talent would have been out of there years ago. But Mateo was a believer. He felt that he owed something to the community, and he was convinced that poor Latinos often didn't get a fair shake from the legal system. Hell, I couldn't argue the point. So he pulled in a modest salary, he drove a Ford compact instead of a BMW sedan, and he fought for the legal rights of the folks in his community.

Despite the fact that he had shredded me in court a couple of times, and had managed to spring at least two guys who I know to this day were guilty, I liked Mateo a lot. And seeing as I was now in jail, I wanted him in my corner.

He was there at the door to my holding cell at seven a.m. sharp, his suit rumpled, but a great big smile on his face.

"Fearsson," he said. "Got yourself in a mess, didn't you?"

It's testament to how tired I was that I'd been lying on a stainless steel pallet and he still woke me from a sound sleep.

"Hey, Mateo," I said. "Still eating tamales, I see."

Mateo was a big guy. Not tall, mind you. Just big. The buttons on his dress shirts always seemed to be straining to the breaking point, and he walked with a bit of a waddle. I would have guessed that he was only a couple of years older than me—maybe in his mid-thirties— but I already worried that one of these days he was going to drop dead of a heart attack.

"Not true," he said, as the guard unlocked the door to my cell. "My wife has me on one of these no-fat, no-carb, no-protein diets."

I laughed and frowned at the same time. "It can't be all of those. That leaves nothing, but water."

He shrugged and made a face. "That's how it seems most of the time. Grab your coat. You're outta here."

I sat up, wincing as I did. My entire body hurt, though whether from the attack at Robo's or from sleeping on a metal bed I couldn't say for certain. "You posted my bond?"

"No bond. No evidence, no real cause, no case. No more jail."

I stood and grabbed my coat. "Really?"

"Yeah." We started walking. "I said something about the Constitution and they got all panicky. Decided they'd be better off letting you go."

"Mateo—"

He stopped, turned to face me. "The only charge that had any legs at all was aggravated burglary. You went into the dead guy's house, and you were carrying a weapon. Given that you knew the guy, given that you found the door unlocked at that hour, given that Kona was willing to vouch for you, it took me about ten seconds to get that reduced to trespassing, at which point they decided you really weren't worth their time."

I patted his shoulder. "You're a good man."

We walked on, following the corridor toward the front of the building.

"You're not supposed to use the P.D.'s office for stuff like this, Jay," he said. "I sprung you for old-time's sake, and because it was Kona who called me. But I have more important cases to deal with, and the office is pretty strapped right now."

"How about I pay you for your time then? Or rather," I said, knowing what he'd say to that, "how about if I pay the office?"

"You've got your own business now, don't you? Private investigations?"

"Yeah."

"How about you do some *pro bono* work for us? I don't have anything in mind right now. But in the future."

I stopped again and held out my hand. "Anytime," I said. "And every time. You understand?"

He shook my hand and grinned. "In that case, you can get your ass hauled off to jail whenever you like."

The jail seemed pretty well lit, but when I stepped outside, I had to shield my eyes from the sun and squint until they were almost closed. I remember as a kid visiting the mountains north of Flagstaff after a winter storm, and the sun on the fresh snow was the same way: so bright that it hurt. The only difference was, on this day it already had to be ninety degrees. I couldn't remember another spring as hot as this one.

When my eyes finally began to adjust, I saw Kona standing across the parking lot with her back to the building. She was talking to someone, and I started toward her.

"I'm parked over here," Mateo said, gesturing toward one of the side streets. He held out his hand again. "Stay out of trouble, all right?"

I shook his hand and grinned. "Thanks again, Mateo. I owe you."

"Buy me dinner, then. Just me, don't invite my wife. I want to be able to eat something."

"You got it."

I started walking toward Kona, knowing that I owed her, too. When I was about halfway to her, she turned to face me, and I saw that she was talking to Billie. I slowed.

Kona laughed at my expression. What choice did I have? I walked the rest of the way to them.

"Hey, partner," Kona said, still laughing. "I called Billie for you."

"I see that."

"I figured you'd need a ride back to your car, and believe it or not, I have more important things to do with my day."

"And Ms. Castle doesn't?"

Billie smiled; she was enjoying this. Who knew that giving me a hard time had become too big a job for one person?

"Sounds like you had a long night," Kona said a moment later, her expression growing serious.

"Even more than you know."

"Billie told me about the club. And I heard that you called the ambulance to Q's place. Plus Robby. That about cover it?"

"Not quite."

Kona's eyebrows went up. "Tell me."

"We off the record? I don't need any more trouble with the PPD today."

She hesitated, then nodded.

"You working another homicide from Mountain View? In the 733?"

She narrowed her eyes. "Yeah, now that you mention it. Antoine Mirdoux, right?" She pronounced his last name like "Murduchs".

"Actually, it's Mirdoux," I said, using the French pronunciation. "Antoine was Creole."

She nodded. "Should have known that."

"Anyway, I made the 911 call from his place."

"What were you doin' there?"

"I talked to Antoine a few days ago, same day I went to see Orestes. Q thought he had some connection to our guy. Turns out he was right. The guy who killed Robby also killed Antoine, and nearly took out Q."

"Robby died of an overdose."

I shook my head. "No, he didn't. There was . . ." My eyes flicked toward Billie. "I saw that color on him, too."

"Damn it," she said. "So, you're telling me I now have three murders that I have to explain to Hibbard and Arroyo?"

"Afraid so. What's happening on your end?"

"Not a whole lot," she said. "I did learn a bit more about Shari Bettancourt."

"Let me guess. She did some kind of community or charity work. Something that involved working with troubled kids."

Kona's jaw dropped. "How the hell did you know that? She'd been working at the free drug clinic in South Mountain for five years."

I nodded. "That figures."

"How?"

"I think that Antoine and Shari, and even Robby Sommer, have been helping our guy pick his targets. Or maybe he's been watching them for potential victims. But it's no coincidence that they're all dead."

"Damn. You've learned more in five days that we did in the last three years."

"Yeah," I said. "Well, don't get all happy just yet. If he's killing them off, that might mean that he doesn't need them anymore."

"You mean he might be done killing?"

I shook my head. "I doubt that. But I think he's been trying to . . ." I broke off, eyeing Billie once more. "I think he's had a specific purpose in mind all along, and if he doesn't need them anymore, that might mean he's succeeded. And that can't be good."

"No, I guess not."

"We have to find this guy, Kona."

"Sounds like you're well on your way to doing that."

"Yeah, if he doesn't kill me first. He nearly had me last night. I'm lucky I'm not lying in the OME with Robby and Antoine."

"How'd you fight him off?" Kona asked.

"I had help."

That took her a minute. Her eyes lit up. "You mean . . . ? He helped you?"

"First time for everything, right? He's taking this seriously."

Kona exhaled through pursed lips. "I guess."

"Hey!" I said, alarm bells going off in my head. I looked from Billie to Kona. "Did you make sure you were off the record before you started talking to her?"

Before Kona could answer, Billie scowled at me. "That's not fair, Fearsson!"

"No, it's not," Kona added. "*She* told *me* we were off the record."

I winced, then rubbed a hand over my brow. "I'm sorry, Billie. I had a long night."

Her expression didn't change, but after a few seconds she nodded.

Kona took my arm and led me a few steps away from Billie. "Listen," she said. "Along those lines, she was asking me some questions while we were waiting for you."

"What kind of questions?"

"She wanted to know if you'd ever spoken to me about magic."

Not surprising. "What did you tell her?"

"Well, I wasn't sure what to say. So I told her that you had, but that you were subject to occasional psychotic episodes, and you'd probably have forgotten all about it by now."

I stared at her. After a minute she started to laugh, as did Billie.

"What did you tell her, Kona?"

"She told me that you had," Billie said, walking over to us. "And she said that as weird as it sounded to her at first, she'd come to believe you." She shrugged. "So I'm wondering if I shouldn't do the same thing. I haven't made up my mind yet, but that's how I'm leaning."

"I like this one, Justis. Don't screw it up."

I had to laugh. "Thanks for the advice."

"I gotta go," Kona said. "You look terrible. Get some sleep, all right?"

"Yeah, I'll try."

We held each other's gazes for a few seconds. "I'll swing by your place after my shift ends," she said. An old ritual tied to the phasings.

"Thanks. See you then."

Kona smiled at Billie. "Nice to meet you."

"You, too."

Billie and I faced each other. After a few awkward seconds, Billie said, "She's great."

I nodded. "She was a good partner. Listen, I'm sorry about what I said. I was out of line."

She shrugged. "You had a rough night."

"Not that rough. I should have known better."

"Come on," she said. "Let's get you out of here. I know you miss being a cop, and hanging out around the city jail probably isn't the best cure for that."

Smart woman.

We started walking to Billie's car, which was parked in a municipal lot nearby.

"You missing work on account of me?" I asked.

"No. I wrote something last night that I scheduled to post this afternoon. I have the day free."

"Lucky for me, huh?"

"How are you feeling?"

"Tired mostly. A little sore from last night."

"Well, Kona's right. You should get some sleep."

We reached her car, got in, and she drove me to Tempe. My car was still there outside Robby Sommer's house. The place was deserted, but the police had left a strip of yellow crime-scene tape across his front door. Billie stared at it now; I could tell she was troubled.

"Who was he?" she asked.

"A drug dealer. He was also Claudia Deegan's boyfriend for a short while."

She nodded, shuddered. "How do you get used to this?"

"Who says I'm used to it?"

She turned to me. "Sorry. I just thought . . . I don't know. You don't seem upset."

"I'm not sure it's the same thing. I'm not going to mourn the loss of Robby Sommer. I don't think the world's that worse off without him. But you never get used to seeing people die, and I have every intention of finding the guy who killed him."

"You think it's the same person who killed Claudia? You think the Blind Angel Killer did it?"

I hesitated, but only for a second. "Yes. And I think he nearly killed me."

"Did he . . . ?" She pointed at Robby's house. "Was this person killed . . . ?"

"With magic?"

She nodded again.

"Yeah, I'm sure he was."

"This is getting weirder and weirder."

"Yes, it is. You know, I really need to get out of the city for a little while, to clear my head. You want to come with me."

"You need to sleep."

I shook my head. "I can't. I slept a little in the jail, and . . . I'll sleep tonight." That was a lie, but the rest was true.

Concern creased her forehead. "You're tired."

"The desert will help. It always does."

Billie continued to gaze at me for a few seconds more. Then she surprised me. "All right."

I smiled. "Good. I need to stop at my office first, then we can drive back out to the monument if you like."

She shook her head. "No, I want to meet your father."

That was the last thing I'd expected her to say. "My father? Billie, that's . . . I usually go to his place on Tuesdays."

"So this week you'll see him twice."

I let out a breathless laugh, shook my head, frowned. Boy, she'd caught me off guard. It had been years since I'd taken anyone out to my dad's place. Kona had come with me once, several years ago, and that had gone well. But still, taking Billie to meet him seemed . . . risky in some way.

"What I told you last night was true," I said. "He has these episodes. There's no telling what state he'll be in when we get there."

"Is he dangerous?"

"Of course not," I said without hesitation.

She shrugged. "Then I'll deal with it."

I didn't know her very well, yet. But I could tell when she had made up her mind.

"All right," I said, getting out of the car. "I need to stop by my office first. Follow me?"

We parked around the corner from the office and I led Billie inside.

"Wow, Fearsson," she said, turning a slow circle in the middle of the room. "I'm impressed."

Wood floors and a fancy coffee machine will do that, I guess.

I keep a fresh set of clothes at the office, just in case. I grabbed these now, and changed in the bathroom. Then I checked the answering machine. I had only two calls—the first was from an insurance company I'd worked for the month before. I'd quit because they were trying to deny a claim I'd told them to pay. Now they were threatening legal action if I didn't resume work on the case.

I glanced at Billie, and she grimaced.

"You get a lot of messages like that?" she asked.

"Not too many," I said. I erased that one and played the next.

"Fearsson?" said a voice on the machine, sounding young and

scared. "You there, dog? I know we said eleven, but . . . but we gotta do it sooner. I'm in trouble here, man. Real trouble. I'll be at my place. Come as you soon as you can."

"Who was that?" Billie asked.

"That was Antoine Mirdoux."

"Mirdoux," she said, her forehead creasing. "You mentioned him to Kona. Isn't he—?"

"He's dead. He was killed last night."

I checked the time on the message. It had come in right around the time I was talking to Kenny Moore in Robo's. I wondered again if Antoine had been trying to set me up, if maybe Red had been trying to lure me into Mountain View and had only resorted to attacking me in the bar when that didn't work. Had he killed Antoine because the kid had failed him? Had he been so angry after failing to kill me that he took it out on 'Toine?

"What's going on in there, Fearsson?"

"What?" I blinked. "In where?"

She walked over and stopped in front of me. Then she tapped my temple gently with her index finger. "That head of yours. I can see it churning away."

I was about to tell her that it was nothing important, but that wasn't true, and I'd had to lie to her too many times already. I didn't want to now.

"I'm wondering if Antoine is dead because of me, because I survived the attack at Robo's."

"Do you think that's possible?"

I shrugged. "I don't know. My mind's muddled." I almost said something about the phasing starting that night, but I stopped myself in time. "I'm working things out," I told her instead.

She nodded, then took my hand and pulled me toward the door. "Well," she said. "Maybe you should do that somewhere else."

"Why?"

"Because if you're right, then this guy is still after you, and I don't want to be here when he tracks you down."

I planted my feet, forcing her to stop. "Aren't you the one who accused me of being paranoid?"

"Yes. But I was also the one who didn't believe in magic."

"And you do now?"

Billie gazed at me a moment. Then she dropped my hand and clapped three times.

"What are you doing?" I asked.

"Come on, Fearsson. 'If you believe in magic, clap your hands'?" She shook her head. "Didn't you ever see *Peter Pan*?"

"A really long time ago."

"You're hopeless." She took my hand again and dragged me out the door.

CHAPTER 19

Against my better judgement, I drove her out to Wofford, wondering the whole way if my dad would be in the same state he was in the last time I visited, or maybe even worse. But as we drove up the dirt road to his trailer, I saw him sitting outside with a book in his hands. He spotted the Z-ster, stood, and waved; always a good sign.

"He seems to be in good shape today," I said.

Billie answered with a vague nod. She was surveying the surroundings. Compared with the Desert National Monument, the area around Wofford was desolate country. A few stunted saguaros grew here and there, and my dad and I often saw hawks and coyotes on the low ridge behind his place. Truth was, I liked it here. It smelled like sage and a person could see for miles in every direction. But I could tell what she was thinking.

"There's nothing out here," she said.

"There's more than you think."

She gave me a "sure, whatever you say," look.

I parked by the trailer and we got out. A breeze blew off the hills, and the heat, which had been stifling in the city, didn't seem so bad up here.

My dad was walking toward us, a big grin on his face. He'd shaved not too long ago, and his clothes were reasonably clean. His t-shirt was even tucked in. "Hello," he said, a hand raised in greeting.

"Hey, Dad. Sorry I didn't call first."

He waved off the apology and took both of Billie's hands in his. "Who's this?" he asked. "And what in God's name is she doing with you?" He'd always been a charmer.

"Billie Castle, I'd like you to meet my father, Leander Fearsson. Dad, Billie Castle."

"It's Lee," he said guiding her to the chair next to his own. "Jay, get us some drinks." He didn't even spare me a glance. I had to smile. This was my dad at his best. We'd been lucky.

I brought out three Cokes, and another chair for me.

"A journalist?" my dad said, as I sat down. "Didn't I warn you about dating people smarter than you?"

I grinned. "Yeah, but that didn't leave me too many options."

Billie laughed.

"Justis," Dad said, his tone stern. "What about rule eleven?"

I shrugged. "Kinda broke that one. But you've met her. Can you blame me?"

"What the hell is rule eleven?" Billie demanded, eyeing both of us.

"My father taught me a lot about being a cop. And he had ten basic rules. Things like, always stick by your partner—"

"That's rule one," he said.

"—Right. And never lend your firearm to anyone, when in doubt call for backup, things like that. Common sense stuff, really." I smiled. "Rule eleven is never become emotionally involved with a member of the press."

"Gets in the way of an investigation," Dad told her. "And more often than not the investigation gets it the way of the relationship. It's just a bad idea." His eyes twinkled. "Most of the time."

"But you're not a cop anymore," Billie said to me.

My dad shook his head. "Rules don't change that much for PIs."

"You must have been very proud when your son joined the force."

"I'm proud of him now, too."

The blood drained from Billie's face. "Of course you are," she said. "I didn't mean . . ."

She looked to me for help, but Dad leaned over and patted her hand.

"It's all right," he said. "I know what you meant. I was proud, though Justis and I weren't as close back then. But in a way I think he's better off now, working on his own. It wears on you being a cop."

He grinned and gave a nod in my direction. "He got to see Randolph Deegan's house, you know. That might not have happened if he'd still been on the job."

Billie nodded and smiled in my direction, but I kept my eyes on my old man.

"What?" he said, staring right back at me. "You told me about Deegan when you were here last time."

"I didn't think you heard," I said, my voice low.

He lifted his binoculars to check out a hawk circling near the road. "I hear everything," he said, his voice matching mine. "I sometimes take a while to process it, you know?"

"Yeah, Pop. I know."

"Red-tail," he said, sounding bored as he lowered the binoculars. "So, Billie, where are you from?"

They started talking, and I sat there and listened. It was more of an interrogation than it was a conversation, but my dad was like that with new people, and Billie seemed to understand. She kept her answers bland—nothing about her father's drinking or her eagerness to leave home. But they got on fine. At one point I retreated into the trailer to get another round of Cokes, but the questioning was still going on when I came back out. Billie was a good sport.

By late in the afternoon, as Billie and I were getting ready to drive back to the city, my dad's spirits were as high as I'd seen them in years.

Billie insisted on cleaning my dad's kitchen before we left. He'd been as insistent about making us sandwiches for lunch—like a proper host, he said—and he'd left quite a mess.

"I like Billie a lot," he told me, when we were alone outside.

"Thanks. So do I."

"Don't mess it up."

I laughed. "You're the second person who's said that to me today. Am I really that bad?"

He regarded me, grim-faced. "You're no worse than I was," he said. "But I'm sure you're not much better, either. You know what I'm saying?"

It had been fifteen years since we'd had a conversation about phasings. But that's what he was talking about. I wondered what full moons were like for him now, with his mind as fragile as it was.

"Yeah, I do," I said. "But I'm not sure that I have much choice."

"I always thought the same thing. Magic seemed so important back then. More important than being . . . whole."

"You think you were wrong to feel that way?" I asked.

He ran a hand over his face. Then pushed both hands through his white hair. "I don't know. Your mother thought so." He stared off to the west, so that the late afternoon sun shone on his face, making his tanned skin appear bronzed, the way I remember it from when I was a kid. "I'm just saying you've got a good thing here. Take care of it as best you can."

He turned to me, and our eyes met.

I nodded. "All right."

Billie stepped out of the trailer, drying her hands on a dish towel. "Well, your kitchen looks a little better, Lee. I'd love to have a couple of hours with it, give it some semblance of organization, but that'll have to wait for my next visit." She smiled and slung the towel over my dad's shoulder.

"You're welcome any time, Billie."

She kissed his cheek. "Thanks."

I gave him a hug and kissed him on the forehead. "Thanks. I'll be out again soon."

"Well, don't come alone." He winked at Billie.

"No, sir."

We got in the car and drove away, raising a plume of dust that billowed like red smoke in the angled sunlight. I could still see him waving from beside the trailer when we turned onto the road toward Wofford.

"Thank you," Billie said softly.

"For what? I think I should be thanking you."

She shook her head. "You didn't know what you'd find out here today. I know what that's like. I remember in high school, coming home from work or from a date, and seeing the lights on in my parents' house. It was the same way. I didn't know if that meant that my mom was up reading, or that my dad was on a bender. There were nights when I'd stay out. I'd walk around the block until the lights went out. If they weren't out by midnight, that usually meant that it was my dad, and I'd go to a friend's house down the street." She ran a hand through her hair. "So, anyway, thanks."

"You're welcome. I'm glad you suggested it. Days like this are pretty rare."

We drove in silence for a while. Then she shifted in her seat so that she was facing me.

"Would you like to have dinner?" she asked. "Just something quiet at my place?"

I glanced at her, and she smiled. Before I knew it, my heart was pounding. I tore my gaze from hers, set it back on the road. She was talking about dinner, but really she was inviting me to spend the night. We both knew it.

"That sounds very nice," I said, a catch in my voice.

She heard it, too. "But?"

"But tonight's no good. I'm supposed to meet Kona at my place after she's off. And then . . . then I have some work I have to do." Lies again. But was this the moment to say, *Can't, I'm going to be temporarily insane starting at sundown*?

"Kona," Billie said, watching the road again. "Were you and she ever . . . ?"

"No. Kona's tastes run in a different direction."

"In terms of race?"

"In terms of gender."

Her eyes widened. "Oh!"

"Can I take a rain check on dinner?"

She nodded and smiled again. "Of course."

We reached the city after the worst of the end-of-work traffic was over. I parked near my office and walked her to her car. I only had another hour and a half before the sun went down and the moon rose. I could already feel myself growing confused. I'd very nearly pulled into the parking space diagonally instead of pulling in along the curb.

I started to say something—I'm not even sure what. But before I could get the words out, she was kissing me. Not like the kisses we'd shared before. This one was deep and passionate, and it made me forget all about Kona and Red and just about everything else. I'm not sure I could have remembered my name for a moment there.

She pulled away after a while, and smiled at me, her eyes still closed, her arms around my neck. "You sure about dinner, Fearsson?"

Fearsson. That was it.

"'Fraid so."

We kissed again.

"Shame," she whispered. "This has been a really nice day." She opened her eyes. "I seem to say that to you a lot."

"It seems that way. Except when I'm writhing in agony on the floor of a bar, or getting myself thrown in jail . . ."

"It's been an interesting week." She got in her car. "Call me. Soon."

"I will."

I watched her drive away, then got back in the Z-ster and drove home. I tried to think about that kiss, the feeling of her lips on mine, her body pressed against me. But thoughts of the phasing kept intruding. The first night was never any worse than the others, but it was no better, either. And I was dreading this phasing more than usual, maybe because it meant that I wouldn't be able to see Billie for three evenings.

I parked in the driveway and managed to remember to collect my mail. But I was feeling more and more addled as I walked up the path to my front door, which may be why I dropped my keys before I could put them in the lock. Whatever the reason, that moment of clumsiness saved my life.

As I bent to pick up the keys I saw a faint gleam of red light seeping through the small space at the base of the door. I straightened and stumbled back a couple of steps, my heart pounding again, though in an entirely different way.

For a split second I thought that it was him, that Red was in my house. But then I realized he wouldn't be glowing like that. This was his work all right, but it was sorcery; I assumed it was a magical tripwire of some sort. A skilled weremyste, someone far more adept than I, could conjure a secondary spell, something that would work like a booby trap. I'd open the door, tripping one spell that would then activate the primary magic. Sophisticated stuff, but I had no doubt Red could handle it with ease. The question was, how could I get into my house without getting myself killed. The sun was setting, the moon was pulling hard at my mind, and I didn't want to be on the streets or with other people when the phasing began in earnest.

I walked to one of the windows and peered inside. Red magic shimmered like fresh blood along the walls, window frames, and doors. He'd managed to mute the glow somewhat, but now that I was aware of the spells, I couldn't believe I hadn't noticed them before I did.

From what I saw, I could only assume that the windows and back door weren't any safer than the front. There was nothing I could do from outside the house. Once inside, I could cover Red's magic with a warding of my own and then trip the spell, to whatever effect. But out here on my tiny lawn, I couldn't see all of his magic, and so didn't know where to place my wardings.

I could think of just one way to get inside: a transporting spell. I had only worked on transporting magic once before, the other day with Namid when I was trying to learn the spell my dad invented. I thought I could pull it off, though. The problem was I didn't know for certain what would trigger the red sorcerer's spell. If it was the opening of a door or window, I'd be fine. If it was mere motion on the other hand, my transporting spell would be the last thing I ever did. I'd transport myself to the living room, and—boom!—no more Fearsson.

I thought about calling on Namid again, but he'd made it clear that he couldn't intervene on my behalf anymore. This time I was on my own. And the sky was darkening.

"What the hell," I muttered.

Three elements: outside in the yard, where I was now; the living room, where I wanted to be; and me. I closed my eyes chanting the words in my head, not caring that if anyone was watching me when I did this, it would seem to them that I'd vanished. After a minute or so, I felt a sudden wave of dizziness and a rush of cold, as if a winter wind had kicked up.

I opened my eyes and found myself in the living room, surrounded by glimmering red magic. With all that I'd seen of Red's conjuring in the last couple of days, I was going to be seeing this color in my sleep. That is, if I survived the night.

I took a tentative step toward the door and didn't blow up, which I counted as a small victory. The next part, though, promised to be far more difficult. First, I warded the house, placing defensive magic all around it, much as Orestes and 'Toine had done with their houses. I tried not to focus on the fact that neither of them had managed to keep Red from destroying the buildings anyway. When I'd finished, though, I couldn't help but notice how weak and thin my wardings looked. My magic had a bluish tint to it; it was almost aqua, to be exact. And most of the time I thought of the color as being pretty deep.

But next to the crimson glow that pulsed from the walls and doors, my conjuring seemed as insubstantial as mist. I could only hope that it would hold.

My next and final challenge would be to trip the magic. Motion hadn't done it, and since it would have been easy to shatter a window from a distance, I couldn't imagine that something so simple would either. In which case, the magic must have worked like a home security system. I had to open something, break the contact, as it were. But of course, I didn't want to be anywhere near whatever it was I opened.

I started by using masking tape on the door, to keep it from moving before I wanted. Then, with the care of a burglar, I unlocked it and secured the latch, so that nothing was holding the door closed but that tape. Finally, I got some cord from the kitchen and tied it to the door handle.

I stood all the way back in the kitchen, but peered around at the door, the cord wrapped around my fist. I was sweating like an overworked horse and my hands were trembling. I checked my wardings once more, to make certain they were in place, and then for good measure, I sheathed myself in magic as well.

Deep breath. And then I yanked hard on the cord.

I'd been expecting something spectacular, and I wasn't disappointed. The force of the explosion knocked me off my feet and made the place quake. Bright yellow flames shot out the door and out a few of the living room windows. I suppose Red wanted people to believe it had been an accident, a natural gas explosion or something like that. And they would have.

I lay dazed on the floor for several seconds. Then I crawled into the living room, my ears ringing, expecting to see the place in shambles. Miraculously, though, my wardings had held. The door was black and smoking, there were new cracks in the walls and ceiling, and several windows were broken. But the damage to the house was minimal considering.

I sat, leaned against a wall, and took a deep breath.

"Justis!"

Kona appeared in the doorway, her weapon drawn, real fear on her face.

"Here," I said from the floor.

She holstered her pistol and hurried over.

"You all right?" she asked, squatting beside me.

I nodded.

"What the hell was that?"

"A present from our friend."

She hung her head and shook it. "I'm really starting to hate this guy."

"Oh?" I said. "He blow up your place, too?"

CHAPTER 20

Kona stuck around for a while and helped me clean up the worst of the mess from Red's pyrotechnics display. I found some old cardboard boxes in the garage and cut out pieces to fit in the window frames in place of broken panes. One of my neighbors called the fire department, but when the engines rolled up, Kona convinced the fire fighters that we had the situation under control. I wondered though if I'd set some kind of city record for initiating 911 calls in a two-day period—Shari Bettancourt's house, the bar, Antoine's house, Q's place, and now this. Not to mention Robby Sommer. Death and mayhem seemed to follow me around.

When we'd done all we could to clean things up, Kona took a seat in the kitchen. I gave her a beer, filled a glass of water for myself, and sat across the table from her. I'd picked up a small scrap of wood from the door, and I was toying with it.

"What's that?" Kona asked.

"Part of my door. Red's magic is still on it."

"Red?"

"That's what I've been calling him. His magic's red, so . . ." I shrugged.

She laughed. "Dude's blowing up your house, killing people right and left, and you've named him like he was some damn pet." She shook her head. "You're a piece of work."

I grinned. "Yeah, I guess I am."

"He knows where you live now," she said, growing serious again.

"That can't be good. Maybe you should stay with Margarite and me tonight."

"I can't tonight. You know that."

"Why not?"

"Tomorrow's the full moon, Kona."

She stared at me for a second, looking lost. Then it hit her. "Oh," she said, sounding like someone had punched her in the gut. "I knew that. That's why I'm here, right?" She shook her head. "Crap." It took her only a few moments to recover. "Well, that's all the more reason you shouldn't be alone. I can stay here with you."

"Thanks, partner, but I'll be all right. And it wouldn't be safe for you, remember."

"Right," she said. "Twice the magic; half the control."

We'd been through this conversation before. I had always appreciated her offers to stay with me during the phasings, but I'd never let her do it. I didn't want anyone around me when I was sinking into the delusions and psychosis, in part because I was afraid I'd hurt someone, and in part because I dreaded being seen like that.

"But," she said, "if this sorcerer—"

"It's full moon for him, too," I reminded her. "He might be strong, but he can't change what it means to be a weremyste." I shook my head. "Red won't bother me tonight."

"Would you stop calling him that, please. It makes him sound like an Irish setter."

"We can call him whatever you want. The fact is, he'll be dealing with his own phasing tonight."

"What about tomorrow morning? And the day after that, and the night after that?" She glanced out at my living room. There was dry wall dust all over the floor and furniture and there were cracks in the walls and ceiling. Kona couldn't see the residue of Red's magic and mine as I could, but that hardly mattered. "I've never tried to tell you how to use your mojo, Justis. I don't know anything about it. But it seems to me you need some help here. You're in over your head."

As if I needed her telling me that. "Yeah, I know. I've been working with Namid, improving my spell work."

"How's that going?" she asked, sounding skeptical.

"I'm alive," I said. "A week ago, I wouldn't have survived what he did to my house."

I didn't tell her that I was still a novice compared to this guy, or that I had no confidence that I could survive his next attack. But I'm not sure she needed to be told.

"All right," she said. "I'm going to assume that you know what you're doing."

I chuckled. "When has that ever been a good idea?" My gaze strayed toward the window. The sky was almost dark. The moon might well have been rising at that moment. "You should go," I said, knowing it sounded abrupt, rude even. Just then I didn't care. "Another five minutes and I won't be much fun to be around."

"There's an assumption there," she said, smiling at me. "But we'll discuss it another time. I should get home to Margarite anyway. I told her I'd met Billie and she's eager for details." She finished her beer and put the bottle in the sink. "Call me in the morning," she said, resting a hand on my shoulder. "I want to know you're all right."

I nodded. "Okay." I didn't really want her to leave, but I didn't want her to stay, either.

She put out her hand. We'd done this a hundred times before, but tonight it felt more final, more frightening. I pulled my Glock from my shoulder holster, removed the magazine, and handed the weapon to her. I was about to be delusional, and who knew what else. Having a weapon in the house would have been dangerous, to say the least. As an afterthought, I pulled off the holster and hung it on my chair.

"Thanks," I said.

"You're welcome."

I sat at the table, staring at the wood grain, and I listened as she let herself out of what was left of my house.

Still I sat, and I began to hear noises. Shouts from out on the street, or maybe from my living room. I shrank back from what I saw at the door, at the broken windows. Red and aqua light played around the edges of the walls and framing. Wardings. I'd used wardings there. Against Red.

I needed to do that again. I'd told Kona—Kona, who had been here only a minute or two before; or had it been longer?

I'd told her that I was safe. That tonight, of all nights, Red couldn't hurt me. Why the hell would I have thought that? What an idiot I'd been!

Standing, I realized that I held something in my hand: a scrap of wood slick with magic, red like blood. I flung it away before it could hurt me and rubbed my fingers on my shirt, expecting them to start burning any second. The red was everywhere. I needed to protect myself from it. I didn't know why, but I did. Wardings. That's what I'd been thinking. Wardings. That was why I'd stood.

But that red magic was already inside. What was the use of warding if it was already here?

I watched the red as I sidled toward the back of the house, my back to the wall. When I couldn't see the red anymore I threw myself down the hallway and into another room. My room. There was no red in here. I closed the door. Locked it.

My room, a shield, and that red magic.

No, those weren't the right elements. Three was the right number. But the elements had to be right, too. My room, the shield, and . . . what? Red himself. I spoke the spell, felt magic surge through me.

The walls shimmered with magic the color of the sea. I sunk to the floor and leaned back against the side of my bed, my eyes closed.

I heard a coyote howl in the distance. Opening my eyes again, I saw sprigs of cinquefoil and clover sprouting from the rug. The ground. I squinted up at the sun overhead, felt its heat on my face and neck and shoulders. A hot breeze touched my skin and I wiped sweat from my brow.

Honeybees grappled with the tiny blooms beside me and a butterfly floated past. Following it with my eyes, I saw it swoop over a patch of grass and then loop back toward a low, shaded path. I inhaled sharply, held my breath, the butterfly forgotten.

The path. It was red, and it wound away from me, cutting through the shimmering aqua light like a knife. Red. He was down that path. I could feel him, close, powerful. Evil, someone had called him. Who had said that?

I followed. I stayed where I was, too tired to move, too comfortable in the clover and grass. But I followed, my mind flying down that path. It led a long way from the grass, over rock and sand and more rock. The grass and flowers were gone, but still the red went on, and I followed, determined now, tired no longer, though still I was sitting, resting.

Like embers the red glowed, hot and angry and my feet ached, my face and neck and chest burned. Heat rose from the path like steam from a boiling pot, damp, rank with the smell of blood. But I followed. After a time a second color bled into the crimson. Green, pale as a forest mist. The colors twined, and I followed, until the green broke free and curled away. I knew that green. I'd seen it before. But I stayed with the red, knowing that was the important color. Time was running short, and I was growing desperate, conscious of the sun dropping like a stone toward the horizon. I tried to run, gasping for breath, my feet leaden.

The path began to climb, steeper and steeper, until I was scrabbling on all fours. An animal, chasing the scent of blood. Other colors joined the red and faded, sweeping in from left and right like swallows angling along a cliff face. Blues and yellows, oranges and golds, something akin to pure light itself, and this one I did know, but it was gone so fast I had no time to guess from where. More greens, more purples. Always they swung away again, these other colors. But the red remained, a gash running through all the rest— raw, livid, fevered. That was the constant, and that was the path I followed.

A bird squawked, shrill and insistent from beside the path. I ignored it, but it called again. Twice, three times. Until I had to stop and search for it.

The phone. The phone was ringing. I picked it up. No sound. At least not at first.

Had I said hello?

"Fearsson?"

I knew the voice, though it seemed to be coming from far away. I could see the red path still, but the sun was setting. I had no time.

"Fearsson? You there?"

"Billie," I said, because that was the name.

"We must have a bad connection or something. Can you hear me okay?"

"Yes."

"I just wanted to tell you again what a great a day I had. I'm so glad I got to meet your father."

I didn't take my eyes off the path. I was afraid even to blink, in case it vanished in the failing light.

"Fearsson?"

"I have to go."

"Oh. I'm sorry. Did Kona come by? Are the two of you still working?"

"No. Kona's . . . she left. The light's almost gone, and I'm losing the path. I can't . . . I have to go."

"I don't . . . You sound funny, Fearsson. Are you all right?"

I had to make her understand; it was important that I explain to her better. But the ribbon of crimson light had faded almost to nothing. And I couldn't find the words.

"Fearsson? You still there?" She sounded frightened now. I could hear the fear in her voice. I was scared, too. The path.

"I can't now," I said, and hung up.

I started up the path again, loose rocks falling away behind me, my hands scraping on the stone and dirt. But I could still see the red and I thought I could see the top.

The phone rang again. The bird. Keening, its voice echoing off the cliffs. But I ignored it. After a time, it stopped.

On and on I climbed. There were no other colors now; only the red. The path was barren, rocky, unforgiving. The drop on either side would have been enough to kill me. In the distance I could see some trees, clustered like cattle in a rainstorm. Mountains rose beyond them, gray and austere. Closer, the terrain rolled like swells on some grassy sea, silvered where the wind blew, bending the grasses so that they gleamed in the pale light.

I slowed as I neared the top, fearful, eager. Far to the west, the sun seemed to teeter on the edge of the world, huge, ovate, its color a match for the path I'd followed to the top of this rise. But I saw nothing. I'd reached the top, and there was nothing. Rock, the lurid glow of that sun, and laughter riding the wind. That was all. The path was gone; it wasn't even behind me anymore.

"What the hell?" I muttered.

I'd been so sure that I was following him. Red. I'd known that he'd be here at the end. So where was he?

"Right here."

I opened my eyes, not realizing they'd been closed. He stood over me. Tall, broad, bald. Eyes as pale as bone. His nose was hooked and crooked. Broken once, maybe. There was something regal about it. His lips were thin and pale, and his chin was dimpled. For so long I'd wanted to see his face, to memorize his features. I stared at him. Stared and stared. I couldn't help myself.

"*Tu aies me cherche, oui?*" he said, his smile cold and cruel. "You have been looking for me?"

For a moment I couldn't bring myself to say anything. At last I nodded. "Yes. But you couldn't come tonight. It's . . . the moon. You couldn't come. And I put wardings on my . . ."

I stopped, because he was laughing. A sound that chilled me, that seemed to make the room colder. The sun was a light again. No heat. I was shivering.

And in that moment I knew. The rest had been delusion, hallucination; whatever you wanted to call it. It hadn't been real. But he was. Red was standing over me in my bedroom. And I was a dead man.

I tried to crawl away from him, my eyes never leaving his face. But he stood between me and my door. I groped for a spell—any spell—that would send him away or shield me from whatever he was about to do. But I could feel the moon pressing down on my mind, crushing memory, knowledge, craft—everything I needed.

"You are resourceful," he said. I remembered the accent from before. Did it even matter anymore that he was French? "I thought you would die from that spell I placed on your house." He glanced from side to side, clearly surprised that the walls around us still stood. "*Tu as fait bien.* You have done well."

I closed my eyes.

My weapon, my shoulder holster, my hand.

Nothing happened.

He laughed again, and I shuddered.

"I do not think it will help you to have that . . . that *gun*." It sounded strange when he said it. "But I do not think I want you to have it anyway." He canted his head to the side. "I do not believe it is where you thought it was. I sense nothing there."

Of course not. I'd given it to Kona. Like I always did.

"The phasing," I said. "It . . . you're not affected?"

"No."

I should have known this. I remembered someone saying that the moons didn't touch him. Who'd told me that? And then it hit me.

"That's what you were doing!" I whispered, amazed at the clarity of my thought. "That's why you killed those kids! You were . . . doing something to make yourself immune to the phasings."

Laughter filled the room, as if blown in on a cold wind.

"You are limited. Almost as much as those with nothing. It is a waste that you should have any power at all." He cocked his head to the side once more. "And yet, you have tracked me and managed to come closer than others. *Tu as un peu de talent, eh?*"

Apparently he thought I had talent. A little, anyway.

"Why did you kill them then? If it wasn't for the phasings, why did you do it? You always kill them on the quarter moon, and you use magic. There's got to be something that you get from them, something that makes you more powerful than you were when you began."

He stared down at me, nodding, his lips pursed now. For an odd moment, his expression reminded me of Kona. "Yes, you are not without some cleverness. A shame then that you have to die."

"Cahors."

Red raised his eyes. I turned, knowing that voice.

Namid stood near my window, his waters as roiled as I'd ever seen them. He was the color of lead, his surface rough as from an unseen wind, like he was covered with scales. His eyes shone as white and hard as the full moon.

"Namid'skemu," Red said, his voice as soft as a kiss, the name rolling off his tongue as liquid and graceful as Namid himself. I wished that I could speak the runemyste's name like that one time. "You should not be here, *mon ami.*"

Namid rumbled, the sound like breakers rolling over a rocky shoreline. "I should not?" he said. "What of you?"

"I am beyond your control now. I am free to do as I please."

"Not here," Namid said. "Not tonight."

Red's smile turned brittle. "You have already interfered once. They will not let you do so again." He shook his head, and even this he did with grace. "No, you cannot stop me. And to prove it, I will kill your little friend while you watch."

I wanted Namid to tell him he was wrong, to laugh at his surety, as Cahors had laughed at me. But instead the runemyste looked down at me, sadness in his glowing eyes.

Cahors stared at me as well, and I felt like a rabbit under the gaze of an eagle. Only more helpless.

I knew better than to think that I could attack him directly. If the moon couldn't touch him, how could I? But I also knew that with the phasing underway, I was stronger than usual. And now that Red had pulled me out of my hallucination, my thoughts were clear enough to conjure. I hoped.

Defend yourself! I heard once more in my head. And the remembered sound of Namid's warning triggered another memory.

Three elements: my magic, a book on the shelf by my bed, Red's head.

The book flew across the room, smacking the myste hard in the back of his head. He spun, as if expecting to see someone behind him.

Before I could cast again, I heard Namid's voice in my mind—for real this time, not a memory.

Ohanko! I can ward your house.

It was all I needed to hear.

Again three elements: Cahors, my bedroom, my lawn. It was the most powerful spell I had ever attempted, but the phasing made it possible, as long as I didn't foul it up.

I didn't. One moment Red loomed over me, eyes blazing in anger, and the next he was gone.

Namid raised his hands, and a clear shimmering shield appeared on the walls of my bedroom.

I clamored to my feet and hurried to the window. Cahors stood outside the house, rage contorting his features.

"You cannot interfere!" he howled. "You challenge me at your own peril, Namid'skemu!"

"My peril?" the runemyste said, keeping his voice low, the way he would have if Cahors had still been in the room. "You are strong, and more than you used to be. But you are no threat to me."

Somehow Red heard him. "You are forbidden to interfere! I know you are!"

"I have done nothing to you," Namid said. "I have merely warded this house."

"That is still interference!"

"Not anymore. The rules have changed. Thanks to you, we had no choice. Surely you did not think that we would stand aside and let you do this."

Red's eyes appeared to burn white hot. "After all you did to me," he said, his voice so low I could barely hear him.

"We did nothing that you did not force us to do."

The man raged in silence, and my face seemed to be scalded by the heat of his glare. I knew that if not for Namid's wardings, his mere glance would have turned me to ash and razed my home to the ground.

I had struggled to keep up with their exchange, but even without the moon's pull, I would have had trouble. How did Namid and Red—Cahors—know each other? Had Red trained with the runemyste, too? Had he once been like me?

"You cannot guard this one forever," Cahors said at last, still staring at me from the lawn. "Your vigilance will slacken, and when it does, I will be ready."

Namid said nothing. Cahors' lips curled upward in a smile that made my stomach turn.

"You know I am right," Red told him. "And you know that he cannot stand against me."

"That has yet to be scryed," Namid said. "As I said, you have changed the rules. Where you are concerned nothing is certain anymore."

"This is, Namid'skemu. This is." He spared me once last glance. "Farewell for now, little weremyste. We will meet again soon, you and I. And we shall see how you do *sans ton ami, oui?*" He laughed again. Then he turned and walked out into the street. An instant later, he vanished.

For several moments, I continued to stare out at where he'd been standing, fearing that he'd reappear, wondering if I'd imagined it after all. Already the moon was dulling my mind again. I felt as though I'd downed a bottle of wine.

"Ohanko."

I turned to face Namid. His waters had softened, though the glow of his eyes remained as intense as it had been when he spoke to Red.

"You're really here?" I asked, sinking to the floor. "This was real? It wasn't just the phasing?"

"I am here. Cahors was as well, but he has gone. You did well. Very well. Are you hurt?"

"No, I'm . . ." I took a breath. "I'm fine. Who is he, Namid?"

The runemyste shook his head. "Tomorrow. In the morning, when you can understand what I tell you. Now you should sleep."

As soon as he said this, I realized that I was exhausted. I nodded. "Yes, all right." I started to close my eyes, then jerked myself awake. "No!" I said. "I never sleep during the phasings. You know that. The dreams . . ." I shuddered.

"You will be all right tonight. I will remain here until you wake."

"You will?" Even on this night, my mind drifting again, I knew how unusual an offer this was.

Namid lowered himself to the floor. To the ground. Sun reflected off his waters. He appeared calmer now, more at peace. "I can guard your sleep, keep the moon from intruding too much, as I am doing now. You will sleep."

"Why would you do this?"

Again he shook his head. "Tomorrow. Sleep now."

The sun shone overhead, and bees buzzed in the clover and cinquefoil. I lay down where I was, my head cushioned in fresh grass, and I slept.

CHAPTER 21

Another reason I didn't like to sleep during the phasings: waking up during the full of the moon was a bit like waking up after a night of heavy drinking. I wasn't sick to my stomach, but my head felt thick and dull, and my muscles were stiff. I'd left the light on all night, and my face felt weird where it had been pressed into the bedroom carpet. If I was going to sleep, why the hell hadn't I climbed into bed?

I sat up, rubbed a hand through my tangled hair. Namid sat cross-legged on the floor a few feet away. His face and body like glass, his eyes bright.

"Ohanko. You slept well?"

"What are you—?" Memories of the night before flashed through my mind, vivid and terrifying. "Crap," I whispered. "It was real, wasn't it? He was here, in my house."

"Yes. It was real."

"And you know him," I said. It came out as an accusation.

"Yes."

"Yesterday, when I told you that the guy was French, and I repeated the name I'd heard Shari Bettancourt use, you knew right away, didn't you? You disappeared pretty quickly to check it out, but you already knew."

"I did not know for certain, but yes, I had some idea that it was the man you saw here last night."

I said nothing, but stared back at him, waiting.

"His name is Etienne de Cahors. He was a druid in Gaul during what you would call the early dark ages. At one time he was a member of my council, but over the centuries he grew resistive. Eventually he began to challenge our adherence to the Runeclave's directives. He was particularly dissatisfied with his inability to use magic directly on your world."

"You mean he's a runemyste?" I asked.

"He was."

"Tell me there's some good news in this, Namid."

"There is not. Somehow he has managed to master the magic that first created him. He has assumed corporeal form and is now free to roam your world. But he retains something of what he used to be. That is why I have been able to keep him out of your home. He . . . well, you would say that he changed the rules."

I remembered Namid saying something similar to Cahors the night before.

"And you guys allowed this to happen?" It was the first thing that came to mind, and I knew as soon as I said it that it wasn't fair, not when one considered all the stupid things we humans had managed to do to the world on our own. "I'm sorry," I said.

"You should not apologize. The Council has asked the same question of itself, and the answer is simple: yes, we allowed this to happen. He has made his displeasure known for a long time. We should have been vigilant and we were not."

"We allowed it, too," I said. "That's what he was doing when he was killing those kids. He was gathering power from them somehow, and using it to break free of what he was. If we'd caught him sooner, we might have stopped him."

"Maybe. Or he might have killed you."

"Wait a minute," I said, my mind still struggling to keep up with all he'd told me. "He's one of you? How come I'm still alive? He should have been able to kill me with a thought. You could, right?"

"As always, Ohanko, you simplify things too much, and you make them too complicated as well. You are most difficult. Yes, my kind are powerful, which is why we place limits on ourselves, limits Cahors has rejected. But you have powers of your own. Your wardings, while still crude and weak, can offer you some protection."

"Is this supposed to reassure me?"

"It is supposed to inform you. Cahors has become something other than a runemyste. We do not know what exactly. But in winning his freedom from the limitations placed on our powers he has weakened himself. Not a great deal, and not forever, but enough it seems to have saved your life a few nights ago. And perhaps again last night."

I nodded, considering this. "All right," I said at last. "Then what do I do?"

"I am not sure that you can do anything," he said, sounding surprised by the question.

"Then what are you going to do?"

"He is part of your world now—"

"So you're not allowed to kill him. You weren't even allowed to ward my house, were you? The rules haven't really changed. You were just telling him that."

"Attacking you in the moon-time is . . . not fair," he said, an admission of sorts. "I could not allow that."

"Not fair," I repeated, chuckling to myself. "And Kona called *me* a piece of work."

We both fell silent. I tried to kick my brain into gear. Despite Namid's doubts, I knew that we had to stop Cahors, and we had to do it soon. Last night, facing Namid, he'd run up against the limits of his power, and he wouldn't be happy about that at all. He was going to kill again in two weeks, when the moon reached its first quarter, and he'd be coming after me before then. I knew too much about him now; he couldn't have me around alerting other weremystes to the danger.

"He's still more like you than he is like me," I said, the thought coming to me with unexpected clarity.

"What do you mean?"

"The phasing didn't bother him at all, just as it doesn't bother you."

Namid regarded me with interest. "True."

"Which means that, comparatively speaking, I'm more of a match for him now than I will be at any other time. That's why my spell worked last night. The phasings are hard on me, but they also make me stronger."

"Even with that, you are not ready to face him. In time, yes. But not yet."

"Then tell me who is. Because we have to do something. I've been watching kids die for three years now, and there hasn't been a damn thing I could do about it. Now I know who's responsible and I'm not going to let him kill again!"

I got up and walked out into the living room. I faltered at the sight of it, having forgotten about Red's magical bomb. But I recovered quickly, went to my jacket and shoulder holster, which were draped over a kitchen chair. I halted at the sight of the empty holster; I'd have to get my Glock from Kona. That was going to be a fun conversation.

When I turned, I saw that Namid had followed me.

"Your weapon—" he began.

". . . Probably won't kill him," I said. "I know. But the other day I took a shot at him and he deflected the bullet."

"And next time you shoot at him he will do the same. It is not difficult magic."

"Would you do it?" I asked.

He hesitated. I couldn't help but smile. I could count on one hand the number of times I'd outthought the runemyste. Okay, I could count them on one finger.

"You wouldn't have to, would you?" I said. "If I shot at you the bullet would pass right through you; we both know it would. But as you said, he's taken corporeal form. He might not be scared of my weapon, but he can't ignore it, either. Not anymore."

"Most interesting, Ohanko. I had not thought of this."

"If I manage to shoot him, he'll be able to heal himself, right?"

"I would expect so."

"But he'll have to focus his magic on doing that. How many spells can he maintain at once?"

"I do not know," Namid said. "Several, I would think. Perhaps more."

I frowned. Several. One to heal himself, one to ward himself from whatever assailing spell I managed to throw at him, and one to kill me. Not the answer I'd been hoping to hear.

"Then how do I beat him?" I asked.

"I am not certain you can. That is what I have been trying to tell you."

"There's got to be some way, Namid. The guy isn't invincible."

"No, he is not."

"How would you defeat him?"

"I would take hold of his magic to keep him from assailing me, and then I would reach into his mind and crush his will."

I shuddered. I'd known for a long time that Namid possessed powers I could barely understand. But in that moment, for the first time, it occurred to me to imagine what it might be like to have the runemyste as an enemy rather than as a teacher and guardian.

"I'm not sure I can do any of that," I said, my tone dry.

Namid smiled. "I would be surprised if you could."

"Where can I find him?"

The runemyste shook his head. "You should not try."

"Where, Namid?"

"I do not believe I should help you in this endeavor."

I stared at him, thinking it through. "You won't have to," I said after a few moments. "He'll find me. As soon as I'm exposed, he'll make the attempt. Normally he'd wait until nightfall, for the phasing to start again, but he knows that you'll protect me then."

"I can protect you now, as well."

"So you're going to follow me around all day?" I demanded.

"I have no interest in spending every moment with you, but I will not allow you to sacrifice yourself to Cahors. It is a senseless act, a waste of your life."

"How do you know I can't beat him?" I asked. "How do you know I'm not supposed to?"

"I have touched his magic. And I have trained you. I believe I know the extent of his power and yours."

"All right, then tell me this: why does he want to kill me?"

"You are a threat to him."

I opened my hands, as if to say, "See?"

He scowled at me.

"Don't blame me," I said. "Your words, not mine. I'm a threat to him. He wants me dead because I know who and what he is, because I have you as my friend, and because I'm a weremyste with a weapon. I can defeat him. But I need you to tell me how to do it."

"And I am telling you, I do not know."

We looked at each other for some time, his pale glowing eyes boring into mine. "You have to let me do this, Namid. Unless you intend to do it yourself."

"You know that I cannot."

"And you know that I can't let him kill again. Not now, knowing what I do."

His waters roughened and for a second I thought he'd grown angry with me. "Yes, all right," he said, sounding more concerned than mad. "You are right. Once you leave here, and once I stop protecting you, he will find you quickly. Your one hope may be that he will not expect you to fight him. He may be weaker now, more vulnerable, but he still thinks of himself as a runemyste. That could be his undoing." He faltered once more before adding, "And you are more powerful than you know. Like your father was. With great power comes great risk. I did not know how strong Leander Fearsson was until it was too late. The training I gave him was not sufficient to save his mind. I have been more cautious with you. As a result, your mind remains strong, but you are not as skilled as you could be. I wish now that I had taught you more. It would have made this day easier for you. Still, you are strong, Ohanko. I believe Cahors knows this. It may be that you can defeat him. As I told Cahors, that has not yet been scried."

"Is that why you saved my life?" I asked. "Because of my dad?"

"I saved you because you can do much good in your world. And yes, because I failed your father. He could have done much good as well. Together, the two of you might have defeated Cahors long ago."

I gaped at him, struck dumb by what he had said. I tried to imagine being on the force with my dad, both of us whole, both of us wielding magic. But the very notion was so far from reality, so far from the life I had known, that no image came to me.

"I have to call Kona," I said, my voice low. "Don't leave yet. I don't want him coming at me before I'm ready."

"Of course." He lowered himself to the floor again and a moment later was as still as an ice sculpture.

I took the phone back into my bedroom and dialed Kona's number.

Margarite answered and I went through enough of the niceties so that I wouldn't sound rude when I asked for Kona. I love Margarite, but at that moment I didn't feel much like chatting.

"You survived," Kona said when she picked up.

"Barely."

"That bad, eh?"

"As phasings go it was all right. But Red showed up. If it wasn't for Namid I'd be dead."

"Damn, Justis! This guy has it in for you, doesn't he?"

"So it seems."

"What are you going to do?"

"What I have to," I said. "I'm leaving the house, going somewhere I know he'll find me. And when he does, I'm going to do my best to kill him. Before I do that, though, I need my weapon."

Kona took a long time to answer, and when she did it was in a tone I knew all too well. "And what does Namid think of this idea?"

"He thinks I'm throwing my life away for nothing."

"That sounds about right," she said.

"What should I do instead? He's coming after me anyway, and Namid can't protect me forever."

"I don't know. Leave town. Get away from here."

"Is that what you'd do?" I asked.

She didn't answer.

"This isn't a guy you run away from," I said. "He can find me anywhere I go. Distance and time don't mean much to him. And besides, if I leave, he'll kill again. Guaranteed."

"He will if you're dead, too. And the rest of us won't stand a chance of stopping him."

"I'm stronger right now than I'll be any other time for the next four weeks. This is my best chance."

"Uh-huh," she said. It was amazing how much sarcasm she could pack into two syllables.

"I'm coming over now. I need my Glock."

"What if I don't give it to you?"

"Then I'll have less of a chance of killing him, won't I?"

"It doesn't sound like you have a much of a chance now!"

"Thanks for the pep talk. Between you and Namid I'm brimming with confidence."

"This is a mistake, Justis. It's suicide and I won't—"

"I'm coming over now," I said, raising my voice, which I almost never did with Kona. "I'll expect you to hand over my weapon when I get there!"

I hung up before she could say more. For a minute or two I stood in the middle of my bedroom, staring at the phone, wondering if she would call back, and not certain whether or not I wanted her to. At last, I tossed it onto my bed, changed my clothes, and headed out into the living room.

"Your friend tried to dissuade you," Namid said from where he still sat on my floor.

"Yeah," I said. "She didn't have any more luck than you did."

"The magic he used on you two nights ago is rudimentary for my kind, though quite effective. A simple shield warding will not work, nor will deflection or reflection. But if you can shield your heart, that might protect you."

I gazed back at him, not bothering to hide my surprise. "Are you trying to help me with this?"

"Of course I am. As I have told you before, if you die it will put to waste all the time I have spent trying to teach you."

"I can use a shielding spell against that magic?"

"Yes, if you shield only your heart. Warding your entire body will weaken the magic too much, but if you focus the warding entirely on your heart it might work."

"I've never done that before. I've never even tried it."

The runemyste shrugged. "You may have to, if you insist on facing him."

I took a long breath. Maybe I was crazy to try this. "All right. Anything else?"

Namid started to say something, then stopped, his bright gaze snapping toward the front door of my house.

"What?" I said, fear gripping my heart. "Is he here again?"

"No," he said. "The woman is."

"The woman?"

He glared up at me. "Your friend. The distraction."

Billie.

"Damn," I whispered. I went to the door and pulled it open.

Billie stood on the path leading up to my house, staring at the burn marks and the squares of cardboard that covered the empty panes of my living room window. She glanced my way as I stepped outside and joined her there, but she didn't say a word. I couldn't even begin to imagine what she was thinking.

"Like what I've done with the place?" I asked. Kind of lame, I know.

She didn't deign to respond.

"I've been pretty tolerant so far," she said instead. "All the talk about magic, that scene in the bar, your night in jail. You know, Fearsson, I've never been with anyone who was arrested." She turned to me. Her face was pale, her eyes hard. "I've been thinking about all the other things that make me like you so much," she said. "The desert. The way you are with your dad. The fact that, when the rest of this crap goes away, you're a lot of fun to be with. You make me think about . . . about everything, in ways I never have before. And I've been getting through this week by thinking that once this case is over, and your life gets back to normal, it'll all be great." She looked at the door again and shook her head. "But there's no such thing as normal with you, is there? It's all like this."

"Billie—"

"What the hell was with you on the phone last night?"

And there it was. The Question. I doubt that she knew it, but she'd come to the very crux of it all: of me, of us, of any future we might have together.

"Was it this?" she said, gesturing at the door. "Were you attacked again? Were you hurt? If so, tell me. I don't know how much more I can deal with, but I know that I can't even try if you won't tell me what's going on."

"Come inside with me," I said, gesturing toward the door.

"Not until you explain what happened last night."

I faced her and our eyes locked. "I will," I said. "But not out here."

"Why? Are you in danger again?"

Yes. So are you. I had a feeling that right then, those words would have sent her away for good. "I don't want to have this conversation in front of my neighbors," I told her instead, which was also true.

She twisted her mouth, but when I walked back up into the house, she followed me. As I closed the door again, a small cloud of plaster fell to the floor, like a tiny flurry of snow. I hoped that she hadn't noticed.

Not that it would have mattered. Taking in the appearance of my living room, making myself see the damage from last night as Billie must have seen it, I felt my heart sink. I wouldn't want any part of this life either.

"Good God, Fearsson," she muttered. "You're lucky you're not dead."

So many secrets. So many lies. I was on the verge of losing her, and I had no idea how to keep it from happening. The truth would drive her away, but I wasn't at all certain that piling on more lies would do any different. And even if I had been, I didn't want to build a relationship on deception and half-truths. So I began there, with the simple statement. *You're lucky you're not dead.*

"To be honest, luck had very little to do with it."

She turned, perhaps hearing something in my voice. "What do you mean?"

I wanted to sit on the couch, but it was covered with shards of glass and dust from the cracked plasterboard.

"When I got home last night, I saw that the same sorcerer who tried to kill me in Robo's had put a spell on my house. The magic's hard to explain, but it was as if he'd rigged a magical bomb to the whole place. If I'd opened the door or tried to break in through a window, it would have blown up, taking me with it."

I could see the skepticism in her eyes. "So what did you do?"

"I did this." I closed my eyes and began to chant aloud. I knew I was scaring her, but with her there in the house, and the phasing underway, I was having trouble concentrating. And I couldn't think of another way to make her believe me. The living room, where I was; the kitchen where I wanted to be; and me. I must have said it eight times before the spell worked. But at last, for the second time in as many days—the third if you count what I did to get Cahors out of my bedroom—I pulled off a transporting spell. One second I was standing in front of her in the living room, and the next I was in the kitchen behind her.

"Fearsson?" she called as soon as I vanished, or at least appeared to. Her voice was high; she sounded terrified.

"I'm right here," I said.

She spun and stared at me, her eyes so wide I almost laughed out loud.

"How the hell did you do that?"

"Magic," I said, smiling.

"I—" She stopped herself. But I knew what she had intended to say.

"You don't believe in magic."

She hesitated. "No, I don't. I didn't." After a moment she frowned. "Can you do that again?"

I walked to where she was standing. "Do I really need to?"

"No," she said, shaking her head. "So you're a . . ."

"I'm a weremyste. Not a very good one. But I'm working on that."

"A weremyste," she repeated. "You're better than most of the ones I know."

I grinned. At least she could still joke. "I used a transporting spell to get from the living room to the kitchen. Last night I used it to get into the house, past the magic of the red sorcerer's booby trap."

"The red sorcerer?"

"Sorry. To those who can see it, magic shows up as a sort of colored light. Different sorcerers have different colors. The guy who's been giving me such a hard time—his color's red."

"All right."

"After I was inside—"

"What color is your magic?"

"Bluish green. Like the sea. Once I was inside, I set up a warding— a shield of sorts. Also magic. Then I managed to open the door to set off his conjuring. If I'd opened the door from outside, I'd have died. I guess Red didn't know that I could do transporting spells."

"I guess not."

"Are you following any of this?"

She shrugged. "More of it than you might think. Last night, after you dropped me off, I spent some time online, looking for information about magic. You'd be surprised at the number of sites there are for people who want to be sorcerers."

I started to respond, stopped myself. "So you already knew most of this stuff."

"Not really. As many sites as they were, they weren't very helpful. They were vague and more New Age than nuts and bolts. None of them said anything about transporting spells or colors or any of that. You should start your own site; you'd get lots of hits." A faint, thin smile drifted across her face, but I could tell that she was brooding on what I'd told her. "A few sites said that you had to be born a sorcerer; others said you could learn spells and train. Which is it?"

"Both. You either have Runeclave blood in your veins or—"

"Runeclave?" Before I could answer, she shook her head. "No. I don't want to know right now. Just go on."

"Either you have it or you don't. But then, you need to learn to use it."

"And you do this by . . . reading books? Talking to other weremystes? Going to Hogwarts while the rest of the world goes trick-or-treating?"

"Mostly you're taught by others."

"So you have a teacher."

Once again, like the night outside of Robo's, I was reluctant to tell her about Namid and the other runemystes. That struck me as a bridge too far. "Yes, I have a teacher," was all I said.

She let it go. "How many of you are there? Weremystes, I mean."

"A lot. Far more than you'd think."

"Give me a number. In the Phoenix metropolitan area, are we talking twenty? Two hundred? Two thousand? More?"

"Probably somewhere between two hundred and two thousand. Those are active weremystes; people who are using their magic. There are more out there—a lot of people have Runeclave blood in them but don't use it. Others have it in them, but it's so weak they're not even aware of it."

"They're not? How can—?" She stopped, staring at me. "Don't you dare tell me that I—"

"No," I said, shaking my head. "I don't see any magic in you."

"Thank God."

She eyed me for several moments. I could see her working it all through, processing everything I'd told her, and all that she had encountered on the net. She was smart as hell, and it wouldn't be long until she caught up with the conversation. And then we'd be right back where we began, which was what I dreaded most.

Sooner even than I'd anticipated, she said, "So when I called, you were still doing magic?"

That was one way around it. Technically, the phasings are caused by magic—my magic—so I could have said that I was doing magic when she called. But again, I didn't want to play games with the truth, not about this. I wasn't even thinking about the relationship, or about our future. I was simply remembering that I'd gotten her in the house by promising to answer her questions. If I couldn't do that much without misleading her, how the hell was I going to make anything else work? I also had a feeling that she was testing me; if she'd read about weremystes, she might well have read about the phasings, too. The strange thing was, I knew how the conversation would end, and still I chose to tell her the truth. I guess I was in love. Nothing else explains the choice I made in that moment.

"No," I said, "I wasn't doing magic. Not really."

"Were you still with Kona?"

"No. She'd left by then."

"Then what? Tell me."

"I was in the middle of a phasing."

Billie frowned. "I found that term last night, in several places, but the sites that mentioned it didn't offer many details."

Not surprising, really. This was the secret every weremyste wanted to hide.

"The word 'weremyste' is pretty similar to the word werewolf," I said. "And our magic works kind of the same way. I can do magic all month long, but when the moon waxes full, I lose control. All of us do. Our magic gets stronger, but our minds weaken."

It crashed over her like a wave. I saw it happen. The color in her cheeks, which had returned during our conversation, drained away again. She took a step back from me, frightened of what she saw. That one step hurt more than anything she could have said.

"Weaken?" she repeated, a quaver in her voice. "What does that mean?" But she knew. I'd seen this coming. A part of me had watched the entire exchange unfold, anticipating every question, every twist and turn that steered us to this point. It was like I'd scried the whole thing. And still, even preparing myself, I hadn't been able to keep my heart from being torn apart.

"It means that I had . . . an episode."

"*What does it mean?*" she demanded again, biting off each word.

I exhaled. "I was hallucinating. I couldn't talk to you because I was too far gone in moon-induced delusions to carry on a conversation."

"The psychological problems you told me about," she said. "The ones that cost you your job on the police force."

"Yes. They're not really psychological problems so much as magical ones."

Billie turned and started toward the door. "I'm sorry. I can't do this. Maybe that makes me weak, or heartless, or something. But I can't do it."

"Billie, wait," I said, walking after her. "All weremystes have this. It's why we hide the fact that we can do magic. It's the price of the power I wield. I could take medication for it, but then the magic goes away, and I need to have access to it."

She was out the door and striding down the path toward her car, but she stopped now, turning to face me again. "You said you had this under control. You said you were seeing someone. A therapist."

"I do get help," I said, cringing at yet another lie, or at least the shadow of one. "Not from a psychologist, but from someone who teaches me magic and helps me through the full moons."

"That's not the same, and you know it." She started toward her car again. "You lied to me, Fearsson," she said over her shoulder. "Or was that some kind of magical lie, so it doesn't count?"

"I told you that the problem never goes away, that I'd learned to control it, to live with it, and that's the truth."

She had nearly reached her car, but she stopped once more and spun toward me. There were tears on her face, though she didn't bother to wipe them away. She might not have known they were there. "You have problems. They cost you your job. And they're still affecting you. You can call them anything you want. You can pretend that you're facing them. But the truth is they haven't gone away, and you haven't learned to control them. That's why you couldn't talk to me last night." She shook her head and started to turn back to her car.

I stepped in front of her. "Billie, please. Let me try to explain this to you. If after I'm done, you still want to leave, then fine. I'll never call you again."

"I can't, Fearsson," she said, crying now. "I just can't. Let's say I believe you. Let's say I accept that the whole magic thing is something more than an excuse not to confront your problems. I still can't live with it. I grew up with an alcoholic. His sickness was everywhere. I'd hear it at night when he was yelling at my mom, or hitting her again. I'd see it in the morning, when I had to clean up the empty glasses and bottles, because he was sleeping it off, and my mom was so scared of waking him that she couldn't bring herself to move, much less take care of his mess. I'd smell it in the afternoon when I got home from school and found him slumped in front of the television with whiskey on his breath. It was all over and I nearly drowned in it.

"Dad always denied he had a problem, and Mom let him. They

spent their entire marriage living a lie, and they nearly dragged me down with them. I know that mental illness is treatable, and I know that people who have problems like yours can lead healthy, normal lives. But first they have to face their problems head on and get help. You won't do that. You're standing there in front of me telling me that it's all right, and clearly it's not." She shook her head. "I can't live that way. I'm sorry."

She started away once more, and I let her go. What choice did I have? I couldn't even be mad at her. She was doing the right thing, the thing my mom probably should have done years before I was born. The thing that might have saved her life. I watched Billie get into her little blue Honda and drive off. Then I went back into the house.

CHAPTER 22

"She is unhappy with you," Namid said, as I closed the door behind me.

"It doesn't matter," I told him, my chest aching. "Like you said, she was a distraction. I have more important things to deal with today."

He gave that little shrug again, and I had to fight an urge to smack him. Not that it would have done any damage.

"You are still determined to go after Cahors?"

"Yes."

I retrieved my shoulder holster from the chair on which it still hung and started to strap it on. Thinking better of it, I pulled an ankle holster from my closet and strapped it on instead. I'd hide my weapon there, under my pants leg. Maybe that would confuse Cahors for all of two seconds. The magazine from my weapon still sat on the table; I slipped it into my jeans pocket.

I tried to think of anything else I might want to have with me, but really all I needed was the Glock. I strode to the door and pulled it open.

"Do you want me to stop shielding you now?" Namid asked.

"Not yet. I need my weapon first. I'll call for you when I have it."

The myste frowned but nodded. I left him there.

It was Saturday and the drive to Kona and Margarite's place in

Mesa took far less time than it would have during the week. When I reached their house, Kona was sitting outside on the front steps. The door to the house was shut. My weapon rested on the cement beside her.

She watched me as I approached, her expression flat, her eyes boring into mine.

"This is a bad idea."

I halted a few paces short of the steps. "Give me a better one, and I'll take it."

Her gaze dipped to the stone path at my feet. "I shouldn't give you your weapon. Maybe if you don't have it you'll be forced to reconsider. I should lock it away inside."

"We both know you're not going to do that."

She looked up at me again. "If you could just—"

"Please don't, Kona. I've been through this with Namid, and I've wrestled with it myself. More people are going to die. He'll keep killing for as long as he wants to live, which is forever. So I have to stop him, or at least make the attempt. I'm not going to convince you, and I don't have time to try. But I can do this. And even if I can't, it's my weapon, my life, my choice."

The muscles in her jaw bunched. "Then go ahead and take it."

"I'd rather you gave it to me."

She turned away once more, her dark eyes welling. A tear slipped down her cheek and fell to the step, darkening the cement. "Damn you," she said in a whisper. But she reached for the weapon and held it out to me, her hand steady. She wouldn't look at me.

"Thank you," I said, taking it. I pulled the magazine from my pocket, slid it home, chambered the first round, and strapped the weapon into my ankle holster. Still Kona kept her gaze averted, tears on her cheeks.

"I have to go."

She nodded, the motion jerky.

I wanted to say more, but no words came to me. At last I turned and walked back toward my car. Halfway there, I halted and faced her again.

"The guy's name is Etienne de Cahors," I said. "He's basically the reincarnated ghost of a druid from medieval France. Q can give you a description. You might need it."

"Justis—"

"Take care of yourself, partner. Give Margarite a kiss for me. I was kind of short with her on the phone earlier."

"Justis!"

I wanted to leave, but she deserved better. "What?"

"Where are you going?"

I shook my head. "I'm not telling you that." I returned to the car, got in, and drove away. Only when I was sure that Kona couldn't see or hear the Z-ster anymore did I steer toward South Mountain Park.

"Namid," I said aloud as I drove.

An instant later the myste was beside me in the passenger seat, his waters roiled.

"You have your weapon now?"

"I do. You can stop shielding me."

"You are certain?"

No. "You've been a good friend to me, Namid, and an excellent teacher. I'm grateful to you."

"You have learned much, Ohanko. I do not know if it is enough to defeat Cahors, but you are a formidable runecrafter. Remember that when you face him."

I nodded. "Stop shielding."

There was no flash of light, no weight lifted from my mind or my body. I had to take it on faith that the myste had done as I asked. He stared at me for a few moments more before fading from view and leaving me feeling more alone than I could remember. First Billie, then Kona, and now Namid. My chest tightened at the thought of my Dad. I should have found a way to say goodbye to him, too. But that was more than I could handle right now. I knew that if I didn't survive the day, Kona would take care of him.

I kept to side roads and avoided the interstates. This was the safer route—if I was on the freeway when Cahors came after me there would be no telling how many people might die. But this way was also slower. Too many intersections; too many traffic lights. I checked my mirrors every few seconds, expecting to see Red pull up behind me, wondering what kind of car the ghost of a Gaulish druid would drive.

I managed to reach the park before he found me, and wasted no time starting up the trail back to the spot where Claudia Deegan's body had been found. Cahors knew the area, but so did I. There might be a few hikers on the trail, but that couldn't be helped. At least I wouldn't be at a supermarket when he found me. I might not be able to keep him from killing me, but I could keep him from taking out a bunch of other people, too.

The hike took me less than half an hour. I was winded and sweating when I glimpsed the yellow police tape and slowed. I'd seen a few people early on, but none in the last fifteen minutes. I was alone, except for Cahors, who I sensed was nearby. I sat on a rock and cleared myself, expecting at any moment to see him materialize right in front of me.

When after several minutes he still hadn't appeared, I started to grow antsy.

"Show yourself!" I called, my voice echoing off the hills around me. "You've been after me for days!

"*Days . . . days . . . days . . .*

"Well, I'm right here . . . !

"*Here . . . here . . . here . . .*

". . . Waiting for you!

"*You . . . you . . . you . . .*"

Nothing.

I bent down and pulled out my weapon, and then left the trail for the thicket beyond the spot where Claudia had been found. If Red was approaching on foot, maybe I could surprise him.

That was the plan anyway.

I felt him strongly now; I knew he was getting close. And he must have felt me, too, because before I saw or heard him, he attacked.

He went for my heart again, and despite what Namid had told me, despite having cleared myself, I couldn't do anything to stop him. One moment I was crouched in that small thicket, my Glock in hand, and the next I was on the ground in agony, my shoulders hunched, my knees drawn up. It felt as though he had ripped open my chest and poured lava over my heart. I couldn't breathe; I was blind, deaf, utterly senseless. There was nothing but me and the pain.

And then his voice.

"You dared call for me?" he said, the words echoing inside my head the way my challenge to him had reverberated off those desert hills. "You believe yourself my equal now, eh? You think you can stand against me? *Tu es un enfant. Tu n'es rien.*"

It shouldn't have been this easy for him. I should have at least put up a fight before dying. But the words for a spell wouldn't come. My pistol couldn't have been more than a foot or two away from my hand, but it might as well have been on Mars.

And then, as suddenly as it had started, his assault stopped. I was aware once more of lying on the ground, dried palo verde leaves in my hair, sand and twigs pressed into the skin of my arms and face. I took a long breath, savoring the absence of pain, bracing myself for its return.

"Come here."

He spoke the words this time, and I felt their power. He was on the path, near where I'd been standing when I called for him. I lifted my head and saw him there. I meant to reach for my weapon. I meant to throw some sort of assailing spell at him. But before I knew what I was doing, I'd gotten to my feet and started toward him. He was controlling me again, his magic pressing down on me. What had Namid said? *I would reach into his mind and crush his will.* That's what Cahors was doing to me, and I couldn't do a damn thing about it.

I walked out from beneath the trees and into the bright sunlight. I couldn't even lift a hand to shield my eyes.

Cahors was grinning at me, no doubt reading my thoughts, relishing my helplessness.

"Stop there."

I halted a few feet from where he stood, my body swaying like a sapling in the wind. A fine sheen of sweat shone on his head and face, but otherwise he appeared unaffected by his hike. He wore black pants and shoes, and a long-sleeve, white, collarless shirt buttoned to the neck. He had to be burning up, but he looked perfectly comfortable. His skin was ghostly pale, a match for his eyes.

He remained still, except for his eyes, which appraised me in a single sweep from head to toe. A faint smile curved his thin lips; he didn't seem too impressed by what he saw. An instant later, the magic was lifted from my mind.

"Well?" he said, spreading his arms wide in a gesture of welcome. "Here I am, little weremyste. Do your worst." He laughed.

"Why did you kill them?" I asked.

He dropped his arms to his sides, the smile leaving his face gradually. "Are we not going to fight, you and I?"

"We will," I said. "But first I want answers. Why have you been killing those kids"

"Surely, Namid has explained this to you."

"I'm not sure he understands."

That brought back the smile, as I knew it would. I was stalling for time, trying to think of how to kill this bastard. But I also wanted to know what he'd been doing. I'd been after the guy for three years; I wanted the truth before I died.

"All right then," Cahors said. "I will answer this for you. And then you will answer a question for me."

I was reminded of the drive out to the desert with Billie, but no sooner had the memory come, than I thrust it out of my mind.

"Sure, fine," I said.

"I took power from them. Power to make myself free, power to give myself a body again, power to keep myself young."

The first two I understood—he wanted to be free of the constraints put on runemystes, and he wanted to take corporeal form. But the last one . . .

"Power to keep yourself young?"

"Yes," he said, sounding too pleased with himself. "When the Runeclave made us runemystes, they took our bodies from us, made us creatures of pure magic. In reclaiming my body, I reclaimed as well my mortality. I would have aged quickly—far more so than would be normal. My body is not from this time. But the magic I take from them—those children—it keeps me young. I will never age. I will never grow weak. I will never die."

"You're immortal," I whispered, my mind reeling.

He merely smiled.

In the next instant, though, I realized that this wasn't what he'd said. The murders were keeping him young. He wasn't immortal, so much as he was dipping into a magical fountain of youth. As long as he kept killing, time couldn't touch him. Which meant that, as long as he lived, the Blind Angel murders would never end.

"And now it is my turn," he said. "Which of them is more dear to you?"

"What are you talking about?" I asked, cold creeping down my neck like a single bead of sweat.

"The two women, the dark-skinned one, and the other, with the long hair. Which of them do you love more? For which of them would you give your life?"

Kona and Billie. He was asking me to choose between them.

"I'd die for both of them. And I'll kill for both, too, you son of a bitch."

His expression hardened, though the hint of a smile still played around the corners of his mouth. "Ah. *Nous combattrons maintenant, oui?* We fight now?"

I said nothing, but instead cast the first spell that came to mind. A fire spell: Cahors, the ground all around him, and flames. Three elements. But even as I cast, I realized that it was a poor choice. Too simple; too obvious. The fire never materialized. Cahors laughed at me.

"You can do better than that, little weremyste."

Before I could say or do anything, I was lifted off my feet and slammed down on my back onto the rocky path. All the air rushed from my lungs, and for several seconds I was too stunned and in too much pain to move.

"I think we will play a little game, you and I," Red said, walking a slow circle around me. "You will try magic on me and then, when your spell has failed, I will punish you. Each time, your punishment will get a bit worse. This sounds like fun, yes?"

I wasted no time trying again. A binding spell this time. It was supposed to immobilize him, as if I had bound him with rope. It didn't.

Red shook his head. "Not very good, I am afraid."

A rock about the size of my fist rose from the ground a few feet from me, rushed at me and slammed into my temple. It hurt like hell, and for several seconds it seemed like tiny white lights were popping inside my eyes. I raised a hand to where the rock had hit me. My fingers came away wet with blood.

I didn't know much assailing magic—I was still learning it from Namid. I tried a blade spell, because it was about all I had left. A knife, my hand, Red's throat. This one failed, too. I braced myself, wondering what he'd do to me this time, still smarting from my last two "punishments." I was already pretty tired of Cahors's game.

But I wasn't ready for this. The skin on my forearm blackened, then blistered, then appeared to melt. I couldn't keep myself from howling as I cradled the arm to my stomach, trembling, my eyes squeezed shut.

"Perhaps you are ready to end our game, little weremyste?" he said, standing just behind me. "Are you ready to die now?"

"Not yet," I said, breathing hard. "Not until I've kicked your ass."

He laughed. "*C'est bon!* I can see why Namid likes you!"

Namid. Hearing his name gave me an idea. I cleared myself again, and visualized a swarm of watery hornets, their tiny clear stingers, and Red's exposed neck and head.

As I'd hoped, Cahors didn't know this one. He started flailing his arms and ducking his head, all the time backing away. I forced myself to my feet and ran back toward the thicket to retrieve my weapon.

I was halfway there when he called, "Stop!"

His magic fell on me like a hammer, staggering me, halting me in my tracks. He made me turn to face him.

"You should not have done that, little weremyste."

There were welts on his head and face, and even a couple on his hands. His pale eyes blazed and his nostrils were flared. I knew that he wouldn't bother with rocks and burns this time. He'd go straight for my heart.

I tried to ward myself the way Namid had told me, but Red had me under his control again. There was nothing I could do to stop it. My chest was aflame once more; even Cahors' magic couldn't keep me upright. The torment seemed to go on forever, until I became convinced that he intended to finish me without another word.

Even as I felt myself starting to panic, though, it ended. I gulped at the air, curled up in a ball, the desert sun feeling like a cool balm after Red's assault.

"What happened . . . to our . . . our game?" I asked, when I could speak again.

"Stand up."

My body tried to resist, but he had taken control of me again. I struggled back to my feet. Even as I did, though, it occurred to me that his attacks on my heart and his control of my will might not be that different. If I could shield my mind somehow, I might be able to keep him out. But first I had to win a moment's freedom.

I tried to open my mouth to speak, but he wouldn't allow it. At least not at first.

"You are trying to say something."

He loosened his hold on me enough so that I could nod.

"Very well." His touch on my mind lightened.

"You're a coward," I said.

He hit me so hard with the back of his hand that I staggered back and fell.

But that was fine with me. It seemed I'd touched a nerve. I made myself laugh, even as I tasted blood.

"Truth hurts, doesn't it, Cahors?"

"Silence!"

"Well, no. As long as you're letting me talk, I think I'll go on. Our agreement was, if I failed, you were to punish me. I didn't fail, did I? But as soon as things don't go your way, you start changing the rules. Like I said, you're a coward."

He was seething. I could see it. He wanted to burn my heart right out of my chest. But I'd gotten to him a little bit. After a moment, he seemed to remember how weak I was and how great an advantage he had over me. He fixed a smile on his face.

"You are right. It was not . . . *juste*. What is your word? Fair! It was not fair of me. You wish to make another attempt?" He opened his hands. "Go ahead."

I didn't have many chances left, and I didn't know how much more of his punishment I could take. Mostly I wanted my Glock. If I could make him think about my magic *and* my weapon, I might have a chance.

And then it came to me. My father's spell. Dual transporting. Shift myself back to the thicket and at the same time retrieve my pistol from where it had fallen. I'd yet to craft the spell with any success, but I knew what had to be done. It was simply a matter of visualizing it, of clearing myself and keeping my thoughts focused.

I began chanting the spell to myself. Seven elements this time; a more complicated spell. Me, the spot where I stood, the thicket, my weapon, my hand, the spot on the ground where it lay, and the simultaneity of the whole thing. That's where I'd messed up in the past, so that was what I concentrated on now.

Cahors was watching me, waiting, no doubt warding himself. As I continued to stand there, seemingly doing nothing, he narrowed his eyes.

"*Qu'est-ce tu fait?*" he demanded, his voice low. "What are you doing?"

I didn't answer. I'd chanted the spell to myself six times, allowing the power of the magic to build. On the seventh chanting, I released the conjuring. I felt that same rush of dizzying cold, as if I had fallen backward into ice water. An instant later, I was standing among the trees, my hand raised to fire. My empty hand.

My damn Glock was sitting in the middle of the path, in the exact spot where I'd been. Within the span of a single heartbeat, he'd spotted me, his eyes locking on mine. Then he looked down at the pistol.

This spell I knew. My weapon, the ground, my hand. Three elements. Simple. One moment my Glock was at his feet and he was bending to pick it up. The next I was holding it in my hand. Without hesitating, I squeezed off a shot.

And as soon as I did, I knew I'd made a mistake. Again. I dove to the side, but Red's reflection spell was, well, faster than a speeding bullet. The slug from my own weapon caught my trailing arm just below the shoulder, spinning my body in middive and causing me to land hard on my back. I lay there for a moment, stunned, winded, gritting my teeth against the white-hot pain in my arm.

I could still hear the echo from my gunshot dying away, and part of me hoped it would bring help. Another part of me hoped anyone who heard it would be smart enough to stay the hell away.

For once, though, I was ahead of Cahors. I had my weapon back, which meant he had no choice but to try to control me again. I sheathed my mind with a warding spell, and half a second later felt his magic reach for me. My shield held, at least for the moment. I crawled behind a tree and fired off a second round. This one came back at me, too, but hit the tree trunk.

He tried for my mind again, and, unable to take control of me, went for my heart. I couldn't protect both, and knew he'd kill me faster if he could burn a hole in my chest. My heart, his magic, a sheath of power. I was growing weaker and colder by the minute. Pain, physical shock, blood loss. But still, the spell worked. I heard him roar his frustration, and then felt his magic bury my mind like an avalanche.

"Come here!" he said. His voice reached me in a sort of weird stereo, once from the path, sounding normal, and a second time inside my head, where it rolled like thunder.

I jerked upright, and walked out of the thicket again, my pistol still in my hand, which hung uselessly at my side. More than anything I wanted to raise my weapon and put a bullet through that bald head of his, but Cahors kept a tight hold on me this time. I didn't imagine I'd have any luck talking my way free.

When I reached Cahors, he held out his hand, and I gave him my weapon. You would have thought it had been his all along. I loathed myself: my weakness, my ignorance, my laziness. Namid had been training me for too long for me to allow anyone—even someone as powerful as Red—to use me in this way.

He regarded the pistol as if he had never seen one up close before, turning it first one way and then another. Then he pointed it at my thigh and fired. Not even his magic could stifle my cry of pain or keep me on my feet.

"A most useful weapon," Cahors said, examining the Glock again while massaging his shooting hand and wrist. "And powerful."

He pointed it at me once more, this time aiming it at my forehead.

I tried the sheathing spell again, desperate to throw off his control. My mind, the shield, his magic.

Cahors shook his head.

"You do not have the power, little weremyste. With time, perhaps, you might have been strong enough to face me. But you are far beyond your depth. *Quel dommage.*"

He grinned. I closed my eyes, knowing I was about to die.

"I think it's time you dropped that weapon and got your sorry French ass away from my friend."

Kona! My eyes flew open. Cahors spun and fired again.

But Kona was hidden behind a good-sized rock, and his aim was wild.

In that moment, though, Red's control over me slipped. And everything started to happen very fast.

CHAPTER 23

I could have gone with another assailing spell, but I didn't think it would work. And I had another idea.

My weapon, his hand, my hand. Three elements. It was so simple, and yet it turned out to be the last thing Cahors expected. I spoke the spell to myself and released the magic. An instant later the Glock was in my hand. I didn't hesitate at all. Still on the ground, I held the muzzle against the back of Red's knee and fired twice in quick succession.

Cahors' howl was like nothing I'd ever heard before. Astonishment, agony, rage; he sounded like a wild animal, one that had never known pain before, and had never expected it would. He collapsed to the ground right in front of me. I had every intention of firing again, of finishing him.

But his magic lashed out at me. No attempt to control this time. No attack on my heart. This was assailing magic, pure and simple. I had no time to ward myself, and I'm not sure any spell I could've conjured would have made a difference. The spell hit me hard in the side, like a fist, or the kick of a mule. I heard a couple of ribs snap, and I crumpled in on myself, gasping, though that made it hurt more.

"Justis!"

I looked up in time to see Kona hoisted to her feet by some powerful, invisible hand. She grabbed at her throat, as if trying to pry away strangling fingers.

283

"Throw away your gun, or she dies," Red said through clenched teeth. He was in pain, but I could see that he was already healing himself. The blood from his leg had stopped flowing. I had little doubt that he would be walking again in no time. I really hated this guy.

"Kill him, Justis!" Kona rasped, fighting for breath. "Never mind me! Just kill him!"

"You know better. You cannot kill me, and you cannot save yourself. But this one is of no consequence. I will kill her if you point that gun at me again. Or you can throw it away, and I will let her go once you are dead. You have my word."

Not that his word was worth anything.

"You'll let her go before you kill me," I said, staring into those pale eyes. "I want to see her walk out of here. You understand?"

Cahors shrugged. "As I say, she does not matter. The gun."

I tossed it away. As soon as it landed, I saw heat waves start to rise from it. I heard several quick pops as the bullets still in the magazine went off. But Cahors wasn't done. The Glock began to glow red, then white. And then it melted into a puddle of steel and plastic.

A moment later, Kona stumbled forward a step, released from his hold on her. She whirled; I knew she was intent on retrieving her weapon. But before she could, she stiffened again.

"No," Red told her. "You will leave, or you will die."

"Go, Kona," I said. "He'll kill you, too. There's no sense in both of us dying."

She stared at me, looking as scared as I'd ever seen her. For all the time we'd worked together, she'd never had to deal with magic in this way. She'd seen its effects; she'd accepted that I could see things she couldn't; she'd even watched me use it to scry. But she'd never witnessed a magical battle, and she'd never been attacked or controlled like this. For the first time in my memory, she was beyond her depth.

"Go," I said again. "This isn't a fight you can win."

Tears dampened her cheeks, shining in the sun. After a moment, though, she nodded.

"Let her go, Cahors," I said. "She'll leave now."

He regarded us each in turn. I saw her expression change as he released her once more.

She continued to watch me, waiting for some signal from me that she should do something. I shook my head.

"Go," I said one last time.

Kona's gaze shifted to Cahors, and her eyes narrowed. "You'd better get the hell away from here," she said, her voice shaking. "Out of Phoenix; out of the damn country. Because the next time I see you, I'll kill you. I swear it."

A rock flew up from the ground near her feet and hit her hard in the forehead, staggering her.

"You should leave now," he said to her. "Before I change my mind."

Her eyes flicked my way again, wide now, questioning. I shook my head once more. She winced, then backed away from us, following the path out of the ravine.

When she had disappeared from view, Cahors turned back to me.

"You should not have hurt me, little weremyste."

My chest seemed to explode in flame. I wouldn't have thought that he could hurt me worse than he already he had, but nothing he'd done to my heart before could compare with this. I heard myself screaming and there was nothing I could do to stop. I didn't want to die. Really I didn't. But at that moment death would have come as a relief. Cahors, though, could read my thoughts, and he must have had other plans for me. The pain stopped.

"No," he said. "No, little weremyste. Your death will not be that easy."

"You know," I whispered, my eyes closed. "I'm pretty sick of you calling me that."

Cahors laughed, but I barely heard him.

I was conjuring again. Same spell as before, but with a slight difference. Kona's weapon, the place where it lay on the rock and sand, and her hand. I repeated it to myself three times, taking as much care with it as I could, and then I released the magic. If it worked, I had a chance. But I'd never tried to send anything so far, and I'd never cast the spell when I didn't know the precise spot for which I was aiming. She could have been anywhere. I knew Kona too well to think she'd left the area. I doubted that Cahors expected her to leave either. He didn't care because he wasn't afraid of her, and he had every intention of killing her once I was dead.

"Are you not going to try to hurt me again?" Cahors asked. "Are you giving up already? I am disappointed."

I knew he was goading me, but I knew as well that Kona needed a bit of time. *If I managed to find her with the pistol.*

I was growing weaker by the moment. My arm and leg throbbed. I'd been shot before, but never twice in one day, and never in the middle of being tortured in so many other ways.

But I had to do something, and I had plenty of reasons to want to hurt him. First though, I needed to protect myself. I started by shielding myself, and then magically flung a rock at him as he'd done to Kona and me. He deflected it toward me, but my shield held.

He raised an eyebrow. "You are learning. But still you have failed again." Red got to his feet. He favored his bloodied knee a bit, but he tested it and it seemed to support his weight. "That is better," he said. "And now, I believe it is time for another punishment."

His foot, my hand, and a good hard tug. He was expecting spells that would hurt him, not trip him. His good leg flew out from under him, leaving only his injured one to keep him up. It didn't. He fell hard on his back.

Still shielded, I sent another rock at his head. This one hit him, opening a cut on his temple.

He swung his leg around and kicked me hard in the jaw, sending me sprawling again. Before I could strike back, he attacked with his magic once more, searing my chest, paralyzing me with pain. He got to his feet, came around, and put his foot on my throat.

"Which will kill you first, little weremyste? Will your heart give out, or will I crush your throat?"

I tried to fight him, but he had me this time. His magic held my mind, his fire burned in my heart, his weight was crushing my windpipe. And I had nothing left. He'd broken through my warding, and I was too weak and too hurt to conjure another.

I thought of Billie, of my dad, and my eyes welled.

The report of Kona's weapon, much closer than I would have thought possible, made me start. Cahors' head snapped to the side, but then he straightened his neck again. Blood gushed from above his ear. He raised a shaking hand to the wound and stared at the blood on his fingers.

A second shot hit him in the neck. A third just behind his eye. And he fell over, landing beside me. He lay still for a moment, but then began to push himself up. Already the bullet wounds were healing over, though he was covered with blood.

My heart wasn't burning anymore; my mind was my own.

I cast a fire spell, the same one I'd tried earlier, the same one he'd blocked with ease. This time it worked. His clothes burst into flame. But he didn't seem to notice. He was still trying to stand. A fourth shot from Kona's pistol hit him square in the back of his head. He collapsed back onto his chest and didn't move again. The blaze I'd conjured began to blacken his skin.

With Kona's help, I crawled a short distance away from him. But then I merely sat and watched as Cahors burned.

"Now I know how they felt when they tried to kill Rasputin," Kona said.

"Yeah." My voice sounded weak. "No kidding."

She squatted down in front of me and looked me in the eye, concern etched on her face. "How are you doing, partner?"

"Not too good," I said. "How'd you find me, anyway?"

"I've been working this case, too, remember. I know where I'd go if I'd wanted Red to find me."

Right.

"The two bullet wounds," she said, examining me. "What else?"

"A burn on my arm, a couple of broken ribs, some bruises. Oh, and my heart feels like it's been shish-kebobed."

She pulled a cell phone from her pocket and frowned at it. "No signal here," she said. "I'll walk back up the trail a ways and call for help as soon as I can."

"Tonight's the full moon, Kona. I can't be in the hospital. They'll think I'm nuts."

"I'll be there. You'll be all right."

"Kona—"

"Justis, you've been shot twice. You're going to the hospital. There's no way around that."

I nodded, knowing she was right. "Yeah, okay." I lay back down, shading my eyes with my good hand.

I must have dozed off, because the next thing I knew, Kona was shaking me awake and the sun was angling across the ravine. I could hear a helicopter in the distance, thudding dully, getting louder by the moment.

"That for me?" I asked, croaking the words. My throat and mouth were dry, and my head was spinning.

She nodded.

I tried to sit up, but she put a hand on my chest.

"Stay there."

I lay back, then turned my head toward what was left of Cahors. "He still dead?"

She laughed. "Yeah. He's still dead. Kevin's on his way, along with Arroyo, Hibbard, and probably half the PPD. You're going to be a hero."

"You shot him, not me."

"Only because you put my weapon in my hand. Nice bit of work, by the way. Scared the shit out of me, but I've got to admit it was pretty cool."

"Starting to like magic, aren't you?" I said, closing my eyes again. The helicopter was close now.

"No," she said, her voice rising. "I don't like it at all. That mojo's going to get you killed someday. You know that. It might have saved your life today, but one of these times—"

I opened my eyes once more. "The craft didn't save my life today, Kona. You did."

She smiled. "Yeah, well, don't tell Hibbard. He doesn't like me as it is."

I laughed. It hurt like hell, but I couldn't help myself.

CHAPTER 24

Once the helicopter landed and the EMTs starting working on me, I lost track of the time. I don't remember the ride to the hospital—I wasn't even sure which one they took me to, though I assumed it was Tempe St. Luke's—and though I have vague memories of trying to fight off the nurses and doctors as they were putting me under for surgery, it's all sketchy. I do know that I slept through most of the night, and that anything I said that made me sound crazy would have been blamed on the anesthetics and pain medication rather than the moon.

When I came to the next morning, groggy and nauseous, Kona was there beside my bed, reading a copy of the *Republic*. She had a bandage on her head and bags under her eyes. I had a feeling she hadn't gotten much sleep.

"You been here all night?" I said. Or tried to. The words sounded as if they'd been scraped from my throat.

"Yeah," she said, smiling and setting the newspaper aside. She scooted her chair closer to the bed. "Margarite was here, too, but she had to go. Something with her dad. She'll be back later. How are you feeling?"

"Like I've been run over by a truck."

"Want me to call for a nurse? They've been trying to wake you all morning, saying you've got to eat something. But I told them to let you sleep."

I made a sour face at the thought of food. "Thanks."

She passed me a plastic container of water and I sipped a little through the built-in straw. It felt good going down, but it didn't help my stomach any. I handed it back to her.

"You're a hero," she told me, picking up the paper again. "Told you you would be." She held up the front page for me to see.

"Blind Angel Killer Dead, Police Say," the headline screamed in that really big banner type usually reserved for presidential elections and wars. Below, in smaller text, it said, "Police, Local Investigator Kill Suspect in South Mtn. Pk." And below that were a pair of photos, one of a cloth-covered corpse that I assumed was Red lying in the ravine, the other an older shot of Claudia Deegan as a smiling, blonde teenaged tennis star. It was a little creepy to see her that way, and maddening to think that years from now, when they talked about this case, she'd be remembered, but Gracia Rosado wouldn't.

"The article say anything interesting?" I asked.

She shook her head. "Not really. I told them the guy was French, so now the media guys and the Feds are wondering whether this needed to be treated as a terrorism case."

"How'd you explain the fact that he'd been burned to a crisp?"

"I said he'd tried to burn us with some unknown liquid, but that he'd lit himself on fire instead."

"And Hibbard bought that?" I asked.

"To tell you the truth, he's so glad this guy is dead, he would have believed anything. He didn't even mind that you helped bring him down."

"It's like he's a new man."

"Well," she said with a frown, "I wouldn't go that far."

We fell silent and I took stock of how I felt. My mind was still dull, the effect of the moon and the painkillers and whatever they'd used to knock me out for surgery. My ribs were a little sore, but my arm and leg, both heavily bandaged, didn't feel too bad. I'd been lucky.

"Justis," Kona said, her tone weird enough to make me look at her. "I called Billie, to tell her what had happened and where you were. She . . . she said she wouldn't be able to make it over to see you. But I had a feeling that maybe there was more to it."

Kona missed nothing. That was one of the reasons she was such a good cop.

"There was," I said, the ache in my chest duller than Red's fire, but no less painful. "She doesn't want to see me anymore."

Kona grimaced. "Why not?"

"She found out that I'm a weremyste, and she knows all about the phasings and what they do to me."

"How'd she find out?"

I met Kona's gaze. "I told her."

For a long time she said nothing. Then she shrugged slightly and picked up the paper again. "I guess you know what you're doing."

"I guess."

Neither of us said anything for a while. I pointed to the water and she handed it to me. I drank a bit more, and this time held onto the container. I was starting to feel better.

"I liked her, Justis," Kona said after some time. "Billie, I mean. I think she was good for you."

"You're not the only one."

She nodded once. "Then I won't say anything more."

She left a few minutes later.

I flipped on the television and watched a Sunday talk show or two and then a Diamondbacks game. Most of it washed over me, but watching anything was better than lying there in silence thinking about Billie.

I wanted to be mad at her. I wanted to tell myself that she'd given up on me too soon, that she should have been willing to deal with the phasings and the magic and everything that came with them. But I knew better. I'd seen what that life did to my mom, and I didn't want that for Billie. If I'd been in her position, I would have run from me, too, and I would have done it days before she did. Relationships were hard enough without all the extra baggage I was carrying.

I survived that second night in the hospital despite some pretty terrifying hallucinations of Cahors. Kona had come back to check on me and when I started saying weird stuff and losing touch with reality, she convinced my nurse to give me some sleep medication. Good thing, too. At one point I started to chant a spell in my head, though later I couldn't remember what kind of spell it was. Chances are, I would have burned the hospital to the ground.

◎ ◎ ◎

When I awoke the next day, I was alone. Of course. Kona had work to do, and she knew that the danger of the phasings was over, at least for a few weeks. The day dragged, the food sucked, and I started bugging every nurse who came in about when I could go home. They all told me the same thing: that I'd have to ask the doctor.

The doctor didn't come in until late afternoon, meaning that I'd have at least one more night there. He gave me a thorough exam, took off my bandages and checked my bullet wounds, both of which seemed to be healing well, and said that I could leave the hospital the next day.

Kona showed up a couple of hours later and we made arrangements for her to take me home around midday. She didn't stay long—she had a new homicide to deal with and was sure she'd be at 620 for most of the night.

I had a quiet evening. With the phasings over and the pain in my ribs a little more manageable, I slept pretty well.

The paperwork and billing took most of the next morning, and by the time Kona came to get me, I was ready to be done with hospitals for good. She drove me home, where the Z-ster was waiting in the driveway—Margarite had driven her home for me. The place still looked like hell—no surprise—and I wondered how I was going to pay for the repairs as well as my share of the hospital bill. I put those questions out of my head, since I knew that I wouldn't be working for a few weeks. No one was going to hire a PI who had only one good arm and leg.

Kona helped me into the house and got me settled in the living room. She'd brought me some food, including some leftovers from a meal Margarite had made, and she stocked my refrigerator while I took in the cracked walls and ceiling, the broken windows, the mess on my furniture and floors.

"You're awfully quiet," she said, emerging from the kitchen after a few minutes.

"I'm wondering how I'm going to get this place fixed up."

"With all that reward money it shouldn't be too hard."

I stared at her. "What?"

"Twenty-five thousand dollars, my friend. From the Deegans, remember?"

I'd forgotten all about it. "But you—"

Kona shook her head. "You know I can't take any of that money. Department regulations. No rewards accepted. That money is all yours. And believe me, Hibbard's good and pissed."

I gave a little laugh. The reward money. Funny how a little thing like that could improve a person's mood.

CHAPTER 25

A couple of days later I drove to Maryvale. I wasn't supposed to get behind the wheel for a few weeks, but I was going crazy alone in my house. Shifting was a challenge with only one good arm and one good leg, but I managed it. I still didn't like going to that part of the city, but I wanted to see how Orestes was doing.

When I arrived, Q was sitting outside in his rocking chair, which, as far as I could tell, was one of the few pieces of furniture to survive Red's attack. He had casts on his leg and arm, and bandages on his head. But he smiled when he saw me get out of the Z-ster, and he raised his good hand in greeting.

"Justis Fearsson, where have you been? With your arm in that wrap you look like Q's twin."

I laughed, hobbling toward him. "How you doing, Q?"

"Q's doin' all right." He gestured at one of the folding chairs. "Sit down, sit down."

I unfolded the chair next to his and sat. I could hear noises from inside the shop and I raised an eyebrow.

"That's Q's boy in there," he said. "He's helpin' Q with repairs."

"I didn't know you had a son."

"Yup," Q said, grinning and sounding proud. "Q got a little girl, too." The grin tightened. "'Course she's with her mama, and doesn't come around as much as Q'd like."

A moment later a sweet-faced kid with short black hair came out of the store, struggling with a trash bag that was filled almost to

295

bursting. He couldn't have been more than thirteen or fourteen years old, and he didn't look much like Orestes. But when Q called to him, he rolled his eyes, the way any kid that age would when his father asked him to do something.

"Come here, boy," Q said. "Justis Fearsson, this is Quincy. One day Quincy will be Brother Q, just like his papa."

Another roll of the eyes and the kid was gone.

"Well, I just stopped by to make sure you were doing all right, Q. I should probably be going." I started to stand, but he put his hand on mine.

"Wait a minute, Jay." Q's voice had dropped, as had his gaze; there was something on his mind. "You know, when a man is hurt, and fearin' for his life, sometimes he'll say crazy stuff. You know what Q's sayin'?"

I wanted to laugh out loud—I knew exactly what he meant—but I managed to keep a straight face. "You mean the other night? You seemed pretty lucid to me."

"No, Q was . . . he was sufferin'. Q had no idea what he was sayin'."

"So then you don't even remember."

"Well . . . no, Q remembers some of it."

At that point I started laughing. I couldn't help myself. "Don't worry, Q. If I need information, I'll be coming to you. And I'll bring cash."

He beamed. "You're a good man, Justis Fearsson. Q's always said that about you."

"Thanks." I limped to the car. "Take care."

After leaving Maryvale, I stopped by the store and with some help from a clerk I managed to buy a few things for my dad. Then I got on Grand Avenue and drove out to his place. For the first time in years, I'd missed my usual Tuesday visit, and after the week I'd been through, I felt a strong need to see him.

He was in his chair when I drove up to the trailer. He glanced over at me, but he didn't wave and he didn't get up. It was hot and windy. The tarp over his chair snapped like a flag and my father sat there squinting against the glare and the dust.

"How are you feeling today, Pop?" I said, stooping to kiss his forehead.

"Not so good," he said. "One of those days, you know? Things seem . . ." He shrugged. "I don't know . . ."

"Muddled?"

"Yeah."

I sat beside him and stared out over the desert.

"It just Tuesday?" he asked.

"No, Thursday. Sorry I didn't get here sooner."

He noticed the bandaging on my arm and leg.

"What happened to you?"

"Got shot."

He cocked an eyebrow. "No joking?"

"No joking."

"What happened to the other guy?"

"He's dead."

My dad nodded and faced forward again.

"Where's that girl you brought out the other day? What was her name again?"

"Billie."

"That's right. Billie. Where's she?"

"We're not together anymore."

He twisted his mouth for a moment. "Phasings?"

He said he was muddled, but he seemed pretty sharp to me.

"How'd you know that?"

"Just a guess."

"How did you do it, Dad? How'd you make things last with Mom for so long?"

"I didn't," he said. "She did. She held on, even when I was too screwed up to do much of anything. I still don't know why."

"She loved you," I said.

"Right. And I'm telling you I still don't know why."

We sat there for a long time, saying nothing, watching the day drift by with the tumbleweed and the dust devils.

"I tried one of your spells the other day," I said, breaking a long silence.

"My spells?"

"Namid said it was yours. Dual transporting—moving myself and putting my weapon in my hand at the same time."

He nodded. "I think I remember that one. Can't do it anymore, but I remember."

"You still conjure?"

"A bit," he said, glancing at me. "Now and then. Just for the sake of doing it."

I don't know why, but it was strange for me to think of my father doing magic. I know that he used to, but I figured he gave it up when he left the force, though, of course, there was no reason he should. I thought about what Namid had said, about how the two of us might have worked together if things had been different.

"So, did it work?" he asked.

"What?"

"The spell. Did it work?"

I shook my head. "No. I moved, but I left my weapon where I'd been."

"Focus on the weapon first."

"What do you mean?"

"When you work the spell, do the weapon first, your move second. That way the pistol gets to your hand before you move yourself. Worst thing that happens is you stay where you are but you're armed."

I stared at him as if he'd done the spell right there. "I thought you said you were muddled today."

"I was, 'til you got here."

I smiled, and he did, too.

"There food in the car?" he asked.

"Yeah."

"Good. I'm outta most everything and I'm starved. I'll make you a sandwich."

I handed him the keys and he unloaded what I'd brought him. After a while he emerged from the trailer with a couple of sandwiches.

We didn't say much more, but I was glad I'd made the trip, and I know that he was, too.

I started the drive back to Chandler a short time before dusk. As soon as I was back on the highway, Namid materialized in the passenger seat, the pinks and yellows and reds of the western sky shimmering in his waters.

"Ohanko."

"Where have you been, ghost? You missed all the excitement."

"I have been speaking with my kind."

It all came back to me then, how he had saved my life in Robo's and warded my house, breaking the most basic rules of the Council of Runemystes. "Did they punish you?"

"They warned me not to act on your behalf again."

"That's it?"

"No. They told me to ask your forgiveness. We were careless and you nearly died. We have done what we can to make certain such a thing does not happen again. But we will remain vigilant, lest others in the council make a similar attempt."

I wanted to ask what they'd done to keep the other runemystes in line, but I knew he wouldn't tell me.

Instead, I asked him something that had been bothering me for the past several days. "Why did he come here, Namid? Why Phoenix of all places? Why didn't he do all of this in France?"

"He could not," Namid said, sounding like I should have known this already. "France is where he was bound into service as a runemyste. To escape that fate, he first had to leave his native land."

I suppose that made sense. "All right, but why here?"

"I cannot be entirely certain," the runemyste said. "He would have required the presence of a university, so that he could find young victims for his magic. He might also have wanted a warm climate, so that his potential victims would be out of doors throughout the year."

"You think he came for the weather?" I asked, incredulous. I thought of Sophie Schaller. I couldn't imagine anyone who had less in common with Cahors; I didn't want to believe that the two of them could have come to Phoenix for the same reason.

"I am merely saying that it is possible," Namid said, his expression remaining the same. "I also think he would have chosen a place with powerful ties to the craft. That might have helped him, too. My people have been using magic in this part of your world for many hundreds of years. And he has known me for a long time."

I hadn't expected that. "He came here because of you?"

"I believe so. In part at least."

I didn't know what to say. "I'm sorry, Namid."

"I believe I should be apologizing to you."

"No," I said. "That's not necessary." I'd never felt sorry for Namid before; it was unsettling. "Anyway," I said after a minute or two, "thank you. For saving my life, I mean. I know you weren't supposed to."

"Of course. Tread like the fox, Ohanko."

I tried to think of some clever response, but nothing came to mind. In the end, I merely nodded, and Namid faded from view.

It was almost dark when I got back to my house, which may be why I didn't recognize the car that was parked out front. I pulled into the driveway and had hobbled halfway to my front door before I noticed Billie standing on the walk. My heart began to hammer so hard in my chest that I was sure she'd see my shirt move.

"I heard you got shot," she said. "It was in the paper."

"Yeah?" Intelligent, I know. But it was all I could manage at the time.

"You all right?"

"Sure. I'm fine."

She nodded, and walked to where I was standing. I hadn't left the porch light on, and only the blue glow of a nearby streetlight kept us from standing in total darkness.

"Can I come in?"

"Why? To tell me again how much you don't want to be with me?"

"That's not fair. Everything I said to you the other day was about how much I do want to be with you. But I'm scared."

Her eyes held mine for the span of a single heartbeat. Then I walked past her to the door, unlocked it, and reached in to switch on a light. I hesitated for an instant, before turning to her and indicating with an open hand that she should come inside. She wouldn't look at me as she stepped by, and I wondered if I would have been better off sending her away. But I followed her into the house and closed the door behind us.

After a few seconds, she turned toward me and took a breath. "You have mental health problems, Fearsson."

"I know that. I'm the one who told you, remember?"

"Of course I do. But I've been researching this, and I've learned a bit more about magic and the phasings. You can actually learn a fair amount once you figure out where to look."

I had an idea of where she was going with this. "Billie—"

"There are drugs. Medications you can take that will keep you healthy. I know about the full moon now, what it does to you. But you can control it."

"It's not that simple."

"Why?" she asked, sounding frightened and angry and so sad it made my eyes sting.

"I tried to explain it to you on Saturday."

"Right. Magic. But wouldn't it be worth it to be whole again, to make those bad times go away?"

"No," I said. "It wouldn't."

She shook her head, a tear rolling down her cheek, and then another. "Damn you! You'd actually choose to suffer this way, wouldn't you? You'd turn your back on a cure and keep going the way you are now."

"Magic is a tool. I need to be able to use it. And after all you know now about what happened to Claudia Deegan, and what almost happened to me, you should understand that."

She shook her head again. "You're too far gone already."

I'd had enough. We could have spent half the night going around and around with this. But I didn't see the use, and I didn't have the energy for it. "You know, Namid," I said aloud. "I could use some help here."

"Who are you talking to?" She sounded scared. If the runemyste didn't show, I'd never see her again.

But a moment later, there he was, shimmering like starlit waters.

"She wants me to start taking blockers," I told him.

"It would be better if you did not," he said. "You can do more good with your magic than without it."

"I know. I want you to tell her that."

Billie took a step back, and I was afraid she'd bolt for the door. "This isn't funny, Fearsson."

"Come on, Namid. Help me out."

"Who is Namid?"

An instant later, his liquid skin rippled, as if disturbed by a gust of wind. Billie gasped.

"He is," I said.

"Good God, what is that?"

"Please. 'Who,' not 'what.' His name is Namid'skemu and he's a runemyste."

"What the hell is a runemyste?" she asked, her eyes riveted on Namid.

"It's kind of a ghost."

"I am not a ghost," he said, making her jump again. "I am a runemyste. And you are a distraction to him."

What a charmer.

"Never mind that. Tell her about the blockers."

"If Ohanko were to take the Abri, he would no longer be able to cast spells. I would rather he train his mind and his magic, and keep his mind clear that way."

"Abri?"

"The medicines that stop magic and protect him from the moon-times. Ohanko calls them blockers."

"But he's sick. Magic is driving him insane."

Namid glanced at me, and a flicker of sadness crossed his watery features. "Yes," Namid said. "As it did his father. Magic is a dangerous tool, and it exacts a cost. As he hones his craft the effects may be controlled. But this is his choice as well as his fate. If he chooses to give up his powers, it must be his decision, and his alone. I cannot force him not to take the Abri; you cannot force him otherwise. For now he has chosen to be a runecrafter, and he must live with the consequences of that choice. So must you."

"No!" Billie said, fear of the runemyste giving way to anger. "Just because you say it's his fate doesn't make it true! You're his friend! If you know where his magic leads, you should tell him to stop!"

"Billie—"

"Yes, I am his friend," Namid said, his voice even as he regarded me again with that same sad expression. "But I am also his teacher, and I have a responsibility to the Runeclave, just as I do to him. Your world is a safer place tonight because of Ohanko's magic. Do you deny this?"

Billie opened her mouth, then closed it again. After a few seconds she shook her head.

"If Ohanko was still a police officer would you tell him to quit rather than put his life in danger?"

"No," she said, her voice low. "But this is different."

"I do not believe it is," Namid said. "There is magic involved, and since you do not understand the craft you think it is different. But is it really?"

Billie narrowed her eyes. "What did you say you were again?"

"A runemyste. My kind guard against the use of dark magic in your world, and we give aid to those who have Runeclave blood in their veins. We teach them to craft, we guide them in this battle against those who would misuse their powers. Ohanko is a runecrafter—a weremyste you would call him—of limited ability. He is learning to become more. But the moontimes will always be hard for him. There is no way to avoid this. Do you understand?"

She considered me, her forehead furrowing. Then faced Namid again. "Will he hurt himself?" she asked. "I've read that sometimes people with magic—they hurt themselves or . . . worse."

"He has not yet."

Billie gave a wan smile. It was kind of nice to see someone else dealing with Namid's cryptic answers and stubborn logic. "So," she said after a some time, "maybe having someone around, someone who might check in on him now and then, wouldn't be such a bad thing."

Namid stared at her for a moment. After a few seconds he nodded, his waters softening. I thought I might even have glimpsed a smile on his face.

"I think I like her, Ohanko."

"I thought you said she was a distraction."

"I may have been wrong."

My mouth fell open. "Well, Billie, that's a first. You've gotten Namid'skemu of the K'ya'na-Kwe clan to admit that he might have been wrong about something."

Billie grinned.

"Your humor is most peculiar, Ohanko. I like her, but you I am not so sure about." He turned to Billie. "We understand each other now about the Abri?"

"I think so, yes."

"Good. Farewell."

He vanished, though for a long time Billie continued to stare at the place where he'd been standing.

"So, what else have you got?" she asked, turning to face me.

"Excuse me?"

"Well, you've got psychological problems, you're a sorcerer, you hang out with that misty-ghosty thing—"

"Runemyste."

"Whatever. I'm wondering if there's more I should know before we go any further."

"Are we going further?" I asked.

She took my hand. "I think I'd like to, yes. But slowly, Fearsson. We've got to take it slowly. I'm in uncharted waters here and I won't lie to you: this all scares me."

"I can understand that. Sometimes it scares me, too."

We stood in silence, our eyes locked.

"So, is there more?" she asked.

"I can't think of anything else. We've covered most of it in the last week or two."

"Well, good," she said. "Because I'm hungry, and I've had enough surprises for a while."

"You want me to make you some dinner?"

"Right," she said. "The one-armed chef. I'd like to see that." She pulled me toward the door. "No, I want you to take me out. No dives this time. Someplace nice."

"The dive was your idea," I reminded her.

"Fine. I'll choose this place, too."

She led me out into the night, and I paused long enough to turn off the light and lock the door, content in that moment to follow her anywhere.

Acknowledgements

The publication of this novel has been a long time in coming and I am indebted to a great many people. Years ago, when I first researched the book, Karen Kontak, of the Phoenix Police Department's Crime Analysis and Research Unit, provided me with much basic information about life in the PPD. More recently, Jeri F., also in the Crime Analysis and Research Unit, helped me sort out the "personalities" of Phoenix's various police precincts and beats. Gayle Millette, of the Phoenix Medical Examiner's Office, gave me invaluable insights into its workings. I am grateful to all three of them for their generosity, their patience, and their professionalism. Naturally, any errors that remain in my depiction of the Phoenix Police Department or the Medical Examiner's Office are entirely my own.

In various stages of preparing the manuscript I have also relied on the expertise of Jennifer Bachman, Larry Jones, and Steve Blount.

I have received feedback on this book from several people, all of whom helped it become a stronger novel. Stephen Pagel read and commented on an early draft, as did Catriona Sparks and James Frenkel. More recent drafts have benefitted from the insights of Kate Elliott, Edmund S. Schubert, Stephen Leigh, and Faith Hunter. And over my years of working and reworking this book, I have received encouragement from Catie Murphy, Misty Massey, A.J. Hartley, John Hartness, Kalayna Price, and all the wonderful folks at Magical Words.

I am deeply grateful to Toni Weiskopf, Jim Minz, Tony Daniel,

Laura Haywood-Cory, and Gray Rinehart at Baen Books, as well as the great folks in their production, marketing, and art departments. I cannot imagine a better home than Baen for this series. I also want to thank Alan Pollack for the very cool and evocative artwork on the jacket.

Most of all, I am grateful to my wonderful agent and fabulous friend, Lucienne Diver, who has stuck by me and this novel through all my struggles with it and all my efforts to make it into the book I knew it could be. Lucienne offered terrific feedback on draft after draft and she continued to believe in Jay Fearsson and his world even when I had my doubts. Without her, this book would not have been published.

Finally, as always, I owe thanks to my beautiful wife and daughters. Without Nancy, Alex, and Erin in my life, nothing else would be worth doing.

—D.B.C.

About the Author

David B. Coe is the Crawford Award-winning author of sixteen novels and the occasional short story. Under his own name he has written three epic fantasy series, as well as the novelization of Ridley Scott's *Robin Hood*. As D.B. Jackson, he is the author of the Thieftaker Chronicles, a historical urban fantasy. *Spell Blind* is the first book in the Case Files of Justis Fearsson. The second novel, *His Father's Eyes*, is already in production. David's books have been translated into a dozen languages. He lives on the Cumberland Plateau with his wife and daughters.